# About the Author

Rachael Johns, an English teacher by trade and a mum 24/7, is the bestselling ABIA-winning author of *The Patterson Girls* and a number of other romance and women's fiction books including *The Art of Keeping Secrets* and *The Greatest Gift*. She is currently Australia's leading writer of contemporary relationship stories around women's issues, a genre she has coined 'life-lit'. Rachael lives in the Perth hills with her hyperactive husband, three mostly-gorgeous heroes-in-training and a very badly behaved dog. She rarely sleeps and never irons.

# Rachael Johns

## Lost Without You

First Published 2018
Second Australian Paperback Edition 2019
ISBN 9781489280961

Published by
HQ Fiction
An imprint of Harlequin Enterprises (Australia) Pty Limited (ABN 47 001 180 918), a subsidiary of HarperCollins Publishers Australia Pty Limited (ABN 36 009 913 517)
Level 13, 201 Elizabeth St
SYDNEY NSW 2000
AUSTRALIA

A catalogue record for this book is available from the National Library of Australia
www.librariesaustralia.nla.gov.au

Printed and bound in Australia by McPherson's Printing Group

*In memory of a very special lady – Alison (Aley) Paine*
*1983–2017*

*A man is lucky if he is the first love of a woman.*
*A woman is lucky if she is the last love of a man.*

# June

June

## Rebecca

No periods, no childbirth and no menopause!

Men have it so much easier than women, thought Rebecca MacRitchie as she stepped out of the shower, grabbed a towel, wrapped it around herself and glared at her reflection in the bathroom mirror.

Take her husband, Hugh, for instance. Although thirteen years her senior, his grey hair made him look distinguished; all hers did was keep her hairdresser in designer dresses. Her daughter, Paige, had tried to reassure her that grey hair was all the rage—apparently some young women were actually dyeing their hair silver. It was nonsensical! Surely they'd be regretting *that* decision later when their first *actual* grey hair sprouted on their head.

Young women and *all* men, none of them knew how lucky they were.

*Geez, Rebecca, you sound like you're ninety, not fifty.*

But it was true. Following a quick shower, Hugh had thrown on his black dinner suit without much fuss and was currently

3

downstairs, no doubt with his feet up in front of the TV watching sport on Foxtel. Whereas a shower was only the beginning of Rebecca's preparation.

She still had to blow-dry her hair, carefully apply her make-up to hide her ever-increasing multitude of wrinkles and pick out a dress that didn't accentuate her middle-aged spread. Normally Rebecca loved nothing better than dressing up, but tonight she was weary and everything simply felt like too much effort.

'Pull yourself together,' she told her reflection. If any night required her best effort this was it!

A shot of excitement fizzed through her at the prospect of what was to come. Tonight was Paige's big night and Rebecca wasn't about to let the odd hot flush or a little bit of dizziness ruin it for either of them. She'd down a cocktail of Berocca and Panadol before they left and she'd be fine.

Forcing herself out of the en suite and into the bedroom, she chose an eighties playlist on Spotify and put her phone on the speaker dock beside the bed. Her favourite tunes from her teenage years never failed to lift her spirits and would surely help get her out of the funk she'd been in these last few days.

Molly, their black labrador, who'd been lazing on the floor by the bed, looked up briefly as Cindi Lauper's voice filled the air, then promptly dropped her head back onto her paws.

'You don't know how easy your life is,' Rebecca told her as she went to select some underwear. She rubbed the towel over her body, trying not to think about how soft it was nowadays. Hugh said there was just more of her to cuddle and he'd love her even if she grew to three times her current size, but that didn't make her feel any better. Discarding the towel on the end of the bed, she pulled on a pair of lace knickers—feel-good underwear had always been important to her. But when she reached for the matching bra, she realised her dress would dictate which bra she could wear and she still hadn't decided on her outfit.

*Bugger it.* With a sigh, she went into her walk-in robe and stared at the row of outfits. Did tonight's celebration call for ruffles or lace? Soft florals or bright prints? Something flowing or something fitted? A dress or a jumpsuit? Usually Rebecca dressed according to mood—one day she'd be a pencil-skirt-and-heels kind of woman, the next day she'd look completely bohemian in colourful floor-length dresses, boots and long, dangly earrings. Hugh would laugh if she told him she had nothing to wear, but the problem tonight was she couldn't quite put her finger on how she felt. She berated herself for leaving this important decision to the last minute—Paige's book launch had been scheduled for months. But then again, until a couple of days ago, Rebecca hadn't known that the launch wouldn't be the only thing they were celebrating.

She smiled at the recollection of Solomon arriving on their doorstep, looking handsome as always but rubbing the back of his neck and blinking as if agitated.

'What a lovely surprise,' she'd said to her daughter's boyfriend as she'd opened the door. But then she'd noticed his worried expression and her heart had slammed up to her throat. 'Oh, Sol, is everything okay?'

For a moment she'd feared something had happened to Paige.

He nodded rapidly. 'Yes. I mean, I think so. I hope so. Can I come in?'

'Of course. You know you're always welcome here.' Rebecca pulled him into a hug and then ushered him inside. 'Can I get you a drink? A beer? Coffee? Milo?'

At that point Hugh had poked his head into the hallway from the living room. 'Sol, mate. Good to see you. Is Paige with you?'

'Uh ... no. She's ... um ...' Solomon, always confident and well spoken, seemed at a loss for words.

'She's teaching one of her art classes tonight, honey,' Rebecca informed her husband.

'Right. Well, to what do we owe the pleasure?' Hugh liked Solomon too—occasionally the two of them went to a footy game together, thankfully they both barracked for the Swans—but those occasions were always prearranged and Rebecca couldn't remember another time Sol had arrived on their doorstep unannounced and without their daughter.

Solomon shoved his hands into his pockets and cleared his throat. 'I know Paige and I haven't been going out for that long ...'

'Haven't you?' Hugh frowned. 'Feels like a bloody long time to me.'

Rebecca smiled. 'Almost two years.'

Solomon nodded. 'And I know I'm a bit older than her.'

'Only a few years,' Rebecca said.

This time Hugh chuckled. 'I'm thirteen years older than Rebecca and we've done alright. Haven't we, love?'

'Let the boy speak,' she said tersely, her heart suddenly light and impatient as she guessed what Solomon was about to say. Or rather *ask*.

'Well, the bottom line is, you know how much I adore your daughter. She's my best friend and also my ...' Solomon paused a moment. 'Well, the absolute best person I know. I want to marry her and I was hoping you'd give us your blessing?'

Rebecca had burst into tears—happy ones—and yanked Solomon into another hug. Of course the answer was yes—not that she believed he needed their permission, but she couldn't help thinking it sweet that he'd come seeking it.

Within seconds she felt Hugh wrapping his arms around them both and when he spoke, she could tell he was all choked up as well. 'I didn't think blokes still came to the parents first, but I appreciate you thinking of us, Sol.'

Solomon let out a relieved chuckle and the three of them disentangled. 'She might not say yes.' But his big grin told them he was positive she would.

And Rebecca was confident too. Until Solomon, Paige hadn't had any serious relationships. Although there'd been plenty of boys chasing her, she was far more interested in pursuing her art and going in to bat for the disadvantaged, but from the moment Paige met Sol, she was a goner. They were perfect together—not only did they make a striking couple but they shared the same values, made each other laugh and you only had to look at them to see the chemistry between them.

Rebecca could always tell when they'd just had sex—it took a good while after for Paige's post-coital glow to diminish—and she felt such satisfaction and contentment that her daughter had a beautiful sex life. She supposed most mothers didn't like thinking about their daughters doing the horizontal mambo. Her own would have preferred she'd stayed a virgin until she was thirty-five.

But finding someone you were both intellectually *and* sexually compatible with was like winning the relationship lottery. Rebecca felt confident Paige and Sol had all the ingredients for a successful, happy life together and she couldn't help being excited at the prospect of a wedding. There'd be so much to organise; Paige would look stunning in practically any style of dress, but what fun they'd have together searching for one.

At the thought of a dress, Rebecca remembered why she was standing in her walk-in robe practically naked. She needed to get a move on or they'd be late.

Finally, she picked out two dresses and laid them out on the bed. One was a black lace knee-length number—the menopausal woman's equivalent of a little black dress—and the other, a maxi dress, in all the colours of the rainbow. But which one would work better tonight? The bright multi-coloured gown was fun and would suit the occasion but she didn't want to draw too much attention to herself when it wasn't *her* night. The black dress might be better, but then again, she didn't want to look like she was going to a funeral.

*Why is this so difficult?*

She fought a yawn and, although excited for the evening ahead, couldn't help thinking how welcoming her bed looked. It was not even six o'clock and already she was struggling to keep her eyes open.

At the sound of Hugh whistling as he padded up the stairs, she snatched her towel back off the end of the bed and covered her nakedness. The last thing she needed right now was him getting frisky.

'You almost ready, honey?' he asked as he appeared in the doorway.

She gestured to the bed. 'I can't decide between these two dresses.'

Hugh frowned as he looked from black to rainbow and back again. 'They're both nice.'

'Nice? I want to look more than bloody nice. Tonight is important. It's not every night your daughter gets engaged.'

'Or launches a book.' Hugh winked, then took a step towards her and put a hand against her arm. 'Are you okay? You look a little off-colour.'

Truth was, Rebecca hadn't been feeling herself for a few weeks now; she'd been off her food—very unlike her—and had found herself short of breath every time she trekked upstairs. 'I'm just tired.'

'Perhaps you need to slow down a little. Cut back on your charity work or reduce your number of students. And maybe you should go see a doctor, you might be low on iron or something.'

'I like being busy. But I'm going to make an appointment with Dr Bell next week. I think I might be menopausal.'

'Ah.' Hugh's lips slowly curved into a smile and he nodded. 'That makes sense.'

It might make sense but it didn't mean she had to like it. 'It's not funny. I'll probably turn into a nightmare to live with. Hot flushes, mood swings, you're in for a real treat.'

'I'm sure I'll cope.' He dropped a kiss on her forehead. 'Now, is there anything I can do to help you get ready? We don't want to be late. Just think, when Paige and Sol get married, we'll finally have the son we always wanted.'

At his words, Rebecca's stomach quivered uncomfortably and she thought of the son she *could* have had. Hugh would have liked a house full of children, but Rebecca hadn't done pregnancy or early motherhood well. Being pregnant, going through almost twenty-four hours of back-breaking labour with Paige had awakened painful memories and led to postpartum depression.

She couldn't bear the prospect of going through all that again, so had decided against any more children.

'Yes.' Rebecca focused once again on the present as she forced a smile for her husband. 'I'm so happy for Paige and Solomon. You choose which dress, I'll quickly do my hair and make-up, and then, let's get this show on the road.'

# *Clara*

As Clarabel Jones curled the ribbon on the present she'd just wrapped for her niece's twenty-first birthday, her mobile rang. Her hand stilled and her heart squeezed as she stared at the device like it were a ticking bomb. Even without glancing at the screen, she knew who it would be. Almost two years since their divorce and Rob still hadn't got the message she didn't want him in her life anymore.

With a heavy sigh, she put down the scissors and abandoned the present. If she didn't answer he'd only try again, or worse, show up on her doorstep. The hairs on the back of her neck rose and she turned slowly towards the front of the house they'd shared for almost twenty-five years as if he were already standing there banging on the front door for her to let him in. Today, *tonight*, was hard enough as it was.

A tear for what could have been slid down her cheek and she swiped at it angrily as she snatched up the phone. 'Hello, Rob.'

'I didn't see you at the cemetery today,' he slurred, already obviously liquored up.

'I went yesterday.' Even as she said this she was annoyed at herself for feeling the need to justify herself. All these years later her heart was still in pieces, and she didn't need *him* making her feel worse.

'I see.' Was that judgement in his tone? 'How are you?'

*How do you think I am?*

She took a deep breath. 'I'm fine, Rob. What about you? How's your mother?'

'Can I come round? You're the only one who truly understands about Laura. We should be together today of all days.'

At the hurt evident in his voice, she felt herself breaking, her resolve wavering. There were times in the past when they had managed to comfort each other through the grief. Times when she'd thought maybe their marriage had a chance of recovering, of surviving. After all, who could possibly understand her heartbreak better than him?

But those times were rare and more often than not he'd turned to a bottle instead. He was going to end up one of those sad, lonely old men who lived on cereal and biscuits (or worse, tinned pet food) and who stunk of body odour because no one ever reminded them to have a shower. Her heart squeezed at the thought, but Rob wasn't her responsibility anymore.

She couldn't, she *wouldn't*, give in to the guilt.

'No, you can't. I'm going out, but even if I wasn't, you wouldn't be welcome here. You need to stop calling me, Rob. I don't want you in my life anymore.'

Silence greeted her declaration. She wondered if he'd finally get the message or if tomorrow he'd have forgotten this conversation.

'Where are you going?' he asked eventually.

She should have hung up, but she'd always found cruelty difficult. 'It's Aoifa's twenty-first birthday so I'm going out to celebrate.'

She waited for the snide remark—about how she could possibly go to a party today of all days—but it didn't come.

'Where is it?'

'Oh, some restaurant in the city,' she lied, because she wouldn't put it past him turning up off his trolley and ruining Aoifa's big birthday bash.

'Say happy birthday to her for me then.' His words didn't sound sarcastic but sometimes it was hard to tell.

'I will. Thank you. Now, I'm sorry but I've got to go.'

'Can I call you later?'

'No. Goodbye, Rob.' And then she disconnected the call.

As Clara went back to garnishing the present, she glanced longingly into the living room at the TV. The urge to curl up on the couch and watch some mindless movie was strong—and no one would blame her if she did—but she knew she'd feel better if she went out. Besides, she loved her niece dearly and wanted to celebrate her birthday with the rest of her family.

It wasn't Aoifa's fault she shared her birthday with the anniversary of her cousin's death.

*Josie*

Laptop on her knee, Josephine Mitreski tapped her neon-pink fingernails on her bedside table as she waited for her husband to FaceTime her. Nik was in Japan, apparently working, but she had a sneaking suspicion he was happier over there than he had been with her for the past few months. It was Saturday night and here she was, stuck in a place they'd moved to because of *his* work, with no family and no one she could really classify as a friend. The most exciting thing she had to look forward to was a phone call from her absent husband and he couldn't even manage to call her at their prearranged time.

Taking matters into her own hands, she punched her finger to the keyboard and dialled him instead. Just when she thought the call was about to ring out, his smiley, gorgeous face appeared on the screen.

'Hey, babe.' His warm voice filled the bedroom and he seemed genuinely happy to see her. Tears immediately prickled at the back of her eyelids.

'You were supposed to call me,' she accused, hating herself for sounding so needy.

'Sorry. I've been busy. Work's insane right now.'

'Never mind.' She leaned back against the pillows and lifted her knees, raising the laptop. 'How are you?'

'Good. Busy.' He glanced over his shoulder as if expecting to see someone. 'Work's demanding, we don't have the same supporting manpower here as in Australia, but it's good experience.' He peered closer to his screen. 'Are you still wearing your pyjamas?'

'No. I just had a shower and put them on.'

'Okay, good.' She bit back her irritation at his obvious relief. Last she checked it wasn't a crime to wear your PJs all weekend. 'What have you been up to today?'

She noticed he didn't ask how she was—probably he didn't want to know the answer. Just as he wouldn't have liked the fact she'd been wearing her pyjamas since she got home from work yesterday afternoon and had no intention of getting out of them until she had to leave the house again Monday morning.

'Oh, you know.' She injected a chirpiness into her voice. 'I went for a walk along the beach this morning, did some shopping, then a bit of housework and a lot of marking—the year elevens and twelves have just done their mid-year exams.'

'Bet you're happy I'm not there distracting you then,' he said with a cheeky grin.

As a high school drama and English teacher, Josie brought a lot of work home, whereas Nik's job as an aircraft engineer didn't require after-hours input. On the nights or weekends she had to do preparation or marking, Nik being home was both a help and a hindrance.

'It's too quiet here without you. I miss you.'

'I miss you, too. I sleep crap when you're not lying beside me, but I'll be home soon. Only seven more sleeps to go.'

*Home?* Even after eighteen months Sydney still didn't feel like home. 'Good.'

This one word was met with awkward silence—the *thing* that had broken them but which Nik didn't like talking about lingered between them like the proverbial elephant in the room.

'Have you heard from your dad lately?' he asked eventually.

Josie nodded. 'He sent an email from some place in the South Pacific a couple of days ago. Sounds like he's having the time of his life, meeting different people every night. Dancing till dawn. You'd think he was seventeen not seventy. Mum would have hated it.'

Nik chuckled. 'Good on him. Maybe we should try a cruise sometime.'

Josie tried hard to hide her horror. She could barely bring herself to get off the couch these days; the idea of being stuck at sea with a couple of thousand strangers didn't appeal in the slightest. 'Aren't cruises for single people, retirees or young families?'

And *there*, without her actually mentioning it, was the elephant. No matter how hard they'd tried, she and Nik didn't fit any of those classifications.

His expression tightened and she noticed little spots of rouge appear in his cheeks. 'I was thinking maybe we could go home for Christmas.'

This time it was obvious the home in question referred to Perth— where his huge extended family and her smaller one still lived—but a trip back to her birth state appealed only marginally more than a journey on the high seas.

'Didn't we just have Christmas?' She tried to make the question sound like a joke.

'It's June, Jose. Besides, if I want time off over the holidays, I need to book now. Some of us only get four weeks a year.'

Her hackles rose. It was one thing people who didn't understand how hard teachers worked making snide remarks about all the holidays they got, but Nik knew better. She was about to remind him exactly this when a voice sounded from somewhere behind him.

'Nikolce, my main man, hurry up! We're ready to go and there's a beer with your name on it waiting.'

Nik glanced behind him again as the owner of the voice poked his head around the door. No one but Nik's grandmother and his mates (when they were taking the piss) called him 'Nikolce'; sometimes Josie even forgot it was his real name. She vaguely recognised the tall, ginger-haired man as one of Nik's colleagues from Perth.

'Give me five,' Nik called back and although he had his head turned away from the screen she imagined him explaining with his eyes that he was talking to the crazy wife and couldn't rush things.

'Hi, Josie.' The guy—she couldn't remember his name—waved from the door. 'How are you?'

'Fine. Hi.' She forced a smile.

He disappeared and Nik turned back to the screen.

'Where're you going?'

He shrugged. 'Dunno. Some of the guys were just gonna head out for a few drinks, but I don't have to … I can stay if you want to chat.'

Yes, she did want him to stay so she wasn't left alone with her thoughts, but she didn't want to be an obligation or a drag.

'Nah, it's fine. You go.' She waved a hand at the screen attempting nonchalance. 'I'm actually going out too.'

'Really?' He sounded sceptical and rightly so because that was complete and utter bullshit.

In reality she planned a night in bed with a bottle of wine and one of her favourite movies from the eighties playing on her laptop. Big bold hair, outrageous fashion, feel-good music and a little Molly Ringwald had been her medicine of choice for as long as she could remember. Now the question wasn't whether she was more in a *Breakfast Club* or *Pretty in Pink* mood, but rather if any of her old faves would do the trick.

'Yep—some of the other teachers are going out for dinner to celebrate the end of exams.'

'Which teachers?'

She thought quickly, naming a couple of young women from the English department and a music teacher she didn't even like. Nik hadn't met many of the people she worked with, so he bought the list hook, line and sinker.

'That'll be nice. It'll do you good to get out.'

'Yes. So you go enjoy your night out and I better get ready for mine.'

'Yeah, you do that.' And then he grinned. 'You might embarrass your colleagues if you turn up to the restaurant in your current attire.'

'What?' She feigned hurt as she gestured to her vinyl-record-covered flannelette pyjamas. 'You don't like these?'

'They're cute, but I much prefer you without anything on at all.'

Once upon a time such words from Nik would have sent shivers rippling through her body, but now all Josie felt was a flicker of irritation.

'I think going out in my birthday suit might embarrass my friends even more. Now, have a good night.'

'You too. I love you. Send me a pic of you all dressed up—it'll make it feel almost like we're going out together.'

'Okay.' She silently cursed this *sweet* suggestion.

17

Nik grinned, blew her a kiss and then disconnected the call.

*FFS.* Cursing Nik's name, she discarded the laptop beside her, then threw back the bedcovers, climbed out of bed, flung open her wardrobe and grabbed the first thing she laid eyes on. She ripped off her PJs, shimmied the dress up over her hips and reached around to zip it up. Her bra was very visible but her gold jacket over the top would fix that for the photo. Ten minutes later, quicker than she'd ever taken to get ready for a night out in her life, her hair and make-up was done, and she fake-smiled at her phone as she snapped a selfie.

Image sent, she made a beeline for the kitchen. Pulling open the fridge, she could already taste the wine on her tongue and couldn't wait for its anaesthetising effects to give her some reprieve from her thoughts. Yet, when she picked up the bottle she was horrified to find there wasn't even enough for half a glass.

Surely she hadn't devoured two whole bottles on her own last night?

A quick survey of her cupboards told her she had and this made her want to drop to her knees and howl. A little voice in her head told her to take a long, hard look at herself and ask when wine had become so important to her.

But a much stronger voice whispered the solution.

*You're all dressed up. Go out and have a drink.*

*Why should Nik be the only one having fun?*

*Paige*

Paige glanced around the gallery section of The Art House in Coogee where she worked and which was currently set up for the launch of her debut picture book. So far there were more balloons than people—not even her own parents had arrived yet. The sales rep from her Melbourne publisher was waiting by the door to greet people when they arrived and the local bookseller had a massive table piled high with the book she'd poured her heart and soul into.

She turned to her boyfriend, Solomon, who stood beside her in a sexy black suit, which was almost as appealing as when he was in full fireman get-up. 'Where the hell are Mum and Dad? They should be here by now. What if everyone bails on me?'

There was nothing worse than throwing a party and having no one turn up. Not that she'd ever experienced such a thing. Paige had always been Miss Popularity and, as an only child, other kids had always been desperate to escape their siblings and hang out at her place instead.

'You know, you're kinda cute when you're anxious,' Sol said with a little smirk. 'It's a side of you I've never seen before.'

She whacked him playfully on the arm. 'I'm not anxious. I'm just … I want tonight to be a success and I don't understand why people can't be on time.'

He chuckled. 'It's barely seven o'clock, they'll be here.' Then he stepped a little closer. 'And by the way, have I told you how gorgeous you look tonight?'

Heat zipped through her as his gaze slid slowly down her body. It was impossible not to smile when Solomon looked at her that way. She felt some of her irritation subsiding and blushed as she recalled how they too had almost been late. 'I think you may have mentioned it once or twice.'

Now, as he dipped his head to kiss her, she squeezed her legs together as inappropriate arousal awoke within her. This was not the time to be getting horny, but at least he'd succeeded in distracting her from the empty room. Whatever happened tonight—even if nobody came—her book was still going to be out in the world spreading its important message and at least she had love in the form of the sexiest firefighter on the planet.

Said hero pulled away from the kiss, put his hand on Paige's shoulders and spun her round towards the entrance to see her best friends coming through the door. 'Told you people would come. Now go, mingle, wow them all with your creative talents. I'll make sure everyone is fed and watered.'

She stretched up and kissed him on the cheek. 'What did I do to deserve you?'

'I ask myself that question every day.'

Paige stuck out her tongue at him. 'Very funny.'

'That's me. Now go.' And he smacked her lightly on the bum as she did so.

'Hello.' She threw her arms around her three besties. 'Thanks so much for coming.'

Karis beamed. 'Wouldn't miss this for the world.'

'This all looks fantastic,' Narelle said as she gazed around the room at the walls lined with framed illustrations from *We All Live Here*.

'Don't forget us when you're famous,' Jaime made Paige promise.

She rolled her eyes. 'As if. Besides, you know that's not why I'm doing this.'

'We know,' Karis said, 'you're spreading an important message. That's why I'm going to go and buy multiple copies, so that when my friends all start popping out babies, I'll have a meaningful gift ready to go.'

Jaime nodded. 'Good idea. I'll do the same. Come on, we'd better go join the queue.'

Paige looked over to see there was indeed a queue in front of the bookseller. People had come! She scanned the room quickly—taking in the faces of folks she'd studied Fine Arts with at Sydney Uni, people she taught in the various classes that ran here, Sol's mum, stepdad and two younger sisters, even the baristas from her local café—but still couldn't see her parents. Where were they? An uneasy feeling settled in her chest and she was considering texting her mother, when Sol's mum, Lisette, caught her eye.

She waved and then gracefully crossed the room, closing the distance between them. '*Ma chérie*, I'm so proud of you,' she exclaimed as she kissed Paige on both cheeks.

Beside her, her husband, Randy, grinned from ear to ear and then pulled Paige into a big hug. 'Congratulations. This is sensational.' He held up three copies of her book. 'I already bought a copy for Lis and me and one for each of the girls.' He gazed adoringly down at Sol's eleven-year-old twin half-sisters who stood beside him. 'Will you sign them for us?'

'Of course.' Paige took the books from him and pulled out the pen she'd popped behind her ear earlier. It was a special one Solomon had bought her as a celebratory gift. She chatted to Callista and Claudette as she signed their books and when she was finished her heart leapt as she looked up to see her parents arriving, with her grandfather and two grandmothers in tow.

'I thought you lot might have forgotten about tonight,' she said, hoping her sharp tone conveyed her disappointment at their tardiness.

Her dad pulled her into a hug. 'Don't be silly, sweetheart. We just wanted to make an entrance.'

In his arms, she felt her annoyance evaporating. His hugs were like medicine for her soul. 'Thanks, Dad.'

She hugged each of her grandparents next and when she got to her mum, she admired the addition of a hot-pink streak in her hair.

'Wow, Mum. Love the new do. Makes you look even younger.'

Rebecca snorted. 'Your dad thinks it makes me look like the teenagers that serve him in Woolies.'

Paige laughed but then frowned as she noticed how sallow her mum's skin was in comparison to the bright colours of her hair and dress. 'Are you okay?'

Rebecca smiled. 'Of course I am, sweet pea.' But then she promptly began to cough, calling herself out as a liar. Was this the real reason they'd been late?

As her dad patted her mother on the back, Paige glanced around for Solomon. He was over by the drinks table, chatting with two homeless guys who attended one of her special charity art classes. 'Water,' she called to him as she pointed to her mother, still hacking as if at any moment she might bring up a lung.

Like the knight in shining armour that he was, Sol arrived pronto with a drink and held it out for Rebecca.

'Thank you.' The one word sounded like a real effort as she closed her fingers around the glass and lifted it to her lips.

'I don't like the sound of that cough at all,' Paige said.

'Sorry,' Rebecca said eventually. 'It's nothing. I must have swallowed air the wrong way.'

Paige raised her eyebrows at her father. 'Is Mum sick?' Her mother wouldn't have let anything keep her from coming tonight.

'She says she's just tired—she has been incredibly busy lately—but also thinks it might be the menopause.' He attempted to whisper this last word but he'd never conquered the art of talking quietly and Paige thanked the heavens above that, due to the excited chatter around them, only her immediate family heard his declaration.

'Oh, dear me,' exclaimed Little Granny, her father's tiny, nearly ninety-year-old mother. 'I still recall when I went through the change. Worst time of my life.'

'It wasn't bad at all for me,' said her other grandmother, whom Paige had always called Jeanie. 'I definitely don't remember coughing being a problem.'

'What's the meno-pause?' asked Claudette and Lisette pulled her into her side and promised to 'tell you later'.

'I'll be fine,' Rebecca said, almost fiercely. 'This is your big night and I forbid you to spend it worrying about me. I've already told your father I'm going to see my doctor next week.'

Paige wasn't mollified, but felt a tap on her shoulder before she could say anything else. She turned to see Louisa—the sales rep—standing behind her.

'Sorry to interrupt, but you've sold so many books already that I thought maybe you could start signing them, get a few out of the way, before we do the speeches. Otherwise you'll be here all night.'

Biting her lip, Paige looked back to her mother and was rewarded with a stern glare. 'You go sign books. Shine like the star you are. I'll be fine.'

'I'll make sure to reserve her a chair.' Solomon winked at Paige, his secret promise that he'd look after her mum.

'Thank you.' She beamed at him and then let Louisa lead her away.

The next half an hour flew as she chatted, signed more books than she could count and smiled for a zillion photos. Eventually she looked up to see Louisa standing in front of the table. 'It's time to launch this book baby.'

Paige jumped to a stand, adrenaline shooting through her limbs. She'd spent the last two weeks rehearsing her speech—this morning she'd said the whole thing by heart to Sol in the shower—and she couldn't wait to finally share her book with all her friends and family.

Louisa took to the mic first. 'Good evening, ladies and gentlemen. I'm Louisa Bradley, the New South Wales sales manager for Red Letter Books. We're delighted to launch tonight *We All Live Here* by talented debut author and illustrator, Paige MacRitchie.'

Heat rushed to Paige's cheeks as the crowd shrieked their applause. Sol winked from the front row where he stood next to her mum and dad, identical smiles on their faces.

'Paige's publisher, Saxon O'Brady, is sorry he can't be with us tonight, but he wanted me to tell you that it's been a long time since an unpublished manuscript has come onto his desk and moved him the way Paige's words and beautiful illustrations have done. All of us at Red Letter Books are super excited about this book and its message, but the best person to tell you about *We All Live Here* is the artist and author herself. Please, let's welcome Paige.'

As the crowd erupted into applause, Paige smiled her thanks to Louisa, then stepped up to the mic and surveyed the gallery. Her heart filled with pride and joy at the crowded room. She took a deep breath and began.

'Firstly I want to thank you all for coming—every person here tonight has been an important part of my life in some way, and it means so much to have you all here with me to launch my first book. Creating *We All Live Here* was a celebration of all my passions— I've been drawing, painting and creating as long as I can remember and you will all know I'm also hugely passionate about advocating for the rights of those less fortunate than myself.

'One night when I was lamenting the state of the world—the way so many people were hard-hearted and close-minded about the plights of others, especially our refugees—Sol said the only hope we have of changing how people think and live is getting to the younger generations. And a light bulb went off in my head. Picture books are read to little kids by parents and grandparents, so it seemed the perfect medium to reach many hearts and generations.'

She paused a moment and took a sip of the glass of water Louisa had placed on the podium for her. '*We All Live Here* is a story of six families who live in the same street and the friendships they make with each other despite their different beliefs, ethnic and cultural backgrounds. This street and these people portray what I want Australia to become—a place where everyone is accepted and considered "normal" no matter the colour of their skin, where they were born, their religion or who they choose to love.'

'Hear, hear!' shouted one of her colleagues as he pulled his boyfriend into his side.

Paige gave them the thumbs up and then continued, talking about the research she did and how each word and illustration in the book was a labour of love.

'The families from *We All Live Here* invite each other into their lives and the end result is that their lives are all richer for knowing and respecting each other. I fell in love with these characters and I hope kids all over Australia will do the same.

'Half of my royalties for this book will be donated to the Refugee Council of Australia and tonight we also invite you to bid in our silent auction for the original illustrations from the book.' She gestured to the artworks that hung around the gallery. 'All profits from the sale of these illustrations will be going to our local shelter for the homeless.'

Once again the crowd applauded. Paige waited for the din to fade, then, slightly aware she sounded like an annoying Oscar winner, she launched into the final part of her speech. She thanked her mum, her dad, her grandparents, Sol's family, her friends and art colleagues for their support and encouragement, and was almost at the end of her thank-yous, when she heard her mum cough.

Trying to ignore the twinge of worry that filled her heart at the sound—her mum was probably simply trying to cover her tears— she trained her eyes on Sol and smiled.

'Until I met Solomon, no one had lived up to my fictional heroes, but Rhett and Darcy pale in comparison to him. He puts up with so much—especially when I'm in the middle of a big art project and this has been the biggest yet.' She had so many more sweet things planned to say (bits she'd left out when reciting her speech earlier to him) but a lump formed in her throat and she found herself suddenly unable to speak as she blinked back tears.

Solomon moved forward and, due to his height and long legs it only took a couple of steps and he was beside her, enveloping her in his strong, perfectly muscly arms.

'I love you,' he whispered.

She smiled as she melted beneath his touch but he held her a mere few seconds before he let go and hijacked the microphone.

'Before we get back to celebrating, there's just one little thing I need to get off my chest.'

What was going on? It was one thing her gushing about him, but people might get bored if this turned into some kind of soppy lovefest.

'Paige has actually been very modest in her ...'

But his words were lost as Rebecca launched into another coughing fit. Paige's gaze left Solomon, anxiety curling round her heart again at the sight of her mother trying to control her barking. Hugh looked anxious also as he patted her on the back and held a glass of water she was too agitated to drink. Instead, Rebecca shrugged him off and waved her hand up at the stage, making gestures for everyone to ignore her and continue.

Paige turned back to Sol—concern that matched her own was etched into his usually smooth forehead.

Then, 'Oh my goodness!' Jeanie shrieked and Paige spun back to face the crowd. The reason for her grandmother's outburst was obvious. Her beloved mother was no longer simply coughing.

She was coughing up blood!

# Clara

The door was open at Siobhan's place in Rosebery when Clara arrived and, as she walked up the garden path, she heard the noise inside. Not loud, disruptive music that the neighbours might complain about but the sounds of her family trying to talk over the top of each other. She smiled at the cacophony, glad she'd come, and was just about to take the first step onto the front porch, when something (or rather someone) jumped out at her from behind a potted azalea.

'Bang, bang, you're dead!'

Her heart slammed against her chest cavity, the bottle of wine almost slipped from her grasp and a word she rarely said fell from her lips as one of her great-nephews aimed a plastic gun at her. Siobhan's lazy golden retriever raised his head where he was sleeping a few feet away but decided she wasn't worth barking at and immediately dropped it again.

'Um-mah,' said four-year-old Dylan. 'You said a bad word.'

Clara tightened her grip on the bottle and hit her tiny tormentor with her sternest expression. 'Of course I said a bad word—you scared me half to death. Does Great Nanna know you have that gun?'

Terror filled his eyes. Clara's mother—Eileen—Dylan's great-grandmother, did not abide toy weapons and as his mother had only been eighteen when she'd given birth to him, both his grandmother and great-grandmother were major influences in his life.

'It's not real.' But he looked sheepishly up at her, his bravado gone.

She dropped down to her haunches so she could address him eye to eye. 'How about we make a deal? I won't tell Great Nanna about the gun, if you don't tell her about my bad word.'

'Okay.' Dylan shoved the gun in the foliage of the pot plant and held out his hand for her to shake.

'Come on, let's go inside. I have to give Aunty Aoifa her present.'

Dylan glanced at the box poking out the top of her handbag as they started into the house, following the hullaballoo down the hallway. 'What is it?'

'You'll see when she opens it.'

Clara waved to some of her teenage nieces and nephews as she passed the theatre room where they were ensconced playing video games. She carried on into the open-plan entertaining area that housed the country-style kitchen, dining and living rooms. Siobhan and Neil's house was large, but even so it struggled to accommodate the number of people milling about. Dylan let go of her hand and snuck away, no doubt to get up to more mischief, and Clara put the bottle of wine and her handbag on the kitchen bench. Engaged in multiple conversations, her family didn't immediately notice her standing there on the edges looking in as if she were watching a show.

Rob, whose family had consisted of himself and his mother, said the Brennans were like some big TV clan, a cast of unique and quirky characters, who always had some drama or other going on. It was true; with four sisters who had all married and bred like rabbits and two parents who embraced their Irish Catholic roots still very much alive, theirs could be a long-running soap opera. They'd had the highs and lows that every such show needed—affairs, teen pregnancy, big weddings, small weddings, a niece who came out of the closet, childhood leukaemia, remission from said leukaemia, divorce ... The dramas were endless but what mattered was that through dark and light times, happy and sad ones, her family were there for each other.

Her mother played the role of matriarch perfectly with her nose always in everybody's business. Her father was a man of few words—currently dozing in the corner—but his wife spoke more than enough for both of them. Clara smiled fondly at her dear old dad, but was quickly distracted by squeals from the other side of the room where her brother-in-law, Ranaldo, was entertaining three-year-old twins, Zoey and Blake, teaching them how to make farting and burping noises.

Most large families had a crazy uncle and a spinster aunt and, from the moment her youngest sister, Bridget, had brought Ranaldo home to meet the family, they'd known he'd fit the crazy uncle role perfectly. Clara had just never imagined herself as the spinster aunt. Well, technically she was a divorcee but that was only semantics— she didn't have any children, and at fifty-three years of age, it would be a miracle of biblical proportions if she ever did.

'Aunty Clara!'

The squeal of her name snapped Clara out of her silent contemplation and she looked up to see the birthday girl pushing past her other relatives to throw her arms around her.

'Happy birthday, gorgeous girl. How did you grow up so fast?'

Aoifa laughed as she pulled back. 'Come meet my new boyfriend, Xavier. Isn't that a sexy name?'

Clara agreed that it was and happily let her niece drag her across the room to where a tall, lanky boy with curly dark hair and an eyebrow ring looked to be receiving a grilling from Aoifa's mother, her grandmother and three other aunties.

'Xav.' Aoifa took hold of his arm and drew him possessively against her. 'I want you to meet my Aunty Clara.'

Xavier's eyes widened. 'Another one?'

The women chuckled.

'This is the last, I promise, and she's my favourite.'

Clara smiled—she suspected she was the favourite aunty of all thirteen of her nieces and nephews and her great-ones as well. She had a tendency to spoil them, but when you didn't have kids of your own, surely you were allowed to indulge your sisters' children a little. She held out her hand. 'Hi Xavier, nice to meet you.'

Despite looking terrified, he had a firm handshake. 'You too. You all look exactly the same. You could be quintuplets.'

It wasn't the first time they'd heard this or something similar. As children, their father had called his five daughters 'my little Russian dolls' and the fact their mother had often dressed them in identical hand-sewn outfits hadn't helped. As adults, they all wore their golden-blonde hair differently but even so, their sea-green eyes and narrow faces made it clear they were related.

Growing up, Clara had always imagined that one day she'd have her own set of real-life Russian dolls, but whoever held the controls upstairs had other plans and instead all she had was a collection of wooden ones. It wasn't that she begrudged her sisters their happiness but why out of five children was she the only one who'd failed marriage *and* motherhood? Had she done something wrong in a past life?

*Stop it!* She hadn't come here to be melancholic and dwell on what she didn't have.

'There's strong genes on my side of the family.' Eileen focused her gaze on Xavier. 'What are *your* family genes like?'

He blinked as she continued, 'I want to know you come from good stock in case you and Aoifa make babies.'

*Always with the babies.*

'Oh, Nanna. Leave poor Xavier alone. I don't even know if I want to have children. I'm only *just* twenty-one!'

'Have I told you all about Ranaldo's mother?' Bridget asked in an obvious attempt to save the birthday girl and her boyfriend from her mother's grilling.

'Oh, yes.' Another sister—Fiona—nodded excitedly. 'You told me but go on, tell them. This is gold.'

And so Bridget shared a story about how her mother-in-law had just run off with a woman she'd met at her bowling club. Apparently her father-in-law was beside himself because who was going to wash his jocks? Aideen (Clara's second-youngest sister) said that sometimes she wished she could do the same.

'Oi, I heard that!' shouted her husband from where he'd been talking footy with his brothers-in-law a few feet away.

Everybody laughed and Clara felt some of the sadness that had weighed her down all day ebbing away. She was glad she'd chosen her family over a date with the TV. She might not have a husband or children, but she was blessed with wonderful sisters, nieces and nephews.

Aoifa led Xavier away from her grandmother and the conversation between the sisters changed to Fiona's angst over her son, Liam, wanting to change from engineering to a drama degree.

'Can you imagine?' The horror on her face would make anyone think Liam wanted to become a male prostitute.

'He's only nineteen. Let the poor boy follow his dreams before life crushes them. Now, Clara, can I get you a drink?'

'Yes, please.' Clara nodded. As much as she loved all her sisters, when Fiona (the oldest after her) started on about something, she could go on forever. It paid to escape while you could, so she followed Siobhan to the kitchen and gleefully accepted a glass of wine.

'How are you doing today, anyway?' This wasn't just your everyday how's-it-going question.

'I'm okay. I'm glad I'm here with all of you.' She took a long sip of her wine just as her phone started buzzing

'Is that yours?' Siobhan glanced towards Clara's handbag on the bench.

She nodded but didn't bother reaching for it.

Siobhan's face scrunched up into a scowl. 'Rob?'

'Probably. I did have to cut him short earlier when he called.'

'It's been two years since the divorce, when he's going to get the message?'

'It's always bad around this time. He doesn't really have a support crew like I do.' Clara let out a heavy breath; she couldn't help making excuses for him.

'And whose fault is that?'

Siobhan was right. Once upon a time he'd had plenty of friends—his band-mates were like brothers—but he'd slowly driven them all away.

Still, Clara ignored her comment. 'I don't know what he wants me to say though. Nothing I've done has helped him in the past.'

'That's why you need to stop trying. Rob will never be able to live a satisfying life until he gets help for his addiction and you'll never be able to get on with yours while he's still lingering in it.'

'I know but …' Breaking free was easier said than done. Clara had always been a helper—it was simply who she was—and there'd never been anyone she wanted to be able to save more than her ex-husband.

'No buts. It's not your responsibility to pay off his bosses, nurse his hangovers, go out searching for him in the early hours of the morning, sign him up to AA and—'

Clara held up her hand 'Okay, okay. I get the message.' She didn't need her sister recapping her disastrous marriage.

'You need to block his number,' Siobhan said, undeterred. 'Take out a restraining order. This has gone on for far too long.'

'A restraining order seems a little drastic—and I'm not sure it would even be possible, he hasn't actually done anything to harm me.'

Siobhan scoffed. 'That's debatable.' And then dived for Clara's handbag.

'What are you doing?' Clara's heart squeezed as her sister grabbed her phone.

Siobhan stared at the screen. 'What's your PIN?'

'Why?'

'Because I'm taking control of this situation. You're always worrying about everyone else. Always making sure *we're* okay, *Rob* is okay, *your patients* are okay, the women you *support* are okay, but what about you? It's my job to worry about you. PIN?'

Clara knew it would be pointless trying to fight this. 'Five. Six. Three. Five.'

Siobhan punched in the numbers as Clara spoke them. 'Bingo!' Then she called across the room to her nephew. 'Liam, how do you block a number on an iPhone?'

If everyone hadn't been privy to this conversation before, they all were now. As Liam asked, 'Why do you want to know?', all Clara's other relatives turned to see what was going on.

Siobhan filled them in and, as usual, Clara's business became a family affair. Liam pushed a few buttons, apparently both deleting and blocking Rob from her phone—she decided not to mention the fact he still knew where she lived—and everyone weighed in on the situation.

'You need to show Rob you're moving on,' Aideen said. 'And the best way to do that is to meet new men.'

'Yes, start going on dates again.' Fiona made it sound as simple as making the decision.

Clara all but snorted. She hadn't dated in over twenty-seven years. Part of her wanted to tell them she didn't need a man in her life but the truth was she missed having someone to come home to. Someone to talk to, someone to bring to family gatherings, someone to warm her feet against in bed on those long, cold wintry nights. Not that she'd ever really had that, not since the very early days with Rob.

After she'd thrown him out the final time, she'd been too raw to contemplate another relationship. Now almost two years on was she finally ready to let someone else into her heart again?

Even if she knew the answer to that question—and she wasn't sure she did—wanting to find a partner and actually finding one were two very different things. 'Where am I going to meet men at my age?'

'You make it sound like you're a hundred, Aunty Clara.' This from Aoifa—she was such a sweetheart.

'Some days I feel it.'

'If you're a hundred, what does that make us?' Her mother gestured to her father, who'd roused himself for this conversation.

The lines around his eyes crinkled as he smiled. 'Whatever makes you happy, love.'

'Thanks, Dad.'

'You could go on a cruise,' suggested Siobhan. 'Aoifa's always telling us we should try one and I've heard they're a great place for older single people to meet.'

'If you don't get seasick,' countered Fiona. She'd always had a weak stomach.

'Or sign up to some kind of club.' This from Bridget.

Ranaldo winked. 'My mum had some luck at lawn bowls.'

'Ooh.' Eileen clapped her hands together. 'I saw Martha Struthers at the funeral of an old friend the other day.'

Martha Struthers was the mother of a boy Clara had briefly dated (if you could even call it that) in high school.

'And she told me that—'

'Let me guess?' Clara interrupted. 'She told you that her son, Michael, is recently divorced and on the market again?'

Eileen nodded excitedly. 'Yes. He was such a lovely boy. You should look him up.'

'No way. I never even liked him when I went out with him. Why on earth would I go back for more?'

In hindsight, Michael—a bit of a nerd—had been another instance of her playing the helper.

'You could join Tinder.' Aoifa smiled at her boyfriend as she snuggled against him. 'That's how I met Xavier.'

Clara raised her eyebrows. She'd heard about Tinder and unless she wanted a sexed-up toy boy, it was not the place for her. And right now, she was done with this conversation.

'Thanks for your concern,' she said in her most authoritative voice. 'But isn't it time for Aoifa to open her presents?'

Everyone approved of this plan so the teens were summoned from the theatre room and they all clustered around the large dining room table to watch Aoifa unwrap her gifts. A pile of discarded paper grew on one end of the table and by the time she'd finished, everyone was starving.

Dinner—a number of different casseroles—was laid out on the island kitchen bench and everyone was instructed to serve themselves and then take a seat. If they could find one. The older generation were seated at the massive table; everyone else had to squash up on the couches or sit on the floor. As the food was devoured, the decibel level in the house rose once again with everyone talking and eating as if it were an Olympic sport.

As usual Clara and her father were the only ones not trying to be heard over everybody else. Her nieces and nephews talked Snapchat, Instagram and other things she didn't understand, while her sisters and brothers-in-law moaned about the hardships of getting teenagers through high school and her mother told them everything they were doing wrong. Clara didn't have anything to say on any of these topics, so as it often did her mind drifted into a fantasy about what her life would have been like if Laura and her other babies had lived. She could close her eyes and still feel her daughter's tiny hand in hers as if it were real.

She tried to swallow the lump that had formed in her throat. Laura would have been the oldest of the next generation, so Clara would have plenty to say on all things parenting. She'd have been the font of knowledge and wisdom for her sisters and all Laura's cousins would have looked up to her and hung off her every word.

Would Laura even be here now or would she be off in some far-flung corner of the globe pursuing her passions? Clara often wondered what they would have been. What her daughter would have grown up to do. Would she have followed in her father's footsteps and gone into the music industry? Or would she have been a doctor? A teacher? A journalist? If Laura had lived would any of them still be living in Sydney or would Rob's career have flourished and taken them further afield years ago? There'd been talk of moving to London before One Track Mind had disbanded.

She could easily visualise this whole other reality about how good her life could have been, if only … But this bubble of bliss never lasted and once again she found herself feeling like an outsider in her own family. She knew they didn't mean to make her feel this way and she wouldn't want them to censor their conversations around her but …

It was a relief when the dog toddled in from outside and slumped under the kitchen table, no doubt hoping that someone would accidentally drop food into his open mouth.

'Hey, boy.' When Clara reached down and scratched his ears, he moved closer to her, settling on her feet. She liked the feel of his heavy body against her legs and wondered if maybe she should get a pet. Then again, pets tied you down, and Bridget's mention of cruises had got her thinking. Maybe she *should* do something crazy like jet off on an overseas holiday. She was only fifty-three; if her parents' ages were anything to go by, she still might have a third of her life left.

Just because the earlier bit hadn't turned out how she'd hoped didn't mean she had to admit defeat.

## *Josie*

Josie locked the door behind her, tucked her wallet, key and mobile phone into her jacket pockets and then started walking fast towards the sea front. Thanks to Nik's love of the ocean, they'd rented an apartment in the coastal suburb of Coogee when he'd accepted the job in Sydney. And although she didn't feel the same urge to reside by the sea as her surfer husband, she had to admit the views were stunning and she loved the restaurants and cafés scattered along the beachfront. Right now, her close proximity to somewhere that sold alcohol was a blessing.

She followed the lights and the sounds of the waves crashing against the shore and in less than five minutes had the choice of the iconic Coogee Bay Hotel or the Pavilion, with its slightly more upmarket bar, depending on which way she chose to go. She'd been to The Pav (as the locals called it) a couple of times with Nik and recalled the sounds of families laughing together from the restaurant downstairs. Scowling at the memory, she dithered only a moment on the corner of Arden and Dolphin Streets before turning in the direction of the hotel. Right now, happy individuals made her cranky, but happy families were even worse.

Her pace brisk, she headed down the footpath, careful not to make eye contact with the Saturday night revellers. When she got to the hotel, she faltered at the entrance. The atmosphere inside simply didn't match her mood. Everyone was talking over pints of beer, barely acknowledging the band that played in the background, and no one had hit the dance-floor.

That's what Josie was in the mood for—dancing off some steam. She could be lost in a crowd while dancing, whereas if she just sat at the bar, someone might try to talk to her. She shuddered at the thought. What had she even been thinking coming out alone at night? How pathetic.

Perhaps she should head home, via the bottle shop of course.

Yet, as she retreated back the way she'd come, other music caught her attention and she glanced up Coogee Bay Road—it came from a place that had only opened a few months ago. She remembered there'd been a flyer in the letterbox and a couple of the teachers from school had been at the grand opening. The consensus was The Inferno (in big flashing lights) wasn't sure whether it wanted to be a pub, a bar or a nightclub but she didn't care what it was as long as it had alcohol, good music and a place where she could dance until she dropped.

Hopefully this combo would mean she'd eventually head home drunk and exhausted and would achieve the slumber that had been eluding her for so long. With this goal in mind, she joined the small queue of people outside and then raised her eyebrows at the bouncer when she got to the front and he asked her for ID.

'I'm thirty-bloody-five!'

'Consider it a compliment, sweetheart.' He winked and gestured for her to head inside.

Josie hated when people she didn't know called her 'sweetheart' but she didn't want to waste precious drinking time telling him off, so she put her irritation behind her and looked around for the bar. If she was in a mood to appreciate the scenery she would have—the décor of low lighting and dark-hued walls scattered with framed photos of celebrated musicians and actors was exactly the kind of thing she adored. This place reminded her of the club she'd been singing at the night she met Nik but none of that mattered tonight. She heard the sizzle of something like fajitas being brought out from the kitchen and turned to see a waitress weaving through people to one of the high tables. They smelt good, but she wasn't here to eat.

Spotting the bar along one wall, she made a beeline for it. Behind a buff barman showing off with a cocktail shaker, bottles of booze lined a mirrored wall—her choices were endless—but all Josie wanted was something that would hit the spot fast.

'What can I get ya, sweetheart?' asked the barman when he'd finished his cocktail magic. She had to admit the drink he'd just handed to a giggly girl beside her looked fabulous.

'Is that strong?' she asked, nodding towards the girl who was turning away.

Buff Barman winked and flashed her a toothy grin. 'Potent.'

'In that case, I'll have one of those,' she said, settling onto the stool.

'Coming right up.'

As the barman set to work, a shadow fell over Josie and someone filled the spot where Giggly Cocktail Girl had been only a moment before. Instinctively she turned to look and saw an older man—perhaps twenty years her senior—hauling himself onto the seat beside her. His dark hair was pulled back in a greasy ponytail and his stubble wasn't of the sexy variety, however something about him made her think he might have been quite good-looking in his prime. He had a kind of *presence* and looked vaguely familiar.

But the best thing about him was that he didn't look hyped up on happy pills like the girl, the barman and the bouncer. His shoulders were drooped and he seemed to radiate defeat.

As if he felt her gaze, he turned his head just enough to meet her eye. 'Hey.'

Josie blinked, startled and vexed that he'd spoken to her.

Without acknowledging Sad Guy's greeting, she turned back to face the bar as the barman placed her fluorescent green potion in a plastic cup in front of her. She handed him a twenty-dollar note, plucked the stupid paper umbrella from the top of the drink and dumped it on the bar, before snatching up the glass and walking off. She stuck the straw between her lips, relishing the slight burn at the back of her throat as the liquid went down.

You probably weren't supposed to drink cocktails like they were shots, but that's exactly what Josie did, so that by the time she reached the dancefloor her plastic glass was empty. She discarded the cup on a nearby table and forced her way into the throng of bodies rocking and bopping along to the latest Calvin Harris.

For the next hour or so the DJ played a mix of tunes from the seventies right up to the songs that were currently hitting the charts and Josie danced with pure abandon. The ear-piercingly loud music drowned out the thoughts in her head and the adrenaline made her feel alive again. When something came on she didn't love, she used the opportunity to grab another drink. Sweat trickled down her neck and she could feel her dress sticking to her back. Her calves ached and she was way too hot in her jacket but it held her wallet and her phone, so in lieu of anywhere safe to leave it, she kept it on.

And kept on dancing, not wanting this buzz to fade.

'Oh my God, I love this song,' she shrieked when eighties hit 'Lost Without You, Baby' blasted all around them.

The slightly stocky blond guy she'd kind of been dancing with gave her a bemused look. 'Who sings it?'

She couldn't help rolling her eyes. 'One Track Mind.'

'Never heard of them.'

'What?' She couldn't believe her ears—this was like admitting you'd never heard of Men at Work or Jimmy Barnes. One Track Mind may have broken up almost thirty years ago but 'Lost Without You, Baby' was almost as much a part of Australia's music history as 'Down Under' and 'Khe Sanh'.

He shrugged and nodded towards her now-empty plastic cup. 'Can I get you another one of those?'

She glanced down and found herself saying, 'Sure. Thanks. Why not?'

Josie watched him closely as he made his way to the bar to grab another. She might be well on the way to drunk, but she wasn't stupid and she wasn't about to have some dude spike her drink. When he returned, they clinked cups—not the same with plastic as it was with glass—and then Josie took a sip. The liquid went straight to her head and for the first time she felt herself unintentionally sway a little.

Her dance partner shot out a hand to steady her. 'You alright?'

'Yeah. Fine.' She nodded, resolving to sip not skol this cocktail.

'Good.' But instead of dropping his hand, he slipped it further around her waist and pulled her against him.

She felt something hard press against her belly and before she knew what was happening, his mouth covered hers and he shoved his tongue inside. Horror washed over her.

*What the hell!*

She yanked her lips from his and palmed her hand against his chest, pushing him hard. He stumbled and surprise flashed across his face.

'How dare you!' If she was going to cheat on Nik, it wouldn't be with someone so ignorant about music. Fury pulsed through her.

'You've been giving me the eye all night. Don't tell me you didn't want me to do that!'

'I didn't want you to do that,' she growled, one unwanted kiss rapidly unravelling all the good the dancing had done.

'Then you're a cock-tease. You don't think I bought you a drink out of the kindness of my fucking heart, do you?'

'I'm not sure what I was thinking but you can have your *fucking* drink!' Josie threw the cocktail—plastic cup and all—at him, before she turned and fled the dance-floor, hot angry tears exploding from her eyes as she ran.

She pulled her jacket around her, suddenly cold and a little scared the jerk might follow her. But damn him to hell for ruining her night. And damn Nik for being far away in Japan.

Weaving through the crowd, Josie barely noticed the people cursing as she bumped into them. She couldn't get out of the pub/bar/club fast enough. She emerged into the night, in desperate need of fresh air, but as she gulped for oxygen, she was hit by the smell of cigarette smoke instead.

Her last cigarette was over two years ago—Nik had convinced her to quit not long after they'd met—but the aroma now assaulted her senses, in a good way. Instinctively she turned to follow the smell and saw that the man attached to the cigarette was none other than Sad Guy from the bar. Leaning against the wall, puffing away as if his life depended on it.

'Do you have another one of those?' she found herself asking.

He looked up, surprise and recognition crossing his face. Then, he straightened a little and shoved a hand into his jacket pocket. Without a word, he conjured a packet of cigarettes and offered it to her. As she took one, he dug out a lighter and did the honours.

'*Man* ... I'd forgotten how good that was.' Josie sighed as the nicotine flooded her body and provided almost immediate relief. So what if it was bad for her? This was an up-yours to the body that kept failing her.

'Have I inadvertently lured you off the wagon?'

'Maybe.' She took another puff. 'But don't think you can give me a lecture, because that would be the pot—'

He held up a hand. 'Relax. I've no interest in lecturing anyone. I'm the last person qualified to judge, besides, I bet you have good reason for faltering.'

She inhaled again. 'Yes, I believe I do.'

Silence reigned between them a few long moments before he broke it. 'Right then, what is it?'

'Huh?'

'Your reason.' He nodded at the cigarette between her fingers.

And, if Josie had been surprised by this stranger's question, she was even more surprised when she found herself answering.

'I'm sad,' she said. 'I'm sadder than I've ever been in my life. I hate my body and I think my marriage is in trouble.'

'That's quite a lot you're shouldering there. No wonder you looked homicidal earlier when I said hello.'

'Sorry. I'm kind of a cow lately, but I can't seem to snap out of it.' She went to take another puff and then realised the cigarette was almost done. Without asking, he lit her another.

'What's the trouble with your marriage?'

'My husband and I have been trying to have a baby. First time we actually got pregnant by accident but I had a miscarriage. I've had another two since.' She didn't know why she was spilling her guts to this man—it had to be the drink—but couldn't help herself. 'Third time I lost the baby at eighteen weeks. She was a little girl.'

Josie spared him the gory details of her uterus being scraped clean but remembered all too clearly how painful and humiliating the experience had been. Her limbs, her heart, every bone in her body grew heavy as her memories plunged her back into despair.

'Fuck.' He let out a long, slow puff. 'No wonder you're feeling like you do. That's just shit. I'm sorry you had to go through that.'

She turned her head to look at him properly. This slightly rough face was the last place she'd expected to find sympathy and understanding but she thought maybe she saw the glint of a tear in his eye. Since her miscarriages—the last one only two months ago, here in Sydney—she'd heard many things from well-meaning friends, colleagues and even family, most of which had made her want to scratch their eyes out.

*It was God's will.* Well, if that was the case, God could go fuck himself.

*It was obviously for the best.* In whose universe?

*The baby is in a better place now.* How could there be a better place than in her arms?

*At least you know you can get pregnant …*

None of her nearest and dearest had a clue what to say, but somehow this unlikely stranger knew exactly the right words. Not to make her feel better but to give validation to her emotions.

She offered him the first genuine smile she'd given anyone in weeks. 'Thanks for listening. I came out tonight to try and numb the pain, but no matter what I do, I can't escape it.'

'You're out on your own?' His question could have been construed as threatening, but it didn't feel that way.

'Yep. Pretty sad, hey? But we haven't lived here long and I don't have any proper friends.' The few she'd begun to make through work hadn't really come to fruition—since losing her last baby, her colleagues seemed too scared to talk to her about anything but school stuff in case they said the wrong thing. She didn't blame them; they probably would.

'Where's your husband tonight?'

'He's in Japan for work. But he's sick of my sadness too. He wants me to get over it and for us to try again, but ...' She sighed, feeling the tears prickling again.

'He *actually* said you need to get over it?'

'Well ... no ... not in so many words, but he doesn't like talking about the babies. And although he says he's sad too, he doesn't act like it. How can he be really? I was the one pregnant. I'm the one who lost a part of me.'

'I don't know your husband, but us blokes process things differently. Don't write him off. I'm sure he's feeling it just as deeply as you.'

She shrugged. 'Maybe.'

'Have you spoken to anyone about your losses?'

'You mean like a counsellor?' She shook her head. 'I'm not really the counselling type. I don't see the point—talking won't change anything.'

'I don't mean some fancy-pants shrink.' He chuckled dryly, then dug his wallet out of his pocket. 'But my wife ... she understands what you're going through. Here's her card.'

With his scrappy clothes, bloodshot eyes, greasy hair and unhealthy-looking skin, this man looked in need of assistance himself. How could *he* have a wife who could help her?

Still Josie glanced down at the card as her fingers closed around it. The name Clara Jones was alongside the logo of Life After Loss, a charity that claimed to support people grieving miscarriage, stillbirth or neonatal death. 'Thanks.'

The flashing lights of an ambulance zoomed past as she slipped the card into her pocket. They both looked up as it screeched to a halt a little further up the road in front of an art studio. Two paramedics jumped out—one carrying some kind of medical bag—and ran into the building.

'Looks like we're not the only ones having a bad night,' the guy said as the paramedics disappeared inside.

She let out a sad laugh. 'True.'

Her mother always said that no matter what you were going through, there was always somebody else going through something worse.

She sighed deeply; while she'd verbally vomited her problems to the man, she had no idea why *he* was out alone on a Saturday night, littering the footpath like some kind of tramp.

'I'm sorry. Here I am unloading my woes to you while I haven't once asked why you're out drowning *your* sorrows.'

The man laughed quietly and then shook his head sadly. 'I no longer need a specific reason to drink, sweetheart. It's just what I do.' He straightened up off the wall and shoved his hands into his pockets. 'Take care.'

And with those words, he walked off, leaving Josie alone, cold, more than a little tipsy, and unsure about whether she was feeling better or worse than when she left home.

## Rebecca

'How are you feeling?'

Rebecca looked up from where she was lying on an uncomfortable hospital bed to see her daughter entering the room. 'Hello darling. Much better. I'm sure this is a whole load of fuss over nothing.'

'I bought you some flowers and some magazines to read. I know how much you like them.' Paige dumped the gifts on the portable bed-table thingy and took hold of Rebecca's hand. 'Sol's just parking the car.'

'Thanks. That's very thoughtful of you,' Rebecca said, knowing Paige couldn't understand why she liked reading about royals, rock stars and fashion. Still, as much as she did enjoy such glossies, she hoped she wouldn't be here long enough to read them.

If she'd had her way, there wouldn't even have been an ambulance last night and she definitely wouldn't now be waiting in the Prince of Wales Hospital for the results of blood tests, chest scans, x-rays, a CAT scan and Lord knows what else they'd subjected her to since her admission. She'd felt like a cadaver that medical students were using to practise everything under the sun on. The number of tests seemed a little over the top for what was likely nothing more than a complication from a common cold.

So she'd coughed up a little blood—okay, even she could admit *that* had scared her a bit—but she'd only fainted *because* of the blood. Rebecca had always had a bit of a queasy tum; when she saw vomit, she hurled in sympathy, and when she saw blood, she got dizzy. Hugh should have known this but by the time she'd come to, someone had already summoned the paramedics. There was probably a perfectly benign reason for her medical theatrics. One of the old dears she delivered Meals on Wheels to had been hospitalised for something similar a few months back—turned out the blood had been from a nosebleed.

Rebecca's eyes went to her daughter's ring finger. Where was the big, shiny, diamond engagement ring that was supposed to be glistening there?

She couldn't remember whether she'd fainted before Solomon proposed or just after. Maybe he *had* proposed but the beautiful ring he'd bought didn't fit properly. Her head hurt as she tried to recall the exact sequence of events last night.

'Where's Dad?' Paige asked as she glanced at the empty chair where Hugh had been in vigil since they'd arrived.

'I made him go downstairs and get something to eat. He was driving me bonkers constantly asking if I was okay, if he could get me anything, whether I was comfortable.'

'He loves you. He's just worried about you. We all are.'

'I know.' Rebecca squeezed Paige's hand. 'I'm sorry for spoiling your night. You looked beautiful, there were so many people there and—'

'Oh, don't be silly,' Paige interrupted. 'Louisa called me this morning and said that after we left everyone was so worried about you and sorry for me that they dug deep into their pockets and bought even more books. More money for the Refugee Council.'

Rebecca forced a smile. As proud as she was of Paige's drive and her vision to improve the world through her art, it was the more personal aspect of last night she was itching to know about.

'At what exact stage of the night did I faint? The last I remember is Solomon coming up to the front to join you … Did he …?' But before she could finish her question, the man himself came into the room with her husband.

'Look who I found lurking around outside,' Hugh said.

Paige stood back to let Solomon greet her mother.

'Hey, Rebecca,' he said, leaning down to give her a kiss on the cheek. 'How you doing?'

She looked into his eyes, trying to see if she could find any answers there. *Did you ask her?* But Sol seemed oblivious to her subliminal message. He went to stand beside Paige, wrapping his arm around her and pulling her into his side.

'I'll be better when they let me out of this place. Paige, go and see if you can find anyone to tell us when that might be.'

'I'm sure they'll let us know as soon as they have any news,' Hugh said.

Rebecca glared at him and then turned back to her daughter. '*Please*, sweetheart.'

'Of course, Mum, I'll go ask at the desk.'

'I'll come with you,' Solomon offered.

'No!' At Rebecca's loud protest all eyes in the room widened at her. 'You stay here. I want … I need … Paige will be fine on her own.'

Thankfully, as she was the one lying in a hospital bed, her loved ones were willing to give her whatever she asked without question. So, after a curious and suspicious glance, Paige went off to look for answers and the men stood like wooden soldiers as if scared to make a wrong move.

'Did you end up proposing last night?' Rebecca hissed.

Solomon and Hugh exchanged a look then Sol turned back and shook his head. 'You fainted before I got the chance.'

'Damn me,' she said, stamping her fists into the mattress.

Hugh put his hand on her arm. 'Relax, honey. The most important thing right now is your health.'

She shook him off as she would a pesky mosquito. 'You have to do it today,' she told Solomon. '*Promise* me, you'll do it today.'

Hugh laughed dryly. 'You seem more excited about Solomon proposing than you were about me doing so.'

She ignored that comment. Although Hugh had sported good looks and a sexy Scottish accent, he was thirty-one—thirteen years older than Rebecca—when he'd moved in next door to her family and this fact had prevented her from thinking about him in romantic terms.

But they'd struck up a conversation when they'd both been out walking their dogs and become solid friends fast. It had been clear to Rebecca from early on in their friendship that Hugh's feelings for her were different to those she had for him. When he'd kissed her, that hunch had been confirmed. Yet, although there hadn't been fireworks or blazing passion on her side, she'd found the experience wasn't all together terrible and they'd started going out.

She'd thought her parents might find the relationship scandalous and had actually been a little disappointed when they told her they approved. A cameraman for Channel Seven, Hugh was a kind, gentle, hardworking man and, most importantly to her parents, he came from a 'good Christian family'. It didn't seem to matter that he only ventured to church for the Christmas and Easter services.

In her mother's words, he would 'make a very suitable husband for her'. When he proposed, Rebecca's 'yes' was as much because she wanted to escape the claustrophobia of living with her parents as anything else.

She wasn't *in* love with him, she didn't think she would ever be *in* love with anyone again, but believed that in time she could grow to love him. And, luckily, she had.

But things were different between Paige and Solomon—their love, every aspect of it, had been the real deal from the beginning. When they looked at each other she saw in their eyes the kind of passion and connection she'd only felt once in her life. And she didn't want anything to get in the way of that.

'I think Paige has enough on her plate right now, don't you? I still want to ask her but—'

Before Solomon could finish his sentence, Paige appeared with two medical professionals in tow. Rebecca recognised one of them as the doctor who'd examined her early that morning.

'Hallelujah!' She'd never been happier to see anyone in her life. The doctors would tell her she had some minor infection, give her some antibiotics and then they could all go home. Solomon could have another go at proposing, Paige would say yes and they could get on with the excitement of planning a wedding.

'Hello, doctors.' Hugh looked much paler than usual. 'Do you have some news?'

The male doctor drew the curtain that separated Rebecca's bed from the others around them. 'We've got the results of your tests. I'm Dr Hodder,' he reintroduced himself and then gestured to the short but thin, dark-skinned woman standing beside him. 'And this is Dr Chopra, from the renal health facility here at the hospital.'

'Renal?' Rebecca breathed.

'Is that to do with kidneys?' Hugh asked. 'We thought she was going through menopause.'

Dr Chopra was so small her white coat swamped her and her stethoscope almost hung to her knees, but she smiled warmly at Rebecca as she spoke. 'The initial tests we conducted showed that you had bleeding into your lungs and so we investigated what exactly was causing this issue. Have you been feeling a little unwell lately?'

Rebecca couldn't answer. She vaguely remembered telling someone late last night about being tired, short of breath and a little off her food, but Hugh stepped in to repeat this now.

'What's wrong with me?' she asked when he was done.

'We believe you have pulmonary-renal syndrome.' Dr Hodder might as well have been speaking in tongues for all Rebecca understood. 'This is quite rare and was likely caused by Anti-GBM disease, more commonly referred to as Goodpasture Syndrome.'

Was she supposed to know what that meant?

'What's that?' Paige asked.

'It's an auto-immune disease in which antibodies attack the basement membrane in the lungs and kidneys, leading to bleeding from the lungs and kidney failure.'

Paige squeaked. 'Kidney failure?' Solomon drew her closer into his side.

'I'm afraid so,' the doctor replied gravely.

Rebecca shook her head. There had to be some mistake. She couldn't have kidney problems. She'd been fairly fit most of her life and, until recently, thought herself in better health than most of her friends. And weren't kidney problems usually associated with a drinking problem? She only ever drank on special occasions. 'How did I get this?'

Dr Chopra took this question. 'Although the precise cause is unknown, it is believed that an insult to the blood vessels taking blood to and from the lungs occurs to trigger the syndrome. Insults can be caused by exposure to tobacco smoke, gene mutations, an influenza infection, sepsis, bacteraemia, to name but a few possibilities. The important thing now is treatment.'

'So this *is* treatable?' Slight relief followed the shock she'd just had.

'What you have is end-stage kidney failure,' Dr Chopra said, speaking slowly as if talking to a child. 'So ...'

'End-stage? You mean ... she's going to ... How can it be *end*-stage? This is the first we've heard about it. She hasn't been sick. Well, not until recently.'

As her daughter's voice escalated, Rebecca's own distress increased. Why had this happened to her? Was she destined to have a short life as punishment for what she'd done in her past?

'Am I going to die?'

'Of course not, love.' Hugh rushed to her side and took hold of her hand. 'She's not, is she?'

'We're going to do everything we can,' Dr Hodder promised, 'to make sure that doesn't happen. I know this is a shock but we also know you'll probably have a lot of questions, so let's give Dr Chopra a chance to explain exactly what we're going to do and let you have some time to process it all.'

Dr Chopra shot her colleague a grateful smile and then took a deep breath before speaking. 'Your kidneys are no longer functioning well enough to meet the needs of your daily life. Kidney disease is usually progressive, however your illness is a rare variety that has reached the end-stage of kidney failure much faster. Our first step is to stabilise your body and this involves plasmapheresis, which basically means separating and removing the plasma from your blood to remove anti-GBM antibodies that are attacking your lungs and kidneys. Then we'll return your red blood cells, white blood cells and platelets, along with a prescribed replacement fluid. To put it simply, we're removing your old plasma and replacing it with a new one.'

Rebecca nodded, unable to speak, wondering if this would hurt, then immediately thinking how stupid that thought was. A little pain would be preferable to the alternative.

'In addition to the plasma exchange,' Dr Chopra continued, 'we'll also start you on immunosuppressants. This first stage of treatment will take about two weeks. During this time, once your organs are stabilised, we'll start you on dialysis.'

'What does that involve?' asked Hugh.

'Dialysis does the job your kidneys are no longer doing—the unit removes waste, salt and extra water to prevent them building up in your body but keeps a safe level of certain chemicals in your blood, such as potassium, bicarbonate and sodium. It also helps to keep your blood pressure at a safe level.'

'And that will make me better?'

'No. Dialysis doesn't cure kidney disease. Your condition means you will require dialysis for the rest of your life, or, if we can find you a suitable candidate, a kidney transplant may be an option.'

Paige's eyes lit up, the terror that had been scrawled across her face since Dr Hodder delivered the news lifting a little. 'You only need one kidney. Don't you?'

'Yes, that's right,' the doctors confirmed in unison.

'So, one of us …' Paige grinned, gesturing between herself and her father, 'can give Mum one of ours.'

'That's definitely something we can discuss in due course,' Dr Chopra said, 'but the first step is stabilising Rebecca's condition, so we're going to start that treatment straight away.'

'How long will that take? Can I take the drugs from home or ...'
Her voice drifted off before she finished the question because the
look on the doctors' faces gave her the answer. This wasn't some
little head cold; this was serious.

'You'll be in hospital at least two weeks,' Dr Hodder told her.
'During that time, we'll establish dialysis and work out a treatment
plan going forward.'

'Two weeks!' She'd been here less than twenty-four hours and
already felt like a prisoner. 'But what about my piano pupils? And
how are we supposed to be planning *their* wedding,' she darted a
glance towards her daughter and future son-in-law, 'when I'm stuck
in hospital that long?'

The moment the words escaped her mouth she realised her
colossal blunder. *Whoops.* She shot Solomon an apologetic glance.
His brown skin meant it wasn't overly noticeable when he blushed,
but she swore his complexion darkened a little now.

'What?' Paige's eyes grew wide as she turned to look at her
boyfriend. 'What wedding?'

As if she wasn't already feeling bad enough, Rebecca felt awful
for stealing Solomon's thunder. She looked to Hugh for help.

He cleared his throat. 'How often will Rebecca have to come to
the hospital for dialysis?' he asked the doctors.

'Two or three times a week.'

'Can't I do dialysis at home? I'm sure I saw something in a
magazine about a dialysis machine you can use at home.'

'There are such machines,' Dr Chopra said, glancing quizzically
from Rebecca to Paige and back to Rebecca again, 'but we prefer to
start you off in hospital. I'm sure you have many questions and we'll be
happy to answer them shortly, but right now, I'm going to go organise
your transfer to the renal health ward. Perhaps you can make a list of

what you'll need from home and someone can go get everything for you. A nurse will be in soon to get you ready. I'll see you on the ward.'

But, despite the bad medical news, getting Rebecca toiletries and spare clothes was the last thing on anyone's mind. The moment the doctors pulled back the curtain, Paige put her hands on her hips and glanced between her mother and Solomon. 'What's this about a wedding?'

*Paige*

'Well?' Paige looked between her mother and her boyfriend.

'I'm sorry. I didn't mean—'

'It's okay.' Solomon gave her mum a forgiving smile, before turning back to Paige. 'Well, this is the last place I planned on doing this and I had hoped on making it a little more special, but ...'

He dropped down on one knee in the middle of the room and drew a small box out of his pocket. 'Luckily I've been too afraid to go anywhere without this since I bought it.'

Looking up at her with his big, beautiful, near-jet-black eyes, he carefully peeled back the lid of the tiny, blue velvet box in his large hands.

Paige sucked in a breath as she gazed down at the most beautiful square-diamond ring she'd ever seen. Her pulse raced at the realisation of what was happening.

'Paige Marie MacRitchie, what can I say?' He grinned cheekily. 'From the day we met, I knew I didn't want to live another day without you. I love everything about you and pretty much find all the same things infuriating. I love your kind heart, your big ideas and the way you can bring almost anyone round to your way of thinking, but at three in the morning, I have to say I prefer my sleep.'

She giggled, having lost count of the number of times she'd woken him up in the middle of the night to tell him something or to ask his opinion on some idea she'd just come up with.

He went on. 'I love the way you click your tongue when you're thinking or concentrating on a painting, except when I'm trying to watch TV. I adore your body, except your cold feet on my bare skin on a freezing night. I love your mind, but your hypothetical questions drive me crazy. No, I have not thought about what I would do if I had to choose between saving my family or saving a whole boat of refugees and neither do I want to.'

She smiled at the way his tone was both doting and exasperated.

'I love the way you clean when you're mad, but not that I can't find anything afterward. I could go on, but all you really need to know is that … When I'm with you, nothing else matters. You make me want to be a better person, you make me want to be someone that deserves someone like you.'

'You *do* deserve me,' Paige whispered, emotion choking her throat at his words.

A glimmer of a smile twisted Solomon's lips. 'In that case … what I'm trying to say …' He blinked and suddenly looked more nervous than ever before. 'Is … Will you be my wife? Will you marry me?'

Torn between terror at the shock of her mum's sudden diagnosis and joy at Solomon's beautiful words, tears trickled down Paige's cheeks. Although she and Sol had been together almost two years and she couldn't imagine herself ever being with anyone else, this proposal surprised her. They hadn't talked about marriage and she'd never placed much value on the institution herself; despite her parents having a good one, it seemed old-fashioned and outdated. Yet, as Solomon's arms wrapped around her and he pulled her down into his lap, Paige knew in no uncertain terms that she wanted to be his wife more than she'd ever wanted anything.

'Yes.' Salty tears snuck into her mouth as she stooped to kiss him. They kissed for a few long moments before she finally pulled back and looked into his now also-teary eyes.

'I'm sorry. I just want to check. Was that a *yes*?'

She nodded, unable to speak past the happy tears flooding her face.

'It had better be,' came her mother's voice from the bed.

She laughed as her father uttered, 'Congratulations.'

'Thanks,' Paige and Sol said in unison, then she nodded to the little box still in his hand. 'You know I only said yes so I can get that ring, right?'

'I suspected as much.' Laughing, he plucked the diamond from the box and slid it onto her finger.

'It fits perfectly.'

'I may have had a little help from your mother regarding size.'

Paige looked to her parents. 'You knew about this?' Well, obviously they must have because it was her mother who'd broken the news only minutes ago, but nothing about today had been predictable.

Her father nodded and his chest inflated with obvious pride. 'Solomon came to us to ask for your hand and then your mother let him take her wedding ring to the jewellers because she knew the two of you have the same sized hands.'

'I see.' The feminist in her felt as if she should reprimand him for asking her parents' permission to marry her—like she was some kind of object to pass from father to fiancé—but the romantic in her loved that he'd gone to so much trouble. She also loved the word 'fiancé' and planned to use it as much as she could over the next few months or however long it took to plan a wedding. 'You're my *fiancé*,' she said.

'And you're *my* fiancée.' He laughed, then kissed her again.

'I'm so pleased for both of you,' said Hugh, coming over to them.

Paige stood and walked into his arms. 'Thanks, Dad.'

'Welcome to the family.' Hugh gestured for Sol to join them. 'You better look after my girl.'

'Da-d!' Paige rolled her eyes but secretly glowed inside.

'I will. She's my whole world.'

'Hey? Don't forget me over here,' Rebecca called from the bed. 'Do I get a hug too?'

Paige rushed over and threw her arms around her mum. 'Of course you do.'

'Congratulations, darling,' she whispered as she held her close and stroked her hair. 'I couldn't have picked a better man for you myself.'

Paige wasn't sure if the tears that streamed down her face were joyful or sad or a combination of both.

'What's the matter, darling?'

Paige sniffed. 'I've never felt so happy and so worried at the same time. I can't believe how sick you are.'

Rebecca, always stoic, scoffed at her words. 'Don't be silly! I'm going to be fine.' Then she nodded towards the magazines Paige had brought with her earlier. 'But, I want you to go buy some bridal magazines to replace those. At least then I can put my hours in this dreadful place to good use. When do you think you'll get married?'

Paige and Solomon looked at each other and shrugged.

'Whenever Paige wants.' Sol grinned. 'We could get married tomorrow if you like!'

'Quite aside from the fact you need to lodge your marriage notice a month before the big day, I'll still be here tomorrow. I'll never forgive myself for forcing you to propose in a hospital, but it'll be over my dead body that you get married in one.'

Paige flinched and, as if she'd just realised what she said, Rebecca slapped her hand over her mouth as her eyes widened.

'There'll be no dead bodies in our family for quite some time,' said Hugh firmly. 'But at least you'll have a funny story to tell your grandchildren.'

*Grandchildren?* Paige surprised herself by smiling at that far-off notion. She looked to Sol. 'You and I will make beautiful babies.'

He chuckled in the deep, sexy, throaty way she loved. 'Let's get married first.'

They stared at each other a few long moments in a manner that would have made her feel nauseous if she had to witness another couple doing it and then her father cleared his throat.

'*But* as excited I am about this engagement, you heard the doctors, Rebecca—why don't you tell me what you need from home and I'll go get it.'

Rebecca shook her head. 'I'll make a list, but Paige should go. She'll get the right things whereas you ...'

Hugh smiled. 'Fair enough. Paige?'

'Of course we'll go.'

'I can't believe what's happening to Mum,' Paige said as Solomon drove his pastel blue Valiant towards her parents' place in Balmain. 'It breaks my heart seeing her lying in that bed looking so vulnerable. I barely remember her having so much as a cold while I was growing up.'

He put a comforting hand on her knee. 'She's a fighter, your mum. I'm sure she'll be fine, but whatever happens, I'm here for you. Don't forget that.'

'Hmm.' Usually if Sol so much as brushed his hand against her, Paige went crazy with desire, but she barely noticed his touch. She dug her phone back out of her bag.

'What are you doing?' he asked as she started tapping away.

'Googling kidney transplants.'

'Do you think that's a good idea? The internet has all sorts of wrong information and the doctors said they'd be happy to answer any questions you have.'

'I'm not stupid, Sol. I can tell the rubbish from reality, but it's good to be informed.'

He didn't reply, just kept his eyes trained on the road and Paige felt suddenly guilty.

'I'm sorry.' She shoved her phone back in her bag. 'I'm just ...'

'I know.' He moved his hand from her knee and took hold of her hand. 'I understand, I care about your mum too and I want her to get well.'

'Thank you,' she whispered, tears threatening again. 'I suppose it could be worse. She could require a heart or lung transplant or something like that, which means someone would have to die for her to live. A kidney transplant has to be much more straightforward, right?'

'I would think so.'

'And I'm sorry your proposal wasn't how you intended it to be. Were you really going to propose last night at the launch?'

He nodded and let out a half laugh. 'I've been planning it for weeks. I went around and gave everyone party poppers to unleash the moment you said yes. Lord, I was hoping you'd say yes. I'd also hired a suite in a flash hotel in the city and had the bed decorated with rose petals and chocolates. I was going to whisk you away and make mad passionate love to you all night long.'

'Really?' He'd never been the gushy gesture type—he was far more likely to show his love by bringing her favourite takeaway to The Art House when she was working late or agreeing to pose naked when she wanted to practise her still life drawing. 'What kind of chocolates?'

'Okay, I *had* booked a hotel room but I lied about the rose petals and the chocolates. And I planned to fuck your brains out the moment we walked in the door.'

Paige snorted and would have elbowed him in the side if he hadn't been driving. 'Solomon Soulie, your mother would wash your mouth out with soap if she heard you speaking like that!'

'When I think about fucking you, I'm not thinking about my mother.'

And with those very naughty words, her *fiancé* succeeded in distracting her from her worries about her mother. 'Drive faster,' she ordered, squeezing her knees together.

By the time Paige and Solomon returned to the hospital with a small suitcase containing all her mother had requested, Rebecca had been transferred to the ward. Although she had a double room, the bed beside her was empty and they arrived to find Hugh asleep and snoring on top of it. Paige's heart squeezed at the sight. The news of her mum's illness had obviously taken its toll on him. Her parents had the perfect marriage and were so attuned to each other that she couldn't imagine one without the other. It would utterly break him if something happened to her mother and he had to learn to live without her.

Shaking her head of that thought, Paige turned her attentions to her mum, who was wide awake and not looking any happier about being confined to a bed. 'Hey. Hopefully we brought everything you asked for.'

'Thanks, my darlings.' Rebecca's smile looked forced.

'Where shall I put this?' Solomon asked.

'Just put it on that movey-table thing there and I'll unpack.' Paige tried to be quiet as she put her mum's things into the cupboard but her father woke up a few moments into the exercise.

'Hello.' He blinked as if disorientated and bolted upright. 'I must have drifted off.'

'Lucky you,' Rebecca said. 'I don't know how you could sleep through all the noise in this place. Hopefully they give me something to knock me out tonight.'

As she said this, a young man rapped on the door and popped his head inside. 'Ready for dinner?'

'Has hospital food improved any in the last twenty-or-so years?'

The man—who didn't appear much older than a boy—blinked; he might not even have been alive twenty years ago. 'Um.'

'Mu-m,' Paige reprimanded. 'Ignore her. Of course she's ready for dinner. Thank you.' As the boy carried a tray tentatively into the room, Solomon whipped the suitcase off the table so he could put it down and Paige spoke firmly to her mother. 'You need to eat to keep your strength up. Your body will be working overtime to fix itself.'

'She's right, love,' Hugh said, sniffing the air in the direction of the tray. 'And it doesn't actually smell too bad.'

Rebecca harrumphed and lifted the lid on the food as the boy all but fled from the room.

'Thanks,' Solomon called after him.

'What are you three going to eat?' Rebecca asked, picking up a bread roll and breaking it in half.

'I'll go see if the hospital café is still open,' Solomon offered.

Her dad decided to stretch his legs and join Solomon on the mission, while Paige continued unpacking and trying to make the room feel a little more cosy.

'I brought a couple of photos for you,' she said, putting two small frames up on the bedside table. One of her parents walking in the Blue Mountains and one of herself and her mother at Paige's twenty-first birthday party.

The others returned just as she finished organising everything.

'Café closed,' Hugh announced.

'But we bought up the vending machines!' Sol held out his hands, which were full of chips, chocolate and lollies. Her dad was carrying a similar haul. It appeared they'd both forgotten about her diabetes. Oh well, she wasn't the one they needed to worry about tonight and she'd make sure she ate enough and properly as soon as she could. There was always the emergency pack of crackers in her bag.

As Rebecca continued picking at her food and Solomon and Hugh began to devour their junk, Paige zipped up the now-empty suitcase and grabbed her handbag.

'Look what I found.' She pulled her parents' wedding album out of her bag as if she were Mary Poppins pulling out the hat stand. 'Ta-dah!'

'Is that what I think it is?' asked Rebecca.

'Oh my,' Hugh exclaimed through a mouthful of Snickers bar. 'We haven't looked through that in years.'

'I know. And Sol hasn't seen the photos, so I thought it would be fun in the light of our engagement for you to tell us about your wedding day.'

'Seems so long ago, I can hardly remember.' Rebecca pushed aside the tray. 'Give it here then.'

Paige handed over the album, which was one of those old ones where you peeled back the plastic and put the photo underneath.

Rebecca lifted the faded gold cover and food was quickly forgotten as the four of them got lost in 1988.

'Geez, that's some dress,' Sol said, pointing at the photo of her mother getting out of a car at the church. Eye-blinding white satin, huge puffy shoulders, pearl beading, lace sleeves, a massive bow at the back and a thoroughly impractical-length train—her mother's wedding dress had it *all* and was the epitome of eighties fashion. Atop her already larger-than-life dark, permed hair was a tulle veil that spread out at the back of her head like a lizard's frill. The bridesmaids were dressed in aqua-green, satin, short strapless gowns, also adorned with gigantic bows, big hair and big earrings.

'We didn't do anything by halves in the eighties. We all wanted to be Princess Di, although I don't think any of us wanted to marry Prince Charles.'

'I think you look gorgeous, Mum. Where did you get the dress? How many did you try on before you found the right one?'

'Actually, I won it. Mum entered me in a competition at a new bridal shop that had opened in the city and she and Dad were over the moon when we won, because his policeman's wage didn't stretch to a fancy wedding. We were on a strict budget.'

'That's right. I'd forgotten that,' said Hugh. 'Lucky you liked it.'

'How could you not like it? And look what a spunk you were, Dad.'

Paige flicked to another page with a photo of her parents cutting their cake. Her father looked like the cat that got the cream in a dashing black dinner suit, white-satin waistcoat and the classic white carnation with baby's breath pinned to his lapel. His cheesy adoring smile made her heart sing and the way he looked at her mother was exactly how she wanted Sol to look at her on their wedding day.

'I'm still a spunk, aren't I, love?' Hugh winked at Rebecca.

She shook her head with a smirk as she flicked to the next page. The photos had yellowed a little but love and fun shone from every image. At the reception, the bridal party sat at a long table, also adorned with bows, aqua and gold balloons, and confetti. It was your clichéd eighties wedding with prawn cocktails for entrée, beef and salmon for mains and a four-tiered fruit cake that apparently looked better than it tasted.

'What song was your first dance to?' Paige asked as she gazed down at her parents locked in a passionate embrace.

Rebecca frowned and looked to Hugh as if she couldn't quite remember. 'Was it "I Should Be So Lucky" by Kylie?'

Paige's mouth dropped open in horror. 'Surely not, Mother.'

Her dad's smile stretched from ear to ear and a glazed look came over his eyes as he said, 'Phil Collins, "Groovy Kind of Love".'

'Oh, that's right. It's coming back to me now. I took hours choosing the playlist and putting all the songs onto a couple of cassettes.'

'If I recall correctly George Michael featured heavily on that list. I think you were half in love with him.'

'I'm still not over his death,' she said, going on to list some of the other songs that had been on repeat on her Walkman around that time, many of which still pumped out of her iPhone speaker dock whenever she cleaned the house.

Rebecca sighed, a sentimental smile sitting on her face. 'The eighties was such a fab decade for music.'

'Did you throw your bouquet?' Paige asked, pointing down at the unsurprisingly enormous (was anything small-scale in the eighties?) cascading bouquet of white and pink carnations. The pink totally clashed with the four bridesmaids' outfits.

'Oh yeah, the bouquet toss was non-negotiable. My single friends would never have forgiven me if we missed that.'

That was a tradition Paige felt weddings could do without and she certainly didn't plan on having it at hers but she loved listening to her parents talk about their special day. And, since she'd brought out the album, her mother hadn't whined once about being stuck there like a prisoner.

A knock on the door interrupted the discussion and a golden-haired nurse Paige guessed to be in her early to mid-fifties entered the room. She wore one of those upside-down watches and a warm smile.

'Good evening. I'm Clara and I'll be your nurse for the night.'

'Hello,' Rebecca replied. 'I *would* say it's nice to meet you but …'

The nurse smiled again as she lifted the clipboard off the end of the bed and peered down at it. 'I understand. This isn't most people's first choice for a holiday. Now I need to do your obs and I'm sorry but visiting hours are over for the day, so you're going to have to say goodbye to your fan club.'

'Okay.' Rebecca nodded, her voice not much more than a whisper, and once again Paige noticed how frail and vulnerable she looked.

'I'm on the late shift at the café tomorrow, so I'll grab some bridal magazines and come to visit you in the morning.'

'And I'll call work and tell them I need a few days off,' said Hugh. 'We won't let you get bored and lonely in here, love.'

They took turns kissing her mother goodbye and even before they'd left the room, Clara had begun to take her blood pressure.

'Do you want to come to our place and have something proper to eat?' Paige asked her dad as they headed for the elevators. Quite aside from the food, she was worried about him going home to an empty house.

'Thanks sweetheart, but I'll be fine. I'm full after all that chocolate.' He chuckled and patted his middle-aged spread. 'I'll have some baked beans on toast later if I get hungry.'

She cringed. Was that what he'd live on if something did happen to her mother? *No*, she refused to think about that option. A kidney transplant would make her mum like new again.

'Maybe I should stay with you tonight,' she said, already thinking about making him up some healthy soup, full of hearty vegetables.

'No. I can look after myself you know. I managed quite a few years before your mother came along. And you should be with Sol tonight, celebrating your engagement and making wedding plans.'

'If you're sure ...' Paige still wasn't convinced.

'I am,' he said as they arrived in front of the line of elevators. 'I promise I'm fine. Your mother is in the best place and I'll rest easy knowing that.'

Sol reached forward and punched the down button.

As they waited, a thought struck Paige. 'Dad—what happened to Mum's wedding dress? Is it packed away at the house somewhere?'

It seemed odd she'd never asked about this before, but she hadn't been one of those little girls obsessed with weddings and dressing up. Much to her mum's chagrin, who'd longed for a daughter to go shopping for clothes with.

He frowned a moment and then scratched his head. 'I think she gave it away to charity.'

'Oh.' Paige's heart sank and she couldn't hide the disappointment in her voice; the grand plan that had entered her head a few seconds earlier was gone as soon as it had arrived.

## Clara

Clara yawned as she let herself into her house just before eight o'clock on Monday morning. Normally following a night shift, she'd eat a quick bowl of porridge, have a shower and fall into bed for a few hours slumber. After thirty-plus years working shift hours, her body was trained to sleep when necessary and she was usually catching z's within minutes of her head hitting the pillow.

Not today.

Although she was her usual post-shift fatigued, her mind refused to switch off. She lay in bed, staring at the ceiling, thinking about one of last night's patients—a woman only a few years younger than herself who'd been diagnosed with end-stage kidney failure. The woman put on a brave face for her family, but the shock of such a diagnosis had hit her hard. Clara had gone into her room in the early hours of the morning, expecting to find her patient asleep but found her in tears instead.

Pulling up the plastic visitor chair, she'd sat beside the woman and listened as she lamented about her situation, asking over and over 'why me?'

Clara didn't have the answers to this question any more than she had the answers to why she'd never been blessed with children or a more stable husband, but she'd tried to comfort the woman as she mourned her healthy body and worried about how her husband would cope if she died. And although Clara was sympathetic, part of her couldn't help feeling a little jealous. At least if her patient died, she'd leave a hole in someone's heart and also a legacy in her daughter. Clara didn't have to worry about leaving anyone behind—sure her parents, siblings, nieces and nephews would be sad but life would go on for each of them—and that didn't give her any comfort.

You never knew when your time was up. She could die tomorrow and when her life flashed before her eyes she'd have nothing to show for it.

*It's not too late to change your destiny.*

She blinked and wondered if she *was* actually asleep and dreaming because such a thought felt far too *woo-woo* to have come from her own head. But it led to her thinking about the conversation she'd had with her family on Saturday night.

As sleep didn't appear to be on the agenda any time soon, Clara threw back her bedcovers, climbed out and set off to make herself a cup of tea.

Her house was almost as big as Siobhan and Neil's, so it was a bit of a hike from her bedroom at the front to the kitchen at the back, but as she headed down the hallway, passing all the other bedrooms, she thought about the vast differences between the two houses. Whereas her sister's house was filled with love, laughter, a constant stream of people and a whole lot of mess, Clara's house was neat and tidy but perpetually cold and quiet.

The size of the house reminded her daily how alone she was.

Over the years she'd tried to fill it with good memories, but she might as well be living in a newly built display home for all its warmth. Or a museum thanks to her various 'collections'. When she and Rob got married they'd had grand dreams and had bought a house as large as they could afford, intending to fill the rooms with children in the not *too* distant future. They'd wanted five or even six, enough for a basketball team Rob had often joked, although she imagined any kids of his were much more likely to form a band.

In those early days, things had been fabulous. After Rob's band were signed by a big record label, they went from playing gigs to touring Australia. When they were home—supposedly working on future albums—the house had been dubbed 'the party house'. It was a rare weekend when the place wasn't filled with people. Clara had adored entertaining and was so proud of Rob, who everyone knew as singer *and* songwriter was the true talent in the band.

But, as their dreams of a family had dried up, so had Rob's inspiration. He stopped picking up a guitar and a pen to work through his feelings and started picking up a bottle and, instead of the house filling with children, all they'd managed to fill the rooms with was clutter.

Clara kept on nursing through their heartaches, but Rob's music suffered big-time. Tired of him always showing up to practice and gigs drunk, sick of him not being able to offer them any good new material, two of his band-mates quit and although the other two stuck by him, their second album (delayed thanks to him) was both a commercial and a critical flop. The group disbanded when they were dropped by their record label not long after and, to the best of Clara's knowledge, Rob hadn't written another song since. Although he'd worked on and off over the years in bars and pubs, he'd never managed to hold down a job longer than a few months. Usually his bosses, who at first were happy to have someone 'famous', had showed him the door when they discovered he was drinking the profits. He never cared much about being fired because the royalties that still trickled in all these years later were enough to keep him in the grog he required.

But whereas Rob drank to numb the pain, Clara bought stuff. There were bookshelves in almost every room, crammed full of paperback novels. At least she read these, but what was the point of everything else?

She owned a collection of bone china teacups and teapots that she didn't even use when her sisters and mother came around for afternoon tea. She had teaspoons, postcards and magnets from the year she and Rob travelled round Australia—an attempt on her behalf to get them to reconnect. Then there were the buttons, the pens, the stamps, the foreign coins, the thimbles, the cat ornaments (because she loved cats but hadn't had one since she was a child), the special royalty edition copies of magazines such as *New Idea* and *Women's Day*. She even had a collection of rolling pins. And that was only the beginning.

Everything was displayed beautifully on shelves throughout the house and even in the spare bedrooms. The rare times Rob was on the wagon, he'd actually been a great handyman and had made cabinets to house all the little things that Clara spent her weekends dusting. She could only imagine the dust that would gather if she actually took her sisters' advice and got a life. If she started 'dating' again—she chuckled at the almost-foreign word—who would maintain her museum?

Her laughter fell flat as an even more horrifying thought struck. What would happen to all her stuff when she died? She didn't have children who'd be lumped with sorting it all out, so her younger sisters or their children would have to do the honours.

And what would they say about her?

*Poor Aunty Clara—she had nothing better to do with her life than collect crap.*

She could just imagine them shaking their heads sadly as they boxed up all her stuff and they'd be right because the only collection she really felt any attachment to was her Russian dolls. Her dad had given her the first—beautifully handpainted blue-and-white ones—on her sixteenth birthday and she had added to it frequently over the years. The rest she could do without.

It was as if a light bulb had gone off in her head.

*I could get rid of it all!*

But then the house truly would feel empty.

The kettle whistled; she couldn't even remember filling it up and, as she poured hot water into her mug and jiggled her teabag up and down, another thought flickered.

*Why don't you sell it?*

Suddenly Clara didn't know why she'd held onto the house in the divorce. Probably because just getting rid of Rob had been effort enough and if she'd downsized then she'd have had to deal with the clutter as well.

Light-headed with excitement, she took her tea, grabbed a packet of Tim Tams from the cupboard and sat down at the table in front of her laptop. As she lived alone, most of the time she ate dinner in front of the TV, so the dining room table had become more of a desk, with bills to pay, other paperwork and books taking up half of it. She rested the tea on last month's issue of the *Australian Women's Weekly* and took a bite of chocolate biscuit as she waited impatiently for her laptop to wake up.

There was so much going through her head, she wasn't sure where to start. Real estate agents, places where she could sell her junk, exotic holiday destinations *or* how to find love in your fifties? Feeling indecisive, she opened four tabs and chose the all-at-once approach. There were young nurses at work who could tap a message out on their phone while at the same time working on three different tasks on the computer.

If the millennials could multitask why couldn't she?

Within half an hour, Clara had a list of local estate agents and had decided that donating her collections to charity was the easiest solution. Siobhan would probably berate her for this decision—saying she could get good money for some of her stuff on Gumtree or eBay—but she didn't need or want money. She needed a life. She wanted freedom, excitement, hope.

The prospect of putting herself out there and opening up to the possibility of a relationship was daunting but there was a lot of advice for women of her vintage in the same position—independent women who were quite capable of looking after themselves but wanted companionship. With a deep breath and shaking hands, she opened yet another tab and typed the most terrifying words of all: 'online dating for over fifties.'

After almost an hour reading the 'why choose us' sections of a number of different websites, she decided to bite the bullet and register for one. She filled in all her details truthfully—no point pretending to be someone she wasn't at her age—then uploaded the most recent photo she could find and pressed submit.

# July

*Josie*

There was a buzz of excitement at school all day (and not just among the students). It was the last day of term and two glorious weeks of holidays lay ahead. Josie's colleagues, who had been sporting dark bags under their eyes the past few weeks, had a spring in their step and were letting their classes out five minutes before the final siren.

Not Josie; she made her year ten English students work to the bitter end.

'Miss!' One of her most annoying students leapt out of his chair and thrust his finger at the window. 'Everyone else is already out. Can we go now?'

'Sit down, Noah.'

Surprisingly, he did as he was told. Probably he didn't want her to give him detention on the last day of school—the mood she was in right now, she would too, if she didn't have to head to the airport to collect Nik.

A heavy ball of dread grew in her stomach at the thought.

She should be excited at the prospect of seeing her husband after almost a month apart, but being with Nik made her feel like a failure. Even on FaceTime, she couldn't look him in the eye. Every time she did she recalled his exact expression each time she'd told him she was miscarrying. Sure, he'd tried to cover over it quickly, always wrapping his arms around her and saying all the things he thought he should be saying—*it wasn't her fault, they'd have another baby, he loved her no matter what*—but he'd never been quick enough to hide the utter disappointment in his eyes.

Her body had killed his babies and she was the murderer of his dreams.

The siren blasted through the school and her students shoved back their chairs and sprung to their feet.

Noah was already halfway to the door when he said, '*Now* can we go?'

'Yes. Go.' She shooed them with her hands.

As the kids streamed past her desk, a few of them whispered loudly to each other.

'What the hell is wrong with Ms Mitreski? She's been such a cow lately.'

'I heard her husband's working overseas so she's probably not getting enough.'

The girls exploded into giggles as they poured out of the classroom. Josie wasn't sure whether they meant her to hear or not, whether they meant to hurt her with their words—she wouldn't put it past fifteen-year-old females—but nothing *they* said could make her feel any worse than she already did. With a deep sigh, she went around the classroom making sure all the windows were shut. The cleaners were supposed to lock up, but so many times the school had been vandalised because one of the windows wasn't shut properly. Or maybe Josie was just dithering.

She walked back to her desk, scooped up her planner and then switched off the lights as she headed out into the corridor. As she dragged her feet towards the staffroom, dodging kids and basketballs and various other things that flew through the air, she passed Jake, one of the younger teachers.

He gave her a super-cheesy grin and lifted his hand to high-five her. 'Woohoo. We made it through another term. Only two more and *sum*-mer.'

'Yippee.' She forced a smile; Jake wasn't much more mature than the year twelve boys.

'What are you up to these hols?' Thankfully he didn't stay still long enough for her to answer, instead continuing on down the corridor high-fiving every student he passed.

She felt like Eeyore right now. Jake was Tigger trying to get everyone to catch his enthusiasm and she just wanted to crawl into a hole and hibernate. Not that donkeys hibernated, but still. Finally, she reached her destination and was relieved to find it empty. She retrieved her handbag, but, as she started towards the door, one of her colleagues entered.

'Oh, hi Jose,' Sarsha said, pulling her long black hair out of its ponytail. 'I thought you'd be gone already. Isn't Nik coming home tonight?'

'Yep.' She hitched her handbag to her shoulder, thankful she had an excuse not to stay and chat. 'I'm heading to the airport now.'

Sarsha flopped into a chair and rocked on it like a kid—the holidays had gone to everyone's head. 'You must be so excited. Does he have some time off too?'

'No, he's back to work Monday.' *Thank God.* If Nik had holidays he'd want them to go out and *do* things together, like bowling.

He thought bowling fixed everything and once upon a time she'd enjoyed playing with him, but the only thing about the bowling alley that appealed right now was the fact it sold alcohol.

'Ah, what a shame. Well, if you get bored and wanna go see a movie, give me a buzz.'

'Okay. I will,' Josie lied as she forced another smile and headed for the door, making a beeline for the staff car park.

She sent a silent prayer of thanks skyward when she made it to her car without further interruption and had the keys turning in the ignition almost before she'd fastened her seatbelt. As she zoomed out of the car park and towards Gardeners Road, she listened to her favourite eighties playlist, but these days even Kylie, Madonna and INXS didn't give her the feeling they once did.

Finally, a good ten minutes from the school and still fifteen minutes or so from the airport, she pulled into a side street and parked. Grabbing her lighter and pack of smokes from her handbag, she jumped from the car and hurried round to the other side so the vehicle could shield her from traffic and possible sightings by students or someone who knew Nik. If it weren't for him she'd smoke while driving, but he had a nose like a hound and would smell her sins the moment he got in the car.

She puffed quickly through one cigarette and immediately lit another, knowing that her husband's arrival home would mean she'd have to quit smoking again. *Damn* him! Nik had never so much as had a puff of a smoke in his life, whereas most of her twenties, due to her working and living in the West End of London, she'd been a pack a day kind of girl. She'd cleaned up her act when she moved back to Perth to 'settle down' and 'get a real job', but when her mother died, she'd turned to drinking and smoking for relief.

Who knew what would have become of her if Nik hadn't come along and dragged her out of the metaphorical gutter? He was like no one she'd ever met before—part geek, part surfer—so different to her previous boyfriends, most of whom had been actors like her and more in love with themselves than anyone else. In Nik she'd found a shared passion for film, someone to make her laugh and someone she could have intellectual conversations with. Until she'd met him she hadn't thought aeroplanes sexy at all, but Nik talking about aviation mechanics and engineering was a surprising aphrodisiac. His love had brought her alive again.

If Nik knew she was smoking now, he'd be so disappointed and likely quote some statistic about nicotine being bad for fertility. Well, duh, nicotine wasn't good for anything but it wasn't like she could do any worse in that department.

Josie was tempted to light up a third but she'd be late meeting his plane. With great reluctance, she climbed back into the car, buried her cigarettes right at the bottom of her handbag, popped half a packet of chewing gum into her mouth and squeezed sanitiser all over her hands.

As she drove closer to the international airport, she thought about the last time she'd been picking Nik up from a work trip. Almost two years ago, only that time he'd been coming home from Sydney and she'd been waiting at Perth airport. How different life had been then—stretched before them like a blank canvas waiting for them to smother it with bright colours depicting their happy life.

She'd fallen into his arms as he appeared in the throng of passengers and they'd stood there, lip-locked, uncaring that they were publicly displaying affection and possibly holding up the traffic in the process. Hands in each other's pockets like the smug-in-love couple they were, they'd walked to the baggage carousel together and he'd been hyped about showing her something he'd found in Sydney.

'What is it?' she'd begged him to tell her as they'd watched the suitcases going round and round. 'Is it something to do with the baby?'

They'd shared a knowing secret look as he'd put his hand on her still-flat belly. Just before he'd flown to Sydney for work, they'd had the biggest surprise of their lives—she was pregnant! Once they'd recovered from the shock, they were both beside themselves with excitement. They'd only been going out a few months, but had been unofficially living together most of that time. When you knew, you knew, right? And Josie had known almost from the moment she'd laid eyes on Nik that he was The One. He'd felt the same; there was only one problem—he was engaged to his high school sweetheart at the time.

Breaking up with his fiancée had created a bit of a family rift—his mother, Vesna, who was originally from Macedonia and held very traditional values, was horrified—but they'd been hoping the baby would smooth things over.

'I'll show you when we get home,' he'd said as he'd lifted his hand off her belly, plopped a kiss on the end of her nose and drew her even closer against his hot, sexy body.

Patience wasn't her virtue, but Nik distracted her with more kisses and as she drove back to her place, he kept one hand on her knee as he raved about his time in Sydney.

'It sounds like you'd like to move there,' she'd said as they walked up the garden path to the little unit she rented in Maylands.

'Actually … the airline has offered me a transfer. It's a promotion, the money's good and I'd like to take it.'

'Oh.' Her chest tightened as if she were having a heart attack. 'I see. Congratulations.' She'd tried to sound happy for him when all she could think was *Where does that leave me? Us? The baby? I have a job in Perth!*

She'd fumbled with her key, trying but failing to get it in the front door lock. As if oblivious to her torment, Nik had placed his hand over hers, turned the key and pushed open the door.

'Thanks,' he'd said, his joy evident in his tone.

She'd walked inside almost on autopilot and he'd carried the suitcase into the lounge room. 'Are you going to come see what I got you in Sydney?'

She'd blinked, having almost forgotten he had something to show her. 'Oh, right, sure, coming!' she'd called, before taking a moment to compose herself. Maybe this wasn't the disaster she thought it to be. Maybe she could go with him? And if not, plenty of people survived long-distance relationships and maybe the job was only temporary.

But, as she'd joined him in the lounge room, she'd gasped.

Standing in front of her wearing a grin almost too big for his face was Nik and he was holding up a wedding dress.

'What is that?'

He'd chuckled. 'I thought that was pretty obvious. I found it in an op shop.'

*Is he a cross-dresser?* had been the first ridiculous thought that entered her head.

'Do you like it?'

And that was a stupid question because on closer perusal she'd realised that not only was it a wedding dress but an eighties one with puffy sleeves, pearls, lace, a bow and a train that took up half the room, and didn't she love everything eighties? 'It's gorgeous, but why did you buy it?'

'I was walking past the shop and it was in the window. When I saw it, I thought of you. And I know it's not usual for a guy to buy his girl a wedding dress, and you'd probably want to choose your *actual* dress yourself, but ...' He shook his head as if he was at a loss for words. 'I thought this would be a fun way to say—'

Gobsmacked, flabbergasted, she'd interrupted. 'Are you trying to propose to me?'

'Yes. I'm doing a shit job of it, aren't I?'

'Oh my God!' Both her hands rushed to cover her mouth as goosebumps spread across her skin. 'Are you serious?'

'Yes.' He'd blinked as if close to tears. 'So ... *will* you marry me?'

*YES*, shouted an excited voice inside her head. If she'd met him in Vegas she'd have married him that very first night, but there were two other pesky thoughts stopping her from shrieking this reply.

'Is this because ...' She'd put both her hands on her stomach. 'Because of the baby?'

'No. Baby or no baby, I want to spend the rest of my life with you.'

Her heart squeezed at his sweet words—Josie had dreamed of getting married as a little girl, but the older she'd got, the less she'd believed in the fairytale/fantasy of meeting Prince Charming and living happily ever after. She'd thought she'd found The One on the set of *Camelot The Panto* but Cameron, who'd played the lead and whom she'd dated for almost two years, had freaked out and split when she'd broached the topic of starting a family. Devastated, she'd come back to Australia, changed careers and thrown herself into the snake pit that was online dating, hoping to meet an entirely different kind of man. Alas, the results were dismal and she'd all but given up hope.

Yet, with that beautiful dress on the couch and the beautiful man standing beside her, she'd found herself starting to believe again.

'Are you sure? I mean ... um ...' She didn't want to remind him that he'd been engaged to someone else until only a few months ago but he guessed what she was thinking.

'Jose,' he'd said, laying the gorgeous gown down on the sofa, closing the gap between them and taking her hands in his. 'I love you. I've never been more certain of anything in my life. My engagement to Danica should never have happened—we were only ever good friends, pushed together by our family. I didn't realise how wrong we were until I met you and it felt so right.'

Her tear ducts had opened at his words, at the absolute certainty in his tone.

'So?' he'd prompted as tears streamed down her cheeks. 'What's your answer? Please tell me those are happy tears?'

'Yes, of course!' And then they'd kissed and laughed and cried and made love, after which she'd tried on the wedding dress. And *oh my* how much she'd loved it.

'It fits perfectly,' she'd exclaimed, smoothing her hands down over the shiny white satin.

'Now,' Nik had replied, 'but—and don't take this the wrong way—you're going to gain a few kilos over the next few months.'

'Then we should get married as soon as possible,' she'd said, twirling round and round, feeling like an absolute princess. She never wanted to take the dress off.

'That suits me, but isn't there some tradition about grooms not seeing the bride's dress before the big day? And I kinda thought you'd want to choose your own dress.'

'I don't care about tradition, I've never been superstitious and I think it'll be extra special walking down the aisle to you in a dress you chose because you knew me so well.'

'Okay.' He'd laughed. 'So, does this mean we're going to have an eighties-themed wedding to match the dress?'

'This is me you're talking to. Were we ever going to have anything else? And it'll be perfect, because after all, if I wasn't singing Belinda Carlisle in that bar the night of your friend's bucks' night, we might never have met!'

'Well, your car still might have broken down and I might still have been driving along at just the right moment ...'

'True—because you and me. It was fate.'

'Still, will you sing for me at our wedding?'

She'd winked. 'If you're lucky.'

'Oh, babe, I consider myself very, *very* lucky.' Then, he'd kissed her again and they'd had a dress rehearsal for their wedding night with Nik slowly undoing the hundreds of buttons at her back. The knowledge that she was about to receive another mind-blowing orgasm was the only reason she agreed to take it off.

That day should have been the beginning of their happy ever after, but so much had changed since that wonderful afternoon that now when Josie thought of it, her heart felt like lead.

A horn blasted behind her and she looked up to realise she'd come to a stop in front of the ticket machine at the airport. Swallowing the urge to give the car behind her the middle finger, she pushed the button for a ticket. The boom gate lifted and she shot into the car park, taking the first available spot she found.

Josie entered the arrivals hall at the exact moment 'landed' flashed up on the information board beside Nik's flight. Her stomach rolled. She couldn't work out whether the butterflies were down to nerves or excitement at the prospect of seeing him after so long. Although she desperately wanted to be able to talk to Nik about her sadness, it made him uncomfortable. The few times she tried to talk about their babies, he got frustrated with her and they usually ended up fighting.

She didn't know if she could handle that anymore. But what was the alternative? Perhaps she could turn, run back to the car and flee her life. Nik would probably be better off without her because he could find someone else, someone who not only managed to get pregnant but to actually hold onto the baby. Someone like his ex-fiancée who had met a new man not long after Nik dumped her and had just announced the birth of twin boys on Facebook. Was that karma? Were Josie's miscarriages her punishment for stealing Nik off Danica? Although she didn't believe in such things, a knot tightened in her stomach at the thought. Had Nik seen that announcement too? Would he be able to help comparing her to his fertile, earth mother ex?

Josie had only stumbled across the post yesterday morning thanks to a friend she and Danica had in common. Mutual friends was the term Facebook used, as if they shared the person like you might share a mug in an office or a book. The moment she'd seen it she wished she could *un*-see it; it had been as if a fist had shot out of her phone screen and punched her in the gut. So strong was her reaction that she'd actually physically thrown up, cursing Mark Zuckerberg as she did so.

'Grandpa!' A shriek from a little boy beside her had Josie looking up to see people starting to emerge into the waiting crowd.

As the door slid open each time, she held her breath for Nik to appear. She watched some film-worthy reunions between lovers young and old, and then finally he did. Their eyes met across the distance, his face birthed a massive grin and he waved as he swaggered towards her, a scruffy Quiksilver backpack hitched to his shoulder as if he'd come from a surfing trip, not a business one. For a brief second she felt a bolt of attraction rush through her body, awakening something inside her that had been dormant for months.

But then he got close enough that she could see right into his eyes and there it was. That *look*. That disappointment. As if she'd only just told him about a miscarriage.

'Man, I've missed you.' He pulled her into his arms and pressed his lips hard against hers.

She tried to relax into him, to kiss him back—maybe if she pretended everything was okay between them, she might actually start feeling and believing it.

'It's good to have you home,' she said when he finally pulled back.

'Japan's great, but I'm so glad to be back.'

She forced a smile. 'I can't wait to hear all about it.'

And, as they walked towards the car park, tell her about it he did. He held her hand with his free one and talked without a break as if he was scared to stop and risk silence between them. He only paused while she paid for the parking ticket.

'You glad it's school holidays?'

'Yep—so ready for a break.' That was what all teachers said, wasn't it?

'You tired?' he asked as they reached the car.

She pressed the button to pop the boot. 'Not really.' Another lie; fatigue was something that plagued her constantly now. It was almost worse than when she was actually pregnant. 'Why?'

'I was thinking we could go out for dinner to celebrate me being home and your holidays. Or, better still we could go bowling?' He winked. 'For old times' sake.'

She drafted a mental list of pros and cons—bowling versus dinner out. At least with the former the actual activity would give them something to talk about. 'Okay, that sounds like fun.'

'Awesome. It's a date!' He slammed the boot and they both got into the car. He was acting over-the-top chirpy, obviously trying very hard to make things good, but every little thing he did irritated her.

'I tried to tag you on Facebook in a "coming home from Narita" post but I couldn't find your profile,' Nik said as she navigated out of the airport. 'Have you unfriended me?'

'No. I deactivated my account. Facebook was giving me the shits.' Or rather all those announcements of pregnancies and adverts in her sidebar spruiking maternity gear and baby paraphernalia were.

'Why didn't you tell me?'

'I only did it last night. It's no big deal.'

'Alright. Well, as long as you're okay.'

Her hands tightened on the steering wheel. *Okay?*

No, she was *not* bloody okay, no matter how much it would be better for him if she was. Not wanting to fight when he'd barely been home five minutes, she bit down on the caustic retort and turned the stereo up instead.

Nik got out his phone. 'I'll book us in for bowling. Six o'clock not too early?'

'No, that's perfect.' The sooner they got it over with the sooner they could slink back home to bed. Of course, that meant she'd probably have to put out—your husband went away for a month and sex was kind of expected on his return. Once upon a time, she'd have been tearing his clothes off the moment they walked in the door (or maybe not even making it that far) and it wasn't that she no longer found him attractive (she wasn't dead) but after so long with sex being for the purpose of procreating, it was now difficult to associate it with anything but.

And if Josie were honest with herself, she was scared. *Terrified* that maybe she *would* get pregnant again—conceiving didn't seem to be her problem—and have to go through yet another heartbreaking loss.

She didn't know whether she or their marriage could survive that.

The thought had tears pooling at the corner of her eyes but she blinked them back and thought of the wine she'd be able to drink at the bowling alley.

# *Rebecca*

'There you are, dear.' The nurse who'd set Rebecca up on the dialysis machine patted her arm and smiled down at her as if she were a two-year-old child. 'Relax and read your book or something, I'll be back soon, but buzz me if you need me.'

It was like a revolving door of nurses around here and there were only a couple Rebecca actually liked—a young guy called Nate and the first nurse she'd met, Clara—but maybe that was more a reflection on her current mood than on them.

She sighed and slumped back into her propped-up pillows as the dialysis unit set to work beside her pumping her blood in and out of her body, whirring continuously with a click punctuating the monotony every few seconds. Although she knew this tall grey *thing* was in essence saving her life, she couldn't help glaring at what she thought looked a bit like an automated teller machine. It was her fourth—or was it fifth? she'd lost count—time receiving dialysis and already the thought of having to do this indefinitely filled her with despair.

The actual process of dialysis was better than she'd imagined but it was so time-consuming. At first it had been hard watching all that blood leave her body, but she was used to it now. The worst part was at the start when they stuck two needles into her wrist to retrieve and return her blood.

'You'll get used to it,' had been the common refrain from all the nurses so far. She wasn't sure she'd ever get used to the needles but she tried to tell herself it was all for the greater good. This process was going to make it so that she could continue to live a 'full, normal, *active* life', or so she'd been told. Personally, she didn't see how being hooked up to a machine two or three times a week for three or four hours at a time—depending on how much fluid weight she gained between sessions—was ever going to feel anything *like* normal.

Her life was so full with teaching all her little music students, volunteering for Meals on Wheels and attending her book club and quilting groups, not to mention spending time with Hugh and Paige, that she didn't know when she was supposed to fit dialysis into it.

Something wet dropped down onto her hand and she realised she was crying. Again. *Dammit.* She reached for the tissues, annoyed— at herself, at her situation, at the world in general. She'd been an emotional mess since her admission to hospital and already gone through two or three boxes of tissues.

But apparently that too was normal. The nurse who'd hooked her up the first time had talked incessantly, quoting statistics at her—sixty per cent of dialysis patients experienced some kind of depression. As if it would make her feel better that she wasn't unique. Even almost two weeks after her diagnosis, Rebecca could still hardly believe she had such a serious, life-threatening condition. And she'd had lots of time alone during that time to ponder her situation.

Hugh and Paige had barely left her side in the first few days and she'd had plenty of other visits from her parents, Hugh's mum and her friends as well. But even though they might want to, her family couldn't put their lives on hold—they'd had to go back to work—and so sometimes she'd found herself with hours on end to simply contemplate her navel. That's when she found her mind going to places she usually didn't allow it to go.

*Dark places.*

She once again glanced over at the photos of her nearest and dearest on her bedside table. Paige was right, these were her favourites, but there was a third hidden in the house that neither her daughter nor her husband knew about. Her stomach churned at the thought. As Hugh was much older than her *and* had a bit of a dicky heart, she'd always assumed he'd die first, but this kidney scare had reminded her nothing was certain. Why had she never thought about what would happen if she died and *they* found it?

What would Paige and Hugh think? Would they ask her parents?

And would her parents tell the truth about the photo she'd been hiding while keeping close to her heart since she was sixteen years old? A photo they'd begrudgingly given to her when they'd told her it would be better to forget and never talk of him again. She'd kept the latter part of that agreement, but as if she could ever forget.

A mother never forgot.

Over the years there'd been times when she'd almost told all. When Hugh had first asked her to marry him, she'd thought about it, believing that husbands and wives should have no secrets. But, as if sensing she was close to coming clean, her mother had sat her down one day and warned her against it. What good would it do? Even if he wasn't angry, he'd want to know details and his curiosity would bring it all back to the forefront. All the pain, all the heartache—not only of having to give away her little boy, but the betrayal of her first love who she'd been so certain would stand by her.

*Wasn't it better to leave the past in the past?*

Her mum had reminded her that the baby had been adopted by a kind, infertile couple who were desperate for a child and would love him as if he were their own. They could offer a more secure home life than she as a single, teenaged mother who hadn't even finished school ever could. Her parents made it clear that giving up her child had been the selfless decision.

'Good afternoon!'

Rebecca's heart lurched as if she'd been caught doing something illegal and she looked up to see Clara coming into the room. Heat rushed to her cheeks and she snatched up a tissue and swiped at her eyes.

'Sorry, I didn't mean to give you a fright,' said the nurse, coming across to the bed. 'I just thought I'd check how you're doing. You must be feeling like an old hand at this now. Beautiful family you've got there.' She nodded towards the photos which had somehow ended up in Rebecca's lap.

'Thanks,' she just managed.

'Are you okay?' Clara asked, frowning slightly. 'I know adjusting to dialysis can take some time but most people have learnt to live with chronic illness before that, whereas you had it thrown on you out of the blue.'

'It was a bit of a shock and I'm going stir-crazy in here. It's making me a little nostalgic.' Rebecca glanced down at the photos again, fighting a sudden urge to tell this near-stranger things she'd never even told her husband. The weight of the secret she'd been carrying all these years felt unbearably heavy all of a sudden.

'Making you what?' Clara prompted, and Rebecca realised she'd said the last few words almost too quietly to be heard.

'I ...' She looked up into the other woman's eyes, which were filled with such kindness and concern. What harm would it do telling her? Weren't nurses bound by some confidentiality clause? Or was that only doctors?

Either way, why would Clara tell anyone her secret?

Rebecca took a deep breath but as she was about to continue, Paige arrived.

'Good morning, mother dear,' she said, practically skipping past Clara to kiss Rebecca's cheek.

'Hi, Clara,' she added and then lowered herself into a chair.

Paige's eyes came to rest on the box of tissues and the pile of used ones next to it on the bed. 'Oh, Mum, what's wrong? Why are you so upset?'

'I'll leave you both to it.' Clara patted Rebecca on the shoulder before quietly retreating from the room.

'Mum?' Paige clutched at her hand.

'I'm okay.' Rebecca forced a smile she didn't feel. 'Dialysis makes me tired and I'm frustrated being stuck here. I keep thinking about all my responsibilities and all the people I'm letting down.'

'Well don't. The world hasn't stopped turning because you're here. Your piano students are probably happy for a few weeks unexpected holiday. Geez, I remember when I was their age and you tried to force me to learn an instrument.'

The look of horror on Paige's face made Rebecca laugh. As much as she'd tried to encourage a love of music—singing and instrumental—in her daughter, Paige's artistic talents always laid elsewhere.

'And I also got a little overwhelmed thinking about all the lifestyle changes I'm going to have to make.' She might be piling it on a little thick but Rebecca didn't want Paige suspecting there was anything but illness upsetting her. 'I was reading the brochure about

living with kidney disease and it all sounds like such a palaver—
I have to cut back on salt, potassium, phosphorus (whatever the
hell that is), alcohol, the list seemed endless. *And* I'm supposed to
exercise.'

'Mum, you barely drink anyway, walking the dog counts as
exercise so you're already doing that and I'll help you with the rest.
I'll eat healthily with you; I could probably do with losing a few
kilos before the wedding anyway.'

'You're perfect as you are. But thanks, my darling.' Rebecca
squeezed her daughter's hand. 'And speaking of my absolute
favourite thing, have you and Sol set a date yet?'

Paige shook her head. 'No. We want to make sure you're well, so
I was thinking maybe we shouldn't rush but wait until after you've
had your transplant.'

'No way!' Rebecca was adamant. Who knew how long they
could be waiting for that? 'Please, promise me you won't let my
illness come into consideration. You said you didn't want a long
engagement and I'll be perfectly able to help you organise a wedding
between these blasted dialysis sessions.'

'Yes, but what's—'

Rebecca guessed Paige was about to ask what the rush was but
she cut her off. 'You could wait for me to get better and something
else terrible might happen.' She knew all too well how things could
be delayed indefinitely if you started waiting for the perfect time.
'Forget about my kidneys, forget about everything else except you
and Solomon—decide when you'd want to get married if there were
no other considerations and set that date.'

'Okay, Mum, I'll talk to Sol about it tonight,' Paige promised.

They wedding-talked a little longer, which helped pass the time
until the original nurse walked in to unhook Rebecca from the
machine.

Hugh arrived a few minutes after the nurse left, carrying a takeaway coffee from her favourite café. 'Here you are, my love.' He placed it down beside her, then leant over and kissed her.

'Thanks, honey. I'm probably not supposed to drink too much caffeine, but if I can't have my coffee, you may as well shoot me now.'

'Mum, don't talk like that,' Paige scolded, then gave her father a hug. 'Here, you sit down.' She gestured to the chair she'd just vacated and perched herself on the end of the bed.

'How was your dialysis today?' Hugh asked as he settled into the seat.

'Fine.'

A knock sounded on the door and they all looked up to see Dr Chopra. She was the reason both Hugh and Paige had come into the hospital in the middle of the day—they'd arranged their schedules so they could be here while Dr Chopra updated them on Rebecca's progress.

'Good morning.' The doctor smiled and then glanced at her watch. 'Actually, good afternoon. We better talk quickly before they bring your lunch.'

Rebecca rolled her eyes. 'No rush. The food isn't anything to get excited by.'

Dr Chopra chuckled. 'Sorry to hear that. Now, how are you feeling after this morning's dialysis?'

'Alright I guess.'

'We haven't had results from today obviously but your waste levels are definitely improving from your treatment.'

'That's good,' Rebecca said hopefully. 'Do you think it's possible I might not have to have as frequent dialysis sessions as you first thought?'

'Sadly not.' The doctor plucked a stylus from her pocket and scribbled something down on the tablet she was carrying. 'Your kidneys won't get better so you need the dialysis to do their job or you'll get sick again.'

Paige piped up. 'But a transplant will fix her for good, won't it?'

Dr Chopra smiled at Paige. 'A transplant should give your mother a new lease on life, but we won't be able to perform the operation until we get Rebecca's disease under control. Both the surgery and the medication we'll use to prevent a rejection can place significant strain on the body, causing problems if you are already unwell, so the earliest we'd be looking at a transplant is six months from now.'

*Six months?* For the sake of her family, Rebecca tried not to let her despair show on her face.

'There are two options regarding kidney transplant,' continued the doctor, 'a living donor or a deceased donor. Right now, the wait time for a deceased donor is about four years, so a living donor is the best option if you can find one. The first step is to test willing family members to look for a match.'

'I'll do it.' Paige shot her hand up into the air like a kid in school. 'Mum and I have the same blood type.'

'I don't think you can, honey.' During Rebecca's endless hours in hospital she'd read all the brochures the doctor had left and googled everything she could about kidney transplantation, discovering that neither Paige nor Hugh were likely candidates.

'Why not?' Paige's expression was one of outrage.

Dr Chopra looked to Rebecca, a slight frown creasing her brow.

'She has diabetes,' Rebecca explained.

'Ah, I see.' The doctor nodded slowly. 'That does rule you out I'm afraid, but even if you were a match *and* suitable, due to your age and the fact you don't have children yet, we'd highly caution against you being your mother's donor. There are higher risks associated with pregnancy for women who have donated, so we don't recommend donation for women who are of childbearing age and haven't yet had a family.'

'Oh.' Paige blinked and Rebecca could tell she was close to tears but trying to hold it together. She shot her a grateful smile.

'What about me?' Hugh asked. 'I know I'm thirteen years older than Rebecca but I'd give her both my kidneys if I could.'

'Your age wouldn't necessarily be an issue if you were a suitable match and in good health,' said Dr Chopra. 'Do you know if you are the same blood type?'

Rebecca answered before he could, not wanting to get his hopes up. 'He's had a heart attack and suffers from high blood pressure.'

The doctor's shoulders visibly slumped. 'I'm afraid that rules you out as well, but we shouldn't lose heart. What about other family members? Brothers? Sisters? Cousins? We'd probably advise against a parent as even if they were suitable, they'd likely be getting towards the end of what we consider optimal donor age. However, a donor doesn't have to be blood-related, so you might have a non-blood relative or a friend who is suitable.'

Rebecca's brother, Anthony, was severely overweight, which she also knew ruled him out and she silently scoffed at the idea of asking a friend. It wasn't like asking someone to borrow a cup of sugar or lend a couple of hundred dollars until payday. Quite aside from the physical aspect, she'd be asking someone to take time off work and put their lives on hold for the operation. And what if they said no? Or worse, what if someone only said yes because they didn't feel they *could* say no? Waiting for a deceased donor or spending the rest of her life on dialysis seemed like a more appealing option than having *that* awkward conversation.

'I'll have a think about it,' she said.

'Good, that's all we need at this stage. I'll leave you a pamphlet about how to approach people and we can talk about it more soon.

It can be daunting having to ask someone, but in general people are willing to help if they can. Obviously, they'll need to undergo extensive testing to make sure they are physically and mentally able to donate, which is why we want you to start thinking of possible donors now.'

'But won't we need to find someone with the same blood type and stuff as Mum?' Paige asked.

'A blood and tissue match is preferred but there are options if you find someone willing who doesn't fit perfectly. Rebecca's blood type is O, which is the hardest to find a match—neither A or B blood types can donate, however if you found a willing donor we could put you both on the Paired Kidney Exchange Program.'

'What's that?' This time the question came from Hugh, who like Paige had been quiet since being told his kidney was of no value.

'It's a register that you and your living donor would be put on to try and match you with other patients and their incompatible donors until we find the right combination where your donor could be matched to another recipient and vice versa.'

'I see.' There was so much to take in and the doctor's words only emphasised what Rebecca had already guessed—that getting better might not be as quick and straightforward as she'd hoped—but hearing it aloud was overwhelming. She fought the urge to cry again, not wanting to make Paige and Hugh feel any worse than they already did.

And then a thought struck—maybe now would be the time to tell them about her secret son. Surely they wouldn't be able to get angry at her when she was so sick and in hospital. But this thought was immediately followed by another.

What if her son was fit and healthy and a blood and tissue match?

Her skin prickled at the thought, but it was a moot point because as if she'd hunt down her child for the sole purpose of requesting an organ. How would that look?

*Oh hi, I'm your mother. Sorry I didn't tell anyone about you or try to contact you until now, but hey, how do you feel about giving me your kidney?*

She laughed out loud at the notion and the others looked at her strangely.

No, she could not tell them—not now—because Paige (who'd always thrown her whole heart and body into any pursuit) would probably make it her mission to hunt down her half-brother and demand he hand over his kidney.

'Sorry.' She coughed. 'I swallowed some air the wrong way.'

*Paige*

Paige barely heard the front door open and Solomon pad into the kitchen where she was sitting on a stool at the counter hunched over her laptop.

'Hello, sexy.' He came up behind her and kissed her neck. 'What's for dinner?'

She glanced at the time on her computer screen—almost seven pm. 'Shit. Sorry. I totally lost track of time.' Generally, she and Sol shared the cooking duties—taking turns depending on who'd be home first. Today, one of the only weekday evenings where she didn't have commitments at the studio, that was her.

'It's okay,' he said, putting his hands on her shoulders and massaging. 'We can go out or order takeaway.'

She moaned and closed her eyes as her head lolled back onto his chest. 'Man, you have talented hands.'

He laughed. 'I think you've mentioned that before. But you're pretty knotted up. How long have you been sitting here?'

'I don't know. A couple of hours?'

'Are you working on the story for the new book?'

'No, this is Mum stuff.'

Sol peered closer at the screen. 'Is that a *spreadsheet*?'

At his surprised tone, Paige laughed—she and Excel had never been friends but it seemed the best way to keep track of potential kidney donors. She turned her head and her heart pitter-pattered at the sight of him in his fireman uniform—*that* would never get old.

'Yes,' she said, focusing back on the task. 'I'm making a list of all our family members.' She pointed at the screen. 'This column has their name, then this one how closely they're related to Mum, and here I'm taking note of any reasons why they might not be a suitable donor. This column is for blood type of those who might be possibilities and this final column is for when we ask if they're willing to be tested.'

'Wow—you've been busy, but I thought you wanted to donate? Aren't you the same blood type as your mother?'

She exhaled her disappointment and then pointed again at the top of the spreadsheet—she and her dad were number one and two on the list, but she'd put their names in red. 'I can't donate because of my diabetes and Dad's out because of his heart.'

'Bugger.'

'I know. I've never hated my diabetes as much as I do right now. Although the doctor said, even without it they'd caution me against being a donor due to my age and gender. Apparently donating can be a risk to fertility. How ridiculous is that? Surely it should be up to me whether I take such a risk?'

And of course she would; her mum was far more important than some children who didn't even exist and might never even get to. If she had to choose between her mother and having kids, there was no choice.

'I guess the doctors know what they're doing,' Sol said. 'Look, how about I have a quick shower, then we grab a glass of wine and you can fill me in on what happened at the hospital and your progress?'

And, despite part of her wanting to continue, wine, Sol and their comfy couch was a combination she couldn't resist. 'That sounds perfect,' she said, pushing to a stand and arching her back into a stretch, 'I've just remembered there's some leftover curry in the fridge from the other night. While you clean up, I'll microwave it for an easy tea.'

'Sounds good. You know me, always up for easy.'

Paige laughed. 'I think you mean you're always easy.'

He slid his arms around her and pulled her in for a smooch. 'Why don't you join me in the shower?' he said a few long moments later when they broke apart and gasped for air.

Her hormones danced a jig. As if she could ever resist the lure of her hot firefighter. 'Good idea.'

She grabbed Sol's hand and they hurried down the corridor to the bathroom.

Not much talking happened in the shower, but by the time she and Sol had finished scrubbing each other clean, Paige was feeling more relaxed and way more positive than she had been all day.

As they poured the wine and reheated the curry, she asked Solomon about his day. He told her about the fun he'd had at Bondi Primary on a school visit in the morning, followed by a nasty car crash on O'Brien Street in the afternoon that had required the jaws of life. Then they sat down on the couch—steaming bowls and full glasses in hand.

'So, how's your list looking so far? Any possibilities?' he asked.

'It's a lot harder than you'd imagine. There's a long list of reasons why people wouldn't be able to donate. Obesity, cancer, previous abdominal surgery, heart attacks and of course diabetes.'

Paige had studied the information her mum had been given that afternoon, looking for a loophole, something that would make her kidney a suitable contender. She hadn't found any such loophole, but she'd practically memorised the list of things that make people unsuitable and she didn't need to bore him with the full list now.

'Do you have to be a relative?'

'You don't even have to be related. Blood type is the most important thing.'

'What blood type is your mother? Not that I can ever remember what I am, but I guess I could ask Mum.'

Paige blinked and turned her head to meet his gaze. 'Are you saying you'd consider giving *my* mum *your* kidney?'

'Buttercup, why wouldn't I help if I could?'

Her heart swelled with love for this amazing man who simply didn't see what the big deal was. His generosity and selflessness were the first things she'd noticed about him (okay, first *after* his incredible good looks and amazing body) when they'd met at a picnic for kids from refugee families. Some of his colleagues who'd come along in the fire truck obviously had places they'd rather be, but Sol was so patient with all the kids, asking each and every one of them to tell him about themselves. He'd stayed long after his mates took off with the truck, kicking the footy around with the children and then helping her and the other volunteers pack up.

She'd offered to drive him home that day and in the confines of her car, their chemistry had come to a head. When he'd invited her inside for a 'drink', Paige had gone willingly. But what she'd assumed would be a one-night stand because she didn't have time for relationships had exploded into something so much more. Sol wasn't a one-night stand kinda guy—he was a take-her-home-and-meet-the-family type and she was helpless against him. His love for his mum, his half-sisters and even his stepdad was clear. Not long after they'd got together, she learnt about his past.

When he was eleven he'd stood up to his father who had been physically abusing his mother for years and then convinced his mum to run away to a shelter with him. Lisette called him her saviour and although Paige herself had never needed him to rescue her, his courage and tenacity were merely two of the many things she loved about him.

She was pretty sure he didn't have any of the ailments that would make him ineligible to be a donor but they were jumping the gun.

'You are a man among men,' she said, putting down her wine and grabbing his face in her hands. She kissed him passionately on the lips, then said, 'but let's see how I go with blood relations first.'

He shrugged. 'Okay.'

'Ooh, there's something else I wanted to tell you,' she said, pushing the worry about the kidney donor out of her mind for now—the transplant couldn't take place for at least six months anyway. 'It's to do with our wedding.'

He grinned. 'I'm liking it already.'

'I want to find Mum's wedding dress and wear it on our big day.'

'What?' The grin faltered. 'Didn't your dad say she gave it away?'

'Yes, I asked him about it again this afternoon. He told me she donated it to a charity fashion parade and at the end of the night they raffled it off. I've spent the last few hours trying to track down the organiser of the fashion parade to see if they have any records of who won it. I actually found her and she said she's currently doing a long overdue cleanout but does still have the minutes from their meetings back then, which might have the name of the raffle winners from that night. She's going to go through them this weekend and call me if she finds a name. Then, I'm going to find the winner and ask if they'll let me buy it off them. I think it would be really special and Mum would be ecstatic to see me walk down the aisle in her dress.'

'Sounds like a lot of trouble to go to and, if Rebecca wanted you to wear her wedding dress, wouldn't she have kept it in the first place?'

Paige's heart sank—she couldn't help feeling annoyed at Solomon; she'd been so excited by this idea.

'I really want to do this,' she said, trying to swallow the lump that had suddenly grown in her throat. 'I can't give Mum my kidney, but maybe I can do this. She's so excited about us getting married and I think this would make it even more special for her.'

'Okay.' He took her hand and squeezed it. 'I understand, and you know I'm happy with whatever makes you happy, I just thought you'd probably want something a little more modern.'

'Mum's dress is a classic, I think it'll stand the test of time. Didn't you like it?'

'Babe, one wedding dress is pretty much the same as the next for me, it's the woman inside it that matters. You could wear a hessian sack and I'd still want to say "I do", but what if you can't find it? I don't want you to get your hopes up and be disappointed. Perhaps we could hire a dressmaker to copy the dress instead?'

But Paige shook her head. 'I can't get the idea out of my head and it's got to be somewhere, right? Wedding dresses don't just vanish into thin air.'

'I guess not. Does this mean you'll want me to wear your dad's suit?' Sol sounded slightly horrified by the idea.

She nudged him in the side. 'No, silly. He probably hired it and I guess we'll do the same for you. It's the dress that matters. It's the dress that makes a statement.'

'And what is the statement you want to make when you walk down the aisle in your mother's dress?'

She took a sip of her wine and pondered this question a moment. 'I want to pay tribute to my parents and their wonderful marriage. That marriage began with that dress and I just feel like it'll be a good omen for our marriage if I wear it as well.'

'Personally, I don't think we need any good omens, but I understand why you want to do this and, if anyone can find it, you can.'

'Thanks.' She snuggled into him again.

'I can't wait to marry you,' he said, dropping a kiss onto her head. 'I know we're already living together and I already come home to you every night and it's not that I want to own you or anything, but I have to admit, I can't wait to be able to say "my wife".' He put on a funny voice: 'Have you met *my wife*? *My wife* and I ... I'll just have to check with *my wife*.'

She laughed. 'I like it when you say that. And I can't wait to be "your wife", which reminds me, do you think we should set a date?'

'I thought you might want to wait until Rebecca was well again?'

'Yes, but planning a wedding, having a date to look forward to will give Mum something to focus on aside from dialysis and her stupid kidneys.' She absent-mindedly ran her fingers up and down his chest as she spoke. 'What do you think about October?'

'*This* October?' His voice and eyebrows went up and she could see him doing the mental calculations in his head. 'That's like ... three months away.'

'Yep—October is usually nice weather, but not too hot.'

'Maybe so, and I don't know much about wedding planning, but I reckon we might find it hard to find a venue on such short notice. Don't these places book up years in advance?'

She nodded. 'That's why I was thinking maybe we could have the wedding on the beach or in a park and the reception in your mum and Randy's backyard—it's big enough and beautiful.'

Sol's eyes lit up. 'Mum would love that. She'd be in her element and it would give her an excuse to redecorate the house like she's been pestering Randy to agree to for the last couple of years. But what if you don't find the dress in time?'

'I've only been on the hunt a few hours and already I feel as if I'm close.' She grinned, excitement building within.

'In that case, we'd better get a move on.' He dug his phone out of his pocket and she watched as he brought the calendar up on the screen and skipped forward a few months to October. 'What day of the week were you thinking?'

'A Saturday I guess. I always find it weird when people get married during the week, don't you?'

'Again, not something I've really thought about,' he said with a bemused smile, then looked down at the screen again. 'But Saturday it is. How's the thirteenth sound?'

'It sounds like our wedding anniversary,' she squealed and almost spilled her wine, which she'd forgotten was still in her hand.

Sol grinned. 'Indeed it does. October thirteenth. Let's do this.'

*Josie*

'Hey babe, I'm heading off now. You have a good night,' Nik said as he entered the lounge room, all dressed in his work uniform of white shirt and navy trousers, and crossed over to the couch where Josie lay sprawled in front of their widescreen TV, remote in hand.

'Thanks, hun,' she replied, pressing pause on *Mystic Pizza* as he bent down to kiss her goodbye. She kept her mouth firmly shut, hoping he wouldn't taste the fermented grapes on her lips. While he'd been in the shower, she'd snuck half a glass of wine from the bottle she'd hidden at the back of the pantry.

'Hope work's good,' she added chirpily.

'I'd much rather stay home and snuggle on the couch with you.'

Nik's 'snuggle' was a euphemism for 'Netflix and chill', which in turn (as she'd learnt from her students) was a euphemism for sex, of which they hadn't had any since he'd returned. That first night, after bowling, he'd actually fallen asleep while she'd been in the bathroom getting ready for bed. Josie hadn't been able to believe her luck. Then, the next day her period had arrived—what had not been a blessing for so long suddenly felt lucky, because it meant she could put off intimacy a little longer. It had been a *long* period, at least that's the impression she'd given her husband.

'I wish you could,' she lied.

'Well, enjoy your movie,' he said and then finally made his move towards the front door.

Josie waited until she heard it shut behind him, then let out the breath she felt as if she'd been holding all day and pushed herself off the couch. She crossed to the window and peeled back the curtain a fraction, watching as her husband swaggered to his car as if he didn't have a care in the world.

There were benefits of Nik working nights—the biggest being that he wouldn't tap her on the shoulder in bed—but it meant long hours together during the day where she couldn't drink or escape outside for a cheeky fag.

As he drove off, a slow smile spread across her face. She let the curtain fall and all but ran into the kitchen where she retrieved the wine bottle from the pantry. She poured herself a large glass, took a long, satisfying mouthful and then headed out onto the back balcony to rescue her cigarettes from their hidey-hole under the foliage of a pot plant.

The moment that first hit of nicotine shot through her, she felt a little better. To hell with the guilt that also came! She was an adult, she could do what she bloody well liked. Thank God for that stranger at The Inferno who'd reminded her of this pleasure. She smiled down at the cigarette and then took another long drag, recalling that night and how good she'd felt dancing her woes away before that wanker had tried to hit on her.

Nothing else made her feel even close to normal the way moving her body to music had. And she craved that feeling again.

*Then go out*, said a voice inside her head.

A little shot of excitement zapped through her body. She took another swig from the glass and went inside to get ready.

Within ten minutes, she was dressed, her hair and make-up passable. Planning to be home long before Nik finished work, Josie didn't bother to hide the evidence of her drinking before shoving her mobile, smokes and apartment keys into her pockets and heading outside. She'd barely lit up another cigarette when Nik stepped out from around the building.

Josie gasped, her free hand rushing to her chest—her heart felt as if it had just been hit with a defibrillator.

'Going somewhere?' Nik folded his arms like a bouncer, his chocolate-brown eyes narrowing as they registered the cigarette.

The obvious blurted from her mouth. 'You scared me half to death.'

No apology was forthcoming.

'You're supposed to be at work.'

He raised one of his thick, dark eyebrows. 'And you're supposed to be on the couch watching *Mystic Pizza*, but instead ...' His gaze trailed up and down her body, taking in her skinny black jeans, pink top and her favourite gold jacket, which matched the sparkly gold boots on her feet. It wasn't an appreciative head-to-toe.

'Where the *hell* were you going?' He glared at the cigarette in her hand. 'And how long have you been smoking again?'

'It's my body, I can do what I like.' Yet even as she spat these words she dropped the cigarette to the ground and stamped it out with her heel.

'Maybe so, but you're *my* wife—and last time I checked that gives me the right to worry, to care. I came back because as I drove away I felt like I was having a heart attack or something. I couldn't stop worrying about leaving you alone and I couldn't shake the feeling that if I didn't go home, something bad was going to happen. I came back to make sure you were okay and ... I find you all dressed up and going who knows where! With who knows whom!'

'I'm allowed to go out if I want to.' But her words sounded childish even to her and her bravado was wavering. This was *not* how she'd envisioned her evening going.

'Yeah, but that's just the thing—you never want to go out, you never seem to want to do anything these days, or is it just that you don't want to do anything with me?' He paused, then raked a hand through his hair. 'Are you having an affair?'

She jerked back as if he'd slapped her. 'Of course not. How could you even say such a thing?'

'What am I supposed to think, Jose?' He threw his hands up in the air. 'When I ask you to go out with *me* you act as if I want you to pluck your own eyeballs out and eat them for breakfast. You flinch when I touch you. You barely even talk to me anymore. I thought it was because you were hurting. I hoped it was the situation, not me, yet you've obviously got plans tonight. If you've got nothing to hide, why didn't you tell me you were going out?'

Her gaze dropped once again to the ground. Tears threatened and she tried to swallow the knot that had appeared in the back of her throat. 'I didn't have *plans*,' she managed eventually. 'I just ...'

*Nope. Lost cause.* Here came the weeping.

'Oh, Jose.' Nik shook his head, then stepped forward and pulled her into his arms. He rocked her against him and cradled her close as tears dripped off her lashes and onto his shirt. 'We need to talk. Let's go inside.'

Her mascara was no doubt streaming down her face now, mixed together with snot and tears—she'd probably scare people if she went out, but the prospect of Nik grilling her about her behaviour didn't fill her with joy either.

'What about your work?' she asked as he unlocked the door and ushered them into the building.

'I called and told them I wasn't coming in,' he said, opening and then kicking their front door shut behind them. 'You're more important. *We're* more important. At least to me.'

Although she heard the dig, she didn't say anything as they headed for the couch.

'Do you want me to get you a drink?' he asked.

Josie thought about the bottle of wine, half drunk and waiting for her on the kitchen bench. *Oh yeah*, she wanted a drink.

'Coffee, tea, a Milo?' he prompted.

She shook her head. 'I'm fine, but you get something if you want.'

In reply, he lowered himself down onto the couch beside her. 'How long have you been smoking and drinking, Jose?'

She blinked. He'd found her in a compromising position with a fag, but she'd been careful not to drink too much when Nik was around.

'I'm not an idiot,' he said as if again reading her mind. It was a really annoying skill. There wasn't supposed to be such thing as *men's* intuition! 'You act differently when you've been drinking—you're more relaxed. Yet, when it's too early for a drink or something, you're all highly strung. But alcohol and cigarettes never made anything better and they're addictive. What happens when we get pregnant again?'

'That's all you care about, isn't it? I'm just a baby-making machine to you.' Her voice rose as her fury grew within. 'And a failed one at that.'

Nik visibly recoiled at her words. 'What? No. I care about *you* but I thought that's what *you* wanted. Isn't a baby what this self-destructive behaviour is all about? You're hurting and self-medicating and—'

'No,' she interrupted, her hands clenching into fists at her sides. He really had no clue, did he? 'Not just *any* old baby. It's about *our* babies, the three we lost. I think about them all the time, but you never want to talk about them. They're real to me, I grieve their loss daily, but you act like the doctors, you act like they were nothing but a few cells. It feels like all you want to do is try and make another one.'

His face crumbled at her words. 'Because I hate seeing you so sad. I'm trying to be strong for you, but you're not the only one hurting. My heart breaks every time I think about it—I loved those babies from the moment you told me you were pregnant—but you know what hurts more?' It was a rhetorical question and he barely paused for breath. 'What losing them has done, *is doing*, to us. We used to be so close, we talked about everything, and now most of the time I feel like I'm living with a stranger.'

His words took her breath away. 'So why didn't you tell me?'

'Because …' His voice broke. 'You're my wife. I'm supposed to be strong for you. I'm supposed to look out for you, to make things better. I feel so fucking helpless. All my life I've been able to fix things. But the one thing I want to fix more than anything—the one person I want to help—I can't. And it kills me.'

By the time he'd finished, Nik's head was in his hands and he was crying. She blinked.

*Her Nik crying.*

He'd never … She couldn't.

Her throat closed over and her eyes stung. *Hold him. He needs you.*

But no matter the voice in her head, her arms felt like lead. She sat there imitating a statue, but then after a few long moments, something flickered inside her, a spark lit by all the times he'd held her on this very couch. She'd cried bucket loads—dams could probably have been filled multiple times over with her tears—yet he'd been bottling all this inside, trying to be strong for her and she'd mistaken his strength for coldness.

Slowly, she lifted her arms and, for what she realised was the first time since her second miscarriage, she shifted closer and wrapped her arms around him. She held him tightly, hoping to give him comfort but also finding her own in the warmth and closeness of his body. Turned out it didn't matter who was holding up who because together they were stronger.

When Nik's tears finally began to wane, she looked into his eyes. For the first time she didn't see her failure, didn't see his frustration when their gazes met, and she questioned whether it had been in her imagination all along. Was what she'd seen actually his own despair, his wretched feelings of helplessness and heartache? They'd been trying to protect each other and in doing so they'd chiselled a giant chasm between them.

'I'm sorry,' she whispered. 'I feel like a failure too. I hate that my body won't do what it's supposed to do. It's not that I don't want you anymore, but I'm scared. What if I do get pregnant again? And what if it ends too soon again? I can't help wondering whether you'll eventually regret choosing me over Danica who obviously has a body that works.'

He scowled. 'What's Danica got to do with this?'

'Don't tell me you haven't heard about her having twins?'

'I didn't even know she was pregnant. Mum and my sisters don't talk to me about her.'

Josie lifted one eyebrow. 'It was all over Facebook.' How could she have seen it and he not?

'We're not friends on there anymore.' Slowly recognition dawned in his eyes. 'Is that why you closed your account?'

'Got it in one. Well, that and the fact that when you want anything badly, social media is a horrible place. Due to weird cyber-algorithms or something I know nothing about, whatever you want is suddenly all you see.'

Nik snatched up her hands and clutched them to his chest. 'I chose you back then and I would choose you again and again. No one gets me the way you do and I hoped you could say the same about me. If we can't have a baby, I'll be sad, but it's you I want more than anything in the world. Do you understand?'

Damn stupid tears threatened again at his words. She wanted him to be enough too but she couldn't help wanting a family. She wanted a little girl with Nik's eyes who was aeroplane-mad and a little boy with her chocolate-brown curls who watched too many movies. Hell, at this stage she'd settle for one *or* the other. She just wanted a little person that was the product of their love.

'I love you,' she said, her heart melting at the intensity of her feelings for him. 'And I'm sorry I've distanced myself recently. I've just never felt such sadness before.'

'I know and I love you, and I'm sad too,' he replied. 'I've hated seeing you suffer through the miscarriages. I know it's taken its toll on your body as well as emotionally on the both of us and it's frustrating that the doctors can't find anything wrong, but never forget, we're in this together.'

'But how many times do we have to go through it? It feels so unfair. Being pregnant is supposed to be a happy time but even that thought now is something I dread because I know there's no guarantee of a baby at the end of it.'

He took a long moment to reply, then, 'You know, there are other options. We could always consider adoption. I understand there's only so much physically you can take—and I don't want to have to watch you go through this even one more time.'

Every bone in her body stilled. She tore her hand from his. She'd contemplated IVF, she'd contemplated admitting defeat and never becoming a mum, hell, at her lowest, she'd even contemplated stealing someone else's baby—not that she'd dare tell Nik that—but not once had the possibility of adoption entered her head.

'How could you even suggest that?'

He blinked—hurt flashed across his face. 'I thought you'd be open to the idea—you've always said you were okay about ...' He shook his head. 'Forget I suggested it. I'm sorry.'

At the expression on his face, Josie's temper cooled. It was a reasonable suggestion.

'No, I'm sorry I snapped. Adoption isn't an easy option anyway—I've heard it can take years to get approved and then even longer to actually get a baby. Besides, I want a little person that's part of you and me. Is that too much to ask?'

'No, not at all.' Nik smiled wistfully and pulled her against him. 'I want that as well. We'll get there. Don't lose hope.'

'I'll try not to. Thank you for coming home tonight.'

'I'm glad I did. Never forget that I'm here for you, but,' he paused and took a breath as if nervous about what he was about to say, 'maybe you should get some professional help.'

'I'm not going to AA. I promise you, I can give up and—'

'I was thinking more along the lines of grief counselling,' he interrupted. 'Talking to someone about our losses.'

At his words, her mind flashed back to that night at The Inferno; she remembered the man who'd given her a cigarette had also given her something else. She'd been wearing this gold jacket that night as well. She slipped her hand into the pocket and her heart did a little jolt as her fingers closed around the lone card. Josie drew it out and held it out to Nik.

His eyebrows moved closer together as they always did when he was focusing on something. 'Life After Loss? Clara Jones?' he read out loud as he took it from her grasp. 'You've already been seeing this woman?'

'No. I just remembered someone gave me this card.'

'Who?'

'You know that night you were in Japan about to go out with your mates and I said I was also going out?'

He nodded.

'That was a lie. I didn't want you to worry about me. But you asked me to send you a selfie and so I had to get all dressed up and then I decided that maybe a night out would do me good. So I walked down to the beach and I went to that new place, The Inferno.'

'On your *own*?'

'Yep. I just wanted to drink and dance and try to forget my pain.'

'Oh, Jose.' Again his voice was soaked with sadness and worry. 'What if something happened to you?'

'I was fine. I'm a big girl and can look after myself. Anyway, I got talking to this man, a much *older* man,' she added quickly, so she didn't give him anything else to worry about, 'and told him why I was upset. He said his wife volunteers for a charity that helps women like me, people like us, and he gave me this card.'

'Well, as much as I don't like the idea of you hanging out with other blokes at pubs, maybe you should give her a call.'

'Yes. I think I will.' She took the card from Nik and put it down on the coffee table in front of them. Then she turned back and climbed into his lap.

He blinked his surprise as she yanked his shirt open at the top two buttons and slid her hands inside, palming them against his hot skin. And Jesus, he felt good. It suddenly seemed absurd that she'd been trying to avoid this. Like dancing, this could wipe her mind of everything else.

'And next time ... you want to go out and dance ...' His voice sounded choked as she stroked her hands over him. 'Promise you'll take me with you?'

'Promise,' she whispered, and then pressed her lips against his.

Neither of them said anything else for a very long time.

*Clara*

Clara sighed as she watched her brother-in-law, Neil, put the last of her boxes into his van. She felt Siobhan's hand gently touch her arm.

'Are you okay?'

'Yes, actually, better than okay.' And it was the truth. She'd worked every available hour over the last couple of weeks, carefully packaging and boxing things. It had been a cathartic experience. As she'd suspected, Siobhan had all but forbidden her from giving the stuff to an op shop, convincing Clara to let her sell it to people who would truly appreciate it.

'And then you can give whatever money I get to whatever charity you want,' she'd promised.

Clara had agreed due to the sheer volume of stuff, which she suspected might overwhelm any charity shop if she dumped it on them all at once. And, since Siobhan's youngest had finished school last year, her sister had been feeling at a loose end; she was over the moon to have a project to stick her teeth into.

'Right then.' Neil dusted his hands on his shirt. 'I'll be off. See you at home, love.'

He and Siobhan had driven over in separate vehicles and both were now at maximum capacity.

She kissed him goodbye. 'Drive safely.'

The sisters stood together as Neil climbed into the van, his forehead red and shiny from all the box carrying.

'Do you have to work today?' Siobhan asked Clara as he started to drive away.

'Not at the hospital.' She glanced at her watch—it was not quite midday. 'I'm on roster at Life After Loss this afternoon, but don't have to be there for a few hours.'

'In that case, do you have time for a celebratory drink?'

'At *this* time of the day?'

Siobhan grinned. 'It's always 5 pm somewhere in the world, but I suppose I could make do with a cup of tea.'

Clara chuckled. 'I'm not sure I have anything stronger anyway. Come on.'

They linked arms and turned back to the house.

'When's the real estate agent coming?'

'Not for a few days. I wanted to have time to clean everything and make the place sparkle after the boxes left, before they took the photos.'

'Good idea,' Siobhan said as they headed into the kitchen.

Clara picked up the kettle and, as she went to fill it at the sink, Siobhan pointed to a couple of cardboard boxes perched on the kitchen bench. 'Oh no, did we forget these?'

'No. I can't sell those.'

'Why not? What are they?' Siobhan lifted back the cardboard flaps on one and looked inside. She picked up a beer can and held it up like it was a dead rat. 'Why on earth have you got all these?'

'They're Rob's. He collected different cans. I'm not sure whether to call him and see if he wants them still or just take them round to Brenda's place.'

'You'll do neither!' Siobhan dropped the can back in the box and then wrapped her arms around it, holding it almost protectively against her chest.

'*You* want the beer cans?' Clara asked, even though she knew that wasn't what her sister meant.

'Very funny. Everyone thinks they're a comedian. For one thing, you no longer have his phone number, remember?'

Clara refrained from reminding her sister that she still had the landline of the house where Rob lived with his mother.

'Personally, I think you should chuck them.'

Perhaps Siobhan was right—if Rob really valued these items wouldn't he have taken them with him in the first place?

'But there's also a box of old vinyl records that I found in the back of the garage and some of his band memorabilia.' Clara gestured to another two boxes further along the bench. 'I can't just toss them.'

She might not have been the music fanatic her ex-husband once was but she knew how rare some of those records were. First albums of groups like INXS, Midnight Oil, The Police, Dragon and Cold Chisel. They'd been his idols but some had also almost become friends for a while. The LPs had been Rob's prized possessions when she'd first met him—his passion, she'd go so far as to say his life—but the last ten years or so, he'd all but turned his back on music.

Siobhan sighed. 'If I were you, I'd sell them and buy myself something nice with the profits but, sadly, you're a much nicer person than me.'

Being 'nice' hadn't got her very far in life but her sister was right—the guilt would eat Clara up if she didn't give them back to their rightful owner. 'Look, if I return these to Rob, then I'm done. That's the last of his stuff in my life and once I sell the house, it'll be like my marriage never even happened, so—'

'So, *I'll* take the boxes back,' Siobhan said in her don't-you-dare-argue-with-me tone.

Knowing her sister, the stuff would sit in Siobhan's boot for a few weeks but at least she wouldn't risk running into her ex by going there herself.

'Thank you, that would be wonderful. And say hi to Brenda if you see her for me.' Clara had always liked Rob's mother and felt a little guilty that cutting him out of her life also meant losing contact with her, but the way Rob was, she didn't see any alternative. It had taken her a long while to understand that with him it had to be all or nothing.

'I will,' Siobhan promised. 'But now, enough about the past. I want to know if you've had any nibbles on the online dating website.'

Oh Lord, Clara would probably regret telling her sisters about that—at least she'd made them swear not to tell their mother. But, knowing Siobhan wouldn't let it rest until she'd given her something, she said, 'Come sit and I'll fill you in.'

As she picked up the tea things and took them to the table, Siobhan carried over the plate of banana and caramel muffins she'd brought with her.

Clara reached for a muffin and took a bite. 'Mmm. These are divine.'

'Maybe you should only have half,' Siobhan said, reaching across as if about to pluck the sugary delight from Clara's fingers. 'If you're entering the dating scene again, you don't want to get tubby because sooner or later you'll need to get naked. It's okay for me 'cos I've been married an eternity and on the rare occasions Neil and I have sex we hardly ever bother to take off our pyjamas, but you'll want to put your best body forward.'

Clara yanked her hand out of her sister's reach. 'I'll eat whatever and as much as I like, thank you very much. If I choose to eat well, it'll be for my own health and well-being, not for some man.' Although she shuddered a little at the thought of getting naked in front of another person again.

*Deep breaths*. There wasn't any rush to jump into bed with anyone—she wanted companionship much more than she wanted sex.

'No need to bite my head off.' Siobhan reached for a muffin herself. 'I was merely offering a little sisterly advice.'

'I know. Sorry.' But Clara took a large, rebellious and comforting bite of her muffin just the same. 'It's all a little daunting to be honest. Online dating wasn't even a thing last time I was in the market for a man. Back then love was a lucky dip; it all seems so orchestrated these days.'

'I think that's a good thing. No more hanging around bars and clubs hoping someone will offer to buy you a drink. I'd usually gone to bed with someone before I worked out how unsuitable they were for me. There were a lot of uncomfortable mornings after before I finally hit the jackpot with Neil. This way you find someone who has the same interests and values before you even meet them in person.'

Maybe Siobhan had a point. Clara couldn't help wondering if she and Rob had met online rather than in the hospital whether they'd have ended up together at all. Probably not. Quite aside from the fact that a nurse and a musician had little in common, imagining such things was pointless as Rob wouldn't have been looking on the internet anyway. Back then, he had groupies falling all over themselves to go out with him. Someone like herself would never have even got close if it hadn't been for his appendix.

She thought back to the evening she'd walked into his hospital room, unprepared for the flirting she was about to encounter, the feelings he was about to evoke. No clue her life was about to change forever.

'Hello,' she'd said with her usual cheery smile as she went over to lift the clipboard off the end of his bed. 'I'm Clara, and I'll be looking after you all night.'

'Looks like my luck's just changed then,' had been his mischievous reply. 'If I'd have known getting appendicitis would lead me to you, I'd have gotten sick sooner.'

And although she'd dealt with plenty of flirty patients before—usually old men who thought it funny—she couldn't recall any quite as good-looking *and* young as this one. And his voice ... It made her toes curl in her sensible flat shoes.

'I need to take your blood pressure,' she'd said, praying that the terrible hospital lighting meant he didn't notice her blushing.

'You can take whatever you like, sweetheart.'

She'd given him a stern look, trying to ignore the fluttering behind her ribs.

'Sorry. It's my natural instinct to flirt with a pretty girl.' He tapped the side of his head. 'And I think I'm still a little bit woozy from the anaesthetic, but I promise to keep my hands to myself.'

'You better,' she'd said, but her heart had hammered in her chest and her fingers shook worse than they had the first time she'd taken anyone's blood pressure. 'So what do you do for a crust?' she asked, trying to make small talk.

'A bit of labouring during the day, but at night I play in a band. One Track Mind. You might have seen us at one of the local pubs.'

'You sing?' That accounted for the voice.

He'd nodded. 'I sing, play guitar, write my own songs. I'm a man of many talents.'

'And modest too.' Yet, although the words sounded arrogant, for some reason he hadn't come across that way. There'd been something almost vulnerable about him, as if he was seeking her approval.

Clara had been lucky (or unlucky, whichever way you looked at it) enough to be on night shift the next couple of nights and, used to late nights, Rob had often been awake when she went in to check on him. In her quiet times, she'd found herself engaging in whispered conversations with him. She'd told him about her family, he'd mentioned his mum and his dreams for One Track Mind to become the next big thing. *We're recording demos at the moment to sub to record companies.*

And although she found him attractive—who wouldn't?—she never suspected he saw more in her than a brief flirtation, simply part of his aspiring rock star act, so she'd been shocked when he'd asked her if she wanted to come see his band.

He'd saved her a spot right up the front of the pub where they were playing and she'd sworn he'd been singing every word to her. Afterwards he'd held her hand as he introduced her to his band-mates, but they'd only stayed for one drink before he'd whisked her away to somewhere quieter. They'd sat in a park and fooled around a little, but most of the time they'd simply talked.

Finally, at almost two o'clock in the morning, he'd taken her home and kissed her senseless on her doorstep. She got the impression he wanted her to ask him in and her hormones were yelling at her to do exactly that, but she didn't want to be just another notch on his bedpost, so she'd summoned all her restraint to resist him.

'I'll call you tomorrow,' he'd promised, and although it had been one of the best nights of her life, she didn't really think he would. His life singing gigs in pubs was light years from her shifts at the hospital. She couldn't imagine what he could possibly see in her when he could have had any number of beautiful girls who understood and were already part of his world.

But the next day she'd come home from work and her flatmate, a fellow nurse called Bonnie, had flashed a yellow post-it note at her. 'Some guy, Ron I think he said, called. He wanted to know if you're free tonight.'

Her fingers had closed around the tiny piece of paper and she'd almost had a heart attack right there in the kitchen.

They'd seen each other again that night, and a week later they'd consummated things. Rob was such a tender lover, so much more giving than the two men she'd previously slept with. She kept waiting for him to tire of her, but instead they grew closer and she started to see the real Rob, the hurting man beneath the cocky musician façade. The crowd might go wild when he sang, he owned the stage at the local pub as if it was a massive concert hall, but when they were alone, he was almost an entirely different person.

They hadn't been together long before he'd opened up about his father's death and the other tragedies in his past. Her heart had broken for him and she'd wanted to make everything better.

And for a while, it seemed like she did.

A few months after they met, a big record label had 'discovered' One Track Mind and, less than a year later, high on the success of his first album, he'd proposed. Their wedding day had been one of the best days of Clara's life, but heartache and tumultuous times were just around the corner.

Now, she couldn't help wondering what their lives might have been like if they'd each married other people. If Rob hadn't got appendicitis, if he'd met and married someone else, someone whose body was compatible with motherhood, would he have been able to recover from the trauma of his youth? Would there have been more than one hit song? Would he have been able to stop at one celebratory drink?

'Clara? Clara! Where are you?'

At Siobhan's loud, urgent question, she blinked. 'What?'

'You went far away. I couldn't reach you.'

Clara could tell her sister the truth but that would only solicit a lecture. And fair enough; hadn't she resolved to move on?

'Sorry, I was thinking about Gregg,' she lied.

Siobhan's eyes sparkled. '*Who* is Gregg?'

Clara took another bite of her muffin before replying. 'Do you remember a guy called Gregg Callen I went to school with? I didn't know him well but we did work on the yearbook together in year twelve.'

Siobhan bit her lip, a look of serious concentration lingering on her face a few moments. 'No, I don't think I do. Don't tell me you've found him online after all these years?'

'Yes, he's one of the profiles that came up as a perfect match to mine. He's divorced too.' Clara didn't tell her sister that Gregg's ex-wife had left him for a woman five years ago. He'd made her promise not to feel sorry for him.

Siobhan leaned forward, eager to hear more. 'And you've been communicating with him?'

'A few emails have been exchanged,' she admitted coyly.

'Well, then, what's he like?' Siobhan asked, her excitement clear in her voice.

So Clara told her sister The Gregg Facts.

He had three grown-up children who were all living overseas; he was planning a trip to Europe in a few months to visit one of them. He wasn't big on watching or playing team sports, but he liked bush walks, reading and watching foreign films. He was a non-smoker and really only drank on holidays, which he said he didn't go on enough of but had made a new year's resolution to fix—hence the upcoming Europe trip.

She liked that he'd decided to get out of his own rut and change his life as well. Although he only lived a couple of suburbs away, they hadn't progressed past emails yet.

'What does he do for a crust?' Siobhan asked when Clara paused for breath.

'He's a high school history teacher.'

Siobhan grimaced a little. 'History? He'll probably bore the pants off you talking about world wars and every single wife of Henry the Eighth.'

'I like history,' Clara said in his defence. And the fact Gregg sounded so different from Rob only added to the appeal. If she was going to contemplate entering a relationship again, she wanted someone solid and stable, not another person she had to mother and look after.

'Well then, in theory he sounds fabulous, but what does he *look* like?'

'Looks shouldn't matter, should they?' Rob had been very good-looking when they'd met and look how that had turned out.

Siobhan rolled her eyes and Clara grabbed her phone to bring up Gregg's profile on the dating website. She smiled as his cheerful face looked up at her and then she turned the phone to show her sister.

'Wow.' Siobhan let out a long, impressed breath. 'He looks a bit like George Clooney—only he's aged better.'

Clara grinned—that was high praise coming from Siobhan who'd harboured a crush on George since she'd fallen in love with him in that awful horror film *Return of the Killer Tomatoes*. 'So have you done the deed yet?'

'Siobhan!' Clara rolled her eyes, thinking it was lucky her sister had coupled up before the advent of the internet, which had changed the face of dating. Siobhan would have been unstoppable if something like Tinder had been available back then. 'We haven't even met face to face yet.'

'What are you waiting for? If he's perfect on paper, then you want to ask him out before some other sex-starved spinster snaps him up.'

'Who are you calling a spinster?'

They both laughed.

Siobhan thrust Clara's phone at her. 'There's no time like the present. Why don't you send him an email right now?'

Clara's heart palpitated at the thought. 'Isn't the gentleman supposed to do the asking?'

'What century are you living in, sister dear? These days men and women have equal rights and that goes for making the first move as well.'

But it wasn't only the prospect of asking that terrified her. The word 'date' sounded so official, so binding, so serious. It sent an actual shiver down her spine. Was she really ready for this?

As if reading her mind, Siobhan softened a little. 'Why don't you just see if he wants to meet you for coffee? That sounds more low-key and you won't be stuck with him too long if he bores you to tears in person.'

'Coffee.' Clara said the word out loud as she pondered it. Maybe she could do that?

'I'll think about it,' she promised Siobhan. She needed time to work herself up to it and no way was she going to do it with her sister watching over her shoulder, making suggestions of what to say.

She pushed back her chair and scooped up both their teacups to show Siobhan that there would be no further discussion on this topic.

'Okay.' Standing, Siobhan picked up the plate with the remaining muffins. 'But don't think about it too long or you'll chicken out, and make sure you let me know the moment Gregg replies. I'll help with your hair and make-up.'

'Deal.' Clara smiled at her sister, making a vow not to tell Siobhan about anything until after it had happened. She was quite capable of making herself look presentable, thank you very much.

*Paige*

Paige sighed as she hung up the phone on the fourth 'R Winters' she'd called that day. There were twenty-four more listed in the White Pages online and she hoped and prayed she didn't have to call them all. She took a quick sip of her water bottle and then punched in number five. It rang and rang and rang. She was just about to give up when someone finally answered.

'Hello?' The voice sounded elderly and a touch out of breath.

'Hi, my name's Paige MacRitchie and I'm call—'

'Do I *know* you?' Now the voice sounded wary as if she were searching for a face to put to the name.

'Oh, no, I don't think so.' Paige laughed nervously. 'I'm trying to track down a Rose Winters who I think may have worn my mother's wedding dress. She might have changed her name when she got married I guess, but I'd love to talk to her about her dress. Is she a relation of yours?'

The woman neither confirmed nor denied this. 'Why do you want to find her?'

'Well,' Paige began, hoping she wasn't wasting her breath on someone who didn't have any answers, 'I recently got engaged and my mum is quite sick at the moment. I want to do something special for her and I think she'd get such joy out of seeing me wearing her wedding dress when I get married.'

'That's very sweet,' said the woman, perhaps softening a little.

'Thank you. But the problem is, she gave it away to charity just after she married my dad in 1988.'

'What did she give away, dear?'

'The wedding dress.'

'Oh, of course, right. And what did you say this dress looked like?'

Paige tried to describe her mother's dress—its beautiful lace, big bow and lavish train.

'That sounds lovely. I've always been a fan of bows myself. My granddaughter got married last year and she could have done with a few well-placed bows to cover her up a little. Why young people insist on wearing such revealing gowns I'll never understand. In my day, we left a little to the imagination.'

'I totally agree, Mrs—? I don't think I quite caught your name.'

'Doris,' she snapped. 'Doris Winters. Now what was it you wanted with my Rose? She's overseas at the moment and I need to go watch *Bold and the Beautiful*.'

'You know Rose?' Paige did a little dance on the spot. Surely this had to be *the* Rose of the fashion parade win.

'Yes, of course I do.'

'Do you know if she got married in a dress she won at a fashion parade?'

'I may be old, but I haven't lost my marbles yet. Rose did get married in a dress she won and it sounds very much like the one you are looking for.'

Paige grinned so hard her cheeks hurt. She could almost feel the dress on her body. Wait till she told Solomon. He'd tell her she should consider a career as a private investigator. If only tracking down a kidney was a matter of following clues like this.

'Wonderful.' She managed to tame her excitement long enough to say, 'Do you have an email address for Rose?' If she was overseas, email might be better than a phone call.

'Email?' The woman asked as if Paige had just requested her daughter's tax file number. 'I don't know anything about emails. She calls me every Sunday at dinner time, but there's no point you contacting Rose anyway.'

'Why not? You don't think she'll want to sell me her dress?'

'She can't sell you something she doesn't have anymore.'

Paige's heart sank. 'What did she do with it?'

'She gave it away two years ago when her husband ran off with his yoga teacher. Never trust a man who is in touch with his chakras, that's my advice.'

'*Oh*. Who did she give it to?' Paige asked, clutching at straws.

'The local Vinnie's op shop,' Doris said as if this was obvious.

Paige felt a flicker of hope within once again. 'And what suburb would that be?'

'Newtown I think—somewhere on King Street.'

'Thanks. I'll check it out.'

'Oh, I doubt it'll still be there after all this time.'

Doris could quite well be right but Paige wasn't one to give up that easily. 'Thank you so much for your time. I really app—'

'Darn it. I've missed the beginning of *Bold*.' And with that the line went dead.

Paige found a parking spot almost right out the front of the op shop Doris had directed her to. If that wasn't a good omen, she didn't know what was.

'Thanks so much for coming with me,' she said, turning to her friend who sat in the passenger seat.

She'd already asked Karis, Jaime and Narelle to be her bridesmaids—to which they'd all squealed excited 'yes'es—but Karis was the only one who'd been able to make today's expedition.

'Are you kidding? Thank *you* for inviting me. These kinds of shops are my jam and I'm always up for an adventure.' Karis, who usually wore beautiful vintage clothes she found in shops such as this one, unclicked her seatbelt and smiled conspiringly at Paige. 'Let's do this.'

Paige beeped the Mini locked and then they crossed the footpath to the big shop, passing two large yellow donation bins as they went. As she looked at the window displays on either side of the door— one full of assorted sporting equipment and the other with blankets and mismatched throw pillows—it was all Paige could do not to skip inside. Her pulse raced with anticipation.

Karis breathed in deeply as they entered the large store. 'Don't you just love that smell?'

Paige screwed up her nose as Eau de Mothballs with a dash of dusty old paper and floor cleaner greeted them. '*Love* is not the word I'd have used.'

Karis laughed. 'Okay, so maybe it's a little musty, but it's worth it for the potential to uncover treasures.'

'I'll take your word for it.'

A wiry woman, hanging up big woolly jumpers on a rack near the entrance, smiled at them. Her name badge announced her as Miriam. 'Morning, loves. Can I help you with anything?'

'Hi,' they replied in unison as Paige took in the organised chaos around them. There were rows and rows of racks crowded with clothing, interspersed with stands stooping under the weight of hats, handbags, scarves and plastic jewellery. Along the walls at the sides and back of the store were shelves and other storage units, almost overflowing with books and board games. There seemed to be lots of mismatched kitchenware and she even noticed the odd broken birdcage among the bric-a-brac.

Karis drifted over to one of the racks and began rifling through rows of dresses that looked like the costume wardrobe from *That '70s Show*. Or at least they would do if Paige tried them on, but Karis managed to not only pull off such clothes but look like she'd just stepped off a Paris catwalk.

'We're looking for a wedding dress,' she said now, loud enough to remind Karis they were on a mission.

'Lovely!' exclaimed Miriam, clapping her hands together. Her eyes went to the sparkling diamond on Paige's finger. 'We have quite a collection of bridal gowns at the moment.'

'Great, but I'm not looking for any old dress,' Paige said, a tad apologetically. 'I'm looking for my mother's dress.'

'Oh?'

She quickly told Miriam everything.

The older woman pressed a hand against her heart. 'Your poor mother. My husband had kidney disease and was on dialysis two long years. It really messes with your life.'

'Is he better now?' Paige asked hopefully. 'Did he get a transplant?'

'He did—my son gave him a kidney in the end—but sadly John had a heart attack six months later and we lost him.'

*Oh geez.* Paige's heart went out to this sweet old woman. 'I'm so sorry.'

'Thank you. It is what it is. We had thirty-six wonderful years together and for that I'll always be grateful. Anyway, let's see if we can find your dress.'

'Karis,' Paige hissed as Miriam turned to go.

Bringing two summer dresses with her, Karis trailed Paige who followed after Miriam to the far back of the store where a mannequin wearing a meringue-style wedding dress stood on a blue box. Not the dress Paige was looking for but the rack on one side of the plastic woman gave her hope. It was crammed so tightly with bridal gowns that you couldn't tell one from another.

'Here, hold this.' She thrust her bag at Karis and immediately began flicking through.

*Nope. Nope. Nope.* There were gowns of every style and colour, dresses from the sixties right through to the present day, but Paige's heart sank as she neared the end of the selection.

Her shoulders slumped and she turned to Karis and Miriam. 'It's not here.'

Her friend frowned. 'Are you sure? You went through them pretty damn quickly.'

'I think I'd recognise my mother's dress,' Paige snapped, fighting tears. It had been a silly fantasy to think that the dress would still be here two years on, but she hadn't known that eighties wedding dresses were in such high demand.

And she'd wanted it so much.

Without a word, Karis stepped forward. As she went through the wedding gowns much more slowly, another woman joined them.

'Miriam,' said the lady with bright rainbow-streaked hair. 'I'm taking a smoko. Can you man the shop for ten?'

'Wait a second, Ramona,' Miriam said, then looked to Paige. 'Have you got a photo of your dress?'

'Yes.'

'Show us. Ramona has been working here so long she's practically part of the furniture and she has a memory like an elephant. If she was here when your mother's dress was purchased, she might remember something about the person who bought it.'

Paige was rapidly losing hope but as she dug the photo she'd taken from her parents' wedding album out of her bag, Miriam gave Ramona the rundown on the situation.

'Here it is.' Paige practically shoved the photo at Ramona, then held her breath and tried to read the other woman's mind as she stared at it a few long moments.

Finally, Ramona clicked her fingers. 'I do remember that dress. It was a stunner. I don't love eighties fashion usually, but there was something special about this one. It reminded me of Princess Di's classic gown. I put it up in the window and in less than an hour, it had sold.'

Paige felt her heart rev. 'Do you know who bought it?'

'I remember it was a man. Pretty young. Tall, dark, handsome, in that clichéd movie-star kind of way.'

'A *man*?' Paige and Karis asked in unison.

Ramona nodded as if this wasn't unusual at all. 'I'm guessing he wanted it for fancy dress. That's what most of our wedding dresses are used for. Guys in drag, theatre productions, hens' night costumes. That kind of thing. Most brides want a new dress, something they can call their own, or they go to a specialist second-hand bridal store where the gowns have been professionally cleaned and made to look new again. Maybe you should try one of them—you might find something similar to your mother's.'

But Paige didn't hear anything past 'Guys in drag'. She shuddered to think of some broad-shouldered sweaty man parading around in her mum's dress for fun. Who cared if he was good-looking! He'd probably stretched, even ripped it, or spilt beer down the front. She fought the urge to burst into tears.

'I don't suppose you remember anything else about this man?' Karis asked, wrapping her arm around Paige. 'Do you have sales records? His name perhaps?'

Ramona shook her head and glanced at her watch. 'Sorry. We might have bank transactions that could give you a clue, but even if we could find something like that from over two years ago, due to privacy, I couldn't give out any such information. Good luck anyway. I'll be back in ten,' she told Miriam before walking away.

Miriam smiled sympathetically. 'I'm really sorry, love. But I hope you find a dress you love just as much and that your mother gets well again soon.'

'Thank you,' Paige managed, still fighting tears. She felt so stupid. Sol had warned her how hard it might be to find *the* dress, but she'd never failed at anything in her life before.

'I'm just going to buy these two,' Karis said, bending to pick up the ugly seventies dresses she'd procured earlier.

'Okay.' Paige tried not to be annoyed that Karis would be walking out with two new outfits while she was leaving empty-handed. 'I'll wait in the car.'

'I was thinking,' Karis began a few minutes later as she fastened her seatbelt. 'If a guy did buy your mum's dress for a costume, then he probably didn't keep it. Maybe he took it back to another shop. So why don't we check out a few more?'

Paige suspected Karis's suggestion was more about her love of scouring charity shops than it was about the dress, but clutched at this new hope. 'Okay, it's worth a shot, I guess.'

'That's the spirit. There's another one just around the corner, we could walk but they have good parking, so I'll direct you.'

True to Karis's word, there was another op shop very close by. They left the car in the car park at the side of the row of shops and went inside. Paige's eyes immediately found a rack of wedding dresses. But the hope that lit in her heart at the sight was short-lived. There weren't as many as there were at the first shop and it took even less time to come to the conclusion that her mother's dress wasn't among them. Karis forced her to show the photo to a woman manning the desk—'just in case'—but not only did she not remember ever seeing such a gown, she was cranky about being interrupted in the game of Candy Crush she was playing on her phone.

'Never fear,' Karis said, linking her arm through Paige's as they retreated back onto the street. 'We've barely scratched the surface of Sydney's opportunity shops.'

But, three hours later they'd scoured every Red Cross, Vinnies, Anglicare, Save the Children, Salvos, Goodwill *and* Smith Family store they could find in the inner west and Paige was ready to admit defeat. It would be impossible to visit *all* the op shops in New South Wales and even then she might come up empty-handed.

'Your mum's not on Facebook, is she?'

'No,' Paige replied. 'She's always refused to sign up—says it's a waste of time, that people don't show their true selves anyway and if she wants to know what's happening in a friend's life, she'll call them. Why?'

A victorious smile cracked across Karis's face. 'I've had an idea.'

When Karis just sat there grinning, Paige prompted, 'Well, go on then, what is it?'

'You put up a post with a picture of your mum's dress. Tell everyone you're trying to track it down and that if they know your mum to please keep it secret from her as this is going to be a surprise. Then you ask people to share it. There's heaps of different groups and stuff that are all about helping people find lost shit, so you can post in those as well.'

'Oh my God!' The heaviness that had been dragging her down since they'd left that last shop suddenly lifted. She felt revived as if she'd downed a can of Red Bull. How many stories had she heard about friends, family, pets and all sorts of other things being reunited through social media? 'Why didn't I think of that?'

Paige dug her phone out of her handbag. She was a fast typist and within moments, she'd tapped out a spiel. As she posted the wedding dress photo to her timeline, she tried to keep her hope and excitement in check. Even if she did manage to find her mother's dress, there was no knowing what kind of state it would be in after all these years, all these owners.

*Rebecca*

Rebecca's gaze fell upon the familiar sight of their house as Hugh turned into their driveway. It felt like she'd been in hospital two long years and her hand was on the passenger door handle before he'd stopped the car.

'Steady on, you don't want to fall and end up back in hospital.'

No way she'd let *that* happen. Excited barks sounded from inside as she headed towards the house, Hugh hurrying after her.

'Sounds like I'm not the only one happy to have you home,' he said as he unlocked the door and pushed it open. Molly exploded from inside and jumped all over Rebecca.

She dropped to her knees and wrapped her arms around the pup. 'Hello, beautiful girl. I missed you too.'

'I'll put the kettle on,' Hugh said, stepping past them to head properly into the house.

'I think I'm going to have a lie down for a bit.' Rebecca glanced around—the house was spotless, even the pile of washing waiting to be ironed that usually lived in a basket near the TV was empty.

Hugh (and perhaps Paige) had gone to a lot of trouble to make sure there was nothing she needed to do.

'Good idea, I'll bring you in a cuppa.'

'Actually, do you mind giving me a few minutes privacy?'

Hugh blinked. 'You don't want me to come into the bedroom with you?'

'Don't be upset. In hospital I've not had a moment to myself—there's always some nurse or doctor or orderly popping their head in. I just need a little me-time.'

'O-kay.' Hugh spoke slowly as if he didn't understand at all, but after the scare she'd given him two weeks ago, he'd be willing to grant her pretty much anything.

'Thanks, hun.' She threw him an appreciative smile and started up the stairs towards their bedroom, Molly pattering closely behind.

Like the rest of the house, this room was immaculate and there was even a bunch of gardenias on the bedside table. She smiled as she crossed the room and then stooped to sniff them. Hugh knew they were her favourite.

As Molly twirled three times like she always did before a snooze and then settled herself down in her favourite spot in front of the bed, Rebecca glanced at the closed door, praying Hugh would respect her request for privacy. Then, taking a deep breath, her hands shaking ridiculously, she went into their walk-in robe, stretched up high on her tippy-toes and pulled down a box she'd labelled 'Old Music Notebooks'. Neither Hugh nor Paige shared her love of music and so they would never think to pry into this box. Besides, it wasn't a lie—the box did contain her old journals, but, right at the bottom, it also housed a whole load of mix-tapes left over from her teenage years, letters, and something even more precious to her than them.

She took the box over to the bed and her breath caught in her throat as she lifted the lid. What if the photo was gone? There was no reason why it should be but suddenly the fear felt real. Without care, she lifted the notebooks that were at the top and flung them on the bed beside her, then rifled through the rest of the box, resisting the urge to look at the tapes from her high school boyfriend—she should have thrown them away years ago. Finally, she found what she was looking for, the old journal filled with the angst-ridden songs she'd written as a teenager. They were all dismal—singing was her skill, not songwriting—but she'd put her heart and soul into them anyway. Ignoring the *R&R Forever* scratched into the front cover in her flowery adolescent handwriting, she flicked straight to the end.

And there it was.

There *he* was—tiny and perfect, a bald-headed angel looking up at her with big, blue, innocent eyes. Well, not at *her*, she'd never got that close to him; he'd been looking up at whoever took the photograph and she didn't know who that was. Maybe a nurse. Certainly she couldn't imagine her mother would have done so.

Tears prickled Rebecca's eyes as she touched a finger to the photo. She let out a long slow breath, one she felt like she'd been holding since she'd thought of this photo in the hospital two weeks ago. This little boy had never been far from her mind these last thirty-five years, but she'd kept him in a box and kept that box buried deep in her heart. Yet now, having come face to face with her own mortality, everything felt like it had changed. Now it was like her long-lost son was actually in that box and that he was knocking on the lid, trying to push it open and get her attention.

Pain throbbed in her forehead and she forced deep breaths in and out, unsure whether her sudden breathlessness was because she was having a panic attack or if it was a symptom of her blasted kidney disease. Either way, this photo couldn't stay here, in the house, where it could so easily be found by someone looking for something else. She didn't know how she'd ever been able to sleep with it so easily accessible.

But what could she do with it? She didn't trust her parents not to 'lose' it and besides, her dad hadn't been in the best of health lately either; she didn't want to put anything else on them.

Did banks still rent out safe deposit boxes? Rebecca wasn't sure if they were actually a thing or if it was just something used in the movies. She could ask Hugh—he always knew stuff like that—but of course then he'd want to know why she needed one. *Google!* The answer landed in her head and she went to grab her mobile only to realise her handbag was still out in the hallway where she'd dumped it when she'd dropped down to hug Molly.

*Bugger.* Why did everything have to be so hard?

In lieu of the internet or her phone, there was only one thing for it. She blinked then wiped her eyes, grateful she hadn't been wearing any mascara. Then, slipping the photograph back into the notebook, which thankfully was small enough to fit in her jacket pocket, she repacked the box and shoved it back on the top shelf of the wardrobe.

Hugh was putting her suitcase outside the door when she opened it. They laughed nervously as if they were strangers colliding in the street.

'That was a quick nap.'

'I've decided I need some fresh air instead,' Rebecca replied, already walking past him into the kitchen where they kept their car keys on a hook. She thought the location ridiculous but Hugh refused to leave them within reach of the front door, saying they'd be easy pickings for burglars there. She plucked her hatchback's key fob off the wall and almost bumped into Hugh as she turned around.

'I could get Molly's lead and we could go for a gentle stroll.'

'I told you, I want to be alone for a bit.' She started towards the front door before he could launch into an argument.

He hurried after her like a blasted shadow. 'Where are you going?'

'I don't know. Just for a drive.'

'I thought you wanted fresh air.'

'Oh, for heaven's sakes, Hugh, you're not my father!'

His face fell. 'I'm sorry. I'm just … worried about you. I don't want you to overdo it. You've been very ill.'

She took a breath and softened. 'Please, just give me ten minutes. I love you and I promise I won't do anything silly.'

'Okay, but don't forget Paige and Sol are bringing dinner round later.'

She squeezed his hand. 'Promise I'll be back well before then.'

On the way to the bank, the photograph felt as if it were burning a hole in her pocket and her mind drifted once again to the information she'd recently discovered. In hospital, late at night with the ward so quiet she could hear machinery beeping somewhere in the distance, when she'd known she couldn't be interrupted by Hugh or Paige or any other friends or family, she'd looked up something she'd never allowed herself to contemplate before.

*How to find an adopted child.*

It seemed fairly straightforward. There was a simple form she could fill in to apply to the Western Australia government department for identifying and non-identifying information about the child she'd given up. She could send it off and in due course she would be rewarded with the adoption information, which would include identifying details about everyone involved—her son, herself and the people who'd raised him as their own.

Then, if she wanted, she could also be placed on the Reunion and Information Register or she could use the information she had to track him down some other way. This day and age, with Facebook—which she'd always steered clear of for exactly these reasons—and all those other online connectors, it had to be easier than ever before to find a long-lost relative.

That thought sent a tingle down her spine. The idea of seeing her boy after all these years was almost impossible to comprehend, but her excitement was short-lived.

Old fears raised their ugly heads.

What if her son was angry and resentful at what she'd done? What if he didn't want to be found? Could she handle a negative response? She'd always believed that it should be his decision to make contact, that she didn't have the right to intrude on the relationship with his adoptive parents, but he was a grown man now and suddenly she wasn't sure if she could spend the rest of her life—however long or short that may be—with the question mark hanging over her head.

Of course it wasn't just herself and her son she needed to think about. She swallowed at the memory of the promise she'd made her ex-boyfriend when he'd turned up all those years ago. Then there was also Paige and Hugh to consider. And her bloody kidneys. Even if she could handle her husband and daughter, she didn't want her son to think her illness was the only reason she'd finally decided to seek him out.

Yet, how else would it look?

Perhaps she could request the information but not act on it until after she was well again. Of course there was no telling how long that would be. Since her nearest and dearest weren't suitable donor candidates, who knew how many months—or even years—it would be until she could have a transplant.

Would she be able to handle having the information at her fingertips and *not* act on it?

Rebecca shot out her hand and pressed the button to lower the window. As fresh air gushed into the car she gasped at it, her head thumping with the enormity of this decision.

Solomon's car was already parked in the driveway when Rebecca returned to her house almost four hours later. Barely before she'd stopped, the front door burst open and Hugh, followed closely by Paige and Solomon, rushed towards her.

'Where the hell have you been?' he demanded, flinging open her car door.

'I told you,' she said as she climbed out of the car and smiled at her daughter and future son-in-law who stood alongside her husband with identical expressions of concern on their faces, 'I needed some me-time. I went for a drive and then a stroll along the beach.'

Hugh pushed his glasses up his nose, something he always did when he was stressed. 'I've been trying to call you for the last two hours. I've been worried sick. I—' He sighed and then yanked her into his arms. 'Thank God you're okay.'

'I'm sorry,' she said, wrapping her arms around her husband, torn between guilt and irritation—she was a grown woman for heaven's sake. 'My phone must be on silent.'

'If you go out again alone ...' Paige's hands were on her hips. 'Then you need to make sure you're contactable. Two weeks ago you were coughing up blood and I know you don't want to admit it, but you're not in perfect health and we can't help worrying about you. Dad and I had visions of you back in hospital and—'

'I'm sorry,' Rebecca said again, extracting herself from Hugh's embrace and giving Paige a hug. 'But you don't know what it's like being stuck in that place, I felt like I was in prison and I just needed to—'

'Are you wet, Mum?' Paige interrupted, pulling back a little and frowning.

'Not really,' Rebecca replied, but suddenly she realised her clothes were a little damp. She shivered involuntarily. That'd be from the stroll she took along the beach. After the bank she'd driven to Bronte, meaning only to sit and think a few minutes but the car had felt as claustrophobic as the hospital. She'd carried her shoes as she walked along the beach and when she hadn't been concentrating a wave had surprised her, splashing water up onto her clothes. The heater in the car hadn't quite had time to dry her off yet.

'Let's get her inside in the warmth,' Solomon said, smiling at Rebecca as if he understood that Hugh and Paige's stressing was annoying.

'Yes, good idea.' She smiled her appreciation as she started up the path. She heard Hugh slam the car door shut and she stopped, closing her eyes in frustration. In all their upset, she'd left her bag in the car. Or maybe it was just her not thinking properly.

'I've got to get my bag,' she said, turning back towards the car again.

Hugh held it up, along with her car keys. 'I've got them. You get inside like Sol said. The heater's on and dinner's ready.'

'Although we might have to heat it up again,' Paige said, disapproval clear in her voice.

As her family ushered her into the house, Rebecca was immediately hit with the usually alluring aromas of Indian cuisine from her favourite local restaurant and while she appreciated the sentiment, she wasn't sure she'd be able to stomach even a mouthful.

'I'm going to have a shower and get into some dry clothes. I'll be quick,' she said and then escaped upstairs to her bedroom before anyone could object or grill her again.

She took the notebook back out of her handbag and returned it to the box on the shelf, not that it held anything of value anymore. Perhaps she should throw it out. Perhaps she should throw away the whole damn box. Why she'd held onto those tapes all these years she had no idea. Not only did she no longer have a device to play them on, but if those particular songs came on the radio now, she always switched stations. The songs that had punctuated her first love now only made her heart ache—like broken promises, they were just words and she didn't need the feelings they evoked.

Vowing to get rid of the tapes later, she had the quickest shower of her life, threw on an old tracksuit and went out to face her family.

The table already laid, Hugh was pouring water for everyone—wine off the agenda thanks to her kidneys—and Paige and Sol were busy opening the lids of the various containers.

'It looks like you bought one of everything on the menu,' Rebecca mused.

Sol winked at her. 'Two of some things. We know how much you love onion badjis.'

'And we know how much you didn't love the hospital food,' added Paige as they sat.

'Thank you.' Rebecca smiled around the table at her three favourite people. 'It's so good to be home.'

They all beamed back at her.

'Eat up,' Hugh said, reaching over and patting her hand.

Still not hungry, in fact very queasy in her stomach, Rebecca put as little food on her plate as she thought she could get away with.

As the men piled their plates high, Paige launched straight into conversation. 'Mum, we've got two exciting bits of news.'

'Oh, wonderful.' Rebecca picked up her fork; she could at least pretend to eat.

'We've set a date!'

For a moment Rebecca had no idea what Paige was talking about. Her blank expression must have given this away for Paige added, 'For our *wedding.*'

'Oh, wonderful,' she said again, beginning to wonder if she'd misplaced all the other words in her vocabulary. She forced herself to smile brightly—this *was* wonderful news. 'What is it? When?'

'October thirteenth, almost three months exactly.'

'Isn't the thirteenth bad luck?' Hugh asked, before shoving another forkful of his favourite beef jalfrezi into his mouth.

Paige rolled her eyes. 'Since when have we believed in stuff like that?'

'True.' Hugh continued eating.

'Well, we've got lots to organise,' Rebecca said. 'Where are you going to have the ceremony? And the reception? It's short notice but I'm sure we'll come up with something.'

'We're gonna get married on the beach and Lisette and Randy have agreed to let us have the reception in their backyard.'

'I'm not sure agreed is quite the right word. Mum's ecstatic about it. She wanted to call a family meeting immediately to start talking about the catering, the music, decorations etc but we thought you might be too tired tonight. We'll have you all round to lunch soon to discuss everything.'

'Wonderful.' Rebecca cringed at her use of that word again.

As she continued pushing her food around her plate, Paige and Sol talked wedding prep. Rebecca tried to make the right noises in the right places, but she was finding it almost impossible to focus. Leaving the photo behind in that safe deposit box had felt a little like abandoning her son all over again and she was struggling to hold it together.

'You alright, sweetheart?' Hugh asked during a rare pause in Paige's wedding soliloquy.

'Yes.' She tried to offer him a reassuring smile. 'I'm more than alright. I'm very excited. Taking it all in. Just a wee bit tired.' May as well milk the damn disease for something.

'We'll make sure you have an early night,' he said.

'Speaking of tiredness,' Paige began, sharing a knowing smile with Solomon before looking back to Rebecca, 'that brings us to our second bit of news.'

'Oh my god! You're pregnant!' Rebecca shrieked, her hand rushing to cover her mouth and her heart jumping as if it had been injected with adrenaline. How many more surprises—good or bad— could she take?

'God, no.' Paige gave Solomon a look of horror and he laughed. 'I'm only twenty-seven, Mum.'

'I'd had ... *you* by that age.' Her chest squeezed, she'd almost said 'two babies by that age'—what a can of worms that would have opened.

'Well, *anyway*.' Paige clearly wasn't going to even discuss the possibility of motherhood. 'What I was trying to say is ...' She paused and looked to Sol. 'Actually, maybe you should tell her.'

He cleared his throat. 'I'm not the same blood type as you, Rebecca, but Paige and I have been looking into the paired kidney exchange program that Dr Chopra mentioned. I'm willing to be your donor, to go on the program and give my kidney to another recipient who has a donor that is your match.'

Rebecca gasped and the tears she'd been fighting since arriving home conquered her.

'Oh, Mum.' Paige pushed back her chair and rushed out of the room.

'Geez,' Hugh said, his tone awed. 'Wow, Solomon. That's ... that's ...' Her husband seemed to be at an unusual loss for words and although there were lots of words swimming around her head, she couldn't speak past her flood of emotion.

Solomon bit his thick lower lip as if unsure what to say or do.

Paige returned to the room carrying a box of tissues. She pulled out the empty chair beside Rebecca, sat and shoved the box under her nose.

'Isn't it wonderful?' she gushed. 'Isn't *he* wonderful?'

At least Rebecca wasn't the only one stuck on the 'W' word, she thought as she dabbed at her eyes with the tissue and tried to rein in her tears. But the word 'wonderful' didn't seem nearly huge enough to describe what Solomon was offering to do.

It was an answer to her prayers.

Dr Chopra had said if she had to go on the deceased donor list, she might be waiting up to four years for a transplant. She wasn't sure how long the wait list was on the exchange program but it had to be better than that.

'Mum, say something,' Paige ordered.

At the excited expectation in her daughter's voice, Rebecca blinked out of her bubble and her heart sank.

Paige and Sol were holding hands across the table—the love, friendship and respect between them as obvious as if it were a physical thing they were clasping onto. What if something happened to him down the track and his leftover kidney failed him? She'd never forgive herself. And how would Paige feel about her then? Sol might be healthy today, but then so was she a month ago and now she needed to rely on dialysis or a selfless offering from someone else to secure her future. Nothing was certain.

A selfish part of her wanted to consider this generous gift but could she risk allowing the centre of her daughter's world to sacrifice one of his organs for her?

'Thank you, Solomon.' Her words came out as a whisper, she was so overcome with emotion. She took a quick breath. 'I can't thank you enough for even considering this, but ... you're so young and I'm not sure I'd feel right about accepting until we've exhausted all other options.'

'What options, Mum?' Paige asked, yanking her hand from his and throwing it up in the air.

'Well …' The last few days Rebecca had been supposed to be thinking about possible friends and family she might approach, but her mind had mostly been elsewhere. A quick survey of hers and Hugh's family had determined that her father was the only known family member with a compatible blood type, but he was eighty and not in good health himself. Hugh's sisters—she could tell—had been relieved they weren't compatible and neither of their husbands had offered to be tested.

'See, Mum,' Paige said after a few long moments of silence. 'This is the best option. Sol's young, fit, healthy and *willing*. Don't look a gift horse in the mouth.'

'But what if Solomon gets sick?' Rebecca looked her daughter right in the eye as she spoke. 'What if I take his kidney and then one day his other kidney fails and he needs a transplant? What if you have kids and I'm responsible for taking their father? How will you feel then?'

Paige blinked as if this thought hadn't crossed her mind, which was probably the case—she'd always been a little impulsive.

Solomon cleared his throat. 'May I say something?'

Rebecca and Paige nodded.

'I appreciate your concern regarding my health, but this isn't a decision I've made lightly. I've done some research of my own and *if* on the off-chance I develop a disease that means I need a kidney transplant myself, because I've been a living kidney donor I'll be given priority status on the deceased donor list.'

Paige smiled victoriously. 'There you go.'

'But,' Solomon continued, 'even if that wasn't the case, it's a risk I'm prepared to take. I wouldn't be able to live with myself knowing that I could have done something to improve your quality of life and didn't. So fine, take your time to think, but don't decline my offer because you're worried about the future. If there's one thing I know is certain about life, it's the *uncertainty* of the future, which is why I prefer to live for today.'

'That's very true,' Hugh said, putting his fork down on his plate as if he too, with all the talk of kidneys, had lost his appetite. 'What do you think, Rebecca?'

Paige and Sol joined him in looking expectantly at her.

'I thank you for the offer and I promise I'll give it some serious thought.'

*Josie*

*What's the point in doing this?*

This question was on replay inside Josie's head as she dragged her feet down the leafy tree-lined Surry Hills street towards Life After Loss.

All the talking in the world wasn't going to fix anything. Nothing could bring her babies to life. And, even though she'd had no mojo to do anything much lately, she could suddenly think of a bazillion things she could be doing instead on the last Thursday of her school holidays. Her hand flickered to her bag, her head and fingers craving the relief of a cigarette, but then she remembered she didn't have any. She'd promised Nik no more smoking, only to drink if they were together and that she'd give this talking-to-someone bizzo a red-hot go.

*Dammit*. She kicked her foot against the footpath and then suddenly realised she'd arrived at her destination.

Like all the other offices on this street, the charity was located in a beautifully renovated old terrace house. The building looked innocuous enough, there were large leafy pot plants in the small courtyard out the front and the windows had lovely white shutters. How could a not-for-profit afford such a property? Perhaps a government grant or a bequest from someone they'd helped? Paige shook her head—what did it matter where the money came from? She was just dithering. With a deep breath, she pushed that procrastination aside, forced one foot in front of the other and headed for the front door.

If this was pointless as she suspected it would be, then she didn't have to come back but at least she could tell Nik she'd tried. The door creaked a little as she pushed it open and a middle-aged woman looked up from behind a reception desk and smiled. 'Good morning.'

'Hi.' Josie swallowed. 'I'm Josie Mitreski. I'm meeting Clara Jones here.'

'Wonderful. Clara won't be a moment. Would you like to take a seat while you wait? And can I make you a coffee or something?'

Josie politely refused the drink, then retreated to the small waiting area and settled in a seat. She felt as if there were a circus of butterflies practising acrobatics in her stomach and hoped she didn't have to wait long or she might chicken out and flee.

'Josephine Mitreski?'

She startled at the call of her name, having not even noticed a woman appear at the edge of the waiting room, and stumbled to her feet. The tall, slim woman who had a slightly wavy, shoulder-length, golden bob smiled warmly at her. 'I'm Clara,' she said as she offered her hand. 'It's lovely to meet you. Come on through.'

A vision of the man who'd given her the business card appeared in Josie's head as she followed Clara down a short corridor; it was almost impossible to reconcile him and this woman as being married. She wore smart black trousers and a blue twin-set, with a string of simple pearls around her neck, whereas her husband with his long hair tied back scruffily had looked like a burned-out rock star.

'Take a seat,' Clara said as they emerged into a bright yellow room with three plush armchairs and generic paintings of beaches and bridges on the walls. Josie wondered if they were chosen because they were two things that could not possibly upset or offend anyone.

'Thanks.' She perched herself on the edge of one of the chairs.

'Can I get a you a drink?' Clara asked, closing the door behind her. 'We have coffee, tea and hot chocolate, or are you more of a soft drink girl? I've got a few Diet Cokes I keep aside just in case.'

Josie's mouth watered at the mention of her favourite drink— during her pregnancies she'd abstained from Diet Coke, not that it had done any good—and she'd got out of the habit of drinking it. 'I'd love a Diet Coke, thanks.'

'Excellent. You get comfortable.' Clara smiled again and then turned to a small fridge in the corner of the room. She retrieved two glasses and two cans of Diet Coke, then put them down on the table between them.

'I can spot a fellow Diet Coke lover from a mile off,' she said as she lowered herself into the chair opposite Josie's. She cracked open her can, then poured it into a glass.

Josie did the same and then took a little sip. Despite Clara's smile, warm tone and attempt to put her at ease, Josie's nerves were rampant but the caffeine hit helped a bit.

'Did you have to travel far to come here?' Clara asked.

'Not too far. We live in Coogee.'

'Have you lived there long?'

'About eighteen months. We moved from Perth.'

'I see,' Clara said, in that way psychiatrists in movies speak when they're analysing someone. 'And do you like it?'

Josie shrugged one shoulder. 'What's not to like?'

'And how did you find me? Did a doctor recommend you talk to someone about your losses?'

Josie shook her head, her stomach growing hard. The small talk had been an obvious attempt to put her at ease but now they were getting down to business. Doctors had suggested she see a counsellor or reach out to an organisation like this one Clara volunteered for, but she'd resisted—believing talking would be futile. 'Actually your husband gave me your card,' she said, thinking of how kind he'd been that night at The Inferno.

'My *husband*?' Clara sounded as if she had no idea whom Josie was talking about.

'Yes, we met outside a pub in Coogee.'

'Ah, that sounds about right. Although he's been my *ex*-husband for two years.'

'He was very kind to me,' Josie said. 'I was in a mess when we ran into each other. He was a good listener. He told me you could help me.'

The older woman leaned forward and put her glass back on the table. 'Well, I'm here to listen,' she said, her warm smile back in place. 'I hope that helps. Would you like to tell me about your miscarriages?'

Josie had mentioned they were the reason for her visit when she'd called and made the appointment, but once again that voice was loud and clear in her head questioning why she was here. *No*, she did not want to tell this stranger anything. Her grip on her glass tightened as emotion clogged in her throat. Her eyeballs stung, telling her she was on the verge of tears.

All the while, Clara's smile—Josie guessed it was supposed to be encouraging—remained firmly in place.

Finally, she broke the silence. 'I'm not sure you know but all of us who volunteer here as parent supporters have suffered our own devastating losses. I'm not going to pretend I know exactly what you're going through, Josephine—'

'Please, call me, Josie. Only my mum ever used my full name.'

'Let me guess? Only when you were naughty?'

Josie found herself smiling, the tightness in her chest loosening slightly. 'Something like that.'

Clara continued. 'Although every parent feels loss differently, I started volunteering because I wanted to help other mothers navigate their grief. I suffered a number of miscarriages and also a stillbirth at thirty-six weeks.'

'Oh God, that's awful.' Josie felt like a fraud sitting here when all her losses had been early enough to be classified as miscarriages, but at the same time she felt a horrific jealousy that at least Clara had been able to hold her baby. 'I've only had three miscarriages,' she said, almost apologetically.

'*One* is too many,' Clara said simply, leaning forward and pushing the big box of tissues on the coffee table towards her.

Josie didn't take one.

'Any loss is devastating. It changes your whole world. It changes you. You've probably found it also changes the way others—people you considered friends—act around you and this hurts. I remember people actually crossing the road to avoid me after the death of my daughter.'

'Yes.' Josie nodded. 'I'm a teacher and I've noticed some of my colleagues leave the staffroom to avoid talking to me.'

'Remember it's not a reflection on you, and it's not that they're trying to be cruel, they simply don't know what to say. The majority of folks don't know how to act around people who have suffered tragic loss.'

'I guess that's why people say you shouldn't tell everyone till after three months. My first miscarriage was at eight weeks,' Josie found herself saying. 'And we'd already told everyone. We went to our obstetrician appointment all excited to get our first ultrasound but,' she blinked back tears, the memories fresh in her head as if it all happened yesterday, 'the doctor couldn't find a heartbeat. I couldn't believe it. I thought I must have heard wrong. I started bleeding the next day.'

Josie swallowed. Clara didn't say a word.

'We didn't tell *anyone* the second time we got pregnant and although we were terrified it would happen again, it was still a shock when it did because the doctor had told us it was very unlikely. It was almost exactly the same time as the first one. Although everyone said there was nothing I could do, I can't help wondering if I'd done something wrong. If I ate something or ...'

'We all wonder that,' Clara said when Josie's voice drifted off. 'But you didn't.'

She shrugged, unsure. 'Third time we got past the *safe* mark.' Her voice filled with scorn on *that* word. 'We did the obligatory cute announcement on Facebook and even started buying stuff. I felt a little nervous about doing so but I was so sick with morning sickness and I never had been with the other two, so it felt like this was it. It was all going to be okay. Only it wasn't.'

A tear slithered down her cheek and she ignored it, hoping if she did so no more would come.

'How far along were you this time?'

'Eighteen weeks, so still technically a miscarriage. The doctor called it a "spontaneous end of pregnancy", but she was my baby.' Josie winced as fresh pain crippled her. 'I'm sorry. Every day I wake up no longer pregnant, not a mum, and I feel as if my heart has been smashed to pieces. All I want to do is cry.'

'And you're allowed to.' This time Clara actually picked the tissue box up and held it out to Josie; she took one and buried her nose in it, making a great big ugly sound.

'It doesn't feel that way,' she said through her sobs. 'Everyone just wants me to snap out of it, but I can't.'

'Of course you can't and neither should you have to. You feel like you'll never be happy again and that's a valid emotion.'

After a long pause, Clara said, 'Did you name your babies?'

'Yes,' Josie whispered. 'We don't know what gender the first one was but I have a feeling it was a little boy. I call him Jamie. The next two were girls, Sophia and Isabelle.'

'They're beautiful names.'

'My husband didn't think I should use my favourite names, in case we have other children, but I felt like my angel babies deserved beautiful names.'

Clara nodded. 'They definitely do.'

At the thought of Nik, Josie recalled how touchy things had been between them. She wondered if that was normal? She wanted to ask if the same had happened between Clara and her husband and that had been the downfall of their marriage.

After a long silence, Clara spoke again as if she could read Josie's mind. 'Are things okay between you and your husband?'

Josie sniffed into the tissue, then held it tightly, scrunched up in her hand. 'Not really. But things came to a head the other night and we finally talked properly.' She explained how Nik had been holding it all inside, because he'd been trying to protect her.

'I'm not a relationships expert or counsellor, and that's not my role, but what you're describing is very normal. Men think we're complicated beasts but they are just as complex. They may feel differently to us as they never actually felt the child growing within them but they feel loss just as deeply. It just manifests in a different way.'

Josie sighed. 'I see that now. I feel so guilty that I didn't see Nik was hurting too.'

'Our organisation has male parent supporters too—fathers who have been through the loss of a child. Your husband might benefit from talking to someone also. Or you could join one of our group support sessions, in which couples talk together about their loss with other couples.'

What Josie thought of that must have been clear on her face for Clara smiled and added, 'It might sound daunting, but a lot of couples find it really helps.'

'We'll think about it,' she said, and found that she meant it.

'You said you moved from Perth. Did you move for work? Or did you come for family reasons?'

'We came for Nik's work—he's an aircraft engineer. But I was happy to move. My mum passed away just before I met Nik and I was missing her so much. My dad's very social and he had lots of friends to look after him but Perth felt wrong without Mum just around the corner.'

And suddenly Josie was crying all over again. The tissues were yanked out at a rate of knots.

Clara let her sob and then when the tears finally started to subside, she said quietly, 'You were obviously close. Was it sudden?'

'A heart attack. No chance to say goodbye.'

'So it's not just your baby losses you're grieving, but also the death of your mother. All that on top of a move, a new job ... I'm so glad you decided to reach out to us.'

'Me too,' Josie said. Although she'd never been one to talk much about herself, she'd found it surprisingly easy to open up to Clara. This other woman might not have been able to bring her babies back, but just talking about them to someone who really understood did make her feel a little better.

When Clara glanced at her watch and said, 'I'm sorry, but we're going to have to wrap this up,' Josie couldn't believe how fast the time had flown.

'When can I see you again?'

'How about next week? I'm guessing you'll be back at school and I also work at the hospital, but I'm here late on Thursday afternoons. Does that suit?'

'Yes. Thank you.'

She usually covered after-school detention on Thursdays. First week back there hopefully wouldn't be too many students misbehaving, but too bad anyway. Someone else would have to cover it; her mental health was more important.

## Clara

The doorbell rang and echoed through the house as Clara slid her second pearl drop earring into its hole. She frowned as she glanced over at the time on her bedside clock. Rob said she was old-fashioned to still have an alarm clock radio, but she liked listening to talkback late at night when she couldn't sleep and it came in useful more often than not. Like now. She sucked in a breath—the nerves she'd been fighting all morning washed over her like a tsunami.

Gregg was fifteen minutes early.

Although she liked punctuality in a person, she'd mentally prepared herself to have another quarter of an hour to practise a greeting and come up with a list of things to discuss, in case the conversation fell flat once they'd exhausted talking about old school acquaintances.

Taking a deep breath, she looked in the mirror and gave herself a quick pep-talk. 'Relax, Clara. This isn't such a big deal. He's just an old friend you're having coffee with. And coffee on a Saturday morning hardly even counts as a date.'

So why had she spent all yesterday afternoon getting beautified? She'd waxed areas that hadn't seen another human in years, had her hair *and* nails done and suffered through a make-up tutorial at the counter in Myer, which ended with her buying more products than she'd probably use in her lifetime. Half of which she didn't even know how to use. She'd spent hours trying on dresses until she'd finally decided on a winter knit with long sleeves. It was a little shorter than she'd usually go for but the sales assistant promised she had the figure to carry it off; now she wondered if the lady said that simply to get a sale. Golly, she hoped she wasn't too overdressed for a coffee date. But the doorbell rang again; there wasn't time to second-guess her outfit.

So instead, she grabbed her handbag, wove her arms into her black velvet blazer and walked down the hallway telling herself she wasn't nervous at all. Trying to ignore the heavy beating of her heart, she summoned her most carefree smile and pulled back the door to …

'Rob?' Clara's heart plummeted to her stomach. 'What are you doing here?'

'You're selling the house?' He spoke loudly, almost shouting and she could smell the liquor on his breath, even at this time of the morning. His long hair wasn't even tied back in his usual ponytail and she shuddered to think of the last time he might have washed it.

She stepped back a little—resisting the urge to look away—but not enough to give him access inside.

'How did you know?'

The real estate photographer had only taken photos the day before; there was no sign up in front of the house yet and she'd been told the listing wouldn't go online until mid-next week.

'Siobhan bought round some of my stuff and told Mum you were clearing out to sell.'

'I see.' It had been almost a week since Clara had given her sister those boxes, but true to her character she'd not delivered them straight away. Talk about timing.

'How could you sell our home without consulting me?' Rob demanded, shaking his hands in the air with each word.

*Oh my God.* He really was delusional. 'Rob, this hasn't been *your* home for over two years now.'

He blinked as if this was the first he'd heard of their separation and she struggled to maintain her exasperation with him. 'Anyway, you have to go now. I'm ... busy.'

'Doing what?' He looked past her into the now-bare house.

'Keep your voice down,' she hissed, not wanting to bring the neighbours out and praying he'd disappear before Gregg arrived. 'I have to go to work.'

He took in her new knee-high boots and then slowly glanced up to her made-up face. 'You don't *look* like you're going to work.'

'Well, I ...' she spluttered, trying to think of how she could get rid of him quickly. Gregg would be here any minute now.

Rob took a step towards the door. 'Let me come in. We need to talk about this, about us, we—'

'No!' She yanked the door shut behind her. 'There's nothing to talk about. Please go.'

But he wouldn't listen. 'I've been trying to call you. Something must be wrong with your phone. I can't get through.'

'There's nothing wrong with my phone. I've blocked your number.'

'What?' His face fell. 'Why?'

Her heart squeezed at his despondent expression but she couldn't do this anymore. She was starting to sweat beneath her winter dress. 'Because we're over, Rob. I'm trying to move on. I don't want you in my life anymore. Please, just go.'

'No, Clarabel.' He reached out and grabbed her arms, using her full name, which he only ever did when he was sweet-talking her. 'Don't say such things. You and me, we've been through too much together. We're made for each other. Give me another chance.'

She didn't think he meant to hurt her but his grip was hard and the pungent smell of his breath almost made her sick. To think she'd considered calling him after that poor girl had told her about their chance meeting.

'Let me go.'

'I can't. I'll change. I'll get help, I'll stop drinking, but life isn't worth living if you're not in it. I've got no one else.'

How many times had she heard these words? She no longer gave any credence to his empty promises and there was nothing but pity left for him in her heart.

'I hope you do get help, but it's too late for us. We've been over a long time.'

It felt like Groundhog Day. How many times would she have to say it for him to accept it?

'No, we're not. We'll never be finished.' He tugged at her arms like a man trying to save himself from drowning. 'Just one more chance. Please, baby.'

'Don't do this, Rob. You're making a scene,' she pleaded just as a navy-blue Lexus parked just in front of her house.

*Gregg.* The vision brought tears to her eyes. This was not the first impression she'd wanted to give him after all these years.

The car had barely stopped before the driver's door flung open and in a few long strides he was on the porch beside them.

'Let her go,' Gregg roared at Rob.

Rob turned his head to glare but still clung to her. 'Who the hell are you?'

'I'm a friend,' Gregg said, 'and I asked you to let Clara go.'

'You don't tell me what to do with my wife!'

'I'm not your wife!'

At these words, Rob did let go, but there was no time for relief. Clara gasped as he turned and took a slug at Gregg.

Gregg dodged to the side and Rob stumbled forward, planting his hands and knees on the ground. Her chest tightened; she felt as if she was having a heart attack.

'Are you alright?' Gregg looked to her, not Rob.

Her hand covering her mouth, she nodded, unable to speak.

'Okay then. Do you want him to go?'

She nodded again, gulping in an attempt to try and stop the imminent tears. This situation was embarrassing enough without adding waterworks to the display, but Rob's physical behaviour shocked her.

'Do you need a hand up?' Gregg looked down at Rob still sprawled on the ground.

'Don't touch me,' Rob growled, scrambling out of Gregg's reach and then using a pot plant to pull himself to his feet. He looked back at Clara and she noticed blood on the top of his lip, as if he'd grazed it on the decking. 'Who is this bloke?'

She swallowed and somehow found her voice. 'He's an old friend. We're about to go for coffee.'

Or at least they were; now Gregg was probably wondering what the hell he'd got himself involved with.

'Are you *seeing* him?' Shock filled Rob's voice as he threw a scorn-filled look at the tall, smartly dressed man now standing beside her.

'That's none of your business, Rob,' she said, finding her strength again. 'Now, can I call you a taxi or are you on the bus?'

Rob said nothing in reply. He simply stared at her a few long moments, then slowly shook his head and retreated. He stumbled again as he took the two steps onto the front path, but somehow, he managed to save himself and, as Clara watched him stagger away down the street, she prayed to God that was the last time she saw him.

'I'm so sorry,' she gushed, turning to Gregg, her face and neck impossibly hot. Thank God Rob hadn't managed to hit him.

'It's alright. You have nothing to apologise for. I'm guessing that was your ex-husband?'

She nodded. If only she could lie. Wiping Rob from her past was proving far more difficult than she could ever have imagined. 'He found out I'm selling the house and, although he has no claim on it, he came to try talk me out of it.'

'Under the circumstances, I'd totally understand if you'd like to postpone our coffee date.'

'No!' Because what if she let him go and he ran for the hills and never came back? This might be an inauspicious start but surely things could only improve from here on in. 'Unless … that is, unless *you* want to.'

Gregg's previously serious expression transformed into a smile and *oh!* That smile took his handsome to a whole other level. How had she never noticed it in school? Perhaps he was one of those people who'd grown into his looks.

'I don't want to,' he said, in a manner that sent shivers down her spine.

'Good.' As relief flooded her, Clara found herself able to smile again. She refused to let Rob ruin her day.

They grinned at each other a few long moments—and then they both spoke at once. 'I can't believe …'

They laughed.

'You go first,' Gregg said.

'I was just going to say I can't believe it's really you. When I saw the name Gregg Callen I remembered you but I thought it was probably someone else anyway.'

'I know. You could have knocked me over with a feather when you popped up on the site. I was actually about to delete my account.'

'Really?'

'Yep.' He grimaced. 'I wasn't having much luck. But then I saw your name and, although your surname was different, Clara isn't a very common name and you looked almost exactly the same as when we were seventeen. I was too terrified to ask you out back then so I knew I'd regret it forever if I didn't at least make contact now.'

'You wanted to ask me out in high school?'

He blushed a little and Clara's heart leapt a little in delight. 'Yeah. But I was such a nerd and ...'

The rest of his explanation fell on deaf ears—she was distracted thinking about how different her life might have been if he had.

'Anyway.' He cleared his throat. 'I did not mean to make that confession within moments of meeting you again. I hope I haven't embarrassed you. Or scared you off.'

She shook her head. *Flattered* would be the more accurate word. 'No, and if that little scene you turned up to didn't scare *you* off then perhaps we should get going.'

'What scene?'

'Thank you,' she whispered with a smile.

He offered her his arm. 'Shall we?'

'Yes, let's.' She hitched her handbag onto her shoulder and slipped her arm into his elbow. Thanks to Rob, the self-locking door was already shut and she just hoped she'd remembered to put her house keys in the bag. But, if not, that would be a problem for Future Her. No way she was going to throw another drama into their first 'date'.

'I thought we could go to the café at Centennial Park,' Gregg said as they walked towards his car, 'but if you'd prefer to go somewhere else ...'

'No. I love Centennial Park. That sounds wonderful.'

He held the passenger door open for her as she climbed into his car. Clara couldn't remember the last time Rob had done any such thing but chastised herself the moment she thought it. If she wanted to have a good time with Gregg, she needed to banish her ex-husband from her mind.

The nerves that had been replaced with anger and shock at Rob's arrival returned as Gregg got into the driver's seat. She racked her mind for something to say. 'I really want to do better than talk about the weather but it's an amazing day for July.'

He chuckled and hit her with another one of his lovely, warm smiles. 'It was bloody freezing when I took Shadow out for his walk this morning.'

Shadow, Clara knew from their many email conversations, was Gregg's dog.

'How old is Shadow?'

'Let's see.' Gregg took a moment, caressing the steering wheel as he reversed out the driveway. 'I got him just after Karan left me, and he was only a pup then, so he must be about five years old now.'

'My sister has a golden retriever about the same age. He must be good company. I sometimes wonder if I should get a pet, but then I'm not sure what I'm going to do with my life or where I'm going to live after selling my house so it seems a little irresponsible to buy one right now.'

'Well, you can borrow Shadow whenever you want.'

Clara smiled. 'Thank you. I might just take you up on that offer.'

'What do you plan to do when your house sells?' he asked as they drove up Oxford Street in the direction of the park.

She relaxed back into her seat. 'That is the million-dollar question. I think maybe I want to take some time off work and travel.'

'Where would you go?'

She thought a moment. 'Well, when I was young, before I met my husband, I was saving to go work overseas—maybe in London—but now, I think I'd like to go somewhere that would take me out of my comfort zone a little more. Somewhere like Africa or South America, where the culture is really different to ours.'

'A girl after my own heart. There's some fascinating historic sites in both those places. South America is on my bucket list too—I'm planning on visiting some of the Pre-Columbian temples and colonial Baroque churches during my long-service leave next year.'

Talking about possible destinations carried them through finding a parking spot and their stroll towards the Homestead, where they both chose fancy cakes to go with their coffees. A sweet tooth was yet another thing they discovered in common.

Gregg patted his stomach. 'Hence why having a dog is a good idea; Shadow makes me get out and exercise.'

From where Clara was standing there wasn't much to pat. For a fifty-three-year-old man, he was in very good shape and she felt her cheeks warm a little at this thought.

When the cakes came, it seemed the most natural thing in the world to dig her fork into his lemon meringue pie and for him to do the same with her chocolate mud-cake. As they ate, the conversation moved from travel to careers to people they'd once both known and finally to sharing horror stories from the hospitals and schools they'd worked in.

'Have you met many of the other women you've interacted with online?'

'Before you I'd met a grand total of two and I'd be hard pushed to say which one was more terrifying. That's why I was considering deleting my profile.'

Clara couldn't help feeling a little buzz that the women who had gone before her hadn't won him over. 'What was wrong with them?'

'This is going to sound terrible, but one had the worst body odour ever. She smelt like a stinky teenage boy and trust me, I've experienced my fair share of them in my career.' He visibly shuddered. 'She might have been a really nice person but ...'

Clara cringed.

'The second woman was a total health nut. We met at a café not unlike this one and she spent the whole time telling me how the food I was eating was not only poisoning my body but also my soul. She said I had a very negative aura.'

'Oh dear. Looks like I got lucky the first time,' she said with a laugh, and then blushed. She didn't want to appear too intense.

But Gregg smiled, reached his hand across the table and then placed it on top of hers. As their skin met something she couldn't quite pinpoint swept over her. Was it ... attraction?

'Look,' he began seriously, 'there's something I need to get off my chest.'

'Oh?' Her heart hitched a beat. What was it? Was he really a woman? No, surely she'd have known *that* in high school. Did he have a criminal past? Did he have some horrific disease, which meant he only had days left to live? That would be just her luck.

'Maybe you should consider getting a restraining order.'

It took her a few seconds to catch on and then she blinked. 'On Rob?'

Gregg nodded solemnly. 'His behaviour looked quite threatening and I don't like to think what might have happened if I hadn't showed up when I did.'

'I can look after myself,' Clara said, feeling a little affronted. Lord knew she'd been doing so for many, many years.

'I'm sorry. I don't mean to overstep. But Rob seemed quite unstable. I hate to think of him hurting you.'

She sighed deeply and conceded, 'He is unstable. But he'd never physically hurt me, not intentionally. It's just ...' The reasons why Rob was the way he was weren't something she wanted to discuss with Gregg right now. In her emails she'd told him she didn't have children but she hadn't elaborated and that wasn't a first date kind of conversation. 'Look, do you mind if we don't talk about this?'

'Of course. I'm so sorry. I shouldn't have said anything.' He glanced at his watch. 'Can I buy you lunch to make up for my blunder or have I stuffed everything up and you'd rather I take you home?'

Clara considered her options. Home to her TV and empty house or spending more time with Gregg? He smiled tentatively at her, making her cheeks heat and insides tingle. If a simple look could make her feel like this, what might a whole afternoon do?

And if she let this one thing ruin their day then once again Rob would have come between her and happiness.

She smiled reassuringly at Gregg. 'Lunch sounds like a lovely idea.'

'Excellent,' he said as the tension in his face fell away to be replaced by another one of his bone-melting smiles.

Lunch, which consisted of lamb salad for Clara and a chicken pie for Gregg, was a success on all levels. There was not another mention of Rob, the food made her mouth water and the wine was delicious, but it was the company that made Clara want to break out in song. She kept forgetting this was a first date because being with Gregg was so easy and enjoyable that it didn't feel new. Or maybe it *did*. That was why it felt so magical.

She tried to put her finger on exactly what it was and then suddenly realised it was the two-way nature of their conversation. For as long as she could remember a conversation with Rob had mostly revolved around him and how he felt about any given situation. Being with Gregg was almost the opposite—he wanted to know everything about her from her family and her work to the mundane things like her favourite foods and television shows.

Dining with Gregg gave her insight into what it might be like to be with a man who didn't have addiction dragging him down. How being with such a man might make her feel more like a woman than she had in years. It was a heady thought and made her glad she'd gone to all the extra effort with her appearance. Gregg made her laugh like no one—man or woman—had for a very long time.

'For a history teacher, you're a pretty funny guy,' she commented, leaning back in her seat and taking another sip of her wine.

'When your wife leaves you for another woman you've got to have a good sense of humour or you'll fall apart. But, I confess I do have secret ambitions about becoming a stand-up comedian.'

'Seriously?'

'Yes. I'd probably be terrible at it but I sometimes scribble down a few ideas in my spare time.'

'I'd love to hear them.'

'Not here. Not when I've only had one beer, but maybe another time.'

'Does that mean we're going to have a second date?' she asked, aware she was blushing like a tomato and sounded like a schoolgirl but thanks to the wine, she didn't care.

Their eyes met and the intensity of his silver-grey gaze had her toes curling in her new boots. 'I certainly hope so.'

A waitress appeared at their table breaking the moment. 'Can I get you another one of those?' she asked, gesturing to Clara's now-empty glass.

Although she wasn't ready for their 'date' to end, it felt wrong sitting here guzzling alcohol while Gregg behaved. 'No thanks. We should probably make a move.'

'Yes, can we get the bill?'

As promised, Gregg paid for everything, even though she protested that she'd drunk more than he had. As they strolled towards the car, he slipped his hand inside hers, which made her instantly warm despite the fact the temperature outside had dropped dramatically.

When they arrived at his car and he let her go to open the door, she almost whimpered at the loss of his touch and the drive back to her place went far too quickly. Gregg walked her to the front door. She dug her keys out of her handbag and then turned to look at him. Standing here with him now felt a lifetime away from that morning when they'd both been here with Rob and she wasn't ready to lose his enchanting company.

*Should I ask him in for coffee? Will he get the wrong idea?*

As these questions whirred round her head, Gregg cleared his throat and spoke first. 'Thank you for a lovely day. I hope we can do it again sometime.'

*Is tomorrow too soon?* In the name of keeping cool, she managed not to blurt this question. 'I'd like that.'

'Excellent.' He smiled, and then, 'Would it be awfully presumptuous of me to kiss you goodbye?'

Simply the way he said the word 'kiss' had her insides liquefying.

# August

## Rebecca

'Are you sure you don't want me to come in with you?' Paige asked as she pulled her car up outside the hospital entrance. 'I was planning on going to the studio and working on some concepts for another book, but there's no rush for that if you need more support.'

'No!' Rebecca hadn't meant to sound so adamant, but she'd been coming here three times a week for almost two months and was well and truly an old hand. More than that, after a whole morning of driving around Sydney with her daughter trying to find a wedding dress, she was actually relieved to be heading into the dialysis unit for a little R&R. 'You go work on your pictures, my illness has already taken you enough away from your work.'

'Alright then,' Paige said as Rebecca climbed out of the car. 'But I'll be back well before you're done, I'll meet you in the waiting room at four o'clock. Have—I'll see you later.'

*Fun?* Rebecca thought as she shut the door and started inside. Lucky Paige had caught herself before finishing that sentence because the mood she was in right now she might have actually snapped.

This morning had been supposed to be fun, but at one stage during the trek from one bridal boutique to the next, she'd had to stop herself grabbing hold of Paige and trying to shake some sense into her. It was all very well wanting to find the perfect gown, but it was almost as if Paige didn't want to find one.

For someone who generally didn't pay much attention to fashion and whose idea of dressing up was wearing knee-high boots with her skinny jeans instead of her usual sneakers, she was being ridiculous!

Today wasn't their first dress-hunting excursion and what Rebecca had been looking forward to had become a kind of torture. Paige must have tried on every gown in the city over the past week or so and none of them had come close to satisfying her. She'd looked like a princess in almost all of them but, according to Paige, they were all either too flamboyant or too revealing, too traditional or not traditional enough. At this rate she'd be getting married in her regular uniform of jeans, a paint-smeared t-shirt and a pair of Converse.

As she approached the entrance of the dialysis unit, she resolved to talk some sense into Paige that very afternoon.

'Hello, Rebecca,' smiled the young woman behind the registration desk as she checked in for her session. 'How are you feeling today?'

'Fine thanks,' she said, deciding not to bore this poor woman with the morning's frustrations. And physically—aside from the tiredness, which could be down to her marathon dress hunt—she was feeling better than she had a couple of months ago. As inconvenient as it had been to reshuffle her lessons and other commitments for her thrice-weekly sessions, dialysis was making things easier that she hadn't even really realised had become hard.

'Excellent. Well, you know the drill. Take a seat and your nurse will be here to collect you soon.'

Less than ten minutes later, Rebecca was settled into position, attached to the machine, blood pumping in and out of her body.

She'd had so many blood tests to monitor her levels of protein, glucose and other things she couldn't keep in her head that these days she barely even noticed the needle go in, and the dialysis unit was beginning to feel like a home away from home.

The first time she'd arrived for treatment, she'd felt like a nervous little girl on her first day at school. She'd been surprised by how many people were actually on the life-saving treatment; people who if she'd walked past in the street she'd never have suspected of being sick at all. People who over the course of a few weeks she'd developed a bond with.

Unlike her family, these people understood how it felt to have to live your life around dialysis appointments and were happy to fill her in on how things worked and share their experiences.

The first person who'd spoken to her had been a man who, with tattoos covering his arms and a long, thick ginger beard, looked like he'd be more at home sitting on a Harley Davidson than a dialysis chair. 'This your first time, love?'

She'd nodded and he'd shot her an understanding smile. At least that's what she'd thought it was but it was hard to tell through his facial jungle. 'Don't worry, love, the first year is the hardest.'

First *year*? She certainly hoped she wasn't here that long, but, unless she agreed to Solomon's generous offer, she quite possibly could be. Her stomach twisted at the thought—she still wasn't comfortable with the idea of Solomon being her donor, but then again, would she be comfortable with the idea of anyone she knew making such a sacrifice for her? It was awful to feel so dependent on someone.

'He's right,' had said an elderly woman whom Rebecca quickly nicknamed Pollyanna. 'We're lucky to live in a country where dialysis is easily accessible or many of us wouldn't be here anymore.'

These two had seemed unlikely friends but, like the other folk that Rebecca soon became familiar with, they'd connected over their shared kidney problems and all seemed to take their situation in their stride. She, Pollyanna, Old Biker Dude and a few others had regular matching appointments and as the machines whirred alongside them, they spoke about their everyday lives.

She'd learnt that Old Biker Dude was actually a retired priest and had never ridden a motorcycle in his life and that Pollyanna wasn't just knitting aimlessly each session, but making something called twiddlemuffs for dementia patients. Her husband of sixty-three years had recently been put in a care facility because he had Alzheimer's and she could no longer look after him properly. Yet still, she was never without a smile upon her face.

Then there was a retired footballer, a librarian about the same age as Rebecca and a young man who was studying film and television at university and had already had one kidney transplant in his teens. It was amazing how much you could learn about a person in the course of a few short hours, and, when those hours repeated themselves two or three times a week, these people came to feel like old friends.

Occasionally, they even talked about their kidney predicaments.

At eighty-four Pollyanna's body was too old to handle a transplant operation but she didn't seem at all daunted by the prospect of spending the rest of her life on dialysis. The librarian was almost two years into her stint on the deceased donor waiting list, which Old Biker Dude was also on. Both of them had mentioned how wrong it felt to be hoping someone would die so they could live free of dialysis. The young student's boyfriend was going to be his donor, but he had another couple of months before his body would be stable enough for the operation. Now the footballer was an interesting case—not able to find a familial match and too impatient to wait for a deceased donor, he'd recently put an advert online and apparently had been inundated with responses.

'Most of them are bullshit,' he told everyone now, 'but I'm going to meet up with this woman next week who seems genuine.'

Rebecca wasn't sure what to think about this possibility—the idea of asking a loved one to donate was hard enough for her to come to terms with, but a stranger?

Why would someone do that for someone they'd never even met?

She was the only one contemplating the Paired Kidney Exchange Program and when she'd told her fellow patients about Solomon's offer, they'd all gushed about what a great guy her daughter must be marrying. Pollyanna understood Rebecca's reticence but the others all thought she was crazy not to jump at her future son-in-law's proposition.

'He wouldn't offer if he didn't want to do it,' had been Old Biker Dude's analysis of the situation.

Each session, once they'd exchanged greetings and caught up with the happenings in each other's lives, there were quiet times where everyone got busy with their own stuff. While Pollyanna knitted, some patients did puzzle books, others read. The footballer played video games on his phone and Old Biker Dude often laughed out loud at whatever he was watching on his. The librarian was using the time to write a novel—apparently she'd spent her whole life dreaming about being a *New York Times* bestseller but had never actually got past the first chapter.

'I guess I was always too scared of failure,' she'd confessed to Rebecca the first time she'd admitted what she was doing. 'But when I got my diagnosis, I suddenly knew that it would be much worse if I died without ever giving it my best shot.'

Sometimes she let Rebecca read snippets of her work-in-progress and it was very good. Rebecca had faith that this time the librarian would finish her book and this made her think about her own dreams.

What would she regret not achieving if she died tomorrow?

The answer was simple. Once upon a time she'd dreamed of being a professional singer or pianist, but not achieving either of those things wasn't something she'd lament over on her deathbed. Careers, material possessions, none of that really mattered in the end. No, she would lie there before taking her final breath, wishing she hadn't given in to her parents' insistence that she give up her baby. A rock formed in her stomach now at the thought. She couldn't change the past, but she could change the future and she'd spent the last two months deliberating on this terrifying fact.

Should she or should she not send off a request for information about her son? Could she live with the ramifications if she did?

Perhaps the more important question was, could she live with herself if she did not?

As Old Biker Dude chuckled beside her and the librarian tapped away on her laptop like her life depended on it, Rebecca took a deep breath and retrieved her phone from her handbag. The online address for the Department for Child Protection Western Australia was imprinted in her head. She typed it in and it only took a few short seconds for the form to appear on her screen.

Not allowing herself any further deliberation, Rebecca started to fill it in.

*Josie*

*Thank God it's Friday.* Josie sank into a bath full of bubbles, relaxed into the warm water and took a sip of her drink. A glass of wine would be the perfect accompaniment right now to her scented candles and the eighties music that blared from the dock next to the sink, but summoning all the willpower she had, she'd poured herself a glass of Diet Coke instead. It hadn't been a bad week but she was exhausted from after-school rehearsals for the upcoming school play and had a mountain of essays she had to get through this weekend.

*No!* She shook her head, refusing to even think about work. Nik would be home soon and they were going out for dinner and then to a movie. It was some action flick she wasn't particularly keen on seeing, but then how many eighties movies had Nik sat through for her when they'd first got together?

Josie smiled at the memory. The day after their eyes had met while she'd been singing in the pub, her car had broken down when she was on the way to the cinema. She couldn't believe it when a car pulled over and out came the man who'd almost caused her to forget the words she'd known off by heart for years.

'Do you need some help?' he'd asked as he sauntered towards her. She saw the moment recognition dawned on his face. 'Hey, you're the girl from last night?'

'Actually, my name's Josie. Nice to meet you.'

'Nik,' he'd said, offering his hand.

It was as firm and warm and lovely as she'd imagined.

He nodded towards her car with its bonnet open skyward. 'So, what seems to be the problem?'

'Do I look like a mechanic?' She didn't say it in a sarcastic tone and when he grinned back, she admitted she had no idea. 'Are *you* a mechanic?'

'I'm an aircraft engineer but I'm not too bad with cars. Want me to take a look?'

'That would be awesome. My dad's not answering his phone and I've got somewhere to be soon.'

'Hot date?' he'd asked as he pushed up his sleeves and leaned in to look at the car. She swallowed at the sight of his tanned, muscly arms.

'Who needs a date when I have Fantales, popcorn and Andrew McCarthy?'

'Andrew McWho?'

'You don't know who Andrew McCarthy is? Actually you kinda look like him, only your hair's darker. He's an actor—he was big in the eighties but he works more behind the scenes now.'

'So you're going to watch a movie?'

'That's right. The local cinema is having a special screening of *Pretty In Pink*.'

'Is that a new release?'

'You haven't heard of *Pretty In Pink*?' She shook her head in disgust. 'You better be able to fix my car or we can't be friends.'

He'd smiled deliciously then. 'I'm pretty certain I can fix this.' He fiddled with something beneath the bonnet. 'Your battery connection just worked itself a little loose. Go turn the ignition, see if it starts now?'

Josie climbed back into the driver's seat and did as she was told. When the engine roared to life, she was kinda disappointed that it probably meant the end of her interlude with Hot Stuff.

'Thanks,' she said, leaning out the open window as he closed the bonnet.

'No worries.' He wandered round to stand by her door and shoved his hands in his pockets. 'Glad to be of service. So, are you meeting friends there?'

'Meeting friends where?' For a moment she was bamboozled by his intense gaze.

His lips curved upwards. 'At the movies.'

'Nope.'

'You're going to the movies *alone*?'

She nodded. 'I read in a magazine once that everyone should go to the cinema on their own at least once before they turn thirty— I did and discovered I liked it. But if you'd like to come with me ...'

Her cheeks burned as she propositioned him. There'd been a couple of brief liaisons with guys since she'd moved from London back to Perth, but mostly she'd been concentrating on her studies, mourning her mother and trying to ignore her broken heart.

'Um ...'

At his hesitation, mortification washed over her. He'd probably just been trying to be nice. 'Guess eighties movies aren't your thing?' she tried to make a joke.

'It's not that.' He shook his head and glanced around as if he was on the run from the law. 'What the hell? I'd love to come with you.'

They'd talked through most of the movie and been rewarded with angry words from other cinema goers and popcorn thrown at their heads, but she'd wanted to know everything about him. He was smart and funny and good-looking and ... *engaged*.

Josie had almost punched him when he'd told her this fact at the end. But at least the kissing and other stuff had only been in her head by then. She'd only known him a few hours but the connection she felt with Nik, she'd never felt before, and she'd been devastated.

A week later, she saw him sitting in the audience again when she was singing. He sought her out on her break and told her he'd broken up with his fiancée because he couldn't get her out of his head. Despite all the voices in her head telling her it was a bad idea, she'd slept with him that night and nothing had ever felt so right.

Things were still not perfect between her and Nik—he was watching her like a hawk and she wasn't sure how long it would take to earn back his complete trust—but they'd been getting better, closer to normal, since she'd started seeing Clara. The bath and candles were part of the self-care Clara had suggested and the 'date nights' were also her idea. Josie had rolled her eyes when she'd raised these suggestions at her second visit.

But Clara was definitely helping. It was such a bizarre thing because all they did was talk—actually Josie did most of the talking and Clara simply listened. She had no miraculous powers that would make Josie able to carry a baby to term, but she'd done more for her than any doctor ever could. They'd seen each other four times now and each time she'd left feeling physically lighter and more able to face the day than when she'd arrived. Each day she felt herself getting a little better. She'd been less snappy with the kids at school. The urges to smoke and drink had been fewer and farther between.

She didn't want to sleep all the damn time. And best of all, she no longer flinched when Nik touched her.

Due to the music, she didn't hear the front door open and almost drowned herself when a shadow appeared behind her in the doorway.

'Holy hell,' she said, placing her hand against her racing heart as she turned her head to take in the sight of her husband, looking movie-star sexy in his uniform, his sleeves pushed up to his elbows revealing his all-year-round tanned skin.

'Sorry, sweet stuff. Didn't mean to scare you.' He eyed the glass in her hand. Did he think there was vodka in there or something?

'It's just Diet Coke,' she said defensively.

'What? *Oh.* Of course it is. No. It honestly didn't cross my mind it would be anything else. I wasn't looking at the glass but rather the naked body holding it.'

Josie wasn't sure whether to believe him or not, but decided to give him the benefit of the doubt. 'How was your day?'

'We had a bit of a problem with one of the planes, but nothing I couldn't fix.' He kicked off his shoes, then crossed to the bathtub and stooped to kiss her on the head. 'What about you? Did you have rehearsals this afternoon?'

'No. Only Tuesdays and Thursdays, thank God.'

Nik slid down the wall and sat beside her, leaning against it. 'I can't wait to see the result,' he said and she smiled because no matter musical theatre wasn't his favourite thing, he hadn't missed one of the school productions she'd been involved in since they met.

'Thanks. By the way, I talked to my dad today.'

'Oh yeah, how is he? Planning another big trip?'

She laughed. 'Actually, he wanted to know what we're doing for Christmas, whether we're heading to Perth or whether he could come here.'

'And ... what did you tell him?'

'I said we thought we'd head home.'

Nik's eyes lit up. 'Seriously?'

She nodded. Being around his sisters and their babies and toddlers wouldn't be easy, but she knew how much being with his family for Christmas meant to Nik and she really was trying to make an effort. 'Maybe Dad could come to your parents' place for lunch with us?'

'Of course he can. You know Mum. The more the merrier.' Then he leaned over the bathtub and kissed her good and proper on the lips. 'You're amazing, Josephine Mitreski. And I love you too.'

She rolled her eyes but glowed inside. 'Feeling's mutual.'

Still grinning, Nik dug his phone out of his pocket. 'By the way, I've got something to show you.' He tapped the screen and turned it towards her. 'That's your wedding dress, isn't it?'

Josie sat up and the water splashed over the edge of the tub as she leaned in to scrutinise the image. It certainly looked like her dress on a pretty, dark-haired woman who appeared to be much younger than she was when she and Nik tied the knot. 'Where'd you get that photo? Who is that?'

'This is the woman who originally wore your dress. She got married in 1988.'

Josie's mind boggled. 'I still don't understand. How'd you get it?'

He tapped the screen again and the photo shrunk, revealing it to be part of a Facebook post. 'A mate from work shared it. This woman's daughter is looking for the dress because she's getting married soon and wants to wear it herself. Her mother is sick and she wants to do something special, something nice for her.'

The post had been shared over one thousand times. If Josie hadn't exiled herself from the online world, she'd probably have seen it herself. She skim-read the details. For someone whose mother was so ill, this Paige seemed very chirpy. She sounded like the kind of person who would put #blessed on the end of every social media post—just the kind of person that made Josie cranky. Especially lately.

'It might not be mine,' she said, flopping back into the bath. 'There were probably hundreds of dresses like that in the eighties.'

Nik shook his head. 'It says this dress was a one-off. It was made by an up-and-coming designer and Paige's mum won it at a bridal expo thing, but then she gave it away to a charity auction. I wonder if anyone else wore it in between then and me finding it for you? It's cool knowing the history of it, don't you think?'

'Hmm …' Josie wasn't sure if 'cool' was the word she'd use. Although her dress was second-hand, or pre-loved as some people would say, she'd never thought much about the person or people who might have worn it before her. It was *her* dress. The dress Nik had chosen for *her*.

'So, shall we message this Paige person?'

Josie frowned. 'Why?'

He shook his head slowly, smiling as if he found her question cute. 'To tell her we have the dress, of course.'

'But it's *my* dress. And it's not for sale.' She wasn't sentimental about a lot of things, but this was different. The day he'd given her the dress was the last time she was truly happy—even though she'd discovered she was pregnant twice again after that, she'd never been able to relax. She wanted to hold onto that little bit of happiness forever.

'You don't have to give it to her. Maybe it can be her something borrowed?'

'But … what if she ruins it? What if we're a different size and she needs it taken in or expanded? What if—?'

'You're not planning on needing it again, are you?' He sounded bemused.

'No. Of course not. But …'

'Look, Jose.' Nik dipped his free hand into the water, taking her wet one in his. 'This woman's mum is sick and she wants to do something special, something nice for her. If we can help, don't you think we should?'

And that's what won Josie over to the idea. She missed her mum so much that she understood the anguish this stranger must feel at her mother's life being in jeopardy. At the same time she couldn't help feeling slightly jealous that this Paige-woman still had a mum to do something special for.

But that was a bitter thought.

An *old*-Josie thought. And she'd promised Clara and Nik that she'd make a concerted effort to curb such negative thoughts. Clara was encouraging her to get outside of her grief, to do things that made her feel good about herself. Things like helping other people. Not that she believed in karma—not really—but maybe doing this good deed would in turn bring something good her way.

She took a deep breath, squeezed Nik's hand and said, 'Okay. She can have it. But only on loan.'

Nik's lips broke into a grin. He lifted his wet hand to her head and drew her lips to his. 'It's the right thing to do,' he said when he finally broke their kiss.

*Paige*

Paige couldn't contain her excitement as she and Solomon drove towards what was hopefully her wedding dress.

In the few weeks since she'd posted the search for her mother's dress she'd had numerous messages from strangers. Each time her heart had leapt in anticipation and then come crashing down a few moments later. She'd had messages from trolls telling her she was un-feminist getting married in this day and age. Lewd messages from men who couldn't offer her a dress but would be happy to offer her something else. A couple of horrible messages saying they hoped her mum died before she found the dress—she couldn't believe people could be so cruel. Messages from dressmakers telling her they could replicate the dress perfectly—for a hefty price. And messages from women who had wedding dresses for sale, never mind that they didn't even bear the slightest resemblance to her mother's.

Until last night, she'd been all but ready to admit defeat and usually docile Solomon had been ready to hunt down some of the senders and slit their throats.

'Relax. We're almost there.' Sol's voice and his hand on her knee interrupted Paige's thoughts. 'But you jumping around in your seat isn't going to get us there any faster and you're distracting my driving.'

'Sorry.' Her heart thumping, she clutched her handbag to her chest and resisted the urge to dig out her phone and read Nik Mitreski's message again. His wife wasn't on Facebook but he'd seen the dress, shown it to her and said it was definitely the one she'd got married in two years ago. Nik sounded like a great guy and the message seemed one hundred per cent kosher but Sol had refused to let her go to the Mistreskis' place on her own. And she was glad of his company.

He removed his hand to switch on the radio and as the latest hit by Ed Sheeran filled the car, Paige tried to focus on it to calm her nerves. What if this was some sick joke? Or what if the dress was similar but not the one she was looking for?

*What if* questions swirled around her head and she felt the beginnings of a headache coming on when Sol finally slowed the car.

'I think this is it,' he said as he parked on the verge out the front of an exposed-brick, art deco apartment building.

Nik and Josie's place was on the ground floor and she could hear music coming from inside one of the lower-level apartments.

'I feel sick,' Paige whispered as they approached the entrance.

Sol squeezed her hand. 'I have a good feeling about this.'

Her stomach flipped and she wasn't sure what kind of feeling she had. She took a deep breath and then pressed the button on the intercom for flat one of six.

The music died within seconds and moments later a deep male voice came through the wall. 'Hello?'

Paige couldn't speak so Sol leaned towards the intercom and announced themselves. 'It's Solomon and Paige, come about the dress.'

'Cool. I'll buzz you in.'

The front door clicked and, as Paige and Sol stepped into the entrance hallway, a door off to the right peeled back to reveal a good-looking couple in their mid-thirties. He wore faded jeans and a long-sleeved Hurley tee and she had on a neon-pink oversized jumper that looked like a remnant from the eighties. Like Karis, this woman looked good in fashion left over from another era.

'Hi,' they said in unison.

'Hi,' Paige managed.

The man, who had to be Nik, offered his hand. 'Nice to meet you both.'

She and Sol shook Nik's hand respectively and then did the same with Josie's.

'Thank you so much for doing this,' Paige said.

'No worries,' Josie said. 'Lucky we don't still live in Perth or it mightn't have been so easy.'

'What?' Paige's heart squeezed. 'Is that where you got the dress?' What if Josie's dress just *looked* similar to her mother's?

Nik took the question. 'No, I was in Sydney for work and saw it in an op shop window. I kinda bought it as a joke and used it to propose but ...'

Paige's heart relaxed again.

'It was love at first sight for me and that dress so although that's not what Nik intended, I wore it for our actual wedding,' Josie finished. 'I have a bit of a thing for the eighties.'

'A *bit* of a thing?' Nik laughed and glanced down at his wife's attire. In addition to the baggy jumper, she wore leopard-print leggings and her dark-chocolate hair was crimped and captured in a high side-ponytail with a bulky purple *scrunchie*. Paige vaguely remembered them from her own childhood. 'That's putting it mildly. I met Jose when she was singing in an eighties bar and I thought she was in costume until we started dating and—'

'*Anyway*,' Josie interrupted, 'Paige and Solomon are here to see the dress.' She stepped back and gestured inside.

They walked straight into a living room that made Paige feel as if they'd stepped back in time. The décor reminded her of her grandparents' place, which her mum often said was in desperate need of a modern makeover.

'Wow, this is ... cool.' Sol glanced around at the framed posters of old singers and movie posters that lined the pink pastel walls. While Paige quite liked the posters, she wasn't such a fan of the orange macramé owl hanging above the TV. The mantel along the top of an open fireplace held a number of framed photographs, but it was the poster of *Top Gun* and another of *Airplane* that impressed Sol. 'I love those movies,' he said.

Nik grinned. 'Me too. Jose and I are both movie buffs. Now can I get you guys a drink?'

'Thanks, that'd be great,' Sol said, but Paige didn't want to waste time making small talk over cups of coffee.

As if a mind reader, Josie said, 'Paige is probably more interested in seeing the dress.'

She nodded. 'Yes, please.'

Nik looked to Solomon. 'Are you going to check out the dress too?'

He shook his head. 'I just came for ...'

'He came to make sure you guys weren't serial killers,' Paige said, filling in the blanks.

They all laughed.

'In that case.' Nik clapped Sol on the shoulder. 'Come this way and we'll leave the women to do their thing.'

While Nik led Sol into the small kitchen off the living room, Josie indicated for Paige to follow her down the short corridor. 'The dress is in our bedroom.'

'Thanks so much for agreeing to let me come see it,' Paige said, feeling nervous and anxious.

'It's fine. I lost my mum a few years ago. She wasn't there on my wedding day, so I understand your desire to do something special for yours.'

Before Paige could offer sympathy about her mother, Josie pushed open the bedroom door and Paige's gaze snapped to the bed where a beautiful white gown lay across the purple bedspread. Tears sprung to her eyes. It was even more beautiful in the flesh than in her mother's photographs. She couldn't believe she'd finally found it.

'Is that it?' Josie asked as the two of them stepped up close.

'Yes,' Paige whispered, reaching out to run her finger over the silk and lace to check it was actually real. Not only did it appear to be, but the silk was still luminous white and not one pearl bead was missing. It had obviously been cared for by its previous owners. 'I've been looking for this dress for ages and ... I can't believe you got married in Perth and yet, it's back here, in Sydney. And we don't even live that far away.'

Josie chuckled. 'I think that's called serendipity. Do you want to try it on?'

'Hell yes.'

Paige let her handbag fall to the floor and was already reaching down to remove her jumper when Josie said, 'I'll give you some privacy but call if you need help with the buttons.'

'Thanks.'

The moment the door shut behind the dress's latest owner, Paige stripped right down to her knickers and bra. Then, she gently picked up the dress—it was heavier than it looked—and turned it over to reveal the gigantic bow at the back. With the greatest care, she undid what felt like hundreds of buttons above it and then held her breath as she lifted the dress, stepped into it and thread her arms through the short, puffy sleeves.

*This was the gown Mum wore to marry Dad.*

She smiled at the thought, but there was no way she could wrangle the tiny buttons on her own, so picking up the skirt to stop herself tripping over it, she crossed to the door and pulled it back a fraction.

'Help required,' she whispered to Josie who was standing there looking at something on her phone.

She looked up and a smile broke on her face. 'Wow. Look at you.'

'I love it,' Paige said, running her hands down the sides, relishing the sensation of lace and silk against her skin. 'It's not even on properly and I love it.'

'It has that kind of effect.' Josie grinned and then made shooing motions with her hands as she ushered Paige back into the bedroom. 'Let's do you up then.'

Paige held still as Josie caged her into the dress, button by tiny button.

'There. Done.' Josie slowly turned her around so she was facing a full-length mirror in the corner.

*Wow.* Her breath caught in her throat. She didn't usually get worked up over clothes but this dress was beautiful *and* it meant something. She'd tried on what felt like hundreds of dresses in the past few weeks and none had come close to giving her the feeling of rightness that washed over her now.

'You look beautiful,' Josie said from behind. 'Is your mother the emotional type? Because if so, I reckon you better have tissues on hand when you show her.'

Paige let out a half laugh, still awed. 'I would have said no, but since she got sick, she's been crying at the drop of a hat.'

Josie smiled sympathetically.

'How much do you want for it?' Paige was willing to pay pretty much any price after the lengths she'd gone to find the dress.

'Oh, it's not for sale. You can borrow it, but I want it back. That's the deal.'

The two women stood there for a moment like two soldiers preparing to battle.

Paige already felt as if this dress belonged to her—it was *her* mother's after all. For a fleeting moment, she contemplated yanking up the train and making a run for it, calling to Sol as she ran through the house, telling him to ready the getaway vehicle. But then she imagined the headlines: *Artist Arrested For Stealing Wedding Dress*—and realised how crazy her thoughts were. Besides, she only needed the dress for one day and she didn't want to push her luck in case Josie refused to let her have it at all.

'Okay. I understand. Do you want a hire fee?'

'Of course not. I just want it back in the same condition it left in.'

'I promise I'll look after it as if it were my own.'

Josie laughed and the tension that had been fleetingly in the room vanished. Still, Paige couldn't quite bring herself to even think about taking the dress off just yet.

'Tell me about *your* wedding?' she said.

'Well, you might have noticed I love the eighties. And, as Nik said, we met while I was singing in an eighties cover band, so when he found this dress, it seemed fitting we continue the theme to every area.' A wistful smile came onto Josie's face as she leaned back against her dresser. 'We went the whole shebang—everything from the outfits to the food, the cars, the music and the table décor was eighties. My bridesmaids wore neon-pink off-the-shoulder gowns. We hired a local hall and decked it out in metallic balloons and neon-pink and orange streamers. At the tables, every guest got either a Rubik's Cube or one of those mini Etch A Sketches. They were so sought-after people were fighting over them and stealing each other's.'

Paige laughed. 'Why do you love the eighties so much? I mean ... if you don't mind me asking. It's just you would have been really young during the actual eighties.'

'No, not at all.' Josie gave a dismissive wave. 'It all started with a project in my first year of high school. For social studies, we had to do a presentation about a decade from the twentieth century and I got the eighties. As I loved drama, I decided to focus on the movies of the era. I watched all the Brat Pack films and fell in love with the music, the fashion, the hair. Everything was a statement piece in the eighties—the Sportsgirl t-shirts and bad hats of the nineties seemed so dull in comparison.'

Paige nodded. She had to concede Josie had a point.

'I think my mum was hoping my love of blue mascara, bright eyeshadow and neon nail polish would fade, but,' she flashed Paige her bright orange nails, 'it hasn't yet. Dressing up, going all out ... makes me feel good.'

'I think you look great,' Paige said, suddenly feeling like the paint-splattered jeans, oversized shirt, sneakers and sensible ponytail she always wore to keep her hair off her face were plain and boring. Her appearance had never been high on her list of priorities; she'd never seen her body as a canvas but preferred to create something *she* could look at. 'I guess you had eighties music at the wedding as well then?' she added.

'Yep.' Josie's eyes lit up again. 'We had an awesome DJ and we danced all night to The Go-Go's, Madonna, Duran Duran ... Oh, and did I mention the *Pretty In Pink*-themed cocktails. They were potent.'

'Do you have any photos?'

'Yes, our wedding album's in the living room. I can show you if you like.'

Paige nodded. 'Please.'

'Be right back.'

Josie left and Paige contemplated taking off the dress and getting back into her normal clothes, but then she remembered the buttons, so spent a few more moments admiring herself in the mirror.

'Here we are,' Josie said, when she returned clutching an album to her chest a few minutes later. 'Shall we sit?' She gestured to the bed and Paige tried to navigate herself and the puffy gown onto the mattress.

'Wait till you have to go to the toilet in it. I needed all three of my bridesmaids to help whenever I had to go to the loo.'

Josie opened the album and, as she flicked through the pages, Paige oohed and ahhed over the vintage orange plastic chairs, the white and chrome tables, the lolly bar with eighties-era sweets and the amazing black cake with pink and orange splashes of colour. Until she'd seen it, she'd thought an eighties wedding sounded a little loud and tacky, but these images looked like a Pinterest photo shoot and everyone looked to be having so much fun. She could almost hear the music blaring from the pages.

'Your wedding sounds so great, so memorable.'

Again, Josie smiled. 'It was. Best day of my life. What plans have you got for yours? Have you guys decided on a theme?'

'No.' Paige bit her lip, suddenly feeling a little overwhelmed. 'Until today I've been so focused on finding the gown that I've let all the other things we should be organising slide. I hadn't even thought about a theme. Do you think we need one?'

'You don't need one, but it makes your day personal and can also make decision-making easier. Do what we did and make it about your passions? What do you and Solomon love? What do you guys do?'

'Well …' Paige thought a moment. 'I'm an artist—I love drawing, painting and creating just about anything but what I love most is sharing art with others. I've recently had my first picture book published and I also run classes at The Art House.'

'Oh, is that that bright yellow place off Coogee Bay Road? I read an article in the local paper about how they offer free classes for homeless people and also children from refugee families.'

'That's the one.' Paige couldn't keep the pride out of her voice— the free classes had been her idea and she'd worked hard to get sponsorship from big companies so they could run them.

'So, tell me about Solomon? What makes him tick?'

'Well, like me, he's passionate about human rights, but he also loves classic cars, football, pretty much all food, and he's a fireman.'

Josie wolf-whistled. 'Fireman. That explains a lot. Those muscles.' She slapped her hand over her mouth. 'Sorry. Totally inappropriate to be thinking those thoughts about your husband-to-be and even more inappropriate to actually say them.'

She didn't actually sound sorry and Paige didn't actually care. She laughed—Sol did have very perve-worthy muscles and she liked people who didn't censor every damn thing they said. 'It's fine. Your hubby's not too harsh on the eye himself.'

'Thanks.' They shared a smile in mutual partner appreciation, then Josie said, 'Where's Solomon from? I mean, what's his nationality?'

'Both his parents are French actually. Their descendants were originally from Louisiana, but both families have been in France since the 1800s. His parents divorced but his mum remarried an American surgeon when he was in his teens and they emigrated to Australia for his stepdad's work.'

'Will you have any tributes to his culture at your wedding?'

Paige blinked. The thought hadn't even crossed her mind but maybe she should ask Lisette if she would like that. 'I'm not sure. Maybe. Oh God, there's so much to organise.'

Josie laughed. 'But it's all fun. Did you also say you write picture books?'

'Yes. And illustrate them. Well, actually I've only got one out so far but I'm working on another.'

'Have you ever spoken to kids about your work?'

'I've done a few story-time readings at local libraries.'

'That's cool, but I actually meant talking to students about the writing and illustrating process? I'm a teacher at Bronte High and my year nine English class are about to study picture books. It would be great if you could come in and they could hear from a real-life author.'

As if Paige could say no after Josie had been so nice about the dress, and why would she want to anyway? She loved talking about her art and the opportunity to inspire a class of teens was just too wonderful to pass up. 'I'd love that,' she said.

'Awesome.' Josie grinned. 'But now, back to the important stuff— your wedding.'

Paige was all ears as Josie spilled her ideas.

'You've got plenty to play with for a theme. You could put crayons and little sketchpads on the tables and ask all your guests to draw you a picture and then you could put them all together in a book. Adult colouring-in books might be a little yesterday but you could design your own colour-in invitation and send everyone a little packet of pencils along with it. Ooh, as a wedding cake, you could have a pile of books instead of your usual tiers. Also, old books bundled together look awesome as table decorations. Or you could have a red, white and black theme to tie in with Solomon's job. And what about arriving in a fire engine? That'd be fun, although if Solomon is

209

into classic cars, then you could work a theme around them instead. Sorry.' Josie paused for breath and gave Paige a sheepish look. 'I'm getting carried away, aren't I?'

'No. No, you're not. Can I hire you as my wedding planner?'

Josie laughed. But Paige was dead-serious—she wanted to put this woman in a box and take her home with her. In fact she was developing a serious girl crush.

'When are you getting married?'

'We've booked the celebrant for October the thirteenth.' There suddenly seemed a lot to organise in such a short time. Was she insane thinking they could do this? 'But that and finding this dress is all we've done so far,' she admitted self-conciously.

Josie snapped the album shut and smiled encouragingly at Paige. 'Don't worry, it'll all come together. Nik and I organised everything in a month. It's not that hard if you know what you want.' Josie glanced at her watch. 'The boys will probably be wondering what we're up to.'

'Yes.' Paige pushed herself up, which took more effort than usual thanks to the weight of the gown. 'Can you help me with these buttons?'

'Sure.' Josie put the album down on the bed and stood. As she began the unbuttoning, she raised the logistics. 'Do you want to take the dress today?'

Paige frowned, she hadn't thought any further than finding the dress. 'Um, well, I don't really want Solomon to see it so I can't take it home. I guess I could take it to Mum's, but I kind of imagined wearing it when I showed it to her.'

'Yes, that does sound more dramatic,' Josie agreed.

Paige turned slightly to look at the other woman. 'I know you're already doing me a huge favour but … would you mind if I brought Mum round here to show her?'

'That's a lovely idea,' Josie said. 'And I guess after that you can store it at her place until the wedding. When do you want to show her? I could do Friday arvo or next weekend?'

A week felt like an eternity away and then there was the issue of her mother's availability. 'Mum teaches piano all day Saturday and Friday afternoon too, I think. Could you do the evening?'

Josie grinned. 'Friday night works for me.'

'Okay, great.' Paige smiled her thanks and this time Josie stayed as she stripped out of the dress. It wasn't uncomfortable changing in front of a stranger—the shared dress had bonded them—and as Paige re-dressed in her jeans, top and jacket, Josie hung the gown back up in the closet and then they went to rescue the men from awkward small talk.

They followed the sound of laughter down the hallway to find the boys sitting side by side on the couch, drinks in hand, feet up on the coffee table as they watched the Dockers slogging it out against the Sydney Swans.

Sol looked up and grinned at Paige. 'Hey gorgeous. How's the dress?'

'Perfect. It's beautiful and fits like a glove.'

'Awesome.'

Someone kicked a goal on the TV and Nik leapt up and shrieked, 'We're making a comeback!'

'Damn.' Sol scowled at Nik but his tone was good-natured.

Josie caught Paige's eye. 'I don't think we were missed at all.'

'Doesn't look like it and I guess I'm driving home,' Paige replied, raising her eyebrows as she nodded towards the near-empty beer bottle in Sol's hand. There were another four bottles on the table making her realise just how long she and Josie had been chatting.

'You can't go yet,' Nik whined, not taking his eyes off the television. 'Solomon and I have a bet going on which team will slaughter the other one.'

211

Paige looked to the screen; the score on the bottom said it could go either way.

'You a football fan?' Josie asked.

''Fraid not. I'd rather give a cat a shampoo and blow-dry.'

Josie snorted. 'Me too.' And then she nodded towards the kitchen. 'Come on, I'll make you a cuppa.'

'That sounds like a very good idea.'

And, while their men bonded over football and beer and bantered playfully over the fluctuating scores, Josie and Paige also had a very pleasant afternoon.

*Clara*

Clara woke on Sunday morning to sun sneaking in through the gaps between the curtains and a man in her bed. A very sexy, naked gentleman who'd had her screaming his name more than once throughout the night. Okay, more than once during the many nights they'd spent together over the last couple of weeks. Gregg might dress like the middle-aged history teacher that he was, but she'd discovered that behind that façade was a funny, wild, sexual beast who had awakened something inside her as well.

She smiled at the thought as she turned her head on the pillow to look at ... What was he? Boyfriend seemed too young for two people in their early fifties. Partner had a long-term connotation and they'd barely clocked three weeks together yet. Lover sounded a little tawdry and although he most definitely filled those shoes, he'd become more to her than just a sex buddy.

As she admired his bare chest, only lightly dotted with still-dark hair, she recalled their first night together, which felt much longer ago than it actually was.

Barely before she'd said 'yes' to Gregg's request to kiss her, their lips had converged and fireworks exploded within her. She couldn't remember which one of them suggested it would be a good idea to move inside, but as the door shut behind them they were already ripping at each other's clothes. Even in her youth she'd never had a one-night stand or slept with someone on a first date; there'd been too much Catholic guilt and fear of getting pregnant instilled in her during her childhood that she'd always taken her time getting to know a guy first. But getting pregnant wasn't a concern these days and Gregg had made her feel so alive that she'd decided to throw caution to the wind.

And it had been worth the risk.

Getting naked with Gregg hadn't been even a fraction of the terrifying she'd imagined it might be when she'd been thinking about taking off her clothes for some faceless, nameless man. She hadn't worried about any of the things she'd thought she would— like her less-than-perfect thighs or whether she was too wild and woolly down *there*.

There'd been no room to think with all the passion and desire pumping through her body and rushing to her head.

*And wow.*

That first night they'd emerged from her bedroom only long enough to scavenge for food and replenish their energy levels so they could go at it again like a couple of teenaged rabbits. Who'd ever imagined sex could be better in your fifties than it was in your teens, twenties, thirties or forties! To think that only a couple of weeks ago, she'd thought she could easily go without for the rest of her life. That notion seemed preposterous now. Not simply because her body hadn't felt this good in years but because her mind and soul felt as if they had been given a new lease of life as well.

And, she enjoyed Gregg's company when he was fully clothed just as much as when he wasn't. Meeting him again after all these years was almost too perfect—*he* was almost too perfect to be true. Handsome, genuinely nice, funny *and* good in bed. More than once she'd pondered the thought that something had to be wrong with him but so far, aside from the fact he slept on his back and snored a little, nothing had surfaced. And so she resolved to stop overthinking things, to stop making mountains where there weren't even molehills and to simply enjoy their time together.

'Good morning.' Gregg looked up at her and she blushed a little at being caught in the act of staring.

'Hi,' she whispered.

'Hi yourself.' He reached out and pulled her into his arms. 'How long have you been awake?'

Clara snuggled into his warm, broad chest, thinking if she died right here right now, she'd die a happy woman. 'Not long.'

'You're not worried about lunch today, are you?'

She blinked, taking a second to realise what he was talking about. Today was the day she'd finally agreed to unleash her sisters onto him; they'd been pestering her for the last two weeks. It was the monthly Brennan get-together—to be held at Bridget's house because it also happened to coincide with a significant birthday for Ranaldo—and Gregg had jumped at the chance when she'd nervously asked him if he wanted to come and meet her family.

'If anyone should be worried, it's me,' he said with a chuckle. 'I might not pass the sister test.'

'You'll pass with flying colours.' Now that he'd reminded her of the occasion, if she was a little nervous it wasn't because she was worried about her family not liking Gregg but more because she hoped he'd like *them*. Meeting the whole Brennan clan at once might be a little overwhelming and they could be intense. Maybe this would be Gregg's imperfection—maybe he wouldn't like her family and, as much as they drove her crazy sometimes, she couldn't imagine a future with anyone who didn't feel comfortable with the important role they played in her life.

'Good.' He kissed her on the forehead. 'Now, shall I make us some coffee?'

Was there anything sexier a man could ask at this time of the morning?

'Sounds perfect,' she said and then reluctantly rolled out of his embrace to get the day started.

Shadow, who had been sleeping on the floor by their feet, roused as they climbed out of bed and immediately hurried over to her. As she bent down to scratch the fur behind his ears, his tail shook furiously.

'I may as well not exist anymore,' Gregg said as he located his pants and tugged them on.

She shrugged and offered him a what-can-I-do smile and he shook his head and smiled back. She'd met Shadow the day after their first date and he'd immediately taken a shine to her. Now whenever Gregg stayed over so did his dog and although he pretended to be offended by the pup's transfer of affection, she suspected him secretly pleased that she and Shadow had become firm friends.

Once they were both dressed and caffeinated, Gregg hitched Shadow to his leash and the three of them set off for a walk up to and around Centennial Park. It was a beautiful day for August and plenty of people were out jogging, riding bikes and walking dogs. When Shadow finally began to tire, they walked back past the local deli and bought *The Sun-Herald*, which they read later while sitting at her kitchen table eating fresh croissants. The whole morning was pretty much the definition of perfection and when the time came to shower and get ready to go to her sister's, they did so together like a couple of teens who had just discovered the benefits of saving water.

Siobhan and Neil were getting out of their car when Clara and Gregg arrived at Bridget and Ranaldo's place in Manly.

'Ooh, you're even better looking in person than you are in your online photo,' were the first words to come out of her sister's mouth when Clara introduced her to Gregg.

'Why, thank you.' Gregg kissed Siobhan on the cheek. 'It's a pleasure to meet you.'

Clara glared at her sister—she'd told them all to be on their best behaviour and here was Siobhan falling at the first hurdle. Neil shrugged an apology for his wife and then offered his hand to Gregg. Introductions were exchanged as the four of them headed inside. The door was open and the noise coming from the backyard told them that's where the family was congregated.

'Wow, this is impressive,' Gregg whispered to Clara as they emerged onto the massive back balcony that overlooked Fairy Bower.

'I know. Both Ranaldo and Bridget work in computers and they created an app or something together a couple of years ago that made them instant millionaires. They bought this house outright.'

They had about five seconds to survey the scenery before all eyes turned to them.

Bridget crossed over from where she'd been barking orders at the birthday boy by the barbeque—although 'barbeque' didn't seem adequate enough for what was essentially a whole outdoor kitchen. She and Ranaldo had embraced the outside cooking experience and thanks to gas heaters in each corner of the balcony and expensive blinds that could shield them from the rain and wind, they ate out almost all year round.

'Why hello,' she said, grinning ridiculously and being not at all surreptitious in her head-to-toe perusal of Gregg. 'You must be Clara's new man.'

'His name's Gregg,' Clara said. 'Gregg Callen. And Gregg, this is my youngest sister, Bridget. Her husband, Ranaldo, is over there in the apron.'

'We thought we'd make the most of this lovely almost-spring-like weather and have a barbeque,' Bridget explained, then leant forward and wrapped her arms around Gregg. 'Welcome to the family. It's lovely to have you celebrating with us all today. We're so happy Clara's finally found someone. She's such a kind, caring, wonderful person and she deserves happiness after her most unfortunate marriage.'

*And you can stop talking now*, Clara silently willed her sister. She glanced around, hoping that someone else would come and save the day. Fiona caught her eye and stepped up to the plate.

'Did you say Callen?' Fiona said, offering Gregg her hand. 'Clarabel Callen, doesn't that have a nice ring to it?'

*Oh my God*. She should have known she couldn't rely on foot-in-her-mouth Fiona. Her sisters were crazy. They weren't even done with the introductions and already she wanted to murder most of them. Besides, after her last experience, she was in no rush to marry anyone.

Although Clara felt her cheeks turn a dark shade of red at her sister's words, Gregg didn't seem fazed.

'Yes, it does, doesn't it? And which one are you?'

'I'm Fiona, and this is my husband Troy.'

By this time, everyone was closing in, crowding around them like they were some rare exhibit in the zoo. Clara suddenly understood how her nieces and nephews felt whenever they introduced a new love interest and she hoped one of them might have some scandalous news to take the heat off her and Gregg.

'Mr *Callen*?' Aoifa squealed. 'Oh my God! Do you remember me? You taught me year twelve history. You were my favourite teacher by far.'

Gregg chuckled as recognition filled his face. 'Aoifa Sanderson. Look at you. What are you up to now?'

'I'm working at a travel agent part-time,' she said, 'and studying psychology at uni, but I'm not really sure what I want to do with my life.'

'You've got plenty of time,' Gregg said, and Clara thought it was lucky he said that to one of Siobhan's offspring, not Fiona's.

'This is my boyfriend, Xavier, Mr Callen.'

As the two men shook hands, Gregg said, 'You're out of school now, call me Gregg.'

The introductions continued and thankfully no one said anything else too mortifying, then Bridget did her hostess-with-the-mostess duties and made sure Clara and Gregg had drinks. Then, while Gregg got chatting to Aoifa and Xavier, Clara's sisters spirited her away to the kitchen and began their assessment.

'I like him,' said Aideen.

The others quickly agreed.

Clara glowed. 'He is pretty fantastic.'

'Definitely an improvement on the last one,' Fiona remarked.

'Yes, he is,' she agreed, still smiling. Her sisters followed her gaze to where Gregg was still chatting away to Aoifa and Xavier, although a few of her brothers-in-law had now joined in as well.

After a while Bridget went off to hurry Ranaldo on the barbeque and Clara's other sisters started fiddling with fancy side dishes in the kitchen. As her culinary skills weren't needed, she went back to Gregg.

'How you doing?' she whispered as she slid her arm around his waist.

'Great. Your family are fantastic.'

When Aoifa and Xavier were dragged off by some of the younger cousins and the brothers-in-law were summoned to help carry plates and food, Gregg said, 'Aoifa was telling me about a short comedy cruise that leaves Sydney and goes up the coast and back. As well as comedy shows on board, there's a workshop you can do with a stand-up comic.'

'That sounds right up your alley,' Clara said. She'd never been much of a comedy fan but Gregg had introduced her to a couple of his favourite comics on Netflix. She'd never laughed more in her life than in the last few weeks.

'She said there's still tickets for the cruise that leaves in just over a week and they're on sale.' He paused a moment, then, 'I was wondering if you'd like to go on it with me. My shout, if you can get the time off work at such short notice.'

'You think you can?'

He nodded. 'Yeah, it's only four days and two are over the weekend, so it shouldn't be a problem.'

Clara pondered the possibility. Going on holiday with Gregg, spending twenty-four hours a day together, would either make her fall even more head over heels or by the end of the four days she'd want to throw him overboard. But everything about her relationship with him had been a whirlwind and wasn't this supposed to be her year of grabbing life by the balls?

She grinned. 'Okay. Why not? I'd love to.'

'Excellent.' He pulled her close and sealed the deal with a kiss.

One of her brothers-in-law wolf-whistled and another shouted 'Get a room!' but Clara couldn't bring herself to be even a teeny bit embarrassed at their public display of affection. She couldn't remember the last time she felt this happy.

'Well, that was a success,' Gregg said, caressing the steering wheel as he turned out of Bridget's street. 'Your family like me so much they're already marrying us off.'

Clara wasn't sure whether to laugh, cry or turn red again. 'I'm sorry about that. I swear they didn't get that idea from me.'

'So you don't *want* to marry me?'

Gregg had to be joking—it was way too early to be having this conversation—but his tone was hard to read and she didn't want to offend him if he wasn't.

'It's not that. It's not you. It's just ...' *Oh Lord.*

'It's alright,' he interrupted with a chuckle, taking one hand off the wheel and squeezing her knee. 'I'm just messing with you. I know things have moved pretty fast between us and I'm not unhappy about what we've got, but I reckon we just enjoy it for a while, don't you?'

She smiled and put her hand on top of his. 'That sounds like a perfect plan.'

Before either of them could say anything else, Clara's handbag started ringing at her feet. She frowned. The only people who ever called her were Gregg and her sisters and she'd just spent hours with them. And Rob. But he no longer could.

'Maybe we left something behind,' Gregg suggested as if she'd just spoken her thoughts out loud.

'Maybe.' She leaned over to retrieve her phone and her frown deepened.

'Who is it?' he asked when she simply stared at it a few long moments.

Her stomach muscles squeezed as a feeling of dread washed over her. 'It's Rob's mother.' She hadn't seen nor heard from Brenda since the divorce.

'I see.' He sounded both surprised and a little put out. Since the episode on her front porch, they'd spoken very little about her ex-husband.

'Are you going to answer it?'

It suddenly crossed her mind that maybe it wasn't Brenda but Rob from his mother's phone. 'No,' she said as the phone stopped ringing of its own accord.

Her high of earlier rapidly diminishing, Clara shoved the phone back in her bag and tried to ignore the prick of guilt. So what if it was Brenda? There was no valid reason for her ex-mother-in-law to be calling on a Sunday afternoon, or any other day for that matter. Unless something terrible had happened to Rob.

She didn't allow that thought to take root. He wasn't her problem anymore.

The phone immediately started ringing again. Reluctantly she retrieved it and this time a different number—one she didn't recognise—flashed up at her.

That feeling of doom grew in her stomach. She'd never been good at ignoring unknown numbers but usually regretted answering them the moment she did.

She pressed the phone up against her ear. 'Hello?'

'Is this Clara Jones?' asked an unfamiliar voice.

'Yes.'

Within two minutes, the voice on the other end of the line explained everything. She was a nurse at St Vincent's and one of her patients—an elderly woman called Brenda Jones—had listed Clara as next of kin. Brenda had fallen at home and badly broken her ankle in two places; she needed some things brought in to the hospital.

'She has a son,' Clara said curtly.

There was a muffled conversation at the end of the phone line, then the nurse came back on. 'Apparently her son is missing.'

'What?' Her grip tightened on her phone. 'Put Brenda on, please.'

Rob's mother was very apologetic about bothering Clara but explained she had no one else to call. He hadn't been home since going out three Saturday mornings ago.

Clara did the calculations—the morning they'd argued about her selling the house. She refused to feel guilty about this timing. 'Have you reported this to the police?'

'Yes, dear. You know what he's like—sometimes he doesn't come home for a night or two, but he's never been away longer than three nights without letting me know, so I called them then. Two officers came round to my place but they didn't seem overly concerned to be honest. Told me they'd put him on some register and would keep an eye out. I'm so sorry to bother you but … I didn't know who else to call.'

When Brenda began to cry, Clara's heart softened. She was furious with Rob but she could hardly leave his mother all alone in the hospital without a clean change of underwear.

'It's okay,' she tried to assure her. 'Do you still have the spare key under the flowerpot out the back? I can go over now and collect whatever you need, then bring it to the hospital straight away.'

Brenda sniffed. 'Oh, thank you. You always were such a good girl. Far too good for my Rob.'

Clara didn't make comment on that.

As her ex-mother-in-law dictated a list, she messily scribbled it down on the notebook she carried in her handbag. 'Be with you soon,' she told Brenda and then disconnected the call.

'What's going on?'

And although she'd vowed to keep her messy past out of her conversations with Gregg, all her good intentions flew out the window. She gave him a no-holds-barred account, starting from the phone call and working backwards to Rob's disappearance, right to the night she'd met him and all their heartbreak and disappointment in between.

'When Rob was seventeen, he got his fifteen-year-old girlfriend pregnant. They broke up and the baby was adopted—he knew he had a son—but her family moved away and Rob never saw her or the baby again. Although devastated, he threw himself into his music as a distraction. When we met, his band were just about to record their first album—it turned out to be a big hit. Especially one song.'

'Would I know the band?'

'Maybe. They were called One Track Mind.' When Gregg shook his head, Clara added, 'You'll have heard their big hit—"Lost Without You, Baby".'

His eyes widened. 'I loved that song. I can never remember who sang it though.' And he burst out in song, 'I've lost my direction, without you ...'

'Everybody did. Most people still do.' Of course they all thought it was just a twisted love song; only a small few knew just how real those words were for Rob.

'Wow.' Gregg was still in awe. 'I can't imagine what it would be like to be famous like that and then fade almost into obscurity.'

'Well, fame isn't all it's cracked up to be—but it brings with it money, which meant Rob was never short on cash for grog. Even years later that song still brings in a reasonable income.'

'So alcohol ruined him?'

Clara nodded. 'To an extent, that was his drug of choice, but he started drinking to numb his pain. He never got over the guilt of letting his baby go. He never stopped wondering what his son was like, if he was doing okay, and he desperately wanted us to have a family. I think he hoped another baby would fill the hole inside him, give him a chance to prove himself as a dad. He was in a good place—his music career was just kicking off when we met—so although he told me about the adoption I didn't realise just how badly this experience had affected him until it became clear we were never going to have children of our own.'

'Can I ask why you couldn't?'

'I had a couple of miscarriages early in our marriage,' she began slowly. 'We had the tests that were available at the time but the doctors could never work out why my body kept rejecting the pregnancies, then finally I almost carried a baby to term.'

'Almost?' Gregg's voice wasn't much more than a whisper.

'We ... I ... found out the baby had died at thirty-seven weeks.' Clara swallowed.

In her head she was back in that room with its pretty lavender wallpaper and the sunshine streaming in through the windows, a ridiculously perfect spring day to have her world shattered. She'd known something was wrong, but she'd hoped. Damn she'd hoped and that had always been her problem. The doctor had been sorry. Everyone had been extremely sorry.

But sorry hadn't helped. Sorry couldn't bring her baby to life.

The lump she'd been trying to ignore expanded in her throat. 'I went through labour knowing ...'

'Oh, Clara. You don't have to say any more.' When Gregg turned and pulled her into his arms, she realised he'd stopped on the side of the road to focus on her. 'I'm so sorry you went through all that.'

No matter that it had happened over two decades ago now, she'd never forget the feel of rocking her dead child in her arms, of watching her tears fall on her pallid skin and hoping they would miraculously revive her. When the nurse had finally tried to take her away, she'd held on, screaming and yelling. Eventually they'd had to sedate her.

She sucked in a breath, trying to stop the tears that threatened at Gregg's kind words and strong, warm embrace.

But it was hopeless. They fell hard and fast.

He reacted quickly, tugging a tissue out of his shirt pocket and offering it to her. 'It's clean. I promise.'

Clara sniffed and managed a 'thank you' as she took it from him.

After a long silence, she said, 'Rob's social drinking got much worse after that, until it stopped being social at all. I think the death of our baby triggered something inside him that brought back all his guilt and sadness over his other child. I kept hoping we would have another baby and that would save him but there were only more miscarriages and eventually I decided it wasn't meant to be. That the pregnancy losses were only making things worse. I tried to help him. For years I tried, but ...'

She'd lost track of the number of times he'd joined Alcoholics Anonymous; he'd never lasted more than a few months.

'But you were dealing with your own grief,' Gregg said, as if that explained everything.

She looked up at him and smiled. What would Gregg have been like in such tragic circumstances? Would he have supported her more than Rob? Would they have been able to support each other? It was almost impossible to even imagine what being with someone who wasn't so dependent was like. Would it have changed who *she* was as well?

'Did Rob ever try to make contact with his son?'

'He didn't really have anything to go on. As far as we know, he wasn't listed on the birth certificate, but I did help him join a couple of groups that try to connect lost family members. Nothing ever came of any of them.'

'How sad.'

'Yes.'

'And now he's missing?'

'Apparently.' But the bitterness she wanted to feel wasn't as strong as her gnawing concern. What if he'd finally done the stupid thing he'd been threatening to do for years and it was all her fault?

*At least then you'd be rid of him once and for all.* She hated herself for that thought.

'You don't believe he's missing?'

She sighed. 'I don't know what to think.' Three weeks seemed too long a time to be lying in some gutter somewhere in a drunken stupor.

'Would you like me to come with you to his mother's place?'

Clara had almost forgotten Brenda's phone call had been what started this discussion. 'I can't ask you to do that,' she said, not after she'd unloaded so tremendously on him and spoiled their almost-perfect day.

'You didn't *ask* me to do anything,' Gregg said gently but firmly. 'I'm offering. Tell me her address and we'll go there now.'

'Thank you.' Clara felt her tears rushing back. For once in her life she was happy to lean on somebody else.

*Josie*

Josie greeted Paige in the high school reception office and pulled her into a hug.

'Thank you so much for coming in at such short notice.' She wasn't usually the hug-to-greet type and they'd only known each other a grand total of six days, but it just felt right with Paige.

'No worries. It's the least I can do for you after you've been so kind about the dress and it's good to see you again.'

'It is,' Josie agreed.

They might be almost eight years apart in age and their artistic talents might lie in different fields, but over a few cups of tea and the shouts of their footy-loving husbands in the background, they'd clicked in a way Josie hadn't done with anyone before. Well, not a woman—she'd had friends growing up of course and still did now, but those friendships had all taken time to mature—the closest she'd ever come to a similar connection was the night her eyes met with Nik's across the busy bar. If she were honest, her almost-instant liking of Paige had surprised her. The other woman seemed so young and idealistic; her chatter about her mum and her upcoming nuptials should have been annoying in Josie's current state of mind but instead she'd found them endearing. And, as the conversation continued, she'd found herself comforting Paige about her mother and even opening up about some of her own heartache.

Why she'd felt comfortable telling Paige about her miscarriages, she didn't know—perhaps it was proof her sessions with Clara were helping—but by the time the football had finished, Paige knew more about Josie than many of her so-called friends.

'Is that your bestseller?' Josie asked as she signed Paige in as a guest on the visitor register and noticed the book under her arm. 'Can I take a quick look before we go meet the kids?'

'Sure.' Paige handed it to her and Josie gasped in delight as she looked down upon the beautifully illustrated cover. Of course she'd googled Paige's work like any responsible teacher would but she hadn't seen a copy of her book in the flesh. 'It's gorgeous.'

'Thanks. I'm really happy with how it turned out.'

'I can't wait to hear you read it to the kids.'

Paige bit her lip. 'I hope they like it. They're a little bit older than my target audience but I have included a few little nuanced things for parents reading it, so they should enjoy those.'

'Trust me, they'll love it—it'll be a welcome change from the last book I made them read.'

'What was that?'

'*Far from the Madding Crowd*. It was before the school holidays and they're still whining about it.'

Josie led her outside and into the throng of students racing between the classrooms from one period to the next. 'Get off your phone or I'll confiscate it,' she warned one of her year nine students as she held onto Paige's arm.

When they got to the classroom, her students were all milling about outside, talking, but they went quiet the moment they saw her visitor.

'All right everyone, inside and sit down quickly,' she ordered. 'As you can see I have someone special here to talk to you today and so we don't want to waste any time.'

They all gave Paige the once-over as they filed inside but then settled in a timely manner.

'As you know we're about to start learning about picture books ...' A couple of the students groaned before Josie could continue, but she shot them both the evil eye. 'I'm hugely excited to introduce you to my friend, Paige MacRitchie, who has recently published her first picture book, *We All Live Here*. Paige is going to talk about the process of writing and publishing. As you are all going to have to choose two picture books to analyse and write an individual essay comparison on and then in groups create your own picture book, I suggest you listen carefully.'

Someone's hand shot up in the air. 'Can we do our essay on Paige's book?'

'No. Stop looking for the easy option, Noah.'

As the kids scrambled for pens and paper, Josie looked to Paige. 'Over to you.'

Paige cleared her throat and smiled at the students—some of them didn't look that much younger than her. 'Hi everyone. Thanks for having me here today. I thought I'd start with a little reading.'

Josie waited for some smart alec to complain about being too old for picture books but thankfully nobody did. And, from the moment Paige peeled back the cover, the kids were enthralled. She put on unique voices for all the characters and Josie wished her drama students were here as they could learn a lot as well. When she finally closed the book, the students cheered and clapped as if she'd just won *Australian Idol* or something.

'Can you read it again?' asked one of the girls.

Paige beamed. 'I'm glad you liked it.'

For the next twenty minutes, she gave them background about herself—how she'd loved books and drawing from a young age and how as she grew older and became passionate about humanitarian causes, she decided she wanted to combine her loves for good. She continued on to talk about how she'd studied her favourite picture books and found they all had certain things in common.

'The main characters all have a problem to solve and the description is minimal. The illustrations are what bring a picture book to life. And just because picture books are short—usually about thirty pages—doesn't mean they're easy.' She spoke about the number of drafts she'd gone through with her publisher and also about the actual publication process.

When the siren for the end of the day sounded, the class let out a collective groan, something Josie hadn't witnessed in all her years of teaching and she found herself as disappointed as her students that time was up.

'Can you come back again?' asked Noah. A number of other students reiterated his request.

Paige looked to Josie as if for permission and Josie said, 'If you have the time, we'd love to have you back when we start planning our own picture books. Your feedback would be invaluable.'

'I'd love to,' Paige said and once again the class erupted into cheers, before waving goodbye as they spilled out the door. 'Wow. They are way more enthusiastic than I remember me or my friends being when we were at school.'

'Trust me, they're not always that way,' Josie replied. 'But I guess passion breeds passion. Thanks for inspiring them.'

'It was my pleasure. And are we still on for tomorrow night?'

'Yep.' Josie grinned. 'I can't wait to see your mum's reaction.' All the bitterness she'd harboured when she heard about Paige and her mother had gone and now all that was left was the joy at being involved in such a special plan.

'Thanks. She's trying to be positive but it's obvious her illness and the monotony of dialysis three times a week is getting her down. She deserves a little happiness.'

With a rendezvous next evening to look forward to, Paige left and Josie started around the room, pulling down the blinds. She was just picking up her bag, when her phone beeped with a message.

It was from Clara: *Really sorry but something's come up and I can't see you this afternoon.*

Josie stared down at the message—she hoped Clara was okay as it seemed unusual for her to cancel at such short notice, but maybe this was a sign? She'd been feeling a lot better these last couple of weeks. Of course she was still heartbroken but Clara's advice to take proper time out with Nik and to do things to make herself and others happy appeared to be doing the trick. Since making a conscious decision to focus on other things aside from her grief, she'd found it easier to get up each morning and she'd handed out a lot fewer detentions at school.

If it weren't for Clara, she'd probably have outright refused when Nik told her about the dress and then she'd never have met Paige. Today, she was so happy that she'd feel a bit of a fraud taking up Clara's time anyway.

But the thought of ending her sessions made her a little sad. She enjoyed her time with Clara—it wasn't only that the other woman provided a safe space for her to talk freely about her grief, but she also really liked her.

Oh well, she didn't have to make any drastic decisions right away. Instead, since she now had a free afternoon, she decided to make a special surprise romantic dinner for Nik. Josie smiled at the thought as she collected her things from her locker in the staffroom and headed for her car.

Fifteen minutes later, she was perusing the gourmet shelves at the local supermarket as she contemplated whether to make beef wellingtons or a rack of lamb with a herb crust when a woman came around the corner and their trolleys collided.

'I'm so sorry.' The words were out of Josie's mouth before she registered she knew this woman. 'Clara?'

Her usually sleek golden bob was tied back in a ponytail, bits of hair were falling out onto her face and she was wearing a tracksuit.

'Josie. Fancy running into you here.' Clara turned red as if she'd been caught doing something illegal. 'I'm so sorry to have cancelled our session at such short notice.'

'It's not a problem.' Josie smiled, wanting to put her at ease. 'I'm feeling really good today. I've made a new friend and she came to school and spoke to my students about picture books this afternoon.'

'Oh, that's nice. How did you meet?'

'It's a funny story actually. About a week ago, Nik came home all excited about something he'd seen on Facebook. There was this woman on there looking for her mother's wedding dress.' She went on to tell Clara the whole story about her gown. 'Turns out the dress was the one this girl was looking for.'

'Hmm ... That's understandable.' Clara nodded and Josie frowned, recognising that the other woman wasn't really listening, but simply making what she hoped were the right kind of noises. She felt as if she could tell Clara she'd signed up for that one-way trip to Mars and the other woman would nod politely and say 'how lovely'.

Although Clara didn't *have* to listen to Josie right now, this distracted behaviour seemed very out of character. Something was bothering her.

Josie reached out to touch the other woman's arm. 'Clara, tell me to mind my own business if you want but … are you okay?'

Clara blinked rapidly, her cheeks flushed darker and she put her hand to her neck. 'I'm f—'

Josie guessed she was about to say 'fine' but the word died on her tongue and instead Clara pursed her lips tightly together and squeezed her eyes shut as if trying not to cry.

The tables suddenly turned, Josie dug into her handbag for the packet of tissues she now carried around permanently.

'Here.' She offered them to Clara with a gentle smile as a woman with two young children looked suspiciously at them as she took a wide berth.

Clara took one look at the packet and burst into tears. 'Oh God. I'm so sorry,' she said, snatching a tissue and dabbing at her eyes. 'This is so unprofessional of me.'

'It's okay. Talking to you has helped me immensely so if you think it'd help you to talk about whatever's bothering you, then I'm more than happy to listen. We could go get a coffee at the café on the corner?'

Clara looked torn between accepting and rejecting the offer and Josie guessed it was because she didn't want to get into trouble with the charity. But she couldn't care less about any rules and protocol that might exist; no way was she going to walk away from Clara in such a state.

'Come on.' She nodded towards the supermarket's entrance. 'I haven't had a good coffee since this morning. We can leave our trolleys here and come back later.'

Clara sighed. 'Okay, if you're sure you have time.'

'All the time in the world,' Josie said; Nik loved her homemade spaghetti sauce, she already had the ingredients for that and it didn't take long to make.

'You're such a sweet girl,' Clara said, a few minutes later when they had ordered their drinks (and some chocolate cake) and were sitting in a corner table at the café. 'I don't want to burden you but I guess I owe you an explanation.'

She didn't owe Josie anything, but Josie didn't say this, understanding Clara needed this excuse to justify opening up.

'As you know, I'm divorced.'

Josie nodded.

'Well, I've recently started seeing someone, a wonderful man.' Clara's eyes lit up a moment, but the joy vanished as quickly as it had come. 'But Rob, my ex, is an alcoholic, and he's never been able to accept we live separate lives now.'

Josie was not surprised by this statement—the man she'd met hadn't looked exactly healthy and she remembered Clara seeming unsurprised that they'd met outside a pub.

'A few weeks ago Rob turned up and there was an altercation. It was awful, he tried to punch Gregg.' Her face went pale at the recollection. 'Once again I told him it was over, and Gregg sent him on his way. As he left, I hoped and prayed I'd never see him again. I've been having such a great time with Gregg the last few weeks—I've felt happier than I have in a long time. I hadn't heard anything from Rob, so I dared to hope that maybe he might finally have got the message. Gregg and I have even made plans to go away on a cruise together, but ...'

Clara paused, sniffed and wiped her nose.

'A few days ago, I got a call from Rob's mother. She was in hospital with a broken ankle and needed some things brought in to her.'

'Ah, and I'm guessing you ran into Rob again?'

'No.' Clara shook her head. 'That's just it. Rob, it seems, has gone missing.'

'Missing?' Josie's head jerked back at this surprising declaration and a waiter chose that inconvenient moment to bring over their order.

'I've given you two spoons to share this delicious cake,' he said with a grin as he put the cake and their coffees on the table. 'Enjoy, ladies.'

'Thank you,' they said in unison, sounding like a recorded message.

'What do you mean, missing?' Josie asked the moment the waiter retreated. Neither of them made a move towards the food or drink.

'He's vanished. The police have listed him as missing but they're not really doing much to try and find him and ...' She sighed heavily again. 'Because he's not available to help Brenda—not that he'd be much use anyway—the task has fallen to me. Gregg and I went to her house and it was in such a state, mess everywhere, dirty dishes growing mould. I couldn't leave it like that, so I've spent the past few days cleaning it up for her.'

That explained the tracksuit and the dirty marks covering it.

'I just came to get some supplies to stock her fridge.'

'That's kind of you,' Josie said.

Clara snorted. 'I don't feel kind. I feel resentful. Don't get me wrong, I like Brenda and I don't blame her, but I just want to move on with my life. And, whenever I feel as if I finally might be free of Rob, something like this happens. I'm tired of all this, I just want closure. For me, for his mother. And I can't leave her to her own defences in her current state. She's got a visiting nurse stopping by once a day to help her, but it's not the same as family. Is it?'

Josie shook her head, knowing that when she was at her very lowest after each of her miscarriages, she'd craved the comfort of her mother.

'I'm sorry, Josie, I shouldn't have told you any of that. I don't know what came over me, but I don't think I'm going to be able to continue with our sessions. I've been volunteering for over twenty years and I hope I've helped, but I'm not sure I have anything left to give.'

Josie's heart clenched—right now she was more concerned about Clara's mental health than her own. Did she have someone else to discuss her woes with? She might not feel comfortable chatting to her new beau about her ex and her ex-mother-in-law.

'I'm so sorry,' Clara continued, 'but I can promise you our other volunteers are lovely.'

'That's okay. I understand. And I appreciate everything you've already done for me. In fact, when I got your message this afternoon, I was thinking that maybe I don't need our sessions anymore. You've helped me accept my grief, not feel ashamed of it and in doing so, you've inspired me to live again. I just wish there was something I could do to help you.'

'Oh, don't be silly, that's not the way this is supposed to work, but I'm glad you're feeling better. Don't hesitate to call the charity's helpline though if you ever feel the need.'

'I won't,' Josie promised, and then an idea landed in her head. 'Can I visit your mother-in-law? Take the burden off you a little.'

Clara blinked. 'You'd do that?'

'Yes. I think I'd enjoy it.' And that was the truth—now that she'd started to think about others aside from herself, she was feeling much better. Helping an old dear could only improve on that.

Clara looked as if she wanted to accept, but, 'I feel like that might be abusing my position as your support person.'

'But you won't be my support person anymore, will you? Please, I'd love to help.'

Slowly, a smile stole onto Clara's face and this time it was in her eyes as well as her mouth. 'Well, if you're sure. That would be a help—I was a bit worried about going away next weekend—and I think Brenda would love it too. She won't be able to get out of the house on her own for a while.'

Josie nodded. 'It's settled then. I'm not taking no for an answer. Now, are we going to eat this chocolate cake or what?'

# Rebecca

Rebecca wondered what her daughter was playing at as she parked in front of an apartment block in Coogee late Friday afternoon. Without any clues as to the why, Paige had demanded she meet her. Rebecca clicked her tongue in irritation and climbed out of her car. She'd been feeling good after today's dialysis session, but as she headed for the building, unease crept into her heart. These days mystery and surprises made her anxious, but Paige had promised this was a good surprise, so she tried to ignore the erratic beating of her heart as she lifted her hand to the intercom.

Then, just before she could press the button, the front door opened to reveal a tall woman with long brown hair tied up in a side-ponytail. The woman, whom she guessed to be in her early to mid-thirties, smiled as if they were old friends.

'Hello. You're Paige's mum,' she said in a sing-songy tone. 'It's lovely to meet you. Come in.'

'Who are you?' Rebecca asked, sounding ruder than she'd meant.

'Sorry.' The other woman laughed and held out her hand. 'I'm Josie, a friend of Paige's. She's … She's here and has something to show you. Come into the lounge room and I'll go get her.'

Before she had a chance to respond, Josie ushered her into the building and the open door of a ground-floor apartment, which went straight into a smallish living room. 'Take a seat if you like.' She gestured to a sofa loaded with bright cushions. 'I'll be back with Paige in a moment.'

Clutching her handbag to her chest, Rebecca glanced around the room. Although not necessarily to *her* taste, it felt warm and personal—the posters and knick-knacks on the walls and shelves told her that whoever lived here loved music, movies and aeroplanes. Her gaze moved on from a cabinet filled with model planes to rest on some photos sitting on the mantelpiece—four frames, two with middle-aged couples in and the other two each with a baby.

She smiled at the first infant lying peacefully on its side; it had a shock of dark hair and one eye open at the camera, but as she focused on the second baby, something nagged at her. She leaned closer and scrutinised the photo, trying to work out what it was.

And then, it dawned.

Jumping back as if someone had tried to strike her, she pressed a hand against her chest. Except for the fact this was in a shiny black frame, it looked almost identical to the one she'd hidden in the safe deposit box at the bank.

*No.* She blinked and shook her head as a coldness snuck under her skin. *It can't be.*

Her illness, her brush with death, had to be making her crazy, delusional even. For so long Rebecca hadn't allowed herself to think about her son, about the adoption, and now she was seeing him everywhere—in almost every thirty-something man she saw in the shops or on the streets she saw something to make her think maybe he was the one. Yesterday, in Coles, she'd almost asked the man stacking tins if he was adopted.

And now she was clutching at this ridiculous straw.

She picked up the frame and, as she studied it, her pulse slowed again. This could be anyone's baby. It was a little fatter than the one in her photo, but now that she looked at it properly, it even looked a bit like the photos she had of Paige, which just proved that all young babies look the same anyway. Especially ones with next to no hair. She'd never have jumped to such a ludicrous conclusion if she hadn't already been feeling so unsettled.

At the sound of footsteps, she put the photo back on the shelf and turned round just as Josie returned.

'Are you ready to see Paige's surprise?'

Rebecca nodded; the photo behind her felt as if it were burning a hole in her back.

Josie turned, beckoned with her finger and, a second later, Paige appeared behind her. She stepped aside so that Rebecca had full view of her daughter in a gorgeous white wedding dress.

'Oh my goodness.' Her hand shot to cover her mouth as emotion rose in her throat. 'You're absolutely beautiful.'

'Thanks, Mum.' Beaming, Paige stepped into the room and did a slow pirouette, Josie picking up the long train and rearranging it as she did so.

Rebecca's gaze fell to said train. 'That dress looks remarkably like mine,' she mused.

Paige and Josie exchanged a look and then both started laughing. 'Mum,' Paige said through her chuckles. 'It *is* yours!'

'What?' Rebecca took a moment to register what she meant. 'But ... How? I gave it away. Years ago.'

'That's a long story,' Paige said.

'And one that needs a celebratory drink, don't you think?' Josie added.

Before Rebecca could say 'hell yes' to the drink and to hell with the fact she wasn't really supposed to be having alcohol, Josie hurried off.

'Are you okay, Mum?'

She blinked. 'Yes, of course.' And summoned a smile for her daughter as she reached down and ran her hand over the silk of the dress. *Her* dress. It was almost impossible to believe and for a moment it distracted her from the photo. 'This is just a little overwhelming.'

Paige closed the distance between them and hugged her. 'I wanted to do something special for you. I look up to you and Dad so much as an example of what a good relationship, a good marriage is, so this just felt right.'

Tears prickled Rebecca's eyes as her daughter held her tightly. Her marriage might look good to those looking in, but could a marriage really be so solid if at its heart was a massive lie? Or at least a huge omission?

'Mum. Don't cry,' Paige shrieked, yanking out of her embrace. 'You'll ruin the dress and then Josie will kill me.'

Josie chose that moment to return with a tray and three flutes of bubbles. *Thank the Lord.* It was all Rebecca could do not to snatch one up and gulp it down.

'What am I going to kill you for?'

'Just Mum blubbering like a baby over the dress.'

'Oh.' Josie smiled, put the drinks down on the coffee table and then conjured a box of tissues for Rebecca. 'Here you are.'

'Thanks.' Rebecca took one, although frankly she would have preferred the bubbles. She was supposed to be overjoyed at seeing her daughter in her wedding dress, but her chest felt tight. Was she having a panic attack?

'You're welcome.' Josie stooped, picked up two of the glasses and handed one to Rebecca and another to Paige. 'Paige said you couldn't drink alcohol at the moment, so I got fake bubbles.'

*Fake bubbles?* Rebecca thought as Josie claimed the third glass for herself. What kind of monster had concocted such a thing? And how much had Paige told this stranger about her medical issues?

'Cheers,' Paige and Josie said in unison, clinking glasses and then turning to clink hers.

'Want to hear the story about the dress, Mum?'

'Go on, then,' Rebecca said, knowing she should be more excited than she sounded. Thankfully the tears seemed to have done the trick—Paige and Josie thought she was all emotional because of the dress.

'Shall we sit?' Josie asked.

Paige and the dress required a whole sofa to themselves, which left Rebecca sitting alongside Josie on the other almost matching, but slightly smaller two-seater.

'So,' Paige began. 'When we were looking through your and Dad's wedding album in the hospital, I suddenly thought how lovely it would be to get married in your dress. I asked Dad where it was and he told me you'd given it away, but after a few days, when I still couldn't get the idea out of my head, I decided to try and find it.'

She went on to explain how she'd actually found the lady who had won it at the charity fashion parade. 'She's divorced now and gave the dress to St Vinnie's a couple of years ago. Karis and I spent a whole day searching all the op shops in the surrounding area but couldn't find it, so she suggested Facebook.'

'And my husband saw Paige's post,' Josie continued. 'Nik was the one who bought it for me from St Vinnie's. I wore it when I got married eighteen months ago.'

'You got married in this dress?' Rebecca couldn't understand why a young woman like Josie would want such an old dress. She herself hadn't given it a thought in almost thirty years.

Josie nodded. 'We had an eighties-themed wedding, so it was perfect.'

'How lovely.' Rebecca tried to focus on the dress conversation but her eyes kept drifting to the mantelpiece. She couldn't help herself. 'Those are lovely baby photos,' she said, standing up and crossing over to them.

Josie gave her an odd look. 'Thank you.'

'Who are they? The babies?' Rebecca tried to sound nonchalant.

'My husband and I,' Josie replied.

Rebecca made a show of picking up the photo of the dark-haired infant first. Now that she'd taken a second look, she couldn't shake the feeling that the baby in the other photo *was* the same baby as the one in the image she'd kept all these years. Just maybe a few weeks older. Could Josie's husband be her son?

'Weren't you just the cutest thing?'

'Oh no, I'm the near-bald one,' Josie said with a chuckle. 'The pretty-looking one is Nik. His mum said even when she dressed him in blue, people thought he was a girl. We tease him about it now but luckily he grew up to be quite good-looking in a much more manly kind of way.'

'I'll attest to that.' Paige grinned and then took another sip of her fake bubbles.

While the girls giggled, Rebecca put the photo down and had to steady herself on the mantelpiece as a giddiness almost knocked her sideways. Although there was an uncanny similarity, the bald baby could not be hers.

*Josie is a girl.*

An almost hysterical laugh shot from her mouth. She wasn't sure whether she was disappointed or relieved. Either way, it was official. She was losing the plot.

'Are you alright, Mum?' Paige put down her glass and stood, her expression concerned. 'Do you need to sit?'

'I'm fine,' she managed, trying to compose herself. Perhaps the kidney failure was a blessing in disguise—whenever she acted weird, everyone put it down to her not feeling well. 'I was just overcome with excitement for a moment. You look so beautiful, sweetheart.'

'Thank you, Mum.' Paige glowed and then looked to Josie. 'You can show her your wedding photo now and we'll tell her about all the ideas you and I have for the wedding.'

'Good idea.' Josie went over to the mantelpiece and picked up a frame that Rebecca hadn't noticed had been lying face down. She gave it to Rebecca. 'Didn't want you to see this before seeing Paige.'

As Rebecca glanced down at the photo in her hand—at the image of Josie in the wedding dress—she did a double take.

It was like staring at her younger self in the mirror.

*Clara*

Saturday morning, Clara parked outside the address Josie had given her in Coogee and leaned over to grab her umbrella from the floor in front of the passenger seat, but when she came back up, Josie was already hurrying down the front few steps towards the car. She was dressed in magenta skinny jeans, silver boots and a sparkly gold jacket. Her bright outfit was a welcome reprieve from the dreary grey sky and monotonous rain that felt as if it had been falling for weeks.

Clara leaned across and pushed open the passenger door, so Josie wouldn't be out in the cold and wet a second longer than necessary. Josie lived a lot closer to Brenda than Clara did—walking distance at a pinch, although not in these dismal conditions.

'Lovely weather we're having, isn't it?' Clara said when Josie slid into the car, dropping her handbag to the floor and holding a Tupperware container on her lap.

'If you're a duck.' Josie laughed and shook her head slightly. Her big gold hoop earrings swung from side to side and water droplets sprinkled over Clara. They both laughed.

'Thanks so much for doing this. It means a lot,' Clara said as Josie secured her seatbelt.

'It's my pleasure. Trust me, going out for tea and cake is a much nicer option than spending the day inside marking essays.'

Clara smiled. When Josie declared she'd bake a cake to take to Brenda's, Clara had objected, but Josie said she found baking therapeutic and who was she to argue with that? 'Nik working today?'

'Yes, he'll be home tonight though and we're going bowling.'

Clara chuckled. She remembered Josie telling her how much Nik adored bowling.

'We're going with our new friends. Nik and Solomon are really competitive, so hopefully we're all still talking after tonight. What about you? Have you got any plans for this evening?'

'I'm seeing Gregg, my new man,' Clara said, feeling her cheeks warm slightly. It still felt weird talking about him that way—she felt far too old to get hot under the collar over a man but when she was around Gregg she felt like a schoolgirl.

'That sounds lovely.'

Before the conversation could lead anywhere else, Clara slowed the car in front of a charming little red-brick house. 'Here we are,' she announced.

'It *is* close to my place.' The garden was a little overgrown and the paint was peeling off the picket fence at the front making it look a little sorry for itself, but with some TLC it could be amazing.

Clara turned into the driveway and stopped the car. The rain was still bucketing down. 'I've got an umbrella or should we just make a dash for it?'

'I'm happy to run. Umbrellas always seems such a palaver.'

'Okay. Let's do it.'

They leapt from the car and ran towards the safety of the front porch where Clara dug a key out of her bag.

'Hello, it's just me,' she called as she ushered Josie into the warmth. She'd instructed Brenda not to worry about the electricity bill but to keep the house toasty; the last thing they needed was her getting pneumonia on top of her broken foot.

It was a small house and the front door went straight into the living room where they found Brenda sitting in her electric recliner watching TV.

'Hello, love.' As she picked the remote off the chair's arm and muted the sound, her eyes went to Josie. She smiled warmly. 'And who are you, my sweet?'

Josie stepped forward as Clara said, 'This is my friend, Josie, and she's brought us cake.'

Brenda's eyes lit up. 'Oh, I love cake. What type?'

'Chocolate. Is there any other?'

Brenda laughed and Clara could tell she and Josie were going to get on like a house on fire, which wasn't surprising. As a teacher Josie was probably used to dealing with many different types of personalities but she seemed the kind of person who could get on with everyone. Clara herself had liked Josie since the moment they met and although she treated all the women she supported the same, she didn't feel as invested in all of them. There was something special about Josie. Although life had knocked her, the way she dressed—not giving a care to current trends but wearing what *she* loved—showed the passionate and charismatic person she was. And the more time they spent together, the more this unique creature had emerged. Even before Josie had cornered Clara at the supermarket and made her talk, Clara had known that Josie was caring and empathetic and it was wonderful to see her smiling again as well.

'How about you two get acquainted.' She took the Tupperware from Josie. 'And I'll go put the kettle on.'

As she headed into the kitchen, Clara heard Josie ask, 'What were you watching?'

'*To Sir With Love.*'

Reaching for the kettle, she smiled as she recalled her own mother's affection for that movie. She was obsessed with the main actor. *What was his name?* Sidney something. It was surprising she couldn't remember it, considering how often the movie had played at home. Her mum had recorded it when it was on TV and then watched it until the video had broken. Years later, Fiona had admitted to assisting in its demise.

When Clara returned to the living room carrying a tray with the tea and cake, Josie and Brenda were in animated discussion about movies.

'I can't believe how many of these I haven't seen,' Josie was saying as she knelt by the cabinet perusing Brenda's movie selection. Before the divorce, Clara had started updating her mother-in-law's impressive collection by giving her some of her favourite films on DVD, but the majority were still on VHS.

'Most of them were long before your time, love,' Brenda said, 'but they're classics. You're welcome to borrow any of them if you'd like.'

'I don't have a video player. Maybe I could come over and watch them with you?' Josie met Clara's eye as she made this suggestion and Clara smiled at her genius. No elderly person liked to be reminded of their need to be looked after, but this way Josie dropping by from time to time wouldn't seem so staged.

Brenda beamed. 'That would be lovely. That's if you haven't got anything better to do.'

'Trust me.' Josie sat down on the sofa next to Brenda's chair. 'There's nothing I like better than watching movies. Most of my favourites are from the eighties but I'd love to be educated about a different era. Now, shall we have a cup of tea?'

Clara played mother, pouring the tea while Josie sliced the cake and gave Brenda an extra-large piece. As they ate, Brenda asked lots of questions and Josie happily entertained her with the story of how she'd met her husband and then with tales from the classroom. Clara found she was enjoying herself much more than she'd imagined she would. She'd forgotten how much she liked Brenda's company. Since the phone call from the hospital, she'd felt irritated at her ex-mother-in-law, but now she found herself fantasising that Josie was her daughter, Brenda the grandmother, and this three-generational catch-up was something they did on a regular basis.

It wasn't that much of a stretch because with her long, dark hair, Josie even looked a little like Rob did when they'd first met.

At that thought, Clara shook her head. No, she didn't want to think about Rob—she wanted to be able to rewrite history, to have met Gregg earlier and for them to have had a child together. A warm, caring daughter like Josie. Of course then Brenda wouldn't be in the equation and Josie really seemed to like Brenda. Clara sighed, thankful that the others didn't appear to notice and chastised herself for once again dwelling on what she didn't have.

*You can't change the past but you can look to the future.*

If Rob didn't come back maybe it would be for the best. She'd look after Brenda and the three of them could fulfil a place in each other's lives that was missing. Josie missed her mum, Clara had always wanted a daughter and Brenda needed family to look after her in her old age. He hadn't come up in conversation today and for that she was grateful; she was sure Brenda would have mentioned if the police had passed on any news.

'I'm going to have to get up and go to the little girl's room,' Brenda announced.

Josie jumped to her feet. 'Here, let me help you up.'

'Thank you, love.' Brenda smiled as Josie reached out to steady her.

Clara grabbed her walking frame. 'Will you be okay going on your own?' she asked, her nursing instincts kicking in.

Brenda chuckled. 'I don't need the use of my foot to pee.'

They all laughed and then, while Brenda went off to the bathroom, Clara and Josie collected the dirty dishes and took them into the kitchen to wash.

'She's a delight,' Josie said. 'I'm having such a lovely time.'

'She's smitten with you as well.' Clara couldn't help smiling at this fact. It was such a relief to have Josie on board because she hadn't told her sisters about Rob's vanishing act or that as a result she'd been taking care of Brenda. Her upcoming cruise with Gregg had been weighing on her mind—she didn't want to have to cancel but she'd been wondering how she could go away in good conscience knowing that Brenda might need her.

'Would you two like to stay for lunch?' Brenda asked when she returned to the kitchen.

Clara looked at the clock on the kitchen wall and discovered that it was indeed that time of the day. They'd been here for over two hours but the time had flown. 'What can we get you?'

'Oh, no, no, no.' Brenda waggled her finger at the two of them. 'I may be getting old and slightly broken, but I can still make a very good toasted cheese sandwich. How does that sound?'

Clara looked to Josie. 'I've got time if you do.'

In reply, Josie pulled out a chair at the small kitchen table and sat.

Clara was relieved to see that Brenda was quite able to get around the kitchen and make a simple meal, or at least a snack. Between the visiting nurse and the odd visit from Josie while she was on the cruise, Brenda would be fine.

After a lovely lunch—toasted cheese might be simple but when cooked by someone else and in good company, it was a real treat—they said their goodbyes and Brenda and Josie made a date to see each other again.

Old woman and young woman exchanged phone numbers.

'Call me any time you need anything,' Josie told Brenda, 'but if I don't hear from you before, I'll be round Tuesday night for our first movie marathon.'

'I can't wait,' Brenda said, giving Josie a hug.

'And I'll bring dinner and popcorn, so don't you worry about anything except choosing the film.'

By the time Clara dropped Josie back off at her place, the rain had eased, the sun was peeking out through the leftover clouds and there was a rainbow in the sky, but even if there wasn't, she would have been smiling. It had been a lovely afternoon.

*Paige*

'Mum, Dad, you're early,' Paige said as she opened the door to her parents just before midday on Sunday. A leg of lamb was in the oven alongside potatoes and pumpkin all roasting to perfection for the big family wedding meeting.

Rebecca leant forward to give her a quick peck on the cheek. 'There's something I need to discuss with you before Sol's parents arrive.'

'O-kay. Come in.' She gave her dad a hug as she ushered them in from the communal landing. 'Sol's in the shower—he went for his run later than usual this morning 'cos we were out late with Nik and Josie.'

Her parents both spoke at the same time.

'Josie's the girl you're borrowing your mother's dress from, isn't she?'

'You and Solomon are seeing Josie and her husband socially?'

'Yes, she's so great. Not only have I found a dress but a new friend.' Paige smiled, thinking about last night. After Nik had kicked all their butts at the bowling alley, they'd gone back to Josie and Nik's place and watched *Top Gun*. Josie and Nik—horrified that Paige had never seen it and many other 'classics'—had vowed to take it upon themselves to educate her one film at a time. 'Sol and Nik get along really well and I feel like I've known Josie forever.'

At that moment, Solomon appeared down the hallway, his hair wet from his shower. 'Thought I heard voices.' He shook hands with Hugh and leaned in to kiss his future mother-in-law on the cheek. 'How are you feeling today?'

'I'm fine.' Her tone was terse and Paige tried to swallow her irritation—Sol was only being polite but her mum hated any reference to her illness. So far she'd refused to discuss his offer of his kidney any further and snapped at anyone who dared to ask how her dialysis was going.

'Mum wants to talk to me about something,' Paige informed him.

'Intriguing.' He wiggled his eyebrows. 'Shall I put the kettle on?'

Rebecca glanced at her watch. 'Actually, I want to talk to both of you. This involves Solomon and I'd like to get it off my chest.'

'Okay.' Sol nodded.

'What it is?' Paige asked, her heart leaping into her throat as she thought of all the terrible things her mum might be about to announce. Maybe the kidney failure wasn't the worst? Maybe she had cancer as well?

'Solomon, if the offer for you to be my kidney donor and go on the paired kidney exchange program still stands,' she said, 'then I'd like to accept it.'

'Oh my God,' Paige shrieked.

'Of course it still stands,' Sol said, grinning. 'Where do I sign up?'

Her parents laughed, then Rebecca said, 'We'll have to make an appointment with Dr Chopra. You'll need to be tested and evaluated to make sure you are physically able to donate and then,

254

if so, they'll put us on the register. The earliest they'll operate is January, so they'll be looking for a pairing match that also works out timing wise.'

'Oh, this is so wonderful.' Paige threw her arms around her mother and didn't even bother trying to fight the happy tears that streamed down her face. 'What made you decide to accept?'

Rebecca hesitated a moment, then, 'The opportunity of getting off dialysis as soon as possible is too good a chance to pass up. I still feel terrible about taking Sol's kidney but if the doctors deem him healthy and they haven't any concerns then ...'

'They won't,' Paige declared, turning from her mother to embrace Sol. She really had the best family in the world and this would only consolidate their bond.

More hugs were exchanged and then her father sniffed. 'Is something burning?'

'Oh shit, the veggies!' But Paige couldn't bring herself to care, she felt like such a weight had been lifted.

As Paige, Sol and her mother were trying to salvage the roast potatoes—the pumpkin was ruined—the intercom buzzed again and her dad went to let Sol's mum and stepdad in. She heard them laughing and talking as they walked towards the kitchen.

'I hope you like your veggies smoky,' Paige said as she kissed her future in-laws in greeting. 'We got a little distracted.'

'Wedding talk?' asked Lisette with a wide grin.

'Not yet. We saved that for you,' Sol said. 'Rebecca has just accepted my offer to be her kidney donor.'

'Oh, wow.' Lisette's eyes teared up; she threw her arms wide and looked between Rebecca and Solomon as if she wanted to hug someone but wasn't sure who. 'That's wonderful news. We're so proud of you, son.'

Randy nodded and clapped Sol on the shoulder. 'Good man.'

'Your son is very special,' said Rebecca.

Hugh nodded. 'We can't thank him enough for giving Rebecca this life-line.'

'Well, we're family now,' Lisette said, 'and family take care of each other.' She and Sol exchanged a look that contained all the years the two of them had been a team, running from his father.

'Shall we eat?' Sol asked, not at all comfortable being the centre of all this praise. He didn't understand why everyone was making such a big deal. If a stranger came up to him in the street and asked for his kidney, he'd probably hand it over on the spot. Just as he gave no thought to his own safety when rushing into a burning building.

Just one of the many reasons Paige loved him.

'Good idea,' she said, silently vowing to show her appreciation later.

When everyone was crowded round the small table, pretending the food piled on their plates was more edible than it looked, Paige got down to business.

Clearing her throat, she picked up her pen and opened her wedding notebook—at the top of each double page spread was the title of something that needed to be decided. Catering. Celebrant. Invitations. Music. Band. Flowers. Decoration. Photographer. Cake. Transport. Bridesmaid dresses. Suit hire. And, last but not least, the guest list. Many of these things she didn't need their assistance with, but she wanted everyone to feel involved.

'That's a good idea.' There was a note of respect in Rebecca's voice as she nodded towards the notebook. 'You're so much more organised than me.'

'This was actually Josie's suggestion. She kept something similar for her wedding and said it helped having everything in one place.'

Her mother frowned.

'Is Josie a friend of yours?' Randy asked.

'She's the girl who wore Rebecca's wedding dress,' Lisette said. 'Remember, I told you this. Paige is going to wear it as well and Josie is letting her borrow it.'

'Ah that's right.' Randy nodded and went back to trying to chisel his lamb.

'She's been a godsend,' Paige said. 'She and Nik had a short engagement as well, so she's given me all sorts of tips to organise things quickly.'

'How long have she and her husband been married?' Rebecca asked, putting her cutlery on her plate as if she couldn't be bothered with the pretence of eating anymore.

'I'm not sure exactly. Can't be longer than two years because that's when the second dress owner gave it to the op shop,' Paige said. 'Anyway, first things first. As you know we want to keep to a strict budget, but we also want the day to be a very special celebration of our love. Having the reception at your place,' she smiled at Sol's parents, 'will keep costs down, but we also want to limit the guest list to just close friends and family, so we don't need to hire too many extra tables and chairs.'

'Are you hoping to have a sit-down meal or something more like a buffet?' asked Lisette. 'I have a friend who has just started a catering company and she's keen to get business, so will do us a good deal.'

'We were thinking more finger food,' Sol replied, looking to Paige for clarification. She nodded. 'Like cocktails and canapés. We want a really fun, casual vibe and that will fit better than a formal sit-down.'

'Do you think your friend will be willing to make food to fit our theme?' Paige asked.

'What theme?' asked both mums in unison.

This was the moment Paige had been waiting for. Her mum was gonna love it. 'Well, since I'm going to be wearing your dress, which was made in the eighties, and since Sol was born in the eighties, we've decided to embrace that era. We're gonna hire a jukebox with eighties hits and have a black and neon colour scheme. The bridesmaids will wear neon green, neon pink and neon purple, the groomsmen will have ties in the same colours and we're hoping to have three cocktails to match.'

'Sounds like fun,' Hugh said. 'If we can't find your mother on the night, all we'll need to do is head to the jukebox. Although you might need to ration her so everyone else gets a chance to pick a tune.'

'Hardi-hah.' Rebecca gave him a look.

Sol chuckled. 'Don't worry, I think Josie will give her a run for her money. That woman has an eighties obsession to rival Rebecca's.'

Everyone laughed, except her mother. 'You're inviting Josie? But you guys only just met.'

'So?' Paige retorted. 'We like them. Plus, she's letting us borrow the dress.'

'Fair enough.' Rebecca shrugged, although her tone sounded like that of a child who hadn't got their own way.

Trying not to let her mother's weird mood get her down, Paige moved to the next item on the list. For the next half an hour, they discussed how they planned to tie in the theme in other areas and came up with a timeline of what needed to be organised and a list of who was in charge of doing what.

'Before we get onto the guest list, I have one more question,' Paige said. 'We've talked a lot about the kind of wedding we want, but is there anything any of you would like us to include?'

'What do you mean?' asked Hugh.

Sol chuckled. 'What Paige is trying to say is would you guys like any nods to your family heritages, either during the ceremony or at the reception? Anything Scottish or French?' he added as he looked from Hugh to Lisette.

'I suppose you could wear the family kilt, but I didn't even do that when I got married.'

'It's your day, do what you want,' said Lisette, 'but it's very sweet of you to consider us.'

'Actually it was Josie's idea,' Paige admitted. 'Until she asked where Sol came from, the thought hadn't entered either of our heads.'

'I can't wait to meet this Josie,' Lisette said, taking a sip of her drink.

Before Paige could say Josie had offered to help them make the invitations, so the two of them would meet soon, Rebecca pushed back her chair, the wooden legs shrieking against the tiled floor. Everyone glanced up at her.

'You okay, love?' Hugh asked, concern furrowing his brow as he too made a move to stand.

'I'm fine.' She waved her hand at him, picked up her plate and then dived for the empty veggie casserole dish. 'Just thought I'd start clearing up a little. Keep chatting. I'll listen while I wash.'

'You don't need to do that,' Sol said. 'We've got a dishwasher; it won't take long to tidy up after and you certainly don't have to help.'

Her mother sighed, her body language like that of a caged bird who'd just missed an opportunity to escape. What was her problem? She'd been so excited about the wedding when Sol first proposed and now it seemed she'd rather do anything except discuss it.

Later, when the dishwasher was packed and everyone was moving into the living room for a post-lunch coffee, Paige cornered her.

'What's going on?'

Rebecca blinked. 'What do you mean?'

'You're acting strange. And I get the impression you've got something against Josie. Didn't you like her when you met her the other day?'

259

'Don't be ridiculous. Why wouldn't I like her? I hardly know her, but neither do you—that's my point—I just think it's a little odd that you're so chummy all of a sudden.'

'I know enough,' Paige responded, feeling defensive. Even when she was a little girl, her mother had never interfered in her friendships. 'I know she's funny, and clever, and kind—three traits I thought *you* also admired in a person.'

'How old is she? She seems a bit older than you.'

'In her early to mid-thirties I think.'

'You think?! But you don't know?'

'No, our specific ages haven't cropped up in conversation. I know she's trying for a family and is worried about her biological clock, but ...' Paige shook her head—this was one of the weirdest conversations she'd ever had with her mother, perhaps with anyone. 'Who cares how old she is? Why does her *age* matter? We're both adults.'

Rebecca's expression softened a moment. 'Josie's having difficulty getting pregnant?'

'Getting pregnant hasn't been the issue,' Paige said, 'but she keeps miscarrying.' She felt slightly bad about sharing such a private thing with her mother, but hoped this knowledge might make her sympathise with her friend.

'That's terrible,' Rebecca whispered. 'Hopefully she has a good family support system.'

'Yes, well, she's getting support from a local charity that deals with miscarriages and stuff. That's helping her.' Paige picked up a box of chocolates that she was going to take into the lounge room to go with the coffee.

'That sounds good, but what about her parents? Do they live nearby?'

'Why are you so interested in Josie?'

'First you accuse me of not liking her and now I'm concerned about her, you're annoyed at *that*. I can't win!' With that she threw her hands up in the air and stormed off to join the others in the lounge room.

Paige looked at the box of chocolates in her hand and wished it was a bottle of wine instead. She had no idea what had got into her mother, but decided to check Google again later and see if one of the symptoms of kidney disease was irrational behaviour and mood swings.

*Rebecca*

'Don't take my baby.'

Physically wrung out from the horror of giving birth—it had been way more painful than she'd ever imagined possible—Rebecca tries to sit up in the bed as she calls to the nurse holding her newborn.

'Can I hold him?'

'It'll be easier for you if you don't. He's healthy. Now rest.'

'I want to see him! You can't stop me seeing him!'

'Calm yourself, Rebecca. He's not your child.'

But, not caring what her mother or the old matron-like nurse thinks, digging deep to find some leftover inner strength, she hurls back the thin cotton sheet, uncaring of the blood dripping from her as she hurls herself at the nurse.

'Give him to me. Let me see him.'

Reluctantly, the nurse turns and, although still gripping the tiny baby, she slowly angles him so that Rebecca can see. Her heart gasps, she feels like she might faint as she stares down at the beauty and *simple perfection of this tiny human. I made him. Pride soars within her. She feels a sense of satisfaction, of cleverness.*

*But, as she reaches out to stroke her finger over its soft, milky skin, its face changes. The nurse is still holding a baby's body but there is an adult face attached. She shrinks back and screams.*

*Looking up at her is Josie.*

'Rebecca?' Hugh's concerned voice jolted her from her sleep and she opened her eyes to see her husband sitting up, looking down at her, his body a silhouette in the light of the bedside lamp. 'Are you okay? Can I get you a drink?'

'I'm …' Her heart still racing, she took a breath. 'I'm fine, I just had a nightmare.'

'Want to talk about it?' he asked, his brow unfurrowing as he reached out to stroke his thumb over her cheek. 'Geez, you're hot. You're burning up. I'm going to get you a glass of water and a cold flannel.'

As he hurried off, Rebecca closed her eyes again and forced deep breaths in and out of her lungs. This was getting out of hand. Night after night that same disturbing scene played over and over in her head. The dream itself wasn't exactly new—over the past thirty-five years she'd often dreamt of that awful day—but its frequency had increased over the past week and tonight the finale had changed.

Tonight, the suspicion plaguing her since Paige had summoned her to see the wedding dress had finally infiltrated her slumber and she'd woken in a cold sweat.

*Josie is a girl. My baby was a boy.*

This had become a mantra the past few days and she said it to herself again now. There was no possible way that Josie was her baby.

*Unless they lied.*

Her whole body turned to ice. No, the notion seemed preposterous—what reason could her parents possibly have had to lie about the sex of her baby all these years? But maybe there'd been some kind of mix-up.

Before Rebecca could think this possibility through, Hugh returned to the room, carrying a glass of water and a carefully folded damp flannel. He perched on the edge of the bed and offered her the drink. Although it was cold, it didn't quench the thirst deep within her. It didn't make her feel any better and neither did the cold cloth when he gently laid it on her forehead.

He appeared to have forgotten about her nightmare and was more concerned about her health. 'You've got a dialysis appointment tomorrow afternoon, don't you? Maybe you should see if Dr Chopra is available and have a chat about how you're feeling. Or do you think we should go get you checked out now?'

It was three o'clock in the morning and she was pretty certain any doctor would discover her to be physically fine, well, aside from her increased heart-rate and the condition they already knew about.

'No.' She put the cloth on the bedside table and forced a smile for her husband. 'Come back to bed. I'm okay.'

Hugh took a moment to acquiesce. 'Okay, but if you're still not feeling great in the morning, I'll take the day off and drive you to dialysis.'

Then he switched off the lamp and climbed in beside her. As he held her close, Rebecca lay there wondering if it was time to confide in him. Keeping it all cooped up inside was driving her insane. But what would she say?

*Hey darling, I know I haven't mentioned this before, but a long time ago, before we met, I had a baby. All these years I've thought I had a son, but now I think maybe I actually had a girl.*

What part of that statement would he hear first? Would he be angry? Hugh had always been such a rational, reasonable person and it wasn't like she'd had an affair or anything. All this had happened thirty-five years ago; he might be shocked, maybe a little hurt she'd kept a secret, but he would recover quickly and then he'd be able to tell her what the hell to do.

'Hugh?' she finally whispered in the dark.

'Mmm.' He already sounded half asleep again.

'If I tell you something big ... will you promise not to get angry with me?'

In reply, he loosened his grip on her and switched on the bedside light. 'What is it?'

Rebecca blinked as her eyes adjusted to the light; she noticed he didn't make any promises. Nausea filled her gut and her mouth went dry.

'What's wrong?' A slight panic crept into his usually calm voice. 'What have you done?'

'I had another baby once.' Just that one statement had tears rushing to her eyes; she wasn't sure she'd even be able to get the rest out.

Hugh shook his head slightly as if perhaps this was a dream. 'I'm sorry.' He cleared his throat. 'Did you say you have another child? Apart from Paige?' She could almost see the cogs ticking in his brain as he tried to grapple with this news. 'How? Before me?'

She managed a nod.

'But you were practically a child when we met. Your parents joked you didn't even have a proper boyfriend before me. I thought you were a virgin!'

'They lied.' About that and who knew what else. And, she herself had never actually told him she was a virgin, but she'd never

265

corrected his assumptions either. Probably not the time to get hung up on semantics.

Hugh slumped back against the headboard and ran his hand through his hair. 'This is a hell of a conversation for three o'clock in the morning.'

'I'm sorry,' she said simply. She'd had over thirty years to come clean—all that time she'd been searching for the right moment and now she could see there was never a perfect moment for confessions like these. How had she ever thought burying it was a good idea? In that moment she hated her parents for making her think it was.

'I guess you better start talking,' he said eventually, his tone chillingly cold. 'Who was the father? What happened to the baby? Was it a boy or a girl?'

'I can answer the first two questions, but the third one is giving me the nightmares.'

'Stop talking in riddles,' Hugh snapped. 'What happened?'

And so she told him.

'I was fifteen when I got pregnant to my high school boyfriend—he was seventeen. We were terrified when we found out but he said he'd stand by me, that he'd support me and the baby, and we'd get married as soon as we were old enough. My parents were horrified—they worried what their church friends would say and Dad thought it looked bad that the sergeant couldn't stop his own daughter from making such stupid mistakes. Robbie and I told them we were in love, but then Robbie got cold feet. He changed his mind and said he didn't want to have anything to do with me or the baby anymore.'

She swallowed—remembering just how painful that declaration had been.

'Without his help, what choice did I have? Mum and I went to stay with an old school friend of hers who had moved to Perth—she told everyone we were going to look after a sick relative. I had the baby there and then gave it up. By the time we returned to New South Wales, Dad had been transferred back to the city from Cobar and Anthony was already at high school in Sydney. Mum and Dad told me to move on as well, to forget about Robbie and remember that the baby was in a better place.'

'And just like that, you forgot?'

'No, of course not.' She sniffed, hurt by the derision in his voice. 'Giving up a child is something you never forget. Giving birth to Paige made it all so real again—the depression I had then was as much about losing my first baby as it was about her or new motherhood.'

'Perhaps you could have told me back then? Maybe I'd have understood better how you were feeling.' Before she could reply, he added, 'So why now? Why at three in the morning do you decide to tell me all this? Is it because you're sick?'

'No. That's not the r—'

'This child of yours,' he interrupted, sitting up straight as if a light bulb had gone off inside his head, 'They might be a kidney match.'

She swallowed, suddenly remembering why she hadn't wanted to say anything until she was well again.

'That's not why,' she said. 'There's no way I would find my child only to ask them for a kidney. That would feel worse than asking a stranger in the street. But being sick brought it all back. It's like they say, when you die your life flashes before your eyes, you think about regrets ... you start to wonder if you should have made different choices. I couldn't stop thinking about him and—'

'And that's why you're telling me? Because you've decided you want to start searching?'

She flinched at the anger in his voice, but shook her head. 'No. I'm telling you because I think I've already found her.'

'Her?' Hugh screwed up his whole face. 'Didn't you just say *him* a second ago? What did you have—a boy or a girl?'

'I thought I had a boy, that's what I was told—that's what I believed—but I never got close, I never held him. All I had was a photo, and then a week ago, when I went to Josie's house with Paige—I saw another photo that looked almost the same as mine. I thought maybe it was her husband, but no, it was a baby photo of Josie and I know it sounds crazy, but she'd be around the same age my child would be, and she looks a little like me. She and Nik got married in Perth so perhaps she was born there, and I recently read about genetic sexual attraction. She and Paige hit it off instantly.'

'Are you saying Paige has a romantic interest in Josie?' His disbelief came through loud and clear.

'No, but they've got some sort of connection and ...' She sighed. 'I just can't get it out of my head that somehow Josie is my child.'

Rebecca wanted Hugh to tell her that she was being crazy—that there was no way Josie was hers. She wanted him to wrap his arms around her and tell her it was okay, that this wasn't going to come between them and he'd help her sort it out. But instead, he turned, threw back the covers, climbed out of bed and stalked from the room.

She sat frozen, wondering if she should go after him as she cringed at the sound of him banging around in the kitchen. When she heard the kettle boiling, she decided to be brave and go out and join him.

Hugh was standing at the bench, stirring a spoon in his mug. 'What are you planning to do now?' he asked, not turning around to look at her or offer to make her a drink.

'I've sent away for information about the adoption, but it might still be a few weeks before I get it.' She didn't mention that she'd phoned the Western Australian organisation responsible for adoption information twice this week to ask, and then beg, if there was any way they could speed up her application. The answer had been no. 'I guess then I'll know for sure.'

'And then what will you do? Do you plan on confronting your child?'

That was a question Rebecca wasn't able to answer. 'I'm not sure. I guess it depends on what the information tells me. If Josie is my daughter—and Paige has become such good friends with her—it's going to be hard to ignore that.'

'What a mess.' Hugh exhaled loudly, put down his mug and buried his face in his hands. Was he crying? Part of Rebecca felt like a weight had been lifted now she'd told him, but by lightening her load she'd complicated his life.

'I'm sorry.' She crossed over to him and put her hand on his shoulder.

He didn't say anything for a long time and he didn't turn to her and hug her like she wanted him to do. 'You know, you could just ask your parents,' he said eventually. 'I think it's highly unlikely that Josie is your daughter. What you've said sounds pretty far-fetched, but at least if you confront them you'll know whether your suspicions have any substance.'

Why hadn't she thought of that before? Probably because until this latest dream, the thought of them lying had never entered her head. She glanced at the time on the microwave clock. Still too early to pay her folks a visit.

'Good idea. I'll do it today. Will you come with me?' Rebecca could face anything if she had Hugh beside her.

'I can't. I've got too much on.'

Those seven words spoke volumes. Rebecca bit her lip, refraining from mentioning that less than an hour ago he'd told her he could take the day off and go with her to dialysis. 'Are you mad at me?'

Slowly, he turned to look at her. 'I'm fucking furious,' he said coldly and then retreated to their bedroom.

Rebecca didn't go back to bed. She made herself a cup of tea, then pulled out her laptop and spent the next few hours searching for information. She'd been too scared to try this before in case somehow Hugh saw her search history, but now everything was out in the open, it didn't matter. Perhaps she could find something about Josie that would set her mind at ease, prove her fears were ridiculous, and then she wouldn't have to confront her parents.

She'd had to stop herself outright asking Paige if she knew if Josie was adopted or what her birthday was. Her daughter already thought she was acting weird—such questions would be a dead giveaway and there was no guarantee Paige had that kind of intel anyway. However much she professed to like Josie, she couldn't know her very well after only a couple of weeks.

But, just like herself, Josie didn't seem to have a digital footprint. She wasn't on Facebook—Rebecca used Hugh's account to check—and when she googled Josie's married name, all she got was something on a school website about a theatre production. It was so damn infuriating, she had to stop herself throwing the laptop against the wall. Josie's husband was on Facebook but he mostly posted photos of planes and the odd bowling score sheet. There was the occasional smiling photo of him and Josie, but of course she wasn't tagged.

When Hugh came into the kitchen just after six am, she still hadn't found anything useful. She offered him a tentative smile, but he refused to meet her gaze as he made himself a coffee. She'd hoped a few hours of sleep would have cooled his fury and that maybe he'd have changed his mind about coming to her parents' place, but judging by the scowl on his face, he hadn't had much sleep or cooled any.

He drank his coffee in silence and went to work earlier than he usually would.

'Have a good day,' she called as he headed down the hallway, but he didn't even respond.

She snapped the laptop shut and glanced at the clock. By the time she had a shower, threw on some clothes and drove all the way to her parents' house in Castle Hill, it wouldn't be too early to visit.

Sweat was pouring off her skin as she parked on their driveway and she was barely managing to control her breathing. Every sensible bone in her body told her she was overreacting—Hugh had said as much. Her parents would probably laugh out loud at her question about whether she'd had a girl, but then at least it would alleviate her fixation with Josie. And, until she knew for sure she wouldn't be able to shut down the adrenaline charging through her body.

Despite the early hour, the back door would be unlocked—you'd think her father's job as a cop would have taught him to be more security conscious, but he'd always thought himself invincible. Usually Rebecca would just let herself in, but since she rarely visited her folks without at least a phone call first—they weren't what you'd call close—she chose to ring the doorbell. When no one came to the door within a minute she rang it again.

'What are you doing here at this hour?' her mother asked by way of a greeting the moment she opened the front door.

Rebecca wasn't in the mood for small talk anyway. 'I've come to ask you a question. Where's Dad?'

'He's still in bed. His angina was playing up overnight, but these days we have no reason to hurry up anyway. I'm going to call the doctor and see if I can get him an appointment later.'

Rebecca didn't have the headspace to worry about her father's heart problems right now, but perhaps this was fortuitous. Her mother had less practice at deflecting uncomfortable conversations.

'Is something the matter? You look terrible. Have you missed a dialysis session? Let me get you a cup of tea.' Her mum reached out to touch her elbow but Rebecca shook her off.

'Did I have a daughter?'

Jeanie blinked and, in the second she hesitated before answering, Rebecca saw panic flash across her face. 'What are you talking about? Of course you have a daughter. Paige is the light of all our lives.'

'I'm not talking about Paige,' Rebecca said, her voice rising. 'The child you made me adopt out. Was *it* a girl or a boy?'

'Why are you bringing this up after all these years?' Jeanie's voice was hushed and she looked over her shoulder as if worried her husband might wake. 'You know the adoption was for the best. You were only a child yourself.'

'Oh my God.' Rebecca staggered back and hit her hip against the hallway table. A vase of flowers fell off and crashed against the floor—she barely noticed the noise or the pain. Her mother was a terrible liar. Or so she'd thought. 'Why can't you just answer the damn question? Tell me the truth? Did I have a boy or a girl?'

Hugging her arms against her chest, Jeanie started to sob. 'We only did what we thought was best—no one wants their teenage daughter to have a baby, everything we did was to protect you.'

'Just! Answer! The damn! Question!'

Her father appeared in the doorway. 'What the hell is going on?' The scowl on his face told Rebecca he was annoyed to have been woken from his slumber. Well, too damn bad. His wrath had nothing on hers.

'Mum's just told me that all these years I thought I had given away a son, but I actually have another daughter.'

Her mum looked as if Rebecca had slapped her across the face.

'What?' Her father's fists bunched and the ugly veins in his neck visibly did the same.

'I said no such thing,' Jeanie rushed, her tone fearful. She'd always been under her husband's thumb.

'But it's true, isn't it, Dad?'

The expression on his face told her everything.

'Stop lying to me. Surely after thirty-five years you owe me the truth. Do I have a daughter?'

Her parents nodded simultaneously, but only her mother's expression showed the slightest remorse. So, Rebecca hadn't been going crazy. Her relief was short-lived.

'*Why?* Why lie?!'

'It was your mother's idea. It was already done by the time she told me, but it impressed me.'

And this surprised her almost as much as the shocking truth. 'What?' She looked to her mum.

'Whenever you mentioned the baby, you called it a girl,' Jeannie admitted and Rebecca remembered the intense gut feeling she'd had at the time. 'I thought because in your head the baby was a girl, you'd be in less pain about giving it up if you thought it was a boy. I was only trying to make things easier for you.'

'Less pain? Easier?' Rebecca was torn between laughing and crying and grabbing hold of her mother and shaking her silly. 'There is nothing but pain when you give up a child. I've spent decades nursing that pain and it would have been the same no matter what the sex of the baby.'

'What's brought all this up now?' her father asked, his voice still irritatingly calm. 'Is it to do with your disease? Your need for a familial donor?'

'It's got nothing to do with that.' She didn't owe them any kind of explanation and Rebecca couldn't bear to look at either of them a second longer.

As she turned and stormed out of the house, her mother still whimpering, her father called out, 'Don't do anything stupid. Remember what's at stake?'

She resisted the urge to spin on her heel and scream at him. *What?* What was he referring to? Her marriage? Her relationship with

Paige? Or was he still worried about the shame this revelation could bring on him, on them? Even after all these years, did he still care about what people would think about his slutty daughter? In 1983, the world was becoming more accepting of sex before marriage and single mums. But her parents and the church they'd belonged to were not.

A few moments later she slammed her car door and sat there in silence, trying to digest what she'd just been told.

Somewhere out there she had another daughter.

Was it possible Josie was that child?

Yes, even without the confirmation from the adoption certificate, even without a DNA test, she knew. In her heart, she'd always known she'd recognise her child if she ever met them, and even before she'd entered Josie's house, she'd had a gut feeling her world was about to change. The question was, what the hell should she do with this information?

*Hugh*. Hugh would have the answer.

Instinctively, she reached into her handbag for her phone, desperate to tell him her suspicions were true, but she stopped herself before pressing 'call'. A tear snuck down her cheek as she recalled his coldness of a couple of hours ago. He'd made it very clear this was her problem. She may have found a daughter but had she lost her husband in the process? She'd never felt more alone in her life.

Registering movement in her periphery, Rebecca glanced up to see her mum heading towards her. Although she needed to talk to someone, she didn't trust herself to let either of her parents be that person, so she put her car into reverse and sped out of the driveway before her mother could get close.

## Clara

Clara was staring at her bulging suitcase wondering whether she'd packed too much for a four-day cruise when a loud banging sounded on the front door.

'Who on earth could that be?'

Gregg had left ten minutes ago to take Shadow to his sister's place and was then going to swing by his house and 'throw a few things into a bag' before coming back to collect her. It was probably one of her sisters come to bid her farewell and offer some unsolicited advice about how to behave on your first trip away with a lover. She rolled her eyes and started for the door.

However, as she got closer, a horrific thought struck: *What if it's Rob?*

This possibility actually made her a little sick. He'd been missing for over a month now and she'd let herself believe he was gone for good. Life was so much less stressful without his drunken messages and phone calls. Her heart pounding, she stopped at the door and stared into the peephole.

The panic whooshed out of her lungs at the sight of a woman standing there. Maybe the new neighbour? Immediately recognising distress on the woman's face, she yanked open the door.

'Are you okay?' she asked, the rescue instincts her sisters teased her about kicking in.

'I'm looking for … Robbie.' But as the woman spoke, recognition flashed in her face. 'Clara?'

It took a few seconds for Clara to click that the woman was a past patient—of course she couldn't remember her name—and then another few seconds to click what she'd said. What did this woman have to do with Rob?

'I'm … I'm not sure I have the right address.' The visitor fiddled with her car keys as she nodded towards the road. 'I found the address for my friend in an old White Pages and it said he lived here. Maybe I should go?'

A ball of dread formed in Clara's stomach. 'What did you say his name was?'

'Robbie. Robert Jones. We were in high school together. Are you his wife?'

'*Ex*-wife.'

'Oh.' The woman looked torn between relief and disappointment. 'Do you have his new address?'

Again Clara didn't know what to say. She didn't want to set this woman on Brenda but neither did she know how much to tell her. 'I looked after you in hospital recently, didn't I?' she asked, buying time.

'Yes, thank you. You were very kind. One of my favourite nurses.'

But that compliment didn't bring the glow it usually would. A suspicion crept into her heart. 'Did you say you and Rob were in high school together?'

'Yes. Do you know where he lives now?' the woman asked again.

*Rebecca*—that was her name. And also the name of Rob's first serious girlfriend!

*Oh my.* Clara grabbed hold of the doorjamb as her suspicions compounded. Even in middle age, this woman looked exactly like Rob's type, much more than Clara ever had. She wore leggings with a long, flowy, tie-dyed tunic and a faded-denim jacket over the top and had a pink streak in her slightly messy, shoulder-length, brown hair. She had to be his high school sweetheart, his first love and the mother of his baby.

A million questions sprouted in her mind. She went with the most pertinent. 'Why are you looking for him?'

'Um.' Rebecca bit her lip as if unsure or unwilling to reveal all.

'Is it about the baby?'

She blinked, but her expression told all.

Clara sighed; part of her wanted to say she had no idea where *Robbie* was and send this stranger packing, but ... All her married life this baby had stood between them. Knowing she'd probably regret this offer, she found herself saying, 'You'd better come inside.'

'Thank you.'

Because Clara had been brought up well, she made them both a cup of tea and offered her guest a seat at the table.

'How much do you know?' Rebecca asked, her fingers gripping around her mug so tightly her knuckles were blue and white.

'I know when Rob was seventeen he got his girlfriend pregnant. I'm guessing you were that girlfriend.'

Rebecca nodded confirmation.

'I know he wanted to make a go of things but wasn't given a choice. I know his baby was given up for adoption against his will and that he never got over it.'

Fury flashed in the woman's eyes. '*That's* his story?'

'It's the truth,' Clara told her, knowing this with absolute certainty, feeling defensive on behalf of her ex. 'Rob may be a lot of things, but he's not a liar. You, however, might not know the whole story. Your father threatened him—he told him if he didn't break up with you, Rob could be charged with sleeping with a minor.'

Rebecca gasped and her tea spilt a little as her hand rushed to cover her mouth. Clara couldn't bring herself to feel much sympathy. This woman had actually done what Clara had never been able to do and birthed him a living, breathing child. Even though Rebecca was as much a victim as Rob in all of this, she found herself harbouring homicidal thoughts towards her.

'Why are you here now?' she asked, her grip tightening on her own mug. 'Have you decided to look for your son?'

Sniffing, as if trying to hold back tears, Rebecca said, 'I should probably be talking to Rob about this.'

Clara snorted—it was kind of a laugh even though she saw nothing funny in this situation. 'Good luck with that. No one has seen him for over a month. He's registered as a missing person.'

'What?'

'Thanks to your father, Rob is a drunk!' Although she knew this was a cruel thing to say, Clara couldn't hold back. All the anger and frustration she'd felt towards her ex-husband, she unleashed on the other woman. 'He never got over losing his son, the guilt and grief he carried with him ruined our marriage and him. For all I know he's finally done what he's been threatening to do for years or even accidentally done himself in. Even if I wanted to, I couldn't tell you where he is.'

'Oh my God.' Rebecca reached into her bag for a tissue. 'I knew my father was a hard man, but I never knew he was such a monster. However, after what I've learnt this morning, nothing surprises me about my parents. All these years, I thought Robbie didn't care. He came to see me once, almost twenty years ago now and—'

'He came to see you?' *That* was news to Clara. She'd always supported him in his desire to look for his son, but aside from the groups she'd encouraged him to post messages in, as far as she knew all *he'd* done was lament. He'd never mentioned making contact with Rebecca. The fact he hadn't confided in her was another stab to the heart.

'He was off his face. He wasn't making much sense but said he wanted to find our baby. I couldn't set someone in such a mess on our child. I made him go away, but promised to tell him if they ever came looking.'

Clara's chest tingled. She put her hand there to steady her heart. 'And has he? Made contact?'

'*She*,' Rebecca whispered. 'We had a girl. The boy was a lie my parents concocted to throw me off the path or something.'

Clara's head spun; this was too much to digest. 'How could you have not known the sex of your baby?'

'I wasn't allowed to hold him. There was a sheet up so I couldn't see the delivery. They took him, *her*, and wrapped her in a blanket. The midwife only let me see her from a distance.'

Clara glanced at the clock wondering if it was too early for a stronger drink. 'So has *she* made contact?'

'No. But I think I've met her.'

Despite not wanting to get involved, Clara couldn't help being curious. Rob's child had lingered in her life like an unsolved mystery for years—could she finally be about to hear the missing clue?

'Well?' she prompted. 'Are you going to tell me?'

Rebecca deliberated a moment but years of nursing people through hard times and her volunteer work had made Clara an expert in reading other people's expressions; she *wanted* to talk. 'It's a complicated story.'

Clara resisted the urge to tap her foot—normally she was a good listener but she didn't have all day. 'I'm all ears.'

'A couple of months ago, Paige, my daughter, got engaged.'

'Congratulations,' Clara said automatically.

Rebecca almost smiled. 'Thanks. Anyway, Paige decided she wanted to wear my wedding dress, but I gave it away to charity years ago. When Paige wants something she doesn't stop until she gets it. She tracked down the second owner of the dress, but she got divorced a couple of years ago and gave her dress to an op shop. Paige and her friend searched high and low, but—'

Clara was getting impatient. 'What's this dress have to do with Rob's baby?'

'She wore it next.' This declaration wasn't much more than a whisper. 'When Paige couldn't find the dress, she put a call out on Facebook. These days it seems social media is the answer to all life's problems,' Rebecca mused, but Clara wasn't in the mood for such observations.

'And?' she prodded.

'Oh.' Rebecca shook her head slightly. 'She found the dress—a woman called Josie got married in it not too long ago. Her husband bought it from the op shop. Josie's obsessed with the eighties so he knew she'd love it.'

But Clara didn't hear the last bit. Something deep in her subconscious twanged. She thought of the Josie she knew—her flamboyant dress style and the passion for eighties movies she'd confessed to Brenda—and then sucked in a breath as she thought of their conversation the day they'd run into each other in the supermarket. Distracted with thoughts of Brenda, Clara hadn't been listening properly when Josie mentioned she'd met a new friend through a wedding dress.

Her chest tightened. Could she have taken this girl unwittingly to Brenda's house? Encouraged them to meet, to talk. Her breathing grew difficult. Was it possible she'd sat opposite Rob's child so many times and not known?

No, Clara didn't want to believe it, but this—this could not be a coincidence.

'I think I know her.'

'You do?' Rebecca blinked. 'How?'

Clara swallowed, not wanting to break Josie's confidence. 'We met through an organisation I volunteer with. I've been helping her deal with … some things.'

'Her miscarriages?'

Cold filled Clara's lungs. That confirmed it—they were talking about the same woman. 'You know about them?'

'Yes. My daughter, Paige, and Josie have become friends and Paige mentioned them. Poor girl.'

'So, Josie wore the dress next and you think she's …' Clara couldn't really wrap her head around what Rebecca was trying to say.

'Yes. I think she's my and Robbie's baby.'

And then she went on to explain it all—how she'd gone to Josie's place to see the dress and seen a photo of a baby that looked exactly like the one she'd given up.

'All newborn babies look similar. Maybe you were mistaken?'

'I know, and at first I thought I was going crazy, but I swear the photos are the same and I also saw a photo of Josie in her wedding dress …' She paused a moment. 'It could have been me. I haven't been able to stop thinking about it since. Finally, I confronted my parents this morning and that's when they admitted I did in fact have a girl. So I have to wonder if I'm right about Josie. Surely a mother would know these things?'

Before Clara could say she wouldn't know, Rebecca added, 'Of course, I could be wrong. It's all just a hunch at this stage, but before I saw the photo, I'd already requested the information, so within a couple of weeks, I'll know for certain.'

Clara tried to think back through her interactions with Josie—had she ever said anything about being adopted?

Even though this whole thing sounded far-fetched, Clara couldn't shake the feeling that Rebecca was onto something. Not only did she look like Rob's type but her eyes, her ridiculously long dark lashes, her bow-shaped mouth and the way her nose twitched when she was upset were all uncannily similar to Josie. They had different chins though.

*Josie has Rob's chin.*

The thought almost knocked her off her chair. How had she never noticed it before? Apparently Rob's father had also had a prominent sticky-out chin and Brenda always said it was the first thing she and her husband had noticed when Rob was born.

But of course, Clara had never been looking for such similarities.

Oh Lord, if this was true, how was she going to act normal around Josie again knowing what she did? And ... *Josie and Brenda.* She'd introduced them herself. Clara's morning muesli churned in her stomach. Talk about timing—for thirty-five years all Rob could think about was one day finding and meeting his child. Now it looked like she'd walked right into Clara's life but where on earth was he?

Until now, she'd not hassled the police to ask what they were doing or even thought about ways she could track him down herself, but she couldn't help wondering if this information would save him. It was too late for them—she didn't want him back—but would there be a sense of satisfaction, of closure, in being able to help him connect with his child?

Then again, Josie was in a tender, emotional state right now. This news could push her over the edge.

'Have you told Josie your suspicions yet?'

Rebecca shook her head. 'No—I came looking for Robbie thinking maybe we could work out what to do together.'

Clara almost laughed—Rob could barely take care of himself, the idea of him being able to even think about everyone else involved in this scenario and make a sensible decision *was* laughable.

'What do you think I should do?' Rebecca asked.

Clara wasn't sure whether her loyalties lay with Rob or with Josie, but they certainly didn't lie with this woman. Then a thought struck—Rebecca said she'd already requested information before seeing the photo. Loathing bubbled within her. 'You need a kidney donor. Is that why you suddenly decided to look for your child now?'

'No, that's not it at all.' Rebecca's words spilled out in a rush. 'I've always buried the adoption because it was too painful to think about, but my kidney failure diagnosis gave me a scare. I realised I didn't want to die not knowing about my son. I mean my daughter.'

Clara wasn't sure whether she believed her or not.

'I'm honestly not after Josie for a kidney,' Rebecca appealed. 'My daughter's fiancé has offered to go on the Paired Kidney Exchange Program with me, but even if he hadn't, I would never ask or expect such a thing of Josie.'

'Maybe not, but how's Josie going to feel finding out her father is missing and her mother seriously ill? The exchange program isn't a sure thing—you'll not only need to find another pair that matches you and your daughter's boyfriend, but the timing also needs to be right. Josie might feel pressured to get tested. As you know, she's not in the best emotional place right now. I think your best bet is waiting for the clarification, and then if Josie is your daughter, you'll need to find out whether or not she has any desire to meet her biological parents. If not—'

'And how do I do that without it being obvious?' Rebecca sounded desperate.

Clara understood she was distressed but she was sick of Rebecca interrupting. She threw her hands up in the air and stood. 'I don't know. This is not my problem! Right now, I'm going on a cruise with my … friend.' She still couldn't bring herself to say partner or boyfriend. 'And I need to finish getting ready, so I'm going to have to ask you to leave.'

'Oh. Okay.' Rebecca's tears had eased a while ago but they looked close to returning now. 'Thank you for your time. Can I give you my number?'

Clara hit her with a look of disbelief.

'In case you learn anything else about Josie or Rob turns up. I'd like to know he's okay and … keep him informed.'

Clara sighed, then picked up a pen and her shopping list pad off the bench and handed it to the other woman. 'Write it here.'

*Josie*

Buttoning up his shirt, Nik walked into the bathroom as Josie retrieved a tampon from the vanity cupboard.

'Bugger,' he said, nodding towards the packet and then taking her in his arms. 'You okay?'

'Yes. I am,' she told him truthfully, but didn't add that she was strangely relieved. The past few weeks she'd finally been beginning to feel like herself again and although part of her desperately wanted to find herself pregnant, the fear of what could happen if she was had been eating her up these last couple of days while she'd been waiting for her period. This felt like a temporary reprieve from that anxiety.

'Do you want me to call in sick to work? We could order in pizza and watch a movie.'

'No, it's fine.' Pizza and a movie were on her agenda, but not with him. 'Remember, I told you, I have plans tonight.'

He raised an eyebrow and started on his buttons again. 'That's right, Saturday night and you're going to hang out with some strange old woman.'

His tone was teasing but there was also an element of disbelief in it. Did he think Brenda was a ruse and really she was off out on the town to drink her sorrows? She made a mental note to take a selfie of them together and send it to him. Perhaps she'd send it to Clara as well, although she wasn't sure whether she'd have reception on the ship.

'She's not strange.' Josie swatted him. 'She's lonely and not very mobile. I'm doing a favour for Clara, but it's actually a real pleasure to spend time with her. I like listening to her stories and it beats sitting home alone with my thoughts. Go, I'm honestly fine and you can't keep cancelling work on my account or you'll have no job left to go to.'

'Alright. Well, you call me if you need to talk or anything, okay?' He kissed her firmly on the lips.

'I will.' She smiled and then shoved him out of the bathroom.

When she was done, she packed some microwave popcorn, a few cans of soft drink and some other treats into a bag and then drove the short distance to Brenda's place.

'Hello, love.' The older woman's face lit up as she opened the door and Josie glowed inside at the knowledge she was making someone's night better.

'How are you feeling today?' she asked as they went into the kitchen, Josie walking slowly to keep in step with Brenda's shuffling.

'Can't complain, but it's lovely to see you, dear.'

Josie smiled; she got the feeling Brenda wasn't the type to complain about much. She'd seen her twice already this week—once for their first movie night on Tuesday, and then she'd popped in yesterday morning on her way to school to see if there was anything Brenda needed her to grab from the shops. But Clara had left her cupboards well stocked and the visits were more about company than anything else. And Josie had meant it when she'd told Nik she enjoyed spending time here; old people had a lot of wisdom to offer if you bothered to pay attention.

'So, what kind of pizza do you like?' she asked now as she put her bags on the table. 'Are there any toppings you definitely don't want?'

Brenda's eyes widened. 'My pizzas are usually in a box from the freezer in the supermarket, I've never had it home delivered before. Is it like a restaurant? Can you really pick and choose what you want?'

'You really can.' Josie stifled a chuckle. 'So what's it to be? Pineapple? Anchovies? Mushrooms? Let's go to town. I'm feeling like indulging tonight.'

'Oh, is something wrong, dear?'

Josie considered telling her about her period but decided that was probably too much information at this stage in their relationship. 'No,' she said, 'I'm all good, but any excuse to indulge I reckon.'

Brenda laughed. Together they concocted a fantasy pizza and then Josie called it in to the local Italian restaurant.

'Next step, the movie,' Brenda said. 'What are you in the mood for?'

'Something funny,' Josie replied. 'Any suggestions?'

'Why don't you come and peruse my collection? I'm sorry but I need to sit down anyway, I can't stand on this foot for long.'

'Oh God, I'm sorry, I should have thought.' Josie ushered Brenda into the living room and helped her into her recliner. She draped a crocheted rug over her knees and then turned her attention to the shelves.

'What's this one about?' she asked holding up a movie called *My Favourite Wife*.

Brenda smiled. 'That was one of the few movies my husband and I agreed on. Generally, he preferred action films.'

'Nik's the same,' Josie said. 'Unless there's a massive body count, he doesn't think it's worth watching. So what's it about?'

'A lawyer whose wife has been missing for seven years. Finally, he marries someone else, and while he's on his honeymoon with the new wife, the old one turns up. She'd been stranded on a deserted island all that time.'

'I'm up for that.' Josie popped it in the DVD player and went off to get the drinks.

'Thank you, dear,' Brenda said when she returned a few moments later. 'It's nice to have company. I really enjoyed watching *The Graduate* with you the other night. It's been a long time since I had someone to watch movies with.'

Josie took to the couch. 'Rob doesn't watch movies with you?'

'Not really. Between you and me, he's not always that good company. I'm not sure how much Clara has told you about him?'

'Not much; she mentioned he struggles with addiction.'

'Yes. He's fond of the bottle alright and that only makes the depression he's battled for years worse. Not that he ever admitted he had a problem.' Brenda sighed sadly. 'I always wondered if things would have been different if his father hadn't died, if he'd had a strong male role model growing up.'

'How did he?' Josie hoped Brenda didn't mind the question.

'In a mining accident. He worked in the Cobar gold mines long before occupational health and safety was a priority. He was underground when a concrete block fell down the raise and crushed him. They tell me it was instant. Robbie was only two.' She nodded to a photo frame above the TV. 'That's them a couple of weeks before Mal died. He was such a good husband and father.'

As Josie gazed at the photo of a young man in faded jeans and a Bonds Chesty singlet with a little boy with what looked like Vegemite smeared on his cheeks, her heart ached for Brenda. She'd lost her love so young and now it looked like she might have lost her only son as well.

'He looks lovely,' Josie said. 'But you were widowed so young, did you never find anyone else?'

'No. It's hard meeting people when you're a single mum with no real family support, but it would have been nice. I always wanted a big family and would have loved more kids.'

A few weeks ago, this admission would have irritated Josie—at least Brenda had managed to have one child—but now she could sympathise; life had a habit of turning out completely different to how you expected or wanted it to.

'I'm not sure Clara told you, but I met your son,' Josie said, wanting to give Brenda something positive to hold onto.

'Oh?'

'Yes. A couple of months ago, we met outside a pub and started chatting. He was a good listener and I poured my heart out to him. He was the one who gave me Clara's number.'

Brenda smiled gratefully at Josie. 'I try not to talk about him in front of Clara. The poor love did put up with a lot. She didn't give up easily and she did her best; she got him into AA a few times but he never lasted. There's nothing anyone else can do for people like Robbie. In the end, they have to help themselves. He's a lost soul but he's got a heart of gold beneath his problems. Such a shame, he was very musically talented, you know?'

This piqued Josie's interest. 'Really? Did he play an instrument?'

'Oh, he played many, but his passion was singing and songwriting. His band did quite well for themselves for a while. There's a picture up there on the wall of them if you want to see it.'

Josie got up and went over to look properly. 'Oh my God,' she shrieked. 'Your son was part of One Track Mind?'

'You know them?' Brenda sounded surprised. 'I thought they'd be long before your time.'

'I was barely born when they were together but I love eighties music and I've actually got their LPs.' There'd been two albums, but the first was the only one anyone remembered. 'I collect them,' she added.

'Wow.' Brenda looked chuffed by this.

'I knew he looked familiar.' She wanted to kick herself—she couldn't believe she hadn't worked out why at the time. Of course if she had, there'd have been no way she'd have spilled her guts to him; she'd have been too starstruck to speak.

'Robbie collected LPs as well. Those boxes over there in the corner are full of them.'

'Can I take a look?'

'Of course. Go ahead.'

Josie crossed to the corner, opened the first box and began rifling through the records. It felt like Christmas as she oohed and ahhed over albums by Queen, Duran Duran, Pink Floyd and many, many more.

But, as she put a Dire Straits LP back in the first box and turned to start on the second, she glanced over to see Brenda's smile had fallen. 'It's so nice to see someone else getting joy from Robbie's things,' she said with a sniff. 'He might not be perfect, but he's my boy and I miss him.'

Josie's heart hurt for the other woman. 'Don't lose hope,' she said, abandoning the record and going across to take the older woman by the hand. 'I'm sure he'll turn up.'

She wasn't sure of any such thing, but she hoped it was the truth for Brenda's sake.

The movie forgotten, Josie held up the One Track Mind album she'd just found. 'Do you have anything to play this on?' she asked, thinking maybe Brenda would quite like to hear her son's voice.

'Robbie's record player is over there, in the other corner. It might be a bit dusty, but I think it still works.'

Josie leapt to her feet, and carried the LP as if it were made of gold. She couldn't believe she was holding Robbie Jones's copy of one of her favourite albums. Why had Clara never mentioned who her ex-husband was? Her school friends had thought her obsession with eighties music crazy and a little embarrassing, but she'd always loved it way more than modern stuff. One Track Mind was a unique sound too. Not quite hard rock, but much rawer than pop.

After a little fiddling, she managed to get it to work and the notes of 'Lost Without You, Baby' filled the air. Brenda smiled again as Josie sang along.

'Was that song about Clara?' Josie asked, turning the music down slightly as the next song began.

'No,' Brenda's one word came out as a whisper.

'Was it about anyone?' Josie would be disappointed to hear that there wasn't some heartbreaking love story behind one of her favourite songs.

'Yes.' Brenda paused a moment, then, 'It was about his son.'

Josie felt her eyes widen. 'But Clara and Robbie didn't have kids.' And she was sure Clara had said the baby that had been stillborn was a girl.

Brenda rubbed her lips together as if unsure whether she should say any more. 'It's never been common knowledge but Robbie's high school sweetheart had a baby. It was adopted out.'

Josie's heart went cold. She'd sympathised with Rob's alcoholism when she'd thought it stemmed from the stillbirth and miscarriages, but adoption … 'How old was he?'

'He was seventeen, but the girl was only fifteen. Under the legal age when she conceived. He was desperately in love with her, as much as any teenaged boy can be, but her parents weren't having any of it. Her father was the local cop—there was rumours in Cobar he was corrupt, or at least a little rough-handed, especially with the Aboriginal folk that were unlucky enough to cross his path. Anyway,' she shook her head, 'let's just say Robbie wasn't given much choice in the matter. Maybe we both should have fought harder to take the baby, but I could barely pay the bills as it was. Robbie would have had to leave school, get a job—between that and being a dad he wouldn't have had time for his music.

'I thought it was the right thing at the time, but it changed him. When he met Clara and his band got the record deal, I thought he was going to be okay. But when they couldn't have children … I think Robbie blamed himself. He figured since he gave up one child, he didn't deserve another.'

A lump grew in Josie's throat. 'That's so sad.'

Not only had Brenda lost a husband and a son, but somewhere she had a grandson she didn't know as well. It made Josie all the more determined to take her under her wing.

'All we can hope is that the baby found a good home, had a good life.'

And although it was something she rarely spoke about, Josie found herself saying, 'I was adopted.'

Brenda blinked. 'Really?'

'Yes. And I landed on my feet with my parents. I bet your grandson did too.'

'Do you know your real parents?'

Josie shook her head, trying not to bristle at the word 'real'—she knew Brenda didn't mean any harm.

When Josie was a kid the possibility of finding her 'biological' family—as was the term her parents used—seemed so far off in the distant future that she never gave it much thought. Maybe she would, maybe she wouldn't. But as the day grew closer where legally she could start a search, she'd come to the conclusion that she didn't want or need to know.

What if things changed when she found her 'biological' mother?

She was so utterly close to her mum and dad that she couldn't bear the thought of their relationship being affected. And she'd read horror stories about adopted kids seeking their roots. Yes, there were some happy endings, but a lot of the time they didn't like what they found.

What if her mum was a druggie? Or in jail? Would Josie feel obliged to help her? Or what if she still didn't want anything to do with Josie? Whenever she thought about possible rejection, she grew so anxious she made herself physically ill. There were simply too many unanswered questions. And, if the woman who'd carried her for nine months wanted to find her, surely she'd come looking?

'My folks always said they'd be okay with me finding them if I wanted to,' she told Brenda, 'but I've just never had that yearning. It was actually kinda cool being the adopted kid. Most of the other kids in my class came from boring two-parent-two-point-three-kid families and I used to love telling them that my parents had chosen me, whereas theirs didn't have a choice. I used to dream there was some kind of baby shop where childless couples went to select a baby from a whole bunch of wailing newborns. A little bit like the cabbage patch, which were where my favourite dolls came from.'

She chuckled and so did Brenda.

'Did Robbie ever look for his baby?' Josie asked.

'He tried. He always wanted to find his son, but his name wasn't on the birth certificate and although he and Clara did what they could to look for him, they never had any luck.'

Before Josie had time to digest this, the doorbell rang signalling the arrival of their dinner.

'I'll get it.' She hurried to the door.

Brenda sniffed the air as Josie returned to the living room with the pizza and garlic bread. 'Hmm, that smells good. I guess we'd better start that movie now too or it'll be very late before it's finished and, unlike you young things, I do need my beauty sleep.'

'Good idea,' Josie said with a smile. 'You press play and I'll go get the plates.'

# September

*Rebecca*

When Rebecca walked into the kitchen after her last piano lesson on Monday afternoon, she found Hugh chopping up vegetables as onion sautéed in the frying pan. Her stomach rumbled at the alluring aroma, but she didn't dare to assume she was included in his dinner plans.

'Good evening.' She cringed at her overly polite tone, her heart halting as she waited to see if he would deem her worthy of a reply. If so, it would be the first time he'd spoken to her since walking out on Friday morning, reeling from the shock of her revelation. He'd been sleeping in the spare room ever since and although she'd tried to talk to him a number of times, he'd shut her down, making it clear she was alone in this situation. In all their years of marriage they'd never gone this long without talking to each other—until this week the record would have been a couple of hours max, and even that had been rare.

How she'd managed to get through three hours of lessons, she had no idea. She'd thought it might help to have something to focus on other than the whole Josie-adoption-Hugh-angry-Robbie-missing situation, but she'd been kidding herself believing she could think about anything else.

'There's a letter for you on the table.'

Rebecca almost jumped out of her skin at the sound of Hugh's voice.

'Thank you,' she said, recovering only a moment because when her eyes came to rest on the plain white envelope with the government symbol in the corner, her heart shot into her throat again. Even without opening it, she could tell what it was and she stared at it long and hard.

'You going to open it?' he asked eventually, his tone making it clear he'd already guessed what it was as well.

Rebecca swallowed, then slid her finger beneath the seal and fumbled to remove the letter. Her heart flopped about in her chest as she read:

*Dear Mrs MacRitchie*

*Thank you for your enquiry. The departmental records have been searched and ...*

Her gaze skipped over the preamble to the important bits.

*Name: Josephine Maria Van Dijk*
*Born: Swan District Hospital, Western Australia*
*Date of birth: 9 April 1983*

The rest of the information blurred on the page as her eyes grew hot and the world began to spin. She steadied herself on the kitchen table and then sank into a chair. She'd known in her heart Josie was her daughter but seeing the truth written in black print was still a bloody shock and she was helpless to stop the flood of tears down her cheeks.

Over the last few days crying had become as much a part of her day as eating, sleeping and breathing. After leaving her parents' place she'd driven aimlessly for a while, not knowing who to turn to in lieu of Hugh and her thoughts had found their way to the father of her baby. To Robbie. She'd felt so affronted that all these years she'd thought she had a boy that she suddenly had an irrepressible urge to let him know the truth.

But she'd gotten much more than she bargained for. Not only had Robbie's ex-wife told her he was missing but Clara had also delivered some unsavoury truths about Rebecca's parents. Now, in addition to her thoughts about Josie, she couldn't get Robbie out of her head. She'd been so consumed she'd almost missed her dialysis session on Friday afternoon.

*What if* questions haunted her day and night.

What if her parents hadn't intervened? Hadn't taken it upon themselves to play God? Would she and Robbie have stayed together? Raised their baby together? Her heart squeezed at the thought. As confronting as it had been to hear about the threat her father had made to Robbie, it made more sense than anything in her life ever had before.

Robbie hadn't abandoned her of his own accord.

And this realisation had brought all her hurt and pain from that time back to the forefront. It broke her heart to think he'd been hurt as much as she had and never truly recovered—at least she'd managed to have a relatively happy life with Hugh and Paige. Robbie hadn't achieved anything like that and now he was missing. Possibly dead. And, from the way Clara had spoken, she didn't care and neither did the police.

A lump formed in her throat again and another barrage of tears followed. Her parents had a lot to answer for. Her mother had tried to call her numerous times over the weekend, but it was a good thing neither of them had shown up at the house, because the way she felt right now she thought she might be capable of physically harming her dad.

'Here.' Hugh's shadow fell over her as he pulled out a chair and sat, offering her a box of tissues as he did so.

'Thanks.' Rebecca tried to pull herself together, not meeting his gaze as she snatched one up—she'd never been self-conscious about crying in front of her husband before but now she worried he'd think her tears were an attempt to manipulate him into sympathy.

'Can I see?'

She pushed The Letter towards him.

Moments later, she heard his sharp intake of breath. 'So, you did have a girl, after all?'

'Yes,' she whispered, trying to halt her tears and not mentioning that if he'd bothered to listen to her over the weekend, he'd have known this. 'Mum and Dad lied.'

And then, because he was still sitting there and she was desperate to talk to someone, she spilled the rest as well. There didn't seem any point in hiding anything now. She told him about her parents' feeble excuse for their lie and how she'd gone to look for Robbie. She relayed her conversation with Clara, her father's inexcusable manipulations to keep Robbie out of her life, the news that Robbie had disappeared, and watched his eyebrows creep closer and closer to his receding hairline as she did so.

'How old was Robbie when all this happened?'

'Seventeen.'

'I don't think he'd have been charged. You might have been underage but you were both at school. The most he'd have got was a rap on the knuckles.'

Even if this was the truth, it wasn't any consolation. If anything, it only made her father's actions—his abuse of power—worse.

Hugh pushed back from the table and stood. Was that it? End of conversation? She couldn't bear it if he continued to push her away. She'd always had Hugh's unwavering support, his love and his friendship. And now that was on the line. Paige might not have noticed yet, but it wouldn't take long before she picked up on the disharmony between her parents. Not only would the rift break Paige's heart, but she'd demand answers and wouldn't rest until she got to the core of the crisis.

'I'm sorry, Hugh.' She grabbed onto his arm. 'I don't want this to come between us.'

His whole body stiffened, she felt his muscles clenching beneath her touch. 'Let me get us dinner and then we'll talk.'

*Dinner?* Rebecca wasn't hungry anymore and she didn't want to give him time to change his mind, but she also couldn't refuse the closest thing to an olive branch that had been offered so far. 'Okay. What can I do to help?'

He stepped away so her hand fell off his arm. 'Nothing. I've got this.'

The next half an hour was excruciating. She took a shower, fed the dog and then sat in her bedroom and read the letter over and over.

In addition to the other information, such as Josie's birth weight and length, it had the names of her adoptive parents. When every word and line was imprinted in her head, Rebecca opened her laptop and searched Josie's maiden name. Whereas the earlier searches for her married name had come up almost blank, pages and pages appeared for Josephine Van Dijk, most of them from theatres in London where she'd appeared in a number of famous musicals.

'Oh my.' Her nerve endings tingled as she clicked on the first image and came face to face with the woman Paige had become friends with. If there'd ever been any doubt that this was her Josephine, there could be none now. She was so beautiful and the knowledge that she'd been a performer like her dad, that a love of music was something the three of them shared, brought tears to her eyes.

Among the websites, she also found an obituary from two years ago for a Natalie Van Dijk and a Facebook page with a number of holiday photos of her widower, Maarten Van Dijk. She wasn't sure what to think of the news that Josie's adoptive mother was no longer alive.

Would that make Josie more or less open to meeting her?

The final line of the letter read: *As of today, Josephine Van Dijk has not requested to be put on the Contact Register.*

Rebecca's heart sank. Surely if Josie had any desire to find her birth parents, that would have been the first step.

Finally, Hugh called her to dinner and Rebecca sat at the table, feeling more like she was eating with a stranger than the man she'd spent almost every day with for the past thirty years.

'This is delicious,' she said, taking a mouthful, despite still having next to no appetite.

'Thanks,' he grunted and then shoved a forkful of pasta into his mouth.

Silence followed a few long moments until Rebecca could handle it no longer. 'Is this going to break us?'

He took his time finishing his next mouthful, laid his fork down in the bowl and let out a long, slow breath.

'I don't know, Rebecca. I'm trying to wrap my head around the fact you've lived with a massive secret all our married life. I keep asking myself why. What does it say about us? Didn't you trust me? Was this the root cause of your postnatal depression?' He shook his head sadly. 'I have so many questions. And all before I even start to think about what happens now you've found your other daughter and what that might mean for our family.'

'I almost told you before we got married. But Mum warned me against it. She and Dad brainwashed me into believing it was better to forget and that talking about it would only bring back painful memories. They made me feel ashamed, made sure I knew how stupid I was to have gotten myself in that predicament, and I didn't want you to think badly of me.'

'Do you really think I would have? I loved you and I wouldn't have held something that happened in your teens against you.'

Rebecca couldn't help but note his use of the past tense. He wouldn't *have*. But did he now?

'I don't know,' she said, working hard not to cry again. 'I was young. I felt shame, guilt, hurt and regret. Not talking about it made sense. Hindsight is a wonderful thing, but all I can say is I thought it was the right thing at the time.'

Now, as she said this, she couldn't believe she'd been so easily led—she despised herself for not putting up more of a fight at every point in the journey.

'Did you *ever* think about telling me? We've been married thirty years. You grew up in that time.'

'Yes. Of course I did. In the nineties the laws changed regarding adoption privacy in WA, I totally freaked out—it meant when adopted children came of legal age they had the right to request identifying information about themselves, about their birth parents. Even with adoptions which were previously closed, like my baby's. I decided then and there to tell you, but then your father died and you were so sad I didn't want to upset you even more. There were still a few years till my child would have been old enough, so I figured I had time, but of course the right moment never came. Something always got in the way as if fate was trying to hold me back. The year my child would have turned eighteen, you had your heart attack ...'

She shook her head, the time for excuses was long gone. 'I can't change the past, Hugh. All I can say is I'm genuinely sorry about keeping this from you.'

'I've never liked your father,' he said.

She blinked. 'Really?'

He nodded. 'There was something about him from the first time we met. I didn't like the condescending way he spoke to you and your mother and there's always been something else, but I couldn't quite put my finger on it.'

She laughed—perhaps they could bond again over the shared hatred of her dad. 'Well, that makes two of us.'

But Hugh wasn't laughing. 'I'm hurt, Rebecca, however the fact that your parents lied to you—first about Robbie and then about the gender of the baby—makes me realise just how much they orchestrated this. I can see you're the victim here, not me, and I want to support you. That's what I want, but I think it's going to take time.'

'I understand.'

'So what happens now?'

'Between us?' She was hoping he'd stop sleeping in the spare bedroom for a start.

'No, I mean what do you do with this information? Do you want a relationship with Josie? And Robbie? How do you feel about him now you know it wasn't his choice to abandon you?'

Rebecca's head hurt with all Hugh's questions. Him not talking to her all weekend had given her plenty of time to think about these things but she hadn't come to any conclusions. And until she'd had the official confirmation, she hadn't felt she could *do* anything. Part of her wanted to drive over to Josie's place right this moment, throw her arms around her and declare herself as her mother, but she knew she might not be well-received.

'I don't know,' she admitted. 'I don't want to upset her and finding out about Robbie's alcoholism and his disappearance might do that. Even if you can forgive me, maybe it would be best just to bury this again. Josie's thirty-five and has never come searching for me—she's not on the contact register, which makes me think she doesn't want to open that box.'

'And you think you can live with that?' He sounded sceptical.

Rebecca swallowed, emotion welling in her throat again. When she'd sent off for this information, she'd thought it would be good to know that her baby was doing okay, what he (well, *she*) did for a crust and if he had a family of his own, but that was before she discovered that not only had she actually had a daughter, but that she already knew her. 'I'm not sure. It will be hard seeing Josie, knowing she's my own flesh and blood while trying to act normal and pretend she isn't. And then there's also Paige to consider. Does she have a right to know?'

How could Rebecca chastise her own parents for lying to her if she then perpetuated the lie by not telling her own daughter? She wanted whatever was best for both her daughters, she just had no idea what that was.

'Hmm,' Hugh mused.

'What does that mean? Do *you* think I should tell Paige?'

'I think you know my stance on secrets—I think Paige deserves to know she has a sister. It'll be a shock, but she's got her head screwed on, she'll cope. However, I don't know Josie, so I can't predict how she might feel or react.'

Rebecca sighed. Why couldn't anyone just tell her what to do?

# Clara

Clara's first cruise should have been exciting, yet from the moment she and Gregg walked up the gangplank, she was distracted. She chose not to tell him about her visit from Rebecca because she didn't want to start their trip talking about Rob, and maybe that was a mistake. Maybe if she'd got it all off her chest, she would have been able to put Rebecca, Rob and Josie behind her.

Instead she tried to *pretend* she was having fun. She oohed and ahhed with Gregg like two excited children as they explored the ship, checking out the many levels with their pools, bars, restaurants, movies theatres and shops. They even glanced into the gym—surprisingly there were a few people already using the facilities before the ship had even left the harbour—and agreed that it was one place they wouldn't be wasting any of their precious time in. Gregg took photos of all the various signs around the ship, making her laugh as he made witty comments about them. He was hoping to come up with a comedy act based on them for the final night when passengers were invited to an open mic session run by the ship's in-house comedians and, despite her mood, she couldn't wait to watch him.

They shared cocktails overlooking the harbour as the ship cast off from the Overseas Passenger Terminal and then had a very lovely dinner in one of the fancy restaurants before going back to their tiny cabin and making love. Gregg was a very attentive lover and usually Clara lost her head the moment he touched her, but she was even distracted during sex.

She'd closed her eyes and tried to focus on his hands and mouth as he talentedly played her body, but damn Rob kept filling her head. Rebecca showing up meant Clara should have been able to pass the Rob/*Robbie* baton to her, but it didn't feel like that. Twenty-five years married was a long time—she'd known Rob most of her adult life and although her head wanted to be rid of him, it was proving harder for her heart to let go. Maybe that was because of Josie.

Maybe if she didn't know Rob's daughter, she'd be able to ignore the revelation Rebecca had delivered that afternoon but she couldn't stop thinking about how happy he'd be if he met her.

'Oh God! Clara!'

She'd opened her eyes and looked into Gregg's. His pupils were glazed over and he was thrusting hard. She could tell he was close to release but was trying to hold on a little longer until she achieved the same pleasure.

*Maybe I should fake it?*

But Gregg wasn't a stupid man, even before she'd thrown herself into this task, he'd stopped moving and pushed up onto his hands. 'Are you okay?'

*Oh Lord*, she'd been caught. 'I'm just feeling a little queasy,' she'd lied, grimacing for good measure. And hoping he wouldn't remember her mentioning earlier her strong stomach and the fact she could hardly feel the boat moving at all.

'Why didn't you say so?' He'd rolled off her and sat up on the edge of the bed, concern filling his eyes. 'What can I do for you? Do you need some water? I could go hunt for some dry crackers.'

She'd shaken her head—a lump forming in her throat at his kindness and thoughtfulness. 'No, it's not that bad, just ...'

'Just me having my paws all over you wasn't helping.' He'd smiled. 'How about we see what movie's on the TV?'

'Yes.' She'd nodded. 'That sounds good.'

And while he'd picked up the remote to flick through the various movie channels on the boat, she'd tried to relax back into the pillows. When Gregg climbed back into bed—having decided on a James Bond film—she'd snuggled into him and vowed to put Rob out of her head.

The next day, they slept until the sun snuck in through the curtains on the portholes and then, over breakfast in the international food hall, they looked through the offerings on the ship's daily program. That afternoon was the first of the two comedy-writing workshops.

'Why don't you have a massage or one of those nail-thingys in the spa place while I'm doing the workshop,' he suggested. 'They might be able to offer you some sort of pressure-spot treatment for sea-sickness.'

'I'm feeling much better this morning,' Clara said. 'Sorry about last night.'

He took her hand and squeezed gently. 'Don't apologise. And, I'm glad you're feeling better, but you still deserve a little pampering. My shout.'

She had to admit a massage did sound appealing and maybe it would help her relax and de-stress. 'Okay. Thank you.'

They finished breakfast, went to the spa to book Clara in for the afternoon and then grabbed their books from the cabin and sat by the pool. Although they thought it a little too cold for a swim, plenty of kids and a few adults were splashing about in the water. The setting should have been so relaxing, but Clara found herself reading the same page over and over again.

'What are you reading?'

'Oh. It's a psychological thriller.' She turned the cover towards Gregg.

'Not very good?' he asked.

'No, it's great.'

'You seem to have been stuck on the same page for over half an hour.'

*Caught. Again.* Her stomach tightened as she gestured towards the kids in the pool. 'I'm finding it hard to concentrate here.'

'Why don't we go see if we can find somewhere more quiet?'

'Good idea,' Clara said, so they picked up their books and headed inside to one of the many bar areas. Except for the woman behind the bar and a man over in the corner setting up instruments on stage, it was deserted. Clara claimed the plush velvet couch in the corner while Gregg ordered the drinks.

As he returned, the music guy picked up one of the guitars and started plucking at a few strings, obviously testing the sound system for later. Her heart clenched as she recognised the notes of 'Lost Without You, Baby'. It was still often played on the radio, which meant she heard it fairly regularly in shopping centres, restaurants and the like. But today it felt like just one more thing working to keep Rob and the Josie–Rebecca problem in her head.

Was he everywhere she went? Would she never achieve any kind of peace?

'Alright ... out with it,' Gregg said.

Clara stiffened. 'Out with what?'

'I just asked you which restaurant you want to try for lunch and it was like you didn't even hear me.'

'Sorry. I was distracted by the musician.'

Gregg frowned. 'He's playing your ex's song, isn't he?'

She nodded guiltily.

'Must be hard hearing it all the time,' he said. 'Ever since you told me about his band, I've been hearing that song everywhere I go.'

She shrugged. 'I've learnt to ignore it.'

'Yet today you noticed,' Gregg said astutely. And then exhaled loudly. 'What's going on? Something has been bothering you since yesterday afternoon. Either you've changed your mind about us but don't want to break my heart when we're stranded at sea sharing a cabin, you're still not feeling well or there's something else. Is it something to do with Rob?'

Clara couldn't help the long sigh that expelled from her lips. 'Yes. I'm sorry. It's not you. Yesterday when you went to drop off Shadow I had an unexpected visitor. My ex-husband's high school girlfriend turned up.'

'The one who had the baby?'

'Yep. She was looking for him because she's recently discovered her parents lied—not only did she not know about the threat they made to Rob but she also just found out they told her she had a boy when she actually had a little girl.'

His eyes bulged.

'I know,' Clara said, still shocked herself. 'But that's not the only crazy thing in all of this.' Gregg didn't say a word as she explained about the hunt for the wedding dress, how Rebecca had met Josie, seen a photo and begun to suspect something weird was going on. He listened as she explained the web she'd unintentionally woven by introducing Josie to Brenda. 'I was beginning to feel really close to Josie and now ...'

Now she couldn't help being a little jealous that Josie might develop a relationship with Rebecca. She wished she could rewind the clock twenty-four hours and not open the door to the woman.

'No wonder you're distracted,' he said when she'd finally finished unloading. 'That's a hell of a story. Why didn't you tell me?'

If only it *was* simply a story—something in a book she'd taken to read on the cruise, instead of her own complicated life. 'I didn't want to burden you. This was supposed to be our weekend; I wanted us to be able to enjoy it without my personal dramas overshadowing everything. I don't want to think about all of this,' she almost screamed these words, 'but I can't help it.'

'I'd rather you be honest and open with me,' Gregg said, reaching for her hand. 'I want to be there for you.'

'But you didn't sign on for *this* mess.'

'That's what relationships are like at our age. You don't get to this stage in life without having a little baggage.'

'Some of us seem to have more than others,' she retorted, a tad resentful. If anyone should be bringing drama into their relationship, it should be Gregg as he was the one with children. The fact she and Rob had never managed to have a family should in *theory* have made their break a clean one.

He raised an eyebrow. 'Trust me, I've got baggage; just nothing has happened to unpack it yet, but if you stick around long enough, I promise to bring plenty of drama to this relationship.'

She laughed at his attempt to make her feel better. 'Thanks. I think.'

'Hey. It's okay. Isn't this kind of stuff what makes life interesting?'

She snorted. 'Maybe. But for just once, I'd like a few boring months. I feel like I've had enough drama and heartache for a lifetime.'

'Maybe you should run away,' he suggested.

'Huh?'

His lovely silver eyes sparkled. 'We could run away together. You could come with me when I go overseas next year. Leave all this behind. As you said, it's really got nothing to do with you anymore. And, if Josie is indeed Brenda's granddaughter, then even if Rob isn't found—even if the worst has happened to him—then Brenda has got other family after all. She doesn't have to be your burden anymore.'

Clara's stomach twisted at what should have been a comforting thought, but she couldn't help feeling sad that maybe Josie would no longer need her either. 'Are you serious?'

He nodded. 'Why not?'

*Why not indeed.* Hadn't she decided recently that she would like to see the world? And she couldn't imagine a better travel companion. He was so easy to be with, so thoughtful and caring. The fact he'd keep her warm at night as well was simply an added bonus. 'I'll give it some serious thought,' she promised.

He smiled. 'Good. But in the meantime, don't shut me out again. I want to be here for you.'

'Thank you.' She kissed him on the cheek and then leant her head against his shoulder. 'I guess for so long I've been used to dealing with stuff on my own. Rob was certainly never any support so I'm not accustomed to having someone to lean on and I didn't want to ruin your weekend.'

'It's *our* weekend,' he said, 'and you haven't ruined it because you're here. That's what matters.'

After that, things did get better. Clara felt lighter having got it all off her chest. Being with Gregg was like medicine for the body, mind and soul and she wished they could stay on the ship forever. But finally, the last night came and Clara found herself trying to calm Gregg's nerves as he psyched himself up to go on stage.

He was too anxious to eat dinner.

'Relax,' she said as they sat across from each other at the ship's Asian fusion restaurant. The food was very good, it was a pity Gregg couldn't enjoy it. 'When you're up there just—'

'Do not tell me to imagine all the audience naked,' he interrupted, jabbing his index finger at her. 'I've never understood how that's supposed to make you feel any better. I'd be embarrassed and wouldn't know where to look.'

She smiled. 'What I was going to say is to remember all these people are strangers. We've been on board almost four days and haven't run into anyone either of us know. At worst you make a fool of yourself in front of me and no one else important ever need find out. But I know that you won't and I'm proud of you for following your dream no matter what happens.'

'Thank you. That means a lot. I'm so glad you're here with me for this.'

'Me too,' she said. It felt good to be able to be a support to him, rather than the other way around for once.

Clara finished her dinner and Gregg managed a few mouthfuls of his grilled wild Chilean sea bass before the time came to head down to the comedy lounge. He chatted to a few people he knew from the workshops as they lined up to register and then he and Clara sat down in the front row.

Soon after, the lights dimmed and one of the ship's comedians welcomed everyone.

'Open mic is my favourite night of the cruise,' she said in a strong American accent. Or was it Canadian? Clara could never tell the difference. 'I can't wait to hear what talent we have on board this time round. This is scary shit getting up in front of people and trying to be funny—trust me, it doesn't get easier—but if you can laugh at yourself then it's a whole lot easier when others are laughing at you instead of with you as well. So relax, have fun and remember we've all gotta start somewhere. Without further ado, I want to introduce this evening's judges, comedians from all four corners of the globe.'

Clara took Gregg's hand—it was shaking—as the judges said their hellos and the first wannabe comedian was called up to the stage. The podgy man who said he was a taxi driver from Darwin talked about farts and snot—it was nothing original but he might have got a few laughs if the average age of the audience was about forty years younger. The next two acts—a male and then a female—were better but if these three were any indication of the calibre of the contestants, Clara felt confident Gregg had this competition in the bag.

'I'm going to get a drink,' she said as the next person took to the stage. 'Can I get you anything?'

'Just some water, please.'

'Okay. Be right back.' She snuck up to the bar at the back of the theatre. As she was ordering her glass of wine, there was a commotion at the entrance as a woman coming in and a man going out almost collided. As the two people side-stepped each other, Clara gasped in recognition.

'Rob?' she called, but he didn't hear her and kept on walking.

*No, it couldn't be.* She shook her head and managed to thank the barman as he handed her the drinks. What would Rob be doing on this ship? He'd never once in his life voiced a desire to go on a cruise. It had to be someone who looked similar to him.

Shaking her head, Clara started back to her seat but her heart was pounding and she couldn't get the image out of her head.

What if in some bizarre twist of fate it *was* Rob? Anger flared within her at the thought that he might have been living it up on the high seas while she was going out of her way to look after his mother.

Before Clara could think about what she was doing, she turned and hurried in the direction the man had gone. Wine sloshed over the rim of the glass and onto her fingers, so she dumped it and the water on the bar and fled into the busy corridor. There were people everywhere, dressed in 1920s garb and chatting joyfully on their way to the Gatsby party on the top level. She wove through them, looking left and right, scrutinising every face and straining her neck as she peered ahead to try and spot the man in question.

Losing patience and hope she was about to give in when she thought she saw him heading up the stairs. She picked up her pace, following the long-haired lout up three flights and out onto the pool deck. Cool air hit her face; it was freezing out here and, aside from the bar over in the corner, the deck was almost deserted.

'Excuse me?' she called as he strode towards the bar and she jogged to keep up. 'Rob! Is that you?'

Clara was panting by the time the man finally turned around. Her heart sank and her shoulders drooped with them.

'Are you alright, love?' His expression was one of concern.

Now that she was close enough, she felt a right fool for thinking this man bore any resemblance to her ex-husband. He was at least ten years younger and the long dark hair was about the only similarity. The anger she'd felt seconds earlier dissipated as frustration flooded into its place. Her eyes burned as she fought a sudden onset of tears.

'I'm sorry,' she managed. 'I thought you were someone else.'

'Not a problem.' The man smiled. 'You have a nice night.'

'Thanks.'

As he continued on his way, Clara remembered what she'd been doing when she'd seen him.

*Oh, please Lord, don't let me have missed Gregg's gig.*

With that thought, she hurried back the way she'd come, almost tripping a number of times in her haste to get to the theatre. The crowd were applauding as she entered and she glanced at the stage to see Gregg beaming as he made his exit.

315

*I've missed it.* Not for a long time could she remember feeling so utterly disappointed in herself. What had she been thinking racing after a Rob look-alike? She was with Gregg now. He was the one that mattered. He was the one who cared about her. Her heart heavy she made her way back to their seats, arriving at the same time as Gregg did.

'What did you think?' His face glowed from the buzz of performance, telling her it must have gone well, but happiness for him warred with self-loathing.

He obviously thought she'd been watching from the bar. She could lie, she could pretend she'd seen, but then what if he asked specific questions about his act?

'Where's the drinks?' he asked, frowning down at her empty hands as they simultaneously lowered themselves into their seats. 'Have you already drunk your wine?'

*Oh God.* 'I'm sorry,' she whispered, because the next act had begun. 'I missed you.'

'What? How?'

'I thought I saw Rob leaving the theatre. I went after him.'

'*Rob*?' His expression was a cocktail of hurt, confusion and curiosity, but mostly hurt.

She nodded.

'And was it him?'

'Can you guys shut the fuck up?' hissed someone behind them before she could reply.

'Sorry,' Gregg muttered and then crossed his arms and turned to face the front, not saying another word.

The next hour was excruciating as Clara sat there beside Gregg watching the rest of the amateur comedy acts. Although, judging by the reaction from the audience, many of the other contestants were good, Clara couldn't concentrate and she couldn't help noticing that Gregg's laughter didn't sound authentic either.

After what felt like hours the MC returned to the stage announcing the end of the acts and congratulating all who got up and gave it a go. 'The judges and I all agree that it was hard to pick an overall winner tonight,' she said. 'We're glad our boss is having a night off or some of our jobs might be in jeopardy. But we've managed to narrow it down to three. Third place goes to Macy Baker for her trip to the hairdresser musings. Second place to Duke Moore for his celebrity impersonations. And taking out the grand prize is Gregg Callen because all three of the judges are kicking themselves for not noticing the humour in those signs before. Congratulations, Gregg, you've won a hundred-dollar voucher and we're sure we'll be hearing more from you very soon.'

As the audience erupted into cheers, Clara stood to hug Gregg in congratulations, but he headed straight onto the stage without even acknowledging her. Her stomach clenched. He was annoyed with her. And rightly so. The people started to flow from the theatre the moment Gregg had accepted his prize but he stayed and chatted to the comedians.

She stood on the edge of the stage and waited for him, thinking that if he hadn't been angry at her, he would have gestured to her to join them.

Finally he came over to her. 'You ready to go?'

Ignoring the brusqueness of his tone, she smiled brightly and leant forward to give him a hug. 'Congratulations. Well done. That's fantastic.'

'Thanks,' he said, stepping back from her embrace quickly.

'Shall we go celebrate with a drink?'

Gregg shook his head. 'I feel like calling it a night. We've got to be up early tomorrow to disembark the ship.'

'Okay. Sure.'

Neither of them said a word as they headed to their cabin and Gregg didn't hold her hand as he usually did either. Once there, he immediately went into the bathroom to get ready for bed and Clara fought back tears. How quickly things could change. This morning she'd been envisioning jetting off overseas with this man, possibly spending the rest of her life with him, now he felt like a stranger.

'I'm sorry,' she said again the moment Gregg emerged.

He sighed deeply and perched himself on the end of the bed. 'Did you find him? Was the man you saw Rob?'

'No. It was silly. He only looked vaguely similar when I got close, but in that moment I felt compelled to check. I wish I hadn't. I'm devastated I missed your comic debut.'

'Do you still love Rob?'

She blinked; his question blindsided her for a few moments. 'No. I'm no longer in love with him. I was furious when I saw him—I wanted to hunt him down and tell him about his mum, about Josie.'

Gregg nodded. 'I understand.'

But Clara knew that understanding and forgiveness were two very different things. 'Thank you. I don't suppose you'd like to give me a private show now?' she asked hopefully.

He shook his head. 'Maybe another day. I'm not in the mood tonight.'

'Okay. That sounds good.' She tried to take comfort in Gregg's reference to another day, but couldn't shake the feeling that things had changed between them.

*Rebecca*

'Hope dialysis goes well this afternoon. I'll see you tonight,' Hugh said as he picked up his lunch from the kitchen bench and headed for the door.

'Thanks.' Rebecca smiled, trying not to dwell on the fact he didn't kiss her goodbye. At least they were talking again.

She wondered what she could do to fill in the time until her appointment and decided to throw herself into some spring cleaning; maybe while she was scrubbing the mould from the bottom of the shower, she'd have some sort of epiphany about how to tell Josie and Paige they were sisters.

Three hours later, the house was as clean as it had been since that day she came home from hospital and Rebecca had come to a decision. She would wait until Paige and Sol's wedding was out of the way. With any luck a paired match would be found for her and Solomon before too long. In that time, hopefully Robbie would turn up, but even if he didn't, once she was well again, she'd be able to tell Josie and Paige the truth without her illness muddying the waters.

Feeling good about this decision, Rebecca was putting away the cleaning things when her phone rang.

'Hello?' she said as she flopped down into a chair at the table, hoping she hadn't overdone the strenuous activity that morning.

'Hi, Rebecca,' said a slightly familiar voice. 'It's Clara. Rob's ex-wife.'

'Oh, hi,' Rebecca managed, her chest tightening as she anticipated why the other woman could be calling. 'How was your cruise?'

'Do you have time to talk?' Clara asked, ignoring Rebecca's question. 'I was thinking it might be good if you come to my place—there are a few things I want to discuss and it might be easier in person. Or we could meet somewhere if that's better for you?'

Rebecca glanced at the time on the microwave clock—there was still a couple of hours until she was due at the dialysis unit and she saw no reason not to spend them with Clara. 'No, your place is fine. I can be there in about half an hour.'

On the drive over, she wondered what Clara might have to say. Had she discovered something else about Josie? Maybe she'd already taken it upon herself to tell her. No, she wouldn't do that. Would she? It was more likely she had news about Robbie. Oh God, perhaps he'd turned up. Or been found. Was he …? That probably wasn't something Clara would want to tell her over the phone.

Her heart thumped as her brain ticked over all the possibilities.

Somehow she made it to her destination without crashing her car or having a nervous breakdown. Clara opened the front door before Rebecca had a chance to knock. The smile she'd always worn in hospital was noticeably absent; now she looked like a disapproving schoolmarm. Clara couldn't be much older than she was but as Rebecca met her gaze she felt like a child who'd messed up big-time.

'Hello, Rebecca. Thank you for coming. Do come inside.'

*You're welcome? My pleasure?* Rebecca wasn't sure how to respond to the other woman's greeting so she left it at 'hi' and then followed her down the hallway into the kitchen.

'Can I get you something to eat or drink?' Clara asked.

'A cup of tea would be lovely, thank you.'

'You're probably wondering why I've called you here,' Clara said a few minutes later as she put a cup of tea in front of Rebecca and then sat down opposite with one of her own.

Rebecca nodded, although she guessed it wasn't a social rendezvous. She'd be very surprised if Clara suddenly conjured a Tupperware catalogue and asked if she wanted to buy any containers.

'Last week when you told me your suspicions that Josie was yours and Rob's daughter, I was obviously in shock and I didn't tell you the whole story.'

'Whole story?' Rebecca frowned. What could Clara possibly have to add?

'Do you remember Rob's mother, Brenda?'

'Of course.' She and Robbie had spent more time at Brenda's place than they had at her parents' because Brenda had been far more accepting of their romance. Rebecca was pretty sure Josie had been conceived under Brenda's roof, but didn't mention this now.

'She recently had a fall and broke her ankle. Because Rob couldn't be found, Brenda called me from the hospital and I've been looking after her—making sure she has everything she needs, checking in on her,' Clara explained.

'So Brenda lives back in Sydney now too?'

'Yes, Rob moved to the city to pursue his music and she followed not long after we got married. There was nothing keeping her in Cobar. And don't get me wrong, I like Brenda but I'm trying to get on with my life and it all became a little overwhelming to be honest. I ran into Josie in the supermarket not long ago, when I was getting some groceries for Brenda. Josie could see I was upset and asked what was wrong. I probably shouldn't have burdened her, I was supposed to be the one helping her, but I found myself unloading. When I'd finished, she generously offered to meet Brenda and take on some of the load. I probably wouldn't have said yes, except I was due to head off on the cruise and I didn't know how I was going to leave when Brenda might need something.'

Rebecca startled as if she'd touched an electric fence. A chill ran down her spine. 'So Josie and Brenda have met?'

'Yes. They hit it off immediately. Josie sent me a photo of the two of them watching movies together on Saturday night.' She picked her phone up from the table, tapped at the screen and then angled it for Rebecca to see.

'Oh my God.' So, not only was Paige besotted with her secret-sister, but now Brenda and Josie were spending time together blissfully unaware of their connection?

'I know I said I wasn't sure if you should tell Josie your suspicions or not, but, if she is your and Rob's child—'

'She is,' Rebecca interrupted and bent to pick her handbag off the floor to retrieve The Letter. But, as she dug around in the bag to no success, she realised that in her haste to leave the house, she must have left it on the kitchen counter. *Dammit*. How could she be so careless?

'Are you okay?' Clara asked and Rebecca looked up to see the other woman frowning at her.

Trying to ignore the unease gnawing at her heart, she dumped her bag back on the floor. 'I was going to show you the adoption information. It arrived yesterday.'

Clara's expression grew pale. 'And ...? Is your daughter called Josie?'

'Josephine. I looked her up online. I found photos of her working in theatre—it's definitely the Josie my daughter, Paige, has become friends with.'

'I see.' Clara let out a long, resigned sigh. 'I've been thinking about this all weekend. Not knowing about his daughter was something Rob never recovered from. I might not be able to find him and let him know, but I can't sit by and watch Brenda and Josie get close, unaware that they are actually family. The guilt of knowing about this is eating me up already, so I think you should tell Josie your suspicions.'

She paused a moment. 'And if you don't, I will.'

Before Rebecca could digest what Clara was saying, her phone started beeping in her handbag. 'That's my dialysis reminder,' she said, glancing at her watch. 'My appointment is in an hour.'

Maybe she could skip it just this once.

'No.' It was as if Clara could read her mind. 'This has been going on for thirty-five years, another couple of hours, or even days, won't hurt. Go to your appointment. It's not going to do Josie or anyone else any good if you end up back in hospital.'

And with those words, Clara pushed back her chair and picked up the tea cups. Rebecca hadn't even touched hers and it didn't look like she was going to get the chance. Decision made. Conversation clearly over. Never mind the fact Clara had in essence just threatened her. Part of Rebecca felt indignant—what right did Clara have to make such a decision?—but a bigger part of her felt relief. Until it was all out in the open, they couldn't be sure how anyone was going to react.

And, until it was, neither could they begin to recover.

The only question was how should she do it? Who should she tell first? Paige or Josie? Perhaps three hours to herself while the machines pumped blood in and out of her body would give her the headspace required to work this out.

'Thank you,' she found herself saying to Clara as she too pushed back her chair and stood. 'I will tell her. Soon. And I'll let you know when it's done.'

*Paige*

'Mum?' Paige called as she let herself into her parents' house. Her voice echoed and a bark sounded from out the back. 'She must be out,' she told Josie as she ushered her friend inside. 'I'll just let Molly in and then grab the album.'

'She won't mind us being here or borrowing it without her permission?' Josie asked as she shrugged out of her jacket.

'Nah, course not.' She led Josie through the house and into the kitchen, where they found the dog—face pressed up against the glass door begging to be let in.

'She's gorgeous,' Josie said as Paige opened the door and Molly rushed over to investigate the visitor.

'She's a pathetic guard dog, but yeah, she's pretty special. Can I get you a tea or coffee?'

'Aren't you a beautiful girl?' Josie looked up from where she was rubbing Molly's neck and making smoochy noises. 'After the day I've had at school today, I could murder a coffee.'

'Coming right up, but just warning you Mum doesn't have a fancy machine.'

'That's fine. As my mum used to say, as long as it's hot and wet, it's perfect.'

Paige laughed, then grabbed the kettle to fill at the sink. 'So what was so terrible about your day?'

'Oh, you know, the usual, kids complaining about …'

But Paige didn't hear the rest of Josie's sentence. Between the kettle and the sink, lying on the kitchen bench, was a letter. At first she didn't think anything of it and was simply about to move it out of the way in case she spilt anything on it, but as she picked it up, she couldn't help taking a closer look. It was from the Department for Child Protection Western Australia and it was about an adoption.

'Oh my God.' Paige's heart crashed into her chest.

Josie looked up from where she was still lavishing affection on the dog. 'Are you okay?'

But Paige seemed to have forgotten how to speak. She couldn't tear her gaze from the letter in her hand.

'Paige?' Josie came up beside her. 'What's the matter?'

Paige looked into her new friend's eyes, still in shock. 'This piece of paper says my mum adopted out a child. When she was a teenager.'

Josie's eyes grew wide. 'Seriously? And you never knew?'

'No.' The shock stimulated her tear ducts and she swallowed to try and stop a flood of them. 'I had no idea.'

'Can I see?'

Without thinking that her mum might not want someone she barely knew looking at her private paperwork, Paige passed the piece of paper to her friend.

Barely before Josie's eyes had dropped to the paper, she too gasped. 'That's me.'

Paige was unable to comprehend Josie's words. 'What?'

'I'm adopted,' Josie told her. 'And before I married Nik my surname was Van Dijk. That's my birthdate and that's the hospital I was born in.'

'*Josephine.*' As Paige said the word goosebumps painted her skin. She'd only ever known Josie as Josie and had been in such shock when she'd first seen the letter that she hadn't even realised the baby on this paper shared the same first name as her friend.

'Yes.' The letter was shaking in Josie's hands.

'That makes you and me sisters.' She swayed a little and tears threatened at this joyful but shocking news.

'Half-sisters,' Josie said, her tone terse. 'I'm sorry, Paige, I've got to go.' Then, she grabbed her handbag from where she'd dumped it on the floor near Molly and hightailed it out of the house.

Only after Paige heard Josie's car reversing out of the driveway, did she realise she'd taken the letter with her. She was deliberating whether to chase after her when she realised her car was still at the café where she and Josie had met earlier to discuss her involvement with the picture book projects. Chat had somehow digressed from how Paige would assist the kids to wedding talk and Josie had mentioned she'd love to see the photos from Rebecca's wedding. They'd decided to carpool, which meant Paige was stranded.

But in lieu of what had just come to light, this seemed the least of her issues. There had to be some kind of mistake.

The kettle whistled and Paige whirled around to switch it off; in the time it had taken to boil, her whole world had changed. And a cup of coffee didn't seem nearly adequate for dealing with this revelation. She yanked open the fridge, relieved to find an unopened bottle of wine on the bottom shelf. After pouring herself a large glass, she sat down at the table—a lot of things might not make sense right now but at least one thing suddenly did. She hadn't been imagining her mother's weirdness around Josie. Had she known the connection when she'd been asking all those questions? How long had she had this information? And did her father know too?

He had to, otherwise her mum wouldn't have left the letter lying around in the kitchen. That felt like a double betrayal. All these years she'd thought them a tight-knit team of three and yet they'd been keeping this ginormous secret from her. She understood that maybe it wasn't the kind of thing you told a child, but she'd been an adult for almost a decade now. And who was Josie's father? Could it be a boy from the band her mum had been in in high school? It had to be—she remembered her mum mentioning the group a few times and her grandparents had always shut the conversation down pronto.

Dammit, who else was complicit in keeping this from her?

She was about to call Solomon and fill him in, when she heard a key in the front door. She and Molly met her dad in the hallway. He took one look at her and his face fell.

'Honey? What's wrong? Have you and Sol had a fight?'

Paige snorted. Right now Sol was the only person she knew she could rely on *not* to let her down.

'No. I found the letter about Mum's *other* daughter.'

*Rebecca*

Rebecca was surprised to see Paige and Hugh sitting at the kitchen table when she arrived home late that afternoon—she hadn't been expecting her daughter for dinner and her car wasn't out the front. She looked at the half-drunk wine bottle sitting between them, then noticed Paige's eyes were red, her lashes damp and her cheeks blotchy as they always were whenever she'd been crying.

She looked from Paige to Hugh and then back to Paige. *She knows.*

Rebecca's knees almost went out from under her. 'You *told* her?' Yet even as her voice rose to ask this question, the answer dawned. *The letter.*

'Don't blame him,' Paige said tersely. 'I found the letter. I can't believe you've lied to me and Dad all these years.'

Rebecca eyed the wine. Surely one small glass wouldn't hurt. Hugh and Paige wouldn't approve but then she was already in their bad books anyway.

'I'm sorry, Paige,' she said, resisting the urge to grab a glass. She took a seat at the table instead, and not a moment too soon—she felt more than a little dizzy.

'*That's* all you have to say for yourself?' Paige's tone made Rebecca feel more like the child than the mother here and she wasn't sure she had the mental energy to defend herself. At least she no longer had to work out how to tell Paige about Josie—three hours in dialysis, she'd been rehearsing different speeches in her head all that time and she hadn't been sure about any of them.

Now she only had Josie to worry about.

Rebecca took a deep breath, hoping oxygen would slow the spinning of her head. What exactly did Paige want her to say?

'What if I was a lesbian and had fallen in love with Josie?' Paige screwed up her face. 'The two of us could have been intimate and—'

'Don't be silly. You're not a lesbian so that's an unhelpful line of thought.'

Hugh raised an eyebrow at her and she knew what he was thinking, that until recently she'd thought she had a son and it could have been a problem if Paige had fallen for *him*.

'How much did you tell her? Did you tell her about Mum and Dad's underhanded behaviour?' Paige had always been closer to Rebecca's parents than she was herself but she should know what kind of people her grandparents were. 'Did you tell her no one ever gave me a choice? Did you tell her about their lies?'

Paige shook her head in obvious disgust. 'You always have a choice, Mum, and anyway, we're not angry about the fact you had a baby, it's the fact you chose to hide it from us all these years.'

Hugh nodded. Paige's anger and indignation seemed to have rejuvenated his, just when she'd thought he was beginning to forgive her.

'When were you planning on telling me?' Her rage was unrelenting. 'When were you planning on telling *Josie*?'

'Soon. Very soon. I've spent all afternoon trying to work out how. I know you're angry but I had to consider how Josie might feel when she finds out. As far as I know she's never tried to look for me, so I need to approach this with sensitivity.'

'It's too late for that.'

Rebecca's heart ground to a halt. 'What?'

'She was with me this afternoon. We found the letter together.' Paige held her chin high, her expression smug as if she was kind of proud of this fact.

Rebecca was winded a few moments, and then, 'How did she react?'

'How do you think she reacted? She was bloody shocked. She's probably wondering why you've suddenly decided to find out about her now.'

'Because,' Rebecca said, 'facing your own mortality is a sobering experience, it makes you—'

'She might be a match!'

For a moment Paige looked full of hope and Rebecca felt heartened by the fact that deep down her daughter obviously still cared about her health, about her, but she couldn't allow her to go down this path.

'That is *not* why I requested that information,' Rebecca said forcefully. 'Even if she is a match, I would never ask her of that. And I forbid you to either.'

'Instead, you're happy to let my fiancé sacrifice his kidney? That's why you suddenly agreed, isn't it? So you could find Josie without her thinking you wanted something from her.' Paige shook her head again. 'Well, you can forget using Solomon's kidney now. It's been withdrawn.'

Rebecca couldn't win and her usually sweet daughter's rage had her stomach squeezing. Was it possible to feel any more worthless? She looked to Hugh for some support but he remained irritatingly silent.

'By the way, who is Josie's father?' Paige asked, almost giving Rebecca whiplash with her quick change in direction. 'There wasn't a name for him on the letter. Is he one of the guys you were in that band with?'

'Yes,' was all she decided to say right now. No matter how angry Paige was, Josie definitely deserved to hear these answers first.

'And do you know where he is? Have you spoken to him? Does he know you've *found* Josie?'

At least she could honestly answer this, 'No. I have no idea where he is these days.' The thought of Robbie lost filled her with sadness—if only he were here right now; at least there'd be one person happy with this revelation.

'Well, do you at least have a name?'

Rebecca forced breath into her lungs. 'I'd rather be the one to tell Josie that. Could you please give me her phone number?'

Paige looked incredulous. '*I'll* call her and let her know you want to talk to her. I'm not about to hand over her number without her permission.'

Rebecca had never felt more like slapping her daughter as she did in that moment, yet at the same time, she couldn't afford to anger her any more. Paige too was hurt and in shock. 'Okay, I understand.'

Silence filled the room a few long moments and Rebecca found herself saying, 'Are you going to stay for dinner? Maybe we could order takeaway.' She wasn't hungry but if her daughter was fed, maybe she'd be in a more amenable mood to listen to Rebecca's side of the story.

Paige and Hugh exchanged glances and then she pushed back her seat. 'Dad, can you please give me a lift home?'

'Sure, honey.' He stood as well.

'Are you right to drive?' Rebecca asked, gesturing to the empty wine glasses on the table. 'I could drive her instead.'

She heard the desperate hope in her voice just as strong as the scorned disbelief in her daughter's reply. 'I'd rather risk my luck hitchhiking than ride in a car with you right now.'

Rebecca looked to Hugh—was he going to let her speak to her in that manner? She waited for the old 'Don't you speak to your mother like that' but instead he shrugged and grabbed his car keys from the hooks on the wall.

As her husband and daughter headed for the front door, Rebecca slumped back in her seat. This whole situation was breaking her heart.

It was time to stop being a coward and start trying to clean up the mess she'd created.

*Josie*

After leaving Paige's mum's house, Josie made a beeline to the nearest bottle shop.

'Have a nice night, sweetheart,' said the bloke behind the counter as he handed over two wine bottles in a brown paper bag. Somehow she managed not to whack him with the package.

'Thanks,' she said. 'And actually can you give me a small pack of Winfield Silver and a lighter as well, please?'

It was illegal to drink while driving, but it wasn't illegal to light up, so she paid for her cigarettes, went outside and did exactly that. She wasn't supposed to be drinking or smoking but these were extenuating circumstances. It wasn't every day you found your biological mother and in the very few times Josie had contemplated the possibility it had never been like this. She'd imagined them connecting through one of the adoption registers, getting to know each other via phone calls or emails first and then finally, one day, maybe meeting in person. And she'd never contemplated the possibility she might meet a half-sibling first.

As she drove, she glanced over at the handbag sitting on the passenger seat as if it were a ticking bomb about to explode—inside was The Letter. What did it even mean? Pausing at traffic lights, she yanked the paper from her bag and stared down at the date. *Last week*. It had only been sent last week. Josie knew enough to know that Rebecca could only have requested the information recently. But why? Why after all these years had she suddenly decided to do something? And was she planning on confronting Josie?

Someone behind beeped their horn, signalling their annoyance that the lights had gone green and she hadn't moved. Josie turned her attention back to the road and drove as fast as she could. Once home, she kicked off her boots and headed for the kitchen where she retrieved the largest wine glass they owned and filled it to the brim. Then, she took the letter, her drink and the rest of the bottle into the living room and sank down onto the couch. She absent-mindedly picked up the remote and turned on the TV.

Just when she'd finally been starting to feel a little better, life had gone and thrown this at her. Oh how she wished her mum were here right now to call for advice. She thought about phoning her dad, but immediately decided against it—this wasn't something she wanted to land on him over the airwaves.

A tear snuck down her cheek and she brushed it away.

There were so many questions whirling in her head. If Rebecca was her mother, who was her father? Maybe she was the product of rape? Bizarrely, the thought had never crossed her mind before but there was no biological father named on the birth certificate.

A whole other glass of wine was required for that thought. This was exactly what she'd feared all her life—that if she dug into her past she'd uncover things she didn't want to find.

Eventually, after almost a whole bottle of wine, she stumbled into the kitchen for a snack. Two-minute noodles were the easiest option and were something her mum often made her when she came home from school; the perfect quick comfort food. Josie put water into a saucepan, drank another half glass of wine while she waited for it to boil and finished the bottle as the noodles cooked to perfection.

When they were done, she grabbed a drainer, carefully—so as not to burn herself—poured the noodles into it and then set the saucepan down on a chopping board. A *glass* chopping board she realised as it instantly shattered. It was like a bomb going off in the kitchen. Tiny shards of glass sprayed everywhere. She dropped the drainer and the noodles all over the floor as she instinctively reached out to retrieve the saucepan. Somehow in doing so, she not only managed to burn her hand on the pan but wedge a large piece of broken glass between two of her fingers.

'Shit, ouch, shit, ouch,' she yelped, bouncing around on the shattered glass. Thank God she was still wearing thick winter socks, which offered a slight layer of protection.

Of course Nik chose that moment to arrive home. She cringed as she heard the door open—not even Mary Poppins would be able to clean up fast enough.

'What have you done to yourself?' he asked as he appeared.

'And a very good evening to you too,' she retorted, then glanced down at her hand to see she was dripping blood all over the floor. Surprisingly, it didn't hurt.

She followed Nik's eyes from her hand to the empty wine bottle on the kitchen bench. 'Don't even start. I found my mother today. Or at least I found out who she is.'

At this declaration she burst into tears.

'What?' He looked momentarily shocked, then he launched into action, grabbing paper towel. 'Let's get you out of this mess,' he said, ushering her out of the kitchen and into the adjacent, small dining room they rarely used.

'It's your fault for making me give Paige the dress,' she sobbed as he gently took her hand in his and surveyed the damage.

'I've no idea what you're talking about. Let's get you fixed up and then you can tell me.' He stuck his tongue out, concentrating hard as he tried to remove the glass from her skin.

'Youch!' she yelped as he succeeded in plucking it out—it was more the visuals than any pain. Her hand felt numb and she hoped it was the alcohol, not that she'd severed an artery or anything.

Nik shoved a wad of paper towel between her fingers. 'Is that a burn too?'

'Oh, yes.' She'd forgotten about that. Guess it must be the alcohol numbing the pain after all.

'You've really done a number on yourself, haven't you? Hold this,' Nik told her, gesturing to the paper towel, before rushing over to the fridge—the glass crunching beneath his shoes—and grabbing an ice-pack. He wrapped it in more paper towel and then pressed it against her hand. 'Cold water would be better, but I think stopping that bleed is more important.'

She nodded and he let out a deep breath.

'So, you found your mother? I didn't know you were even looking.' His tone was slightly accusing as if this was just another thing in a long line of things she'd done recently to let him down.

'I wasn't,' she said indignantly. 'I was at Paige's mum's house this afternoon with her and—'

'That blood isn't stopping,' Nik interrupted, gently peeling back the now-red paper towel. 'I think we're gonna have to take you to the hospital. I reckon you need stitches.'

'No,' she groaned. After her miscarriages, she hated hospitals and they'd all think her some stupid drunk who'd got sloshed and then injured herself. All those weeks of being sober wouldn't mean a thing.

But Nik wasn't taking no for an answer. Within minutes, he'd bundled her—and two more rolls of paper towel—into the car and they were on their way.

'Okay, I'm all ears,' he said.

'Well,' Josie began. 'So. Paige and I found a letter.' Her head started to throb, so much for the anaesthetising qualities of alcohol—and suddenly she felt like she might throw up. Telling him the rest of the story was not an option right now.

'A bottle of wine will do that to you,' Nik said dryly as she tried to stop herself from hurling all over their car. She thought she deserved a little more sympathy considering the circumstances.

When they arrived at the hospital, Nik helped her out of the car and she leaned on him as they headed inside. He dumped her in an uncomfortable plastic chair, grabbed a cup of water for her from a dispenser in the corner and then went to register at the arrivals desk. By the time he returned, Josie's nausea had settled a little and she managed to get the gist of the story out.

'So let me get this straight,' he said when she'd finished, 'you wore your mother's wedding dress when you got married?'

*Oh good grief*—until that moment she hadn't even thought about that connection.

'*Biological* mother,' she corrected him. Thinking of Rebecca as anything else felt not only weird but also a betrayal of the woman who'd raised her. Her *real* mum.

He shook his head slowly and scratched his chin as if still trying to get this straight. 'Fuck, Jose,' he said eventually and then pulled her against him. 'Why didn't you call me?'

'I'm not supposed to interrupt you at work unless it's an emergency.'

He pulled back slightly and gestured to the blood still seeping through the paper towel and all over his shirt. 'I kinda think this fits.'

'I guess I wasn't thinking straight.'

'It's okay,' he said. 'Geez. So does Rebecca know you know? How do you feel about this?'

'I guess Paige would have told her by now—I've had missed calls from her and someone buzzed the intercom this evening, that could have been Rebecca, but I pretended I wasn't home.'

'I wonder who your dad is. Are you even the slightest bit curious?'

'Of course I am,' she snapped. 'But …' Before she could continue, she glanced upwards and her gaze caught on a sign on the wall.

*ARE YOU AN ORGAN DONOR?* was in big bold print and beneath it a list of all the reasons you should be.

'Oh my God.' Realisation dawned hard, fast and cold.

'What?' Nik asked, looking worriedly to her hand.

'That's why Rebecca has suddenly decided to look for me!'

Nik frowned; although she was the one half-cut, she had to explain it to him.

'Remember why Paige wanted to find the wedding dress?' It was a rhetorical question but Nik nodded as she continued. 'Because Rebecca is sick. She has kidney failure and needs a donor to save her.'

He took a moment and then, 'That fucking bitch. How dare she!'

Josie found herself torn between the rage Nik felt and heartbreaking pain. For the briefest of moments she'd thought maybe her biological mother wanted to find her because she actually cared but the timing was hard to ignore. Tears came to her eyes.

'Josephine Mitreski?'

They looked up to see a stern-looking nurse standing a few feet away.

'Coming,' Josie said, rising to her feet and almost falling right back down again. Nik caught her and assisted as they followed after the nurse.

She hoped the hospital would give her some very good drugs that would make her sleep very well and when she woke up she'd discover this had all been a dream, like one of those badly written stories some of the kids in her class dared to hand in.

## Paige

Paige was in full-swing cleaning mode when Sol arrived home from work just after midnight.

'Do *not* enter the kitchen!' she screamed as he came to a grinding halt in the doorway.

He held up his hands as if the mop she was wielding in hers was a weapon. 'What's happened?'

'You will not even believe it,' she told him, dumping the mop in the bucket. 'Turns out Josie is my sister.'

His eyebrows caved inwards and he shook his head slightly. 'What? Josie and Nik, *Josie*? But you don't have a sister.'

'So I thought,' she replied, her grip tightening on the mop handle as her rage burned strongly. 'Turns out, Mum had a baby when she was sixteen with her bad-boy musician boyfriend that Jeanie and Grandpa didn't like. Her parents helped her "take care of it"—Mum and Gran went to stay with Jeanie's sister in Perth and she had the baby there, then adopted it out.'

'Jesus. I didn't think stuff like that still happened in the eighties. Your poor mum. Did she want to give the kid up?'

Paige ignored his sympathy for her mother. 'Well, as you said, it was the eighties—forced adoption was a thing of the past.' She'd checked that this evening just to be sure. 'So if she really wanted to keep it she could have.'

'This is big news.' He nodded towards the mop. 'Want to abandon that and come talk while I shower? I stink.'

She glanced around the kitchen; one corner still hadn't been done. 'How about you shower while I finish up. You hungry?' Not that she wanted to dirty up her now-pristine kitchen but, despite her mood, she wasn't a beast.

Sol shook his head. 'Nah. We had to go to a small house fire tonight and we stopped for burgers on the way back to the station.'

'Okay.' She nodded. 'I'll be in soon.'

Sol walked out of the en suite with a fluffy white towel wrapped around his waist just as Paige was coming into the bedroom. As he finished drying himself and pulled on some boxers, she flopped onto the bed.

'How did this all come to light?' he asked, coming to sit beside her. 'Did Josie or your mother tell you?'

'Neither,' she began, curling her legs up on one side of her and leaning into him. She told him about her and Josie finding the letter.

'Geez, and how's she handling this?'

'Who? Josie?'

He nodded and Paige shrugged. 'I don't know. She left almost as soon as we found it. And then Dad came home and he explained everything. I tried to call Josie tonight a few times but she's not answering.'

'Understandable. Give her time. So, what did Hugh say?'

Paige repeated their conversation almost word for word—how he'd only known about the adoption a short time, how apparently her grandfather had threatened her mum's boyfriend with prison or something if he didn't cut all ties with her, and how they'd lied about the gender of the baby. 'All these years Mum thought she had a boy.'

'That was a pretty shitty thing for your grandparents to do,' Sol said. 'Plenty of people have kids at sixteen and make fine parents. Doesn't sound like they gave your mum much choice, and what about the bloke? I'd be furious if someone kept me from my baby like that.'

Paige let out a frustrated breath. She hadn't given a thought to the father. 'Maybe so, but that's ancient history. The fact remains Mum went out of her way all these years *not* to tell us about her other child. I'm not sure I can forgive her.'

'Don't you think you're overreacting a little bit?' He sounded slightly bemused by all this.

*Overreacting?* She turned to glare at him. 'How would *you* feel if you found out you'd had another sibling all your life and nobody ever bothered to tell you?'

He considered this a moment. 'I guess I'd be a little upset, but then I'd think about how my mum must have felt having a baby when she was still practically a child herself and how painful having to give it up and never see it again must have been. I'd try not to make it all about me.'

'Excuse me?' She felt her cheeks flush. 'What are you saying?'

'I'm saying think about Rebecca—she must have been carrying a lot of pain, anguish and maybe guilt throughout the years. Why do you think now, all of a sudden, she's decided to get information about the adoption?'

'Apparently her health scare prompted it all. She didn't want to die not knowing, but when she was going to tell all of us I have no idea. Oh, and the reason she changed her mind about accepting your kidney was because she didn't want her child to think that's why she wanted to find them.'

His eyes widened. 'She said that?'

'Well, not exactly but why else the sudden turnaround?'

Sol frowned. 'I guess that makes sense. A lot of people who are hurt in fires or lose their houses report that their brush with death made them reassess a whole load of other things in their lives.'

*Whatever*. Paige was in no mood to listen to statistics about strangers. Fires and adoption were nothing alike. 'Anyway, I told her the offer is off.'

'What offer?'

'The offer of your kidney of course.'

'Um.' Sol lifted his hand from her knee. His stern expression was one she'd rarely seen aimed at her. 'Don't you think that's something you should have run by me first? My kidney, my decision.'

'You're *my* fiancé—you wouldn't have offered if it wasn't for me. If we weren't together you wouldn't even know Mum needed a kidney.'

Sol puffed out a breath as if he was trying not to lose his cool. 'Look,' he said, 'I get it, you're upset, you're still in shock, maybe you're a little jealous of Josie too, of the fact you weren't actually your mum's first child, so maybe we should both calm down a little bit and sleep on—'

'I'm not jealous of Josie!' she interrupted, outraged. 'I like Josie—she's not the one who lied all these years.'

Sol raised an eyebrow. 'Don't you think you're being a little harsh? You're normally so empathetic to the plights of others, can't you give your mum the same courtesy?'

'What?' She shook her head in anger. 'You can't compare Mum to the people I champion! They haven't chosen their circumstances but Mum *chose* to keep this secret.'

'Rebecca obviously thought she had good reason to do what she did,' he said evenly.

*Was he kidding?* 'So, you think secrets are okay in relationships? In marriage?'

'I don't think life is as black and white as all that.'

'Do you have secrets from me?'

'No. You know everything about me, but I haven't got something tragic like your mother had in her past and no one has ever told me anything in confidence that they didn't want you to know.'

Paige couldn't believe her ears. She opened her mouth, then closed it again. Was he really saying that if someone asked him to keep a secret from her he'd consider it?

Enraged, she grabbed her pillow and stood.

'Where are you going?' Sol asked.

'To sleep on the couch.'

'Don't be ridiculous.'

'I'm not being ridiculous,' she retorted. 'I just thought you'd be a little bit more supportive and I can't believe you and I have such fundamentally different views on honesty in marriage.'

'Paige. Let's talk about this.'

But, no longer in a mood for conversation, she continued towards the door.

'You stay here,' Sol called. She heard his feet land on the floor indicating he was getting out of bed. 'I'll take the couch.'

And because he was the one in the wrong and being so damn unsupportive, she decided to let him. 'Okay,' she said, stepping aside so he and his pillow could walk through the door.

He had the audacity to say 'goodnight' as he passed, but Paige didn't say a word; she simply slammed the door behind him and then burst into tears.

Of course they'd had disagreements before but this was the first time either of them had slept on the couch since they'd moved in together. The shit had got real today—she'd needed his support, for him to be on her side, and instead he'd all but called her irrational and selfish and made her question if they really knew each other at all.

## Clara

Wednesday morning, Clara was baking a carrot cake to take to Gregg—the way to a man's heart and all that—to apologise for ruining their cruise, when her phone rang. Although she hadn't stored Rebecca's number in her contacts, she immediately recognised it and was tempted not to answer. *This woman* had brought nothing but pain and heartache to her life. In some ways Rebecca and her baby had felt like the third person in her marriage, like Camilla had been to Charles and Di.

'Rebecca?' she said—not bothering with niceties.

The other woman made no attempt at small talk either. 'She knows.'

'How did she take it?'

'I don't know. I said she knows, but I didn't tell her.'

Rebecca was talking in riddles. 'What do you mean? If you didn't tell her, then who did?'

'No one,' she whispered. 'You know how I didn't have the adoption information in my bag yesterday? Well, Josie was at my place with Paige and they found the letter.'

'Oh my goodness. How did she take it?'

'I'm not exactly sure. Paige refused to give me Josie's number, so I went to her apartment but if she was there she ignored my attempts at the intercom and this morning Solomon, Paige's fiancé, called me. Josie's husband phoned and asked him to ask Paige and me to give Josie a little time; she'd contact us when she was ready. Nik said Josie had taken it pretty badly—I'm really worried about her but I want to respect her wishes. Do you think you could check in on her for me?'

*What a shambles!* Of course Clara would call Josie, but it wouldn't be for Rebecca. 'Yes, okay. I can do that.'

'Thank you. And can you let me know when you've spoken to her?'

Rebecca sounded desperate—why couldn't Clara bring herself to feel sympathy? Because now, knowing about Rob's visit to Rebecca the year Josie turned eighteen, she couldn't help resenting her for turning him away.

Still, Clara found herself promising to call with an update once she'd made contact with Josie. She disconnected and stared at the phone. Perhaps an in-person visit would be better. People could pretend to be okay over the phone but face to face it was harder to hide true emotion. And something told her that although today was a 'school day' Josie might not have made it in to work.

'Sorry, Gregg,' Clara said to herself as she finished smothering the cream-cheese icing over the cake and then popped it in a container to take it round to Josie's. She'd make it up to him some other way.

Decision made, she drove to Josie's apartment.

She pressed their button on the intercom and held her breath as she waited for a reply.

'Hello?' came a wary male voice a few moments later.

She leaned closer to the wall. 'Hello. Is that Nik? I'm Josie's friend, Clara. I've brought her some cake.'

'Um ... that's nice, but I'm sorry, Josie's not feeling very well today. I'll tell her you stopped by.'

'Can you just tell her I'm here and ask if she's up to talking to me?'

He gave a deep sigh. 'Can you wait a sec?'

'Of course.' Luckily with spring finally here, the weather had improved and it wasn't too cold waiting outside on the doorstep.

About thirty seconds later, Nik's voice came back through the wall. 'I'll buzz you in.'

The door in front of her made a click sound and she pushed it open. An incredibly good-looking, dark-haired young man, whom Clara immediately guessed to be Josie's husband, was waiting for her in the hallway between the ground-floor apartments.

He offered her a warm, welcoming smile and then lowered his voice. 'Josie told me who you are. Thanks for all you've done. She's been doing quite well, until a setback yesterday.'

'I understand. That's why I'm here.'

He frowned, but then Josie called out, 'I hope you're not giving Clara the Spanish inquisition!'

'Sorry,' he called back through the open door, then indicated for her to follow him into the apartment.

'Hey, Clara.' Josie was sitting on the sofa, her legs curled up beside her, hugging a cushion to her chest. She once again looked like the shell of a woman she'd been the day they met. And, her hand was wrapped in a bandage. What had she done to herself?

'Oh, sweet darling.' Clara's heart felt as if it could burst with love for this girl. She rushed over to her, sank down beside her and pulled her into her arms. 'It'll be okay.'

Josie's whole body racked with sobs as Clara held her a good five minutes until they finally subsided.

'How did you know to come?' Josie asked eventually.

'Rebecca called me,' Clara said. 'I know you said you needed time and didn't want to see anyone but I just wanted you to know I'm here for you. If you want to talk, we can or if you'd—'

'Hang on.' Josie blinked and pulled out of Clara's embrace. 'How did Rebecca know to call you?'

Clara's heart stopped—Josie had no idea of her connection to all this. *Oh boy.*

She glanced up at Nik. 'Do you think you could make us a cup of tea?'

He looked to Josie for the go ahead—no way was he going to leave her if she needed him.

Josie nodded, and Nik hesitated as if he still wasn't sure whether to go, before finally leaving the room.

She settled herself on the other end of the sofa as she tried to work out where to start. It might not be her place to tell Josie about Rob, but how else could she explain why Rebecca had called her?

'I met Rebecca a couple of months ago when she was admitted to hospital for her kidney problems, but unbeknownst to us we had a prior connection.' Clara swallowed—there was no easy way to say this. 'Rebecca and my ex-husband were high school sweethearts. About a week ago, she turned up on my doorstep looking for him because …'

Josie gasped and her bad hand rushed to her chest. She winced in pain. 'Rob's my father, isn't he?'

'Yes, honey.'

'Oh my God.' She covered her mouth with her good hand and her face contorted as if she were close to tears. 'That means Brenda is my grandmother?'

'She is.'

'Does she know?'

350

Clara shook her head. 'No. When Rebecca and I realised the connection, I told her she had to tell you because I believed you and Brenda had a right to know what you were to each other, but you found the letter before she had the chance. I was waiting until you knew to see if you wanted me to tell Brenda.'

Josie blinked. 'But Brenda told me about Rob's adopted baby—he was a boy.'

At that moment, Nik returned with tea on a tray. He took one look at the tears streaming down his wife's face and glared at Clara. 'You're supposed to be making her feel better.'

Josie waved a hand at him. 'It's okay. This isn't Clara's fault.' Then she looked to Clara and sighed deeply. 'Can you tell him?'

'Of course.'

Nik put the tray on the coffee table and went to perch on the sofa's armrest beside Josie. He plucked a tissue from the box already beside them, handed it to his wife and then wrapped an arm around her.

The tea on the table went cold as Clara filled Nik in and answered both their questions. She told them about Rebecca's parents—the threats and the lies—and how Rob had never recovered from giving Josie up.

When she was finished, Nik ran a hand through his hair. 'Jesus. And now your husband's missing, isn't he?'

*Ex-husband.* Clara didn't bother correcting him. 'Yes. He has been registered as a missing person for just over a month.'

Nik raised an eyebrow. 'Funny, I don't remember hearing about his disappearance in the news or anything.'

'There was a short article in the paper the week after he vanished, but apparently there are almost forty thousand people reported missing in Australia every year. The police simply haven't got the resources to give each one the necessary time and I guess, rightly so, children and teenagers are their priority. Rob's track record with depression and alcoholism means ...' She was going say it meant he'd probably chosen to disappear or worse come to a nasty end with no one to blame except himself, but this was Josie's father they were talking about now.

Nik finished for her. 'It means they don't think there's anyone else involved or that he's been a victim of crime.'

'Exactly.' She nodded and offered him a grateful smile.

'At least I know where my urge to drink in a crisis comes from now,' Josie said wryly.

'You had a mishap, that's all. You'll get back on track.' Nik reached for her hand.

At that moment his phone started ringing. He dragged it out of his pocket and glanced down at the screen. 'Will you be alright if I take this? It's my boss.'

Josie smiled. 'I'm fine. Clara's here.'

Again, Clara's heart swelled. She was so relieved Josie hadn't shot the messenger, so to speak.

'Are you up for a piece of cake?' Clara asked as Nik went into the kitchen to take the call. 'Not to blow my own trumpet or anything, but I'm pretty sure I make the best carrot cake in Australia.'

'In that case, how could I resist?'

Clara cut two slices using the knife Nik had brought in on the tea tray—someone had really trained him very well—then handed one to Josie on a small plate.

'Oh my God. This is amazing,' Josie said through a mouthful after taking the first bite.

Clara grinned. 'Told you.'

'I wish you were my biological mother,' Josie declared, her eyes suddenly misting again.

'Oh, precious, precious girl.' Clara took the plate from Josie, put it down on the coffee table and then wrapped her in a massive hug.

Tears came to her own eyes. How she too wished this were the case. 'If I was, I would never have let you go.'

They embraced for a few long minutes before Josie finally pulled back and said, 'Would you come with me to see Brenda?'

'Now? You want to tell her today?'

'Yes. But do you think she'll be able to handle the shock?'

'I think she'll be overjoyed, but, if there are any emergencies, don't forget I *am* a trained nurse.'

When Nik returned they told him of their plans and he insisted on coming with them. So as not to scare her new grandmother, Josie had a quick shower, made herself presentable and then they were on their way.

*Josie*

Things were getting more and more surreal by the second, Josie thought as she and Nik followed Clara to Brenda's place.

'You okay?' he asked. 'Sorry, stupid question.'

'I am. I'd actually been starting to wonder about maybe looking a bit into my birth, perhaps even trying to track down my parents.'

'You had?' Nik sounded rightly surprised.

'Yep. You know that night I found out who Brenda's son was?'

He nodded. After getting home from Brenda's, Josie had lain awake in bed for hours waiting for Nik, to fill him in on the exciting news that her new friend was the mother of one of the singers she'd obsessed about in her teens.

'Well, talking about adoption with Brenda made me realise how complicated it could be and I've been thinking more about my own situation than I ever have before. I was planning to talk to you about the possibility of sending off for information but I wanted to wrap my head around it first.'

'I understand. But I guess you don't have to go to all that trouble now.'

'Hmm.' There was that, but Josie still didn't know how she felt about the decision being snatched out of her hands.

Before either of them could say any more on the matter, Clara turned into Brenda's driveway and Nik stopped behind her. Josie found herself excited and nervous all at once. It felt as if she were about to meet Brenda all over again, only this time there was so much more at stake.

The three of them stood on the small porch a few moments later and Clara rang the bell. They hadn't phoned ahead to warn Brenda of their visit, so didn't want to let themselves in and risk giving her a fright. Knowing that with her dodgy foot, Brenda wouldn't be able to hurry to the door, they waited impatiently until she finally did.

'Well, isn't this a lovely surprise,' she said as she pulled open the door. 'I wasn't expecting either of you today, was I?'

'No, this is an unscheduled visit,' Clara said as Brenda's eyes went to Nik.

'And who is this handsome young thing?'

He chuckled as Josie introduced him. 'Brenda, I'd love you to meet my husband, Nik.'

'Pleased to meet you.' Nik offered the older woman his hand. 'Josie has told me all about you.'

Brenda blushed, obviously pleased. 'I hope good stuff.'

'Very good.'

'Can we come in?' Clara asked, interrupting the polite chit-chat, for which Josie was glad.

'Of course.' Brenda shuffled sideways to make way for them. 'I was about to make myself a toasted cheese sandwich, would you three like one or have you already eaten?'

Josie wondered if her grandmother—*grandmother*—lived only on toasted cheese sandwiches and looked to Clara for direction. Was this a food kind of occasion?

'That would be lovely but I insist on helping you make them since we've landed on you unexpectedly,' Clara replied.

They followed Brenda into the kitchen and Clara made good on her promise. Josie felt on edge sitting idle at the kitchen table but she couldn't be much help with her hand anyway.

'What have you done to yourself, dear?' Brenda said, when they sat down to eat.

'Oh, this?' Josie shook her hand and winced. 'Had a little cooking accident last night. Needed a couple of stitches but I'll be fine.'

'Is that why you're not at work today, then?'

Again Josie and Clara exchanged glances.

'Oh goodness,' Brenda exclaimed, turning pale as her hand rushed to her chest. 'You've heard something about Rob. That's why you're here, isn't it?'

'Not exactly,' Clara began, 'not anything recent anyhow—but this visit *is* about Rob.'

And then—thank goodness because Josie wasn't sure she'd have been able to get the words out without crying—she explained it all, Brenda's eyebrows getting closer and closer to the grey hair at her forehead with every word.

'Are you telling me Josie is my granddaughter?'

'Yes.' Josie could barely say the word as tears rushed to her eyes.

'Oh my, I think I might have a heart attack,' Brenda said and then burst into tears herself.

'Please don't.' Josie pushed back her seat and rushed around the table. She crouched next to the older woman, but when she opened her mouth she couldn't find words to convey her feelings. Brenda also appeared to be at a loss. They reached out and hugged each other.

Josie rested her head on her grandmother's chest and cherished the feeling of Brenda's arms wrapped around her, tears falling into her hair.

'Is it really true?' Brenda whispered eventually.

'Yes. As Clara said, Rebecca got the adoption information on Monday. And although your son isn't listed there, he was the father of her baby. Robbie is my dad.'

It was the first time Josie had said—or thought—'dad' in terms of her biological father. She loved the man who raised her, he was mostly definitely her father in all the ways that mattered, but she felt an unexpected affinity with Brenda's son. It wasn't only the music thing. Her mind boggled at the fact they'd actually had a conversation—it seemed cruel they'd met without any clue what they were to each other. So many times in the last few months she'd thought back to that kind stranger outside The Inferno.

Guilt pricked her heart at the thought that maybe if she'd searched for her parents as so many other adopted children yearn to do, she'd have found Rob and Rebecca before it was too late.

'Oh my sweet, darling boy.' Brenda stared at Josie as if looking for her son inside her. 'He would have been so proud of you. And your love of music … the two of you are so alike.'

A lump formed in Josie's throat at Brenda's use of the past tense. No, she couldn't bring herself to accept that Robbie was gone for good. She wanted to meet him properly, she wanted to talk to him again, to help him get the help he needed as he'd inadvertently helped her.

'We have to find him,' she said with conviction. 'Surely there's more the police can do. Maybe we can start a Facebook group. There's loads of pages and groups dedicated to missing persons. We can start a page for Robbie and ask our friends and family to share it. Someone is sure to see it who has seen Robbie and if not, people all over the world will keep a look out for him for us.'

'But you're not on Facebook anymore,' Nik said unhelpfully.

Josie glanced over at him—she'd almost forgotten he and Clara were here. Obviously she would reinstate her account. 'Can you go get my laptop?'

'What?' He blinked. 'Now?'

'Yes. There's no time like the present. We don't know what kind of state Robbie could be in, so the sooner we can find him and get him any help he needs, the better.'

Nik still didn't move. 'You're probably going to have to tell your dad.'

And it clicked he was talking about her adoptive father. Josie's shoulders slumped—she'd been riding along on adrenaline, thinking only of finding Robbie, but not of her father who would likely see her post and want answers.

'I'll call him now. Do you mind if I use the lounge room for some privacy?' she asked Brenda as she pushed to her feet.

'Not at all, dear. I just hope he's sitting down when you talk to him.'

Josie smiled. 'I'll make sure he is.' Then she turned to Nik. 'What are you waiting for?'

He stood. 'Okay, okay, I'm going.'

While Nik went to fetch the laptop and Clara made a cup of tea for Brenda, Josie called her father. She wasn't sure how he was going to react, but all she could focus on was finding Robbie. Suddenly that was the only thing that felt like it mattered.

'Sweetheart,' he exclaimed as he answered the call, 'this is a lovely surprise. How are you?'

They usually only phoned each other on the weekends—a call during the day during the week was definitely an anomaly.

'I'm … complicated,' she said, aware she sounded like a Facebook relationship status.

'Is something wrong?' He sounded worried and she wanted to put him at ease but also be careful not to hurt his feelings.

'Dad,' she began, 'I know I always said I didn't want to find my biological parents, but I've changed my mind.'

'Really? What's brought this on?' He didn't sound disappointed, merely curious.

And so she told him—about the dress, meeting Paige, and Clara and how that had led her to Brenda. 'I felt a connection with all three women almost immediately upon meeting them, but until Monday, I didn't know why. Then, when I was at Paige's mum's house with her, we found a letter containing all the details of an adoption. My adoption.'

The craziness of this situation didn't get any less crazy the more times she heard or told the story. Her dad was no less shocked than anyone else had been as she filled in the rest of the particulars.

'Whatever happens, you'll always be my dad, but I need to do this. I need to at least try to find Robbie—not only for my own sake, but also for Brenda's. She's lovely, you'd like her.'

'I understand, darling,' he said. 'You know your mother and I have always been supportive of whatever decision you made regarding your birth parents.'

'You didn't just say that to make me feel better?'

'No, honey. We love you exactly the same as we would if we'd conceived you ourselves, but we always felt grateful to the two strangers who created you. It's distressing to hear your adoption wasn't as legitimate as we were led to believe and my heart aches for that poor man.'

'Thank you, Daddy.' She hadn't called him that since she was a little girl. 'I love you.'

When Nik returned ten minutes later she was disconnecting the call. 'It's all done,' she told him as she all but snatched the laptop from his hands.

'That was quick.'

'You know we don't mince words in our family.'

'And he's fine with it?'

'More than fine. He says he'll share the post and get his friends to as well.'

'I see.' Nik still didn't look convinced of her plan. She saw his Adam's apple rise and fall as he swallowed. 'What if you can't find Robbie? Or worse, what if you get bad news?'

Josie knew he was really asking whether she was strong enough to be able to handle either of those scenarios.

'Look,' she said, reaching out with her good hand to touch his arm, 'I know you're concerned because you care and I love you for it, but I have to do this.'

'Okay.' Nik's lips twisted into a resigned grin. He knew that once Josie set her mind on something there was no use trying to convince her out of it.

The next hour was all go in Brenda's kitchen. The table was cleared, the laptop set up at one end and the Facebook page created. When Josie said they needed a couple of recent photos of Robbie, both Clara and Brenda looked contrite.

'Sorry. I cleared all photos of him off my phone when we got divorced.'

'My camera broke a few years back and I never worked out how to use the one on my phone,' said Brenda. 'I think the most recent photo I have is from his fortieth birthday. Remember we had a nice dinner at your place, Clara?'

Clara nodded.

An eleven-year-old photo wasn't ideal, but it was better than nothing. 'Do you think you could find it?' Josie asked.

'Yes—it's the one the police took to use but they brought the original back again. It's in a frame in my bedroom.'

'I'll go get it,' Clara offered.

Josie tried not to give in to the tingling in the back of her throat as she stared down at the photo of Robbie, her biological father. The resemblance between them was clear—and the physical attributes she didn't get from him, she knew came from Rebecca.

She didn't know how to feel about Rebecca. Whereas she'd instantly clicked with Paige and then Brenda, and she felt a burning urge to find Robbie and connect with him, she hadn't felt any such thing towards Rebecca. Not when they'd met at her house or even now that she knew about their biological link. Maybe this was because she didn't trust her. Rebecca had only recently been inspired to look into the adoption, whereas Robbie had always wanted to do so. Josie couldn't shake the suspicion that Rebecca's need for a donor had influenced that decision.

For a moment she found herself wondering if she was perhaps a match—just for interest's sake—but she quickly put this idea out of her head and focused on the task at hand. And, as she snapped the photo of Robbie with her phone and uploaded it to their newly created Facebook page, she had another idea.

'I wonder if we could get the media interested in our story?'

*Rebecca*

Rebecca had a rule—no answering her phone while teaching piano lessons—but when it rang while seven-year-old Balthasar Rafferty (whose parents thought he was a prodigy) was torturing the ivories late Wednesday afternoon, she pounced on it. Her ribcage squeezed around her heart as Clara's number flashed up at her. She'd been on edge all day waiting for this phone call, or better still, waiting to hear from Josie herself. It had taken all her willpower not to call the other woman or try to visit Josie again, but she'd told herself she needed to be patient. For her daughter's sake.

'Stop,' she barked at Balthasar now as she answered the call. 'Hello? Clara?'

'Hi, Rebecca.' The other woman sounded irritatingly calm as if Rebecca's whole well-being didn't depend on this call.

'Did you talk to Josie?'

'Yes,' Clara said. 'She's with me right now actually and she'd like to speak to you.'

'Great.' The word came out as a squeak as Rebecca's heart contracted so much it hurt. She'd never felt so terrified in her life. 'Put her on.'

Rebecca pressed her index finger against her lips telling Balthasar to keep quiet as another voice came onto the line.

'Hi. Rebecca?'

'Yes,' she whispered, fighting tears at the sound of Josie's beautiful voice. 'How are you?'

'I'm ... okay,' Josie replied. 'This has been very overwhelming but I'm coming to grips with it. I was wondering if you'd like to meet? Well, I know technically we already have met but properly this time. I'd love to ask you some questions.'

'Yes, of course. Where?' Balthasar's dad was due to pick him up in fifteen minutes and she could easily cancel her last two lessons of the day. 'Would you like to come here or do you want me to come to you?'

'I was thinking maybe we could meet for coffee on the weekend.'

*The weekend?* She bit her tongue to stop her sigh of disappointment. The two days left until then felt like an eternity right now. Still, she couldn't rush Josie. She'd waited thirty-five years, surely another couple of days wouldn't break her.

'Okay. Great.' She cringed at the sound of her overly chirpy voice. 'Saturday or Sunday? I can come to Coogee.'

'That would be great,' Josie said, and then named a café on Havelock Avenue. 'How's ten o'clock Saturday morning?'

'Perfect.'

Josie offered a short 'I'll see you then' and the line went dead.

Rebecca stared at the phone in her hand.

'Are you okay?' Balthasar asked and Rebecca realised she was crying.

'Oh.' She blinked and snatched a tissue out of the box on top of the piano. 'Yes. Fine. It's just allergies. Keep playing.'

'My little brother has allergies to peanuts,' Balthasar said, his fingers making no move towards the keys. 'If a peanut even goes near him he could die. Are you going to die?'

'No. Not today anyway.'

Appeased by her answer, Balthasar began on 'Mary Had a Little Lamb', getting all the notes wrong and out of order. She should correct him—his parents were paying good money—but she didn't have the mental energy to do so.

By the time she emerged from the piano room after two more lessons, she was well and truly craving a stiff drink. She'd been good thus far and managed to steer clear of any alcohol since her diagnosis, but Dr Chopra had said if there was a special occasion one drink shouldn't do too much harm, as long as it was counted within her normal fluid allowance.

If finding your long-lost daughter wasn't a special occasion, Rebecca didn't know what was.

However, when she entered the kitchen to find Paige helping Hugh with dinner preparations, her heart leapt and thoughts of a drink faded. If Paige was here for dinner, she couldn't be too angry.

'Hello, sweetheart,' she said, crossing the room to hug her daughter. 'What a lovely surprise.'

Paige dodged her embrace and looked to Hugh. 'Do you want me to set the table, Dad?'

'That'd be lovely, thanks hun,' Hugh said as he turned over the steaks on the electric grill.

Maybe Rebecca did need that drink after all. She crossed over to the fridge. It would be interesting to see if either her daughter or her husband made comment when she poured herself a glass.

If not, she'd know they'd completely given up on her. Yet, when she grabbed the bottle of white wine that had been in the fridge for months, she found it half empty and screwed up her nose in annoyance. This must have been what Paige and Hugh had been drinking the other day when she found them fuming over the letter together and now it would no longer be fresh.

There was no point in wasting her naughty glass of wine on old goods. She sighed and opted for water instead.

'How was your day, Hugh?'

'Not bad. Busy. What about yours?'

Although his tone sounded friendly enough, normally when she asked about his day he gave her a lot more—often telling her funny stories about the people he'd had to film.

'The same.' She took a sip of her water and sat down at the table. 'I got a phone call from Josie.'

That got both Hugh *and* Paige's attention.

'And?' they asked as they looked at her properly for the first time since she'd entered the kitchen.

'We're going to have brunch together on Saturday to get to know each other better.' That hadn't exactly been the way Josie had sold it, but Rebecca hoped it was the beginning of some kind of relationship.

'I'm seeing her tomorrow,' Paige said, and it was like she'd picked up one of the steak knives she'd just laid on the table, plunged it into her mother's heart and twisted it back and forth.

'That's great,' Rebecca managed. 'You did always want a sister.'

'Yes, and Josie's great,' Paige said. 'But we'll never be able to make up for all the years *you* kept us apart.'

At her daughter's accusatory tone, the knife went even deeper. Maybe Rebecca deserved Paige's wrath but it still hurt. 'I'm sorry,' she said, knowing those two words weren't even close to being enough. But what else was she supposed to say? She couldn't rewrite the past, even if she wanted to. And if she did, Paige might not even be here anyway.

'Whatever.' Paige turned away again. 'What else can I do to help, Dad?'

Hugh asked her to mash the potatoes and while they finished prepping the meal, Rebecca racked her mind for something to say. Did her daughter just need time? Rebecca already had to be patient about Josie, she wasn't sure she had enough in reserve to be patient about Paige as well.

When the plates were served and Hugh and Paige joined her at the table, she thanked them for the meal and then said, 'Have your bridesmaids had their fittings for the dresses yet?'

Paige rewarded her with an icy glare. 'There might not even be a wedding anymore.'

'What?' Rebecca dropped her fork to her plate. 'Why?' Panic set in at the thought that somehow Paige and Solomon had fallen out because of her.

'I'd rather not talk about it,' Paige said, before shoving a forkful of mashed potato into her mouth. 'Yum, Dad, this is delicious.'

'Thank you, sweet pea.'

Rebecca looked to Hugh for some kind of clarification, but all he said was, 'Paige is going to stay with us for a couple of days. Her bed's all made, isn't it?'

'Of course. Although no one's slept in it for a while, the sheets might be a bit musty. I can put fresh ones for you on after dinner.'

'The sheets will be fine as they are.'

The table fell quiet again. Rebecca tried to eat but Hugh's usually delicious mashed potato and gravy felt like she was swallowing gravel.

'How's the new book going?' she asked in another attempt at conversation.

'I haven't written or drawn anything in weeks.' And Paige's tone indicated she didn't want to talk about this either. She snatched up her phone and started tapping away on it.

Rebecca waited for Hugh to say something—mobiles at the dinner table had always been against the rules, something he'd implemented after filming a segment about family values—but he said not one word.

'Oh wow,' Paige exclaimed breaking the awkward silence that had descended upon the table.

'What is it?' Rebecca asked.

Paige looked to Hugh as if Rebecca wasn't even there. 'Josie's new Facebook page has already been shared over a thousand times.'

Hugh looked impressed. 'The power of social media never fails to exceed expectations.'

'Um, could one of you please fill me in?'

Paige let out a sigh as if irritated by this question but replied nonetheless. 'Josie and her grandmother have started a Facebook campaign to try and find her dad.'

'To find Robbie?'

'*Yes*,' Paige said in a tone that said Rebecca was stupid.

A million thoughts collided in Rebecca's head. Josie had gone to Brenda before even bothering to call her. She couldn't make time to meet her until the weekend but she'd already spent who knows how many hours throwing herself into finding her biological father? That hurt. And why was Rebecca the last one to find out about this? Josie had obviously filled Paige in on *everything*. Even Hugh already knew.

The answer was crystal clear. *Clara*. She'd obviously presented Josie with a skewed version of events—no doubt focusing on the 'poor Robbie' aspect. She could tell Clara didn't like her, but Robbie wasn't the only victim here and Rebecca longed for the chance to plead her case to their daughter.

Should she beg Josie to meet her sooner than the weekend?

'I can't believe you never mentioned you knew someone famous,' Paige accused. 'That you went out with him. You had a baby with him!'

That old chestnut again. Rebecca was getting irritated at being the villain here.

'He was hardly famous,' she snapped.

'I think he had one more hit song than you've ever had,' Paige retorted.

Once again Rebecca looked to Hugh for support, but once again he didn't come through. The tears that had never been far away these past few weeks threatened, but she refused to cry in front of them.

'Thanks for dinner,' she said, pushing back her chair to stand. She scraped her barely touched meal into the bin, dumped the plate into the dishwasher and then stormed off to her bedroom.

She'd thought Hugh might come after her, but when five minutes passed and neither he nor Paige appeared, Rebecca grabbed her laptop. She'd created a Facebook profile before she'd really thought the decision through. Now all her secrets were out in the open, there was no longer any reason for her not to be there. It was a lot easier than she'd imagined and within ten minutes she was sending friend requests to everyone she knew, including Hugh, Paige and Solomon.

This time when she searched for Josie, she found her immediately. For a brief moment she wondered why she'd been elusive before but then another quandary took precedence. Would Josie be annoyed if Rebecca requested *her* friendship? Would she feel it was an invasion of privacy? Would she feel pressured to accept even if she didn't want to?

This was so stressful—no wonder she'd stayed away from this world for so long. With a deep breath, she clicked the button to request Josie's friendship. There. It was done now and the ball was in her court.

Trying to ignore the loud, erratic beating of her heart, she went on to search for the group or whatever it was that Paige had mentioned. Typing the words 'Robert Jones Missing Person' immediately brought up the correct result. She gasped as she clicked the link and a photo of him sitting in front of a birthday cake ready to blow out the big four-oh candles greeted her. Couldn't they have found a more recent shot?

He hadn't aged particularly well but beneath the crusty exterior she could see the boy she'd loved and feelings she'd been battling for years swamped her. She'd tried to put him out of her mind, but he was always there lingering in the crevices. Sometimes when she was making love with Hugh, she even closed her eyes and thought of Robbie instead. Her cheeks heated and guilt filled her heart, but it quickly made way for sadness.

'Oh Robbie. Where are you?' She reached out and touched her finger to his face on the screen. A tear slipped down her cheek. She'd always felt slightly smug that Rob's band hadn't hit the real big time—it had seemed like just deserts for choosing music over her and their baby, which is what she'd always felt he'd done—but now she knew the truth, her heart ached.

He'd been so talented.

The last thing he should ever have been was a one-hit wonder.

The bedroom door opened and she snapped her laptop shut and then swiped at her cheeks.

Hugh raised an eyebrow. 'Paige has gone to bed.' And then he went into their en suite presumably to ready himself for the same.

Rebecca put her laptop away and waited for him to return.

The en suite door opened. He padded over to the bed without making eye contact, then climbed under the covers and reached for the Lee Child book on his bedside table.

'So what happened between Sol and Paige?' she asked.

Hugh inhaled deeply, exhaled loudly and then snapped the book shut. 'They argued over your little secret.'

Her throat tightened. 'But why?' She couldn't work out what bearing this had on her daughter's and future son-in-law's relationship.

'Apparently Paige was upset over the discovery you have another child, she has a sister, and Sol wasn't as supportive as she thinks he should be.'

Rebecca frowned. 'What did he say?'

'He seems to believe some secrets are okay in relationships—he stood up for you and got really angry when Paige said she'd retracted his offer of a kidney. He said it wasn't her decision to make.'

Rebecca had forgotten about that—her kidney problems had paled in comparison to everything else, if it wasn't for the reminders in her phone she'd likely have missed dialysis—and guilt swamped her at the realisation that she was the reason for the problems in her daughter's relationship. Whatever happened, it suddenly became clear that she couldn't take a kidney from Solomon. She'd go on the deceased donor list; dialysis wasn't that bad anyway. Right now it was almost preferable to being in her own house; at least at the hospital people didn't give her the cold shoulder and look at her like she was pond-scum.

'I'm going to talk to her,' she said, throwing back the covers.

'I wouldn't advise it. She needs a little time to cool down. You've said sorry. What else are you going to say? She'll talk when she's ready.'

Rebecca was torn between heeding his advice and telling him where to go. After an internal debate, she flopped back against her pillows.

'What were you doing on the computer before?' he asked.

The question startled her and she floundered around in her head for an answer that wouldn't upset him.

'I joined Facebook,' she said because the moment he checked his phone, he'd see her friend request anyway.

'So you could check out your old boyfriend?' His tone was caustic.

She felt defensive. 'Okay, yes, I did check out the page that Josie has set up. Now I know the truth about what happened all those years ago, I'm devastated for Robbie. And I can't help feeling upset that Josie has gone to all this trouble already to try and find him when she can't fit me in until the weekend.'

Hugh didn't appear to hear this last bit. 'How am I supposed to compete with a rock star?'

'He's not a rock star,' she scoffed, 'and you're not competing with anyone. You're my husband.'

'Yes, but the question is, would I be if your parents hadn't intervened?' He looked her right in the eyes as he said this. 'I've always felt I loved you more than you loved me, Rebecca, but all these years I didn't know why. Now I do.'

His words stunned her. She'd always overcompensated, making a big show of how happy she was with Hugh, making sure Paige knew her parents loved each other, and he'd never questioned any of it before. Was it true he'd always felt like this?

In her shock, she took too long to reply.

Her whispered, 'That's ridiculous, I do love you,' was said to his back and she wasn't sure it held the conviction it should.

*Paige*

When Paige headed into school on Thursday morning, nerves she hadn't felt the first time swirled in her stomach. She placed a sweaty hand on her stomach, trying to fight the nausea that rose within as she waited for Josie to come meet her in reception.

Yesterday evening she'd led her mum to believe that Josie had contacted her and *wanted* to meet her today, but that wasn't exactly the truth. Although Nik had asked them to give Josie space, Paige had already been scheduled in to help the students with their picture book projects today and so yesterday she'd used that as an excuse to reach out to her sister.

*In the light of everything that's happened, do you still want me to come to school tomorrow? x Paige*

One hundred and twenty excruciating minutes later Josie had called.

'Thanks so much for getting in touch. I had the day off work today but I'll be back tomorrow and I don't want to disappoint the kids. They're really looking forward to working with you again.'

'Okay, great,' Paige had said, her heart leaping at the fact her sister hadn't cancelled. *Her sister!* 'And ... how are you today? I know this is a bit of a shock for all of us.'

Josie had chuckled lightly. 'That's one word for it, but I'm doing better than yesterday.'

And that's when she'd filled Paige in on everything and Paige had realised that the adoption shock was only the beginning of the revelations. Perhaps she should have let her mother explain a little more before she'd asked her father to drive her home.

Yet, although their conversation on the phone had been comfortable enough, Paige was terrified things would have changed between her and Josie now.

The door to the reception opened and in walked the woman herself—Josie looked pretty much the same as usual, except for her right hand was wrapped in a bandage.

'Hey, Paige,' she said.

'Hi.' Paige offered her a tentative smile. The last few times they'd met, they'd greeted each other with an easy hug but neither of them did so today. 'What did you do to your hand?'

Josie lifted her arm and looked down as if she were seeing her hand for the first time. 'Oh, this?' She shrugged. 'It was a silly accident—I'll fill you in later. The kids will be waiting.'

Her introduction was brief, then she gave Paige the nod to start doing the rounds and retreated to her desk.

Paige had to admit some of the kids had unique and clever ideas— there was a surprising amount of talent among the testosterone and body spray—but she struggled to give them her full attention. Her gaze kept drifting to Josie who was tapping away on her laptop.

*That woman is my sister!*

They'd clicked almost instantly so in some ways this thought wasn't a stretch of the imagination, but the knowledge left Paige questioning everything she thought she knew. Her whole identity felt as if it had shifted. All these years she'd thought she was an only child and all along her mum had another daughter. She had a sister. She *was* a sister.

And her parents' marriage wasn't the perfect relationship she'd always thought it to be.

'So do you reckon someone will publish our book?' asked one of the boys—Paige thought his name was Noah—jolting her from her thoughts.

She summoned a smile. 'I love your enthusiasm, but most publishers want to see a finished manuscript not simply an idea from a debut author before they offer a contract.'

'Okay, miss. Promise I'll do you proud.'

While Noah got into actual writing, Paige moved onto the next student and tried to focus on them rather than Josie. The period seemed to last forever but finally the siren went and the kids gathered up their things. Within thirty seconds the room was empty, leaving Paige and Josie alone again.

'They're really great kids. I'm amazed by some of their ideas.'

'The thing about kids is that they—well, at least this bunch—believe they're awesome and that they can do whatever they set out to do. The real world hasn't ground them down yet.'

Paige sighed deeply—until a few days ago, she'd felt like one of these students.

'Thanks for coming in,' Josie said, starting around the room to pull down the blinds. 'It really makes a difference for them to have you here—it's inspiring.'

'It's my pleasure.' Paige paused a moment then cleared her throat, which felt as if her heart was lodged there. 'Have you got time for a quick coffee?' She sounded like a teenage boy asking his crush to the school ball, but she wanted to know where she stood with Josie. If they were still friends.

Her sister hesitated a moment, then nodded. 'That would be great. Give me five to pack my things and I'll meet you at Harpers by the Beach.'

'Sounds good.'

'Sorry I'm late,' Josie said, when she arrived and flopped into the seat opposite Paige. 'I got caught up talking to someone at school.'

'It's fine. I haven't anywhere else to be.'

A few moments of uncomfortable silence lingered between them, until Josie finally said, 'Well, I guess we have a bit to talk about.'

Relief flooded Paige. 'Yes. How are you digesting the news?'

Josie held up her bandaged hand. 'I freaked out at first, hit the bottle and then burnt and cut my hand trying to make a snack.'

Paige winced. 'Ouch.'

'I'm not proud of my behaviour but then I'm not sure how you're supposed to react when you unexpectedly stumble upon the details of your birth while hanging out with the half-sister you never knew existed.'

Paige offered a wry smile.

'What about you? What did you do when I fled?' Josie cringed. 'And sorry about rushing off and leaving you without a car. I wasn't thinking straight and it didn't dawn on me until the next day how selfishly I behaved.'

'It's fine. I understand. Dad came home not long after and told me everything he knew—he'd only just found out as well. Neither of us can believe Mum kept you a secret all these years. And then she came home and tried to justify her actions. I've never felt such fury

375

in my life. I couldn't listen to another word of her pitiful excuses for what she'd done to you, to us, so Dad took me back to collect my car. Then I drove home and Solomon and I had a massive fight.'

Paige's eyes grew suddenly hot and her lungs ached—could they be feeling relayed pain from her heart? She couldn't just ignore what Solomon had said but how could she let it go either?

Josie reached her good hand across the table and put it on top of Paige's. 'What did you guys fight about?'

Paige swallowed, choking back tears as she gave her the rundown.

'Sol's a match for your mother?'

'No.' Paige explained about the Paired Kidney Exchange Program. 'It's the worst fight we've ever had, and I think it might be the last. How can I marry a man who has such fundamentally different views on marriage to me?'

'Men.' Josie shook her head in sympathy and retrieved her hand.

'Yes.' Paige rolled her eyes and tried to laugh. 'Anyway, I still can't believe Mum kept you a secret all this time. I'm sorry. If I'd known you existed, I'd have looked for you years ago.'

'I've known there's a possibility you existed for a long time,' Josie said, her tone almost apologetic. 'I knew my biological parents had me in their teens and that there was a chance at least one of them had other kids, but I never wanted to look.'

'Never?' Paige couldn't imagine being able to live with such a mystery. 'Didn't you wonder what your folks were like? Didn't you want answers to so many questions? Not knowing would have driven me insane.'

'No. It might sound hard to believe but I never did. I had a great childhood and I felt very close to my adoptive parents—I didn't want to do anything that might jeopardise that.' She paused as a waiter with a hipster beard and thick-rimmed black glasses arrived at their table.

'Are you ladies going to order drinks?' Although he smiled and sounded chirpy enough, the message was clear—if they weren't going to buy something, they shouldn't be occupying a table.

'Oh, sorry.' Josie made a move to stand. 'What can I get you, Paige?'

'I'll have a hot chocolate, please.'

The waiter held a hand out to Josie indicating she should sit. 'It's okay, we don't usually do table service, but I'll put your order in and bring your drinks over. Looks like you're deep in important conversation.'

He had no idea.

They both uttered their thanks and Josie sat down again. 'I guess I thought if my parents wanted to find me they would, but that if I went looking there was the chance I might discover something I'd rather not know.'

'Like what?' Paige asked.

'Like I had drug addicts or serial killers for parents. Or that I was the product of rape. That my parents were dead or ...'

'Missing?' Paige prompted when Josie didn't finish her sentence.

Josie nodded. 'And I guess my worries were warranted, because my father turns out to be a depressed alcoholic and my mother is fighting a serious illness. Not exactly rainbows and unicorns.'

'Well at least you're doing something to find him,' Paige said, not really knowing what to say to that. 'I shared your Facebook page.'

'Thanks. I saw.'

'I don't suppose you've had any leads yet?'

Josie shook her head. 'No, but I shared the page to a whole host of news and current affairs shows and have sent messages to their enquiries pages, asking if any of them would be interested in doing a story on Robbie—his music career, the adoption and the fact he's missing.'

'That's a great idea.'

Josie's shoulders sagged a little. 'I know it's early days but I haven't heard back from any of them. I have to admit I thought people would be more interested, what with Robbie being famous and everything.'

Paige didn't admit that although she knew One Track Mind's hit song, she wouldn't have been able to name the band it belonged to. She so desperately wanted to do something to make her new sister happy. 'I'm not sure if I've mentioned it, but my dad works for Channel Seven. I could ask if he had any contacts who might be able to do that?'

Josie's eyes lit up. 'You think he'd help?'

Paige swallowed. She wasn't sure how keen he'd be to help find his wife's first love, but she also knew he could never bear saying no to anything she asked. 'Of course he will,' she said—and if not, she'd go into the station and convince his colleagues herself.

'Thank you, Paige. I don't really know what else we can do.'

Paige glowed inside. 'It's my pleasure. I'll talk to him tonight.'

Josie's expression turned serious. 'I think you and Sol will get through this, but do you think he'll stay on the kidney exchange program with Rebecca if you do break up?'

Paige shrugged. 'Probably. He's like a bloody saint. If Jesus were alive, Sol would give him a run for his money.'

Josie snorted. 'Saint Solomon. It has a nice ring to it.'

But Paige wasn't in the mood to laugh. 'Why?' she asked.

'Why what?'

'Why do you ask if Sol will still donate?'

Josie glanced down at the table. 'You said there were no family donors? I can't help thinking that maybe the only reason Rebecca looked for me was because of the kidney, if she hoped maybe I'd be a familial match?'

'I asked her that too,' Paige admitted, her heart aching for Josie. 'Mum's adamant that's not the reason she requested the information, but I don't blame you for being sceptical. She says you're going to see her on the weekend?'

'Yes.'

'You don't sound all that excited about the meeting.'

'I'll be honest,' Josie said. 'I don't know how to feel about Rebecca. The position of mother is already taken in my heart.'

While part of Paige understood, there was one thing she didn't quite comprehend. 'But you're going to great lengths to find Robbie,' she said. 'Don't you have such a great relationship with your adoptive father?'

'No. No, it's nothing like that,' Josie rushed to assure her. 'I adore my dad. But Robbie always wanted to find me. Your grandparents threatened him with prison if he didn't let me go and he never got over that.'

Paige gasped and pressed her hand against her heart. 'Prison?'

'Yes. Your mum was underage when they slept together.' Before Paige could even begin to try and digest this news about her beloved grandparents, Josie added, 'Brenda and Clara both confirm that he's lived his whole life thinking about me, whereas Rebecca had spent hers hiding me.'

Her dad had told her this part and while she couldn't argue with the facts, it was still awful to hear about her grandparents being the villains in this story. She'd been so angry at her mother, but for the first time, she felt some of that anger towards her grandparents instead.

'I also want to find him for Brenda, for his mother. She's such a sweet lady and she deserves to know what has happened to her son.'

'I understand. And I'm sorry.'

'None of this is your fault. One of the best things in all of this is that we've found each other.'

Paige held her breath as she said, 'So you *want* us to be in each other's lives?'

Josie gave her a look. 'I thought I'd already made that clear. Things are complicated with Rebecca and weird with Robbie, but it's different with you and Brenda. I knew you both before this revelation and I'd already begun to fall in love with you guys. Sure, it's weird adjusting to the knowledge that we're related but I want you both in my life. You and me? We're sisters. That's if you want us to be.'

'I do,' Paige whispered, a tear escaping as her lips cracked a smile. 'I definitely do.'

'Good.' Josie's eyes were also glistening and she grinned as she reached across the table and took hold of Paige's hand again. 'It'll be okay. This has been a shock but we'll work through it—you'll set things straight with Solomon. While I don't agree with him on the secrets in marriages thing, he has got a lot of other good points and I'm sure you can educate him. But you guys are too good together to throw your future away on your first serious fight. Trust me, relationships are hard, *life* is hard and it's probably gonna throw a whole lot more drama at you.'

Paige knew Josie wasn't talking about the whole adoption surprise now, but about her miscarriages and her yearning to have a baby with Nik. This may have been the first real speed-bump in her relationship with Sol, but she suddenly knew that there was no one she'd rather ride life's highs and lows with than him.

'So you think I overreacted as well?' she asked.

Josie shrugged. 'I think you acted in shock. We both did.'

'And maybe I owe Sol an apology?'

'I'm not going to tell you what to do, but I think it's definitely worth talking to him a bit more before turning your back on him. Believe me, good men aren't that easy to come by. We all make mistakes and in the end we're also allowed differences of opinion, even with those we love—life would be pretty boring if we all thought the same about everything, don't you think?'

Paige nodded. 'And I think you just offered me your first bit of sisterly advice.'

'I did, didn't I?' Josie grinned and sat up proud and tall. 'How'd I do?'

'Well, if I were a teacher and marking your efforts, I'd give you an A-plus.'

They both laughed, then Paige said, 'If Solomon still wants to marry me after all this, will you be my chief bridesmaid?'

'Oh Paige.' Josie covered her mouth with her hand and took a few moments before adding, 'There's no *if* about it and I'd be delighted.'

## *Clara*

Shadow barked as Clara approached Gregg's front door on Friday afternoon. She smiled at the sound—she wasn't sure what reception she was going to get from his owner, but at least she knew the dog would be happy to see her. Clutching a Tupperware container with the second carrot cake she'd made this week to her chest, she lifted her free hand to ring the doorbell.

She didn't have to wait long before the door opened and a bundle of black fur burst from inside, almost knocking her onto the ground.

'Oh Shadow, it's lovely to see you too,' she laughed as she tried to regain her balance and keep hold of the cake, all the while looking up to try and gauge Gregg's response.

'This is a surprise.' The fact he didn't say 'nice surprise' left an empty feeling in the pit of her stomach.

They hadn't seen each other since his hasty departure after dropping her back at her house on Tuesday. After her thwarted attempt to apologise Wednesday morning, she'd called him last night to fill him in, but the call had gone straight to voicemail, so she'd decided to land unannounced today and try her luck.

'I remember you saying how much you like carrot cake,' she said, holding out the container like some kind of peace offering.

'Thanks.' Gregg took it with a nod. 'I do. Would you like to come inside and have a slice with me?'

'Yes. Yes, I would.' She smiled her relief—for a few moments there she'd thought he was going to send her and the cake on their not-so-merry way.

Gregg stepped aside to let her in but Shadow had other ideas; he was still jumping up all over her, sniffing and licking as if it were an event in the canine Olympics and he was in serious training.

Gregg chuckled. 'Looks like Shadow missed you.'

'Only Shadow?' She sounded needy even to her own ears but she couldn't resist the question.

'I may have missed you too,' he conceded with a near-invisible nod of his head.

Feeling bold, Clara used this little nugget of encouragement to step close, stretch up on her tippy-toes and kiss him on the lips. His mouth felt warm and familiar and although it had only been three days since they'd departed the ship, it almost felt like decades since she'd seen him. She sighed in happiness as his arms came around her and he deepened the kiss and she didn't even care about the Tupperware container digging into her back.

Clara found herself thinking that maybe they should migrate to the bedroom for what the young folks called 'make-up sex' when Shadow nudged his way in between them. They both laughed and pulled back.

'I think the dog thinks you came for him,' Gregg said.

Clara smiled and reached down to ruffle Shadow's fur. 'Maybe I did, but the cake I made for you. It's an apology.'

'It's alright, I was probably unfair. I think the nerves and the adrenaline were playing havoc with my head. And I guess I was a little bit jealous that you chose Rob over me.'

She appreciated Gregg's words, but he was not the one in the wrong here. 'That's sweet of you. I was really excited about being there but my mind wasn't fully on the cruise. And you've got to believe me, it wasn't that I chose Rob over you but I couldn't get the revelation about his baby out of my head. I wasn't thinking straight when I thought I saw him and I lost my head a moment. That was unfair to you, to us, but I've taken steps to fix that and I promise that your next live gig, I'll be there with bells on. I'll even bring my whole family along as a cheer squad.'

'That will require a pretty big venue,' he said with a chuckle, and then nodded towards the kitchen. 'Come on. I'll put the kettle on.'

Clara nodded, trying to swallow her disappointment at his suggestion. The kiss had awoken her libido and she'd been hoping they could talk in the bedroom after she'd given him a different kind of apology altogether. She made a mental note that if she ever needed to grovel to Gregg again, she'd dig out some fancy lingerie—not that lacy knickers had ever really been her style—rather than her baking utensils.

Gregg gestured for Clara to go down the hallway ahead of him. Shadow, twigging that there might about to be food on offer, rushed ahead of the both of them.

'Take a seat,' Gregg said, nodding towards the bar stools at his kitchen counter as he put down the Tupperware and went for the kettle.

'Can I get plates for the cake or anything?'

'No, just sit,' he said, and so she did as she was told.

Gregg's kitchen was clean, tidy and well-ordered and she knew from experience that it wasn't because he didn't use it. No, he was a skilled cook—she'd been treated to his culinary talents—and he pulled out fine china plates now to put the cake on. She had similar plates at her place but in all the years they'd been married, Rob had never used them—he probably hadn't even known where they were kept. These differences between her ex-husband and her new man kept popping into her head and she wished they'd just bugger off.

*Of course* they were different—that was the point. Gregg was ten times the man Rob was.

'What did you mean when you said you've taken steps towards getting Robert's dramas out of your head?' Gregg asked as he made her tea in exactly the way he knew she liked it.

Heat rushed to Clara's cheeks—could he read her mind? She was unsure how to answer, until she remembered what she'd said to him in the hall only a few minutes earlier.

'Oh.' She couldn't help sighing in relief and immediately hoped he didn't notice. 'Well, after missing your gig on the ship, I realised that I couldn't just pretend I didn't know about the connection between Josie and Brenda—Rob's mother—when I was the one who'd introduced them. I knew that until it was out in the open, I wouldn't be able to focus on anything else—like us.' She smiled. 'So, that morning when we got back, I called Rebecca and told her to tell Josie the truth or I would.'

'I see.' Gregg sounded impressed. He pushed a fine china cup and saucer that matched the plates towards her and then picked up a knife to slice the cake. 'And, has she?'

'In the end, she didn't get the chance. Josie found out herself.'

'What?'

And while she filled Gregg in on Paige and Josie's discovery of the letter, he cut a portion of cake for each of them.

'Geez,' he said when she'd finished. 'And how did the two of them take that?'

'They were both in shock—obviously Josie knew she was adopted but she'd never attempted to search for her biological parents and Paige had no idea her mother had ever had another child.'

'Things like that always come out in the wash eventually,' he said. 'So do you feel better, less crazy, now it's all out in the open?'

She laughed. 'Much.' And then took a satisfying sip of her tea; it was starting to go cold but that didn't matter—the most important thing was that she and Gregg were talking again.

'How did Josie react about Robert?'

'Actually, considering how emotional she already was when I told her, she took it surprisingly well. She wanted to go round and tell Brenda immediately and it was quite beautiful watching the two of them realise what they were to each other.'

Gregg was quiet, then, 'Hang on. Why did *you* tell Josie? Wasn't it Rebecca's place to do so?'

'Well, she would have told her if it had all happened properly, but as Rob's name isn't on the birth certificate, Josie didn't find out about him in the letter. Rebecca called me to tell me that she knew and asked me to go check she was okay. Of course Josie wondered how I knew what was going on and that's when I had to give her the truth about her father.'

'Poor girl.' Gregg shook his head. 'Must have been a shock to find out that her father is a missing person.'

'Yes, but I think it helped Josie to learn that Rob never wanted to give her up, that he never forgot her and always wanted to find her. And now she's determined to find him.' Clara couldn't keep the excitement out of her voice. 'We've launched a Facebook page to look for him and Josie's hoping to speak to the media and get some attention that way.'

'We?' Gregg asked. He'd been reaching for another slice of cake but he dropped his hand to the bench. 'I thought the idea of telling

Josie the truth was that she and Brenda would have each other and you'd be free of the whole situation? Free to move on, to focus on other things.'

Clara blinked, not sure what to say. How could she explain that she couldn't just turn her back on Josie now? Not after all they'd been through together. 'Yes, I know and I will, but Josie and I have become friends—she's almost like the daughter I never had. I can't just—'

'She's Rebecca's daughter,' Gregg interrupted. 'Rebecca and your *ex-husband's.*'

Clara felt heat rush to her cheeks. 'I *know* that,' she said, 'but right now she needs emotional support as she comes to terms with her situation. I can't just abandon her and Brenda.'

'So, how long does this go on for? What happens when—*if*—Robert is found. Are you just going to step back out of Josie's life then?'

'I guess that will depend on the outcome.' She swallowed. 'I hope he's found and that the two of them have the chance to develop a relationship. I hope finding out about Josie gives Rob the motivation he needs to get the help I've always wanted him to get, but he's an alcoholic and Josie might still need support to deal with that.'

'Right,' Gregg said, and Clara couldn't read his tone but the way he folded his arms across his chest told her pretty much everything she needed to know.

Still, she asked, 'What's that supposed to mean?'

'You said you've had enough of all the drama associated with Robert,' he said, 'but it seems to me you keep chasing after it. You've told Brenda and Josie they're related now, that could be it, but instead, you've got caught up in some kind of campaign to find your ex-husband. It makes me wonder if it's really Josie you want to find him for or yourself?'

'Well, of course I want to find him,' she snapped. 'This is why I'm in support of this campaign. We all deserve to know—one way or the other—but it doesn't have to come between *us*. Not now it's all out in the open.'

'Am I just expected to stand by while you throw your heart and soul into finding your ex-husband?'

'You make it sound like I'm going to set out on an expedition and search the country by foot, looking far and wide for him. I'm not doing any such thing—I'm simply sharing a few Facebook posts for Josie and supporting her and Brenda through the search.' She threw her hands up in the air. 'Was all you said about everyone our age having baggage and you being okay with that a lie?'

'I'm okay with baggage, Clara—truly I am—but I'm not okay with competing with a ghost, especially one who might not even be dead!'

She flinched. 'You're not competing with Rob. We broke up years ago.'

'And yet,' he shook his head sadly, 'he's still very much a part of your life. You can't seem to let him go. I'm sorry, but I already care about you a great deal and I'm not prepared to risk my heart on someone whom I don't think is as invested in me as I am in them. I spent my whole marriage not being someone's first choice and I'm not going to waste the last years or decades of my life in another relationship where I don't come first in my partner's life.'

'What are you saying?' she whispered.

'You're already first to me, Clara. Can you say the same about me? Do you choose us or do you choose them?'

She couldn't believe he was actually giving her a choice—no, an ultimatum.

Part of Clara didn't think this was fair, but another part wanted to tell Gregg that she *would* put him first—she wanted this, she really wanted the normal, drama-free relationship he was offering—but if she turned her back on Josie and Rob, she wouldn't simply be choosing Gregg. She would be denying the essence of herself. Gregg said he cared about her but he cared about the person he wanted her to be, not the person she was.

And thus, she couldn't give him the answer he was looking for. 'This is me, Gregg,' she said simply as tears came to her eyes. 'Apparently it's always been my biggest flaw, but I can't help it—I help the people I care about. It's who I am. If you can't accept that, then I guess we don't have a future after all.'

Gregg nodded, sighed and offered her a sad smile. 'I'm sorry, Clara.'

'So am I,' she said, sliding off the bar stool and collecting her bag off the end of the bench.

Gregg and Shadow saw her to the door—even Shadow seemed to have lost his zest as if he understood what was happening.

Gregg leant forward and gave her a brief but tight hug as they stood in the open doorway. 'Goodbye, Clara. And good luck.'

'You too, Gregg. I hope to see your name in lights one day.' She couldn't help the tears. It had been pretty near perfect while it lasted. In the end, she wasn't sure who dumped who, but it didn't really matter. Again 'dumped' wasn't a word that seemed to suit their generation, but she certainly felt bereft by what had just happened. Maybe she was stupid choosing Josie over Gregg— maybe Rebecca and Josie would hit it off and Josie would no longer need her—but, beneath the surface, this wasn't what this was about.

'Thanks.'

She stooped down and ruffled Shadow's ears for the last time. 'Goodbye, Shadow.'

Clara was halfway to Siobhan's house when her mobile rang. The number that flashed up on the car stereo screen was her real estate agent's. She sniffed furiously and tried to swallow her tears as she accepted the call. 'Hello?'

'Hi Clara,' boomed the agent—he didn't seem to have it in him to talk quietly. 'Good news. I've got a buyer for your house.'

'Really?'

'Indeed I do!' When he told her the offer, she couldn't believe her ears. It was well above what she'd told him she'd consider. And a real boon in the cooling housing market.

'Wow,' she managed, while silently wondering what she'd been thinking. Looked like she may have lost her boyfriend and her house in the space of a day; no, an hour! Where was she going to live?

The agent gave her the details and said he'd email her the paperwork to sign. 'Unless you want to take it to auction after all?' But he laughed as if she'd be stupid to do so when the offer on the table was already so good.

'No, that will be fine,' Clara told him.

She'd barely disconnected the call when her phone rang again. 'What now?' she muttered as she glanced down to check the caller ID. *Josie.*

Despite the fact she'd just broken up with Gregg because of the arrival of this woman in her life, her heart leapt.

'Guess what?' Josie exclaimed, the second Clara answered the phone.

'What?' Clara asked, a tingle of something sparking in her chest at the excitement in her friend's voice.

'*This Is Sydney* are going to do a story on Robbie!'

'Seriously? Oh my goodness, that's wonderful.' Perhaps it was her age, but she still had more faith in the power of TV than she did in the power of social media.

'I know nothing might come of it, but it feels right to try. Nik's working tonight so I'm going round to Brenda's to watch *Flashdance*. We were wondering if you'd like to come and join us?'

'You know what? That would be great. And I've just found out I've sold my house, so I'm in the mood for celebration.'

*Rebecca*

Saturday morning, Rebecca awoke to the aroma of coffee on her bedside table and sat bolt upright in bed. Panic set her heart racing.

'What time is it?' she called out to Hugh, who was already retreating from the bedroom and then immediately kicked herself for not first saying 'thank you'.

'Thanks,' she added hastily as he turned slowly.

'You're welcome.' He offered her a small smile. 'It's only eight-thirty. You've still got an hour before you have to ... go out.'

*Thank God.* She let her head fall against the back of the bed as she reached out like a zombie for the mug and took a long, satisfying sip.

'I didn't want to wake you any earlier as I know how restless your night was.'

Restless slumber was her norm these days, but last night had been particularly bad. Rebecca had tried not to toss and turn, not wanting to disturb Hugh, however she'd obviously failed dismally in this task.

'Sorry.' It felt like a word she'd been saying an awful lot lately. Maybe she should get it stamped in permanent ink across her forehead. 'I should have slept in the spare room.'

He shrugged. 'It's fine.'

But things between them felt anything but fine. And the fact he'd known she couldn't sleep and hadn't asked if she wanted to talk about it only reaffirmed this. They were like flatmates who only had enough money for one bed so shared under duress. The morning coffee he delivered her now felt more like a habit than the devotion it had once been. He asked her about her day but they made small talk rather than deep and meaningful conversation and she couldn't help feeling on edge around him. They didn't feel *even* anymore. Her actions had hurt him big-time. Although she hadn't had an affair, Rebecca's secret had caused the kind of rift she imagined infidelity might and she almost wished Hugh would do something crazy like go sleep with someone else to even the playing field.

But that wasn't his style—he was noble, solid and dependable, which only made her feel worse.

'What have you got planned today?' she asked, perhaps a tad too brightly.

'Not much. Thought I might take Molly for a walk and go buy the paper.'

'Sounds good,' she replied, almost wishing she could offer to go with him.

'I'll let you get ready,' he said and started to go.

Her heart sank—this polite conversation was really getting her down—but just as he reached the bedroom door, he turned back. 'Good luck with Josie today.'

'Thank you,' Rebecca said as he retreated. Her words came out barely more than a whisper and she had to squeeze her eyes together

393

to stop from crying. His few words meant a lot but there was no time for tears right now.

Hugh whistled for Molly. Rebecca heard him chatting to the dog downstairs as he clicked on the leash. She downed a few more mouthfuls of coffee and then threw back the bedcovers. He might think an hour was more than enough time to get ready and go meet Josie, but she did not want to be late. Although she'd technically met her daughter before, that day seemed so long ago now and this was the first time they were going to be face to face alone. Her insides twisted with a mixture of terror and excitement.

She longed for things to go well and she hoped for them to develop some kind of relationship, but understood that this too might take time.

Baby steps—just the same as with Hugh and Paige.

With that thought, she stripped bare and showered in record time, before putting on the clothes she'd laid out last night. In the end, she'd gone with a pair of smart capris, a floaty top and her old faithful denim jacket. She slipped on her loafers and then looked at her reflection in the mirror. Did she look too casual? If Josie was feeling anything like Rebecca she probably wouldn't even notice what she was wearing, but suddenly Rebecca decided sandals would work better with her outfit.

Her shoes were in a bit of a mess in the walk-in robe and it was only after she'd rummaged through the pile that she remembered she'd packed away her sandals and other summer shoes for the winter. They were stored along with the rest of her and Hugh's summer clothes in Paige's old bedroom.

She hurried into Paige's room—considering she'd only stayed there for one night, it was a mess, but even if Rebecca wanted to get angry about it, she couldn't, because her daughter was still giving her the silent treatment. She tried not to dwell on this; the important thing was that Paige had moved back in with Solomon, which meant she could tick Paige-and-Sol-problems off her list of things currently giving her an ulcer. As if she needed any more health issues than the whopping one she already had.

Rebecca thanked the gods when she found the sandals easily and was slipping them onto her feet when she noticed something amiss.

The wedding dress was gone!

Her heart stalled. For the past few weeks the dress had been hanging in Paige's old wardrobe because she didn't want to have it at home in case Solomon saw it in the flesh.

Knowing it was futile—a wedding dress was hard to miss—Rebecca quickly rifled through everything else in the walk-in robe in case she'd missed it. Which of course she hadn't.

*So where the hell is it?*

Had someone stolen it? No, that was absurd. Who would break into their house and steal a thirty-year-old wedding dress? Rebecca placed a hand against her racing heart; Paige must have taken it when she left. But this thought didn't placate her anxiety at all.

The wedding wasn't for a few weeks, so why would she have done such a thing? Had she taken it back to Josie? Was the wedding off, after all?

*Oh Lord.* She'd never forgive herself if that were the case.

Or maybe Paige had simply decided that she didn't want to wear it. Maybe she no longer wanted to wear her mother's dress, because she no longer wanted anything to do with her mother.

Trying to ignore the sensation of acid burning in her stomach, Rebecca raced back into the bedroom and snatched her mobile phone off the bedside table. But Rebecca's call went straight to voicemail. Paige never switched off her phone—not even when she went to the movies. It always had to be on silent, just in case. Heaven forbid she might miss a new Facebook notification.

Of course, she was still avoiding her!

Rebecca tried Sol next but his phone was also switched off—she got his usual message about probably being at work and him calling back as soon as he could. She didn't leave a message but tried Hugh instead. Maybe he'd been home when Paige had taken the dress. Five seconds later she heard her husband's phone ringing in the kitchen. She went out hoping to meet him back from his walk, only to discover he'd left his mobile on the table.

*Damn him!* Didn't anybody understand the concept of a *mobile* phone?

Out of the corner of her eye, she saw the time on the microwave—somehow the last forty-five minutes had gotten away from her. Bugger it, she didn't have time to worry about this right now. Still feeling sick, she grabbed her keys and handbag and headed out to the car. Maybe Josie would know something about the dress.

Realising she was now running late, she drove as quickly as she could to the beach and then praised the Lord when she scored a street park not too far from the popular café. Finally, something was going right. Hoping this was a good omen for the few hours ahead, she walked briskly to her destination.

The mouth-watering aromas of freshly baked pastries and brewed coffee hit her even before she entered the building but the moment she stepped inside she forgot all about them. Josie was already there, sitting at a table in the corner flicking through one of the free magazines. Rebecca wondered if she was actually reading it—she knew in her current state of mind, she wouldn't be able to take anything in. With a deep breath, she tucked her mobile phone into her handbag and walked towards her, feeling as if she were entering a lion's den. This was her and Robbie's daughter. And she was beautiful.

*Do not cry*, she told herself as she got closer.

As if sensing her approach, Josie shot to her feet as Rebecca arrived at the table.

'Hi,' they both said and then stared at each other awkwardly a few—long—moments. What was the etiquette in this situation? As much as Rebecca yearned to wrap her arms around her long-lost daughter and hold her close, she didn't think they were at that stage yet, but a handshake felt far too formal for flesh and blood.

Josie was the first to break the silence. 'Do you want to sit?' she asked, gesturing to the chair on the other side of the wrought-iron table.

'Yes. Thanks. Sorry I'm late,' Rebecca lowered herself into the seat, cringing at the sound of herself apologising again. 'I didn't mean to be, but I got caught up unexpectedly.'

'It's fine, I only just got here anyway. Lucky I managed to nab this table.'

'Yes, good score.' They both laughed nervously and although Rebecca hadn't been planning on asking Josie about the dress right away, she felt the need to explain.

'I was late because I noticed the wedding dress was missing from my walk-in robe and I tried to call Paige to see if she'd taken it, but I couldn't get through to her. I don't suppose she's mentioned it to you?'

Josie frowned and then shook her head. 'I haven't spoken to her since Thursday, although we did message each other yesterday morning and she didn't mention anything about the dress.'

'Hmm.' An uneasy feeling settled in Rebecca's stomach. 'I hope she and Solomon are okay.'

'I know they had a fight, but she told me yesterday that they were good again. I'm sure there's a perfectly reasonable explanation. Maybe she took it to get dry-cleaned or something?'

'Yes, you're probably right.' Rebecca shook her head. 'I'm sorry. I just wanted this meeting to be perfect and I'm annoyed at myself for being late. Let's start again. Can I get you a drink and something to eat?'

'Just a Diet Coke, please.'

'Coming right up.' Rebecca picked up her bag and went to place their orders at the counter. Despite the Saturday morning queue, the staff were accustomed to busyness and she didn't have to wait long.

When she returned to the table she decided to get straight to the point.

'I'm so sorry you found out about our relationship the way you did. I imagine you have questions for me and I promise to do the very best I can to answer them properly, but before I do, can I just say one thing?'

Josie nodded.

'I do not have any ulterior motives in requesting that information. I know you know I'm sick and need a kidney donor, but that is *not* why I decided to find out about you. I was careless with the letter, but I never wanted you or Paige to find out that way and I planned to wait until after I had the transplant to make contact with you. Obviously discovering you were already part of our lives complicated things and I'm so sorry for any hurt I've caused you.'

Josie's expression was very hard to read—Rebecca didn't know if her daughter believed her or not.

'I'll never try to replace the mother you already had, but I'd love for us to get to know each other better and to have some kind of relationship. However, if that's not what you want, I promise I'm going to respect your wishes.'

'Thank you,' Josie said. Then, 'I do have a few questions.'

Ignoring the butterflies in her stomach, Rebecca nodded. 'Go ahead. I promise I'll answer them all honestly and as best I can.'

'How did you feel when you discovered you were pregnant?'

Josie's question surprised Rebecca—this was not what she'd been expecting. She smiled wistfully as her mind flashed back to that day.

'Terrified,' she said honestly. 'But then I told Robbie and he wasn't angry, he didn't run for the hills. He made me believe everything would be okay. We planned to get married—I thought that would please my parents too—Robbie said he'd get a job and we fantasised about a future with our baby. We fell in love with the idea of you fast and with him by my side, I felt like I could conquer anything. I wasn't even that scared about telling Mum and Dad.' She swallowed. 'I'm not sure how much Clara or Paige have told you about what happened next?'

Josie shrugged one shoulder. 'Clara told me that Rob was threatened by your father, that he never wanted to leave you or let me be adopted. That the guilt and the regret drove him to drink and that he always wanted to find me. She told me that he tried to look for me and even asked for your help at one stage but that you refused to look. That you didn't want to.'

'It's not that I —' Trying not to show her anger towards Clara, Rebecca started to explain but Josie interrupted.

'*Paige* told me you kept me a secret her whole life, so I guess that's why you didn't want to help Rob. That's why you turned him away?'

Rebecca felt sick; she could tell Josie wasn't going to make this easy for her.

'Robbie hurt me when he abandoned us,' she begun. 'Whatever his reason—and I now know that this wasn't his choice—he broke my heart. He left me with no alternative but to do as my parents told me was best. I felt so alone back then, I blamed him for losing you but I also felt ashamed and guilty about it all. Because of this I listened to my parents when they told me I should leave the past where it was. I thought about you constantly and of course I dreamed of finding you, but I didn't think it was my right. There were many times I almost told Hugh, but I guess shame held me back. Not shame that I'd had you, but shame that I'd given you up. And the longer I kept the secret, well, the harder it became to tell.'

'So you loved him?' Josie asked.

'Robbie?'

'Yes.'

A wave of nostalgia washed over Rebecca as she thought of her first love. 'Oh yes, I loved him so much.' She swallowed, determined not to cry as she'd promised herself she'd keep it together in front of Josie. 'I know people write teenagers off as not knowing what true love is, but I'm a fifty-year-old woman now and I can tell you that I genuinely loved your father. They say you never truly get over your first love and that's my truth. He was sexy, smart, he made me laugh, he treated me like a princess and he was a hell of a talented musician. Paige tells me you're interested in music too?'

Josie nodded as she sipped her drink through the straw. Then, 'Do you wish things had been different? Do you wish you and Robbie had ended up together?'

Rebecca couldn't help her heavy sigh. That might just be the most difficult question anyone had ever asked her.

'Yes and no,' she said eventually. 'I wish I hadn't lost you; I wish my parents hadn't tried to play God; I wish Robbie hadn't lived with such torture and turmoil; I wish I'd been braver and looked for you earlier, but I can't wish Paige or Hugh away. My life might not have been how I dreamed it would be at fifteen, but I've had a pretty good one and I hope you have too.'

'I have—or at least my childhood and adolescence were good. Maybe if they hadn't been, I'd have come looking for you myself, but my adoptive parents were the best. They weren't musical at all themselves, but they supported my passion and dreams in that area and everything else. They gave me every opportunity I wanted. I couldn't have asked for a better family.'

This brought a lump to Rebecca's throat—it was good news, the best, but she couldn't help the jealousy towards this other couple who had been blessed to bring up her and Robbie's daughter. 'I'm glad,' she said simply.

'Are things okay with you and Hugh now?'

'I don't know. We're trying to make them that way again, but he's hurt that I kept you from him. And rightly so.'

'Did you really always think I was a boy?'

Rebecca blushed at how stupid Josie's question made her sound. 'Yes. I wasn't allowed to hold you when you were born and I never thought to question what anyone told me. It was only when I saw that photo in your house ...' She paused to dig into her bag for the identical one, which she'd recently retrieved from the bank safe, and laid it down in front of Josie. 'That I started to wonder. All my life I've scrutinised any males that were about your age, looking for something, anything that reminded me of myself or Robbie. Now I know why I never found anyone.'

'But you'd decided to look before you saw the matching photo.' Josie pushed the image back across the table, accusation in her tone. 'If not because you needed a kidney, then why?'

'Have you ever been diagnosed with a serious illness before?' When Josie shook her head, Rebecca continued. 'It's pretty frightening.

And it's exactly as the books and movies say—it makes you look back on your life with a fine-toothed comb. I started thinking about what I'd achieved and what things I regretted. I could only think of one regret, but it was a pretty damn big one. *You*.'

Although she'd promised herself she wouldn't cry, she couldn't help the tear that escaped and she didn't try and brush it away.

'Suddenly I couldn't think about anything else. I was supposed to be worrying about my health but all I could think about was my son, well, you know … I knew I had to come clean and I knew I had to find out if you were okay. That's honestly all I need to know. If you don't want anything else from me, I'll accept that, but please, tell me, are you okay?'

*Josie*

Josie took a few long moments and another sip of her drink before answering Rebecca's question.

'Yes, I'm okay.'

She could see the relief on the other woman's face. 'Good. I'm glad.' Rebecca did this weird sniff-smile thing. 'Is there anything else you want to ask me?'

'I'd love you to tell me more about Rob.' She hadn't wanted to ask Clara too many questions because although Clara had been fantastic about all this, she knew she carried a lot of pain where her ex-husband was concerned and wasn't sure she'd be unbiased anyway. And although Brenda had given her wonderful insights, she got all melancholic whenever she talked about her son, so Josie didn't want to raise the topic of Rob unless she did. As One Track Mind was together long before the internet, in this instance, Google hadn't been much help either.

Perhaps this woman could even have something that might give Josie a clue as to where Rob might be.

Rebecca blinked. 'Sure. What do you want to know?'

'I dunno.' Josie shrugged. 'What did he eat for lunch? Aside from music, what was his favourite subject at school? Did he have any favourite movies? I've seen his collection of LPs, but which singer or band inspired him?'

Rebecca laughed at the rush of questions and then sucked in a quick breath before replying. 'Vegemite and cheese sandwiches with egg.' She made a face. 'It's what he brought to school every single day and I thought it was disgusting. I refused to kiss him unless he brushed his teeth afterwards, so he ended up bringing a toothbrush to school.'

Josie couldn't help smiling.

'Sorry,' Rebecca said, 'perhaps a little too much information. Now what did you ask next? Oh, school. Well, he wasn't bad at maths and science but he was really, really good at woodwork. The teacher tried to convince him he should become a carpenter, but he was so gung-ho about being a rock star that he wouldn't consider anything else.'

'Paige mentioned you were a singer and played the piano—if Robbie was a couple of years older than you, he would have been in a higher grade at school; did you meet through your music?'

Rebecca nodded. 'Yep, although the country school we went to wasn't that big and he only lived down the road, so I knew him before then. But when Robbie and his mates decided that the way to success was to have a female singer in their group, they called auditions. I already had a crush on him—pretty much every girl in the school did—and so I saw this as my chance to a) become a star and b) get the guy. And let's face it, at fifteen, the latter was way more important to me.'

'And they chose you?'

'Yes. The rest of the guys were a bit immature—always cracked obscene jokes around me—but Robbie was serious about his music

404

and gave them what-for whenever they became a bit inappropriate with me. He started to walk me home after band practice and we became friends first, but we became much more than that pretty fast.'

Josie didn't know if Rebecca realised it but her eyes lit up whenever she spoke about Robbie—it was clear to see how much she'd loved him and she couldn't help feeling a little sorry for her husband. 'Was the band One Track Mind?'

'No.' Rebecca shook her head. 'Aside from Robbie and me, no one else was really serious about a music career. I'm not sure what happened, but a few years later he appeared on the scene with a new bunch of guys. No token female this time. Guess they realised boy bands were a better bet.'

'So you kept track of him?'

'I wouldn't say I kept track of him, but every radio station was playing that song. It was hard not to follow his progress. I really thought they were going places after "Lost Without You, Baby" hit the charts, but then they just seemed to fade away. That was Robbie's worst nightmare—being a one-hit wonder.'

*And he wouldn't have been if it wasn't for you.*

'He and Clara suffered a number of miscarriages.' Josie decided not to mention the stillbirth. 'And Robbie fell into a deep depression; she thinks it all stemmed from when I was adopted.'

'I know,' Rebecca whispered. 'It breaks my heart to think of him like that. He was always the life of the party, but he was never one of the ones sneaking alcohol into said parties; he was too driven. What happened to him is a tragedy and I'll never forgive my parents for what they did.'

'Me neither,' Josie said, but she didn't add that she wasn't sure if she could forgive Rebecca either. Not only for turning Robbie away when he came to her in desperation, but also for allowing her parents to have their way in the first place. She tried to put herself in Rebecca's position—being fifteen and pregnant—but she couldn't imagine ever giving up a child, not when she so desperately wanted one. No matter how many times Rebecca told her she was young, heartbroken and coerced into the adoption, it didn't change the facts.

*She* had allowed others to take away her baby.

And that was something Josie would never have done. Having felt another human growing inside her, having experienced the agony of losing that life, she knew she would have fought until her last breath to keep her baby. Even if she was only a child herself.

Perhaps, Rebecca had actually been relieved to be rid of her.

'Paige told me about the campaign you've launched to search for Robbie,' Rebecca said. 'I think it's a great idea. I shared the page and I can't help thinking about what else we might do. Perhaps we could hire a private investigator?'

*We?* That sounded expensive and Josie wondered if Rebecca was planning on funding it; if so, how would her husband feel about that? Even if she liked the idea, there was no way she and Nik could afford one and she didn't think Brenda had a wad of cash stuffed up the chimney.

'And ...' Rebecca paused a moment as if unsure of what she was about to say. 'I could ask my father if he knows anyone in the police force in the missing persons unit. I think he kind of owes us a favour, don't you?'

Rage and resentment erupted like a volcano within her and almost burst right from her mouth. *That* was the understatement of the century!

Somehow she swallowed the urge to tell Rebecca she could shove her despicable father where the sun don't shine—that this was too little, too late—but maybe that would be cutting off her nose to spite her face. She didn't want anything to do with her biological grandfather and she couldn't understand why Rebecca would want that either, but if he did have any kind of police power or could at least find out what they were doing on the case, how could she turn that down?

'You'd do that?'

Rebecca nodded rapidly. 'Of course. I haven't spoken to him since I confronted them about your gender, but I'm willing to do anything I can to help find Robbie. I'll go see Dad this afternoon.'

'Thank you,' Josie said. 'And thanks to Paige and your husband, I got a call from a producer at *This Is Sydney*. She was super enthusiastic about doing a piece on missing persons and Brenda and I are being filmed next week for it. If someone has seen him or knows where he is, hopefully this will spur them to get in contact with us or the police.'

Rebecca blinked. 'Hugh helped you?'

'Yes, Paige asked him if he could put the word out at his work and someone got in contact with me almost immediately.'

'That's great news,' Rebecca said, although her voice wavered a little. 'And it's lovely you've connected with Brenda. And Paige. She speaks very highly of you.'

'Yes. They're both great,' Josie said, feeling uncomfortable with where this conversation was going. Although Rebecca had said she didn't expect anything from Josie, she could tell from her biological mother's tone that she hoped they too might be able to play happy families. And while this conversation had been enlightening in many ways, she simply didn't feel any desire to repeat it on a regular basis.

'Would you like some lunch?' Rebecca said. 'My shout.'

Josie had almost forgotten they were sitting in the middle of a busy café and the last thing on her mind was her stomach. 'Actually,' she said, glancing at her watch, 'I've got to go.'

She made no excuse about where as she picked her bag up off the floor and stood.

'Oh.' Rebecca stumbled to her feet. 'Okay. Well, thanks for meeting me. It was lovely to talk to you. I'll let you know what my father says.'

'Thank you,' Josie said and then turned and fled before Rebecca could ask if they could see each other again.

'How was it?' Nik asked the moment she walked in the door. He was lounging on the couch, watching football.

'Exhausting,' she said as she kicked off her shoes and then flopped down beside him.

He picked up the TV remote and muted the footy, which considering the Dockers were playing was a massive sacrifice. God, she loved him. 'Good exhausting or bad exhausting?' he asked.

'Both.' She leaned her head against his shoulder and sighed deeply as he pulled her close against him.

'You wanna talk about it?'

'It was weird,' she said. 'When Rebecca first arrived it felt a bit like a job interview—hers not mine. She was nervous and I found myself trying to put her at ease, even while being a little irritated by her. Then, when she was talking, when she was telling me about getting pregnant and being forced to give me up, I kept forgetting that the baby she was talking about was me. Like logically I know she's my mother but I just don't feel anything for her.'

'That's understandable.' Nik squeezed her hand. 'You might share DNA but you only just met; real relationships take time.'

'She asked me if I was okay. That's what she wanted to know—and I said yes, when we both know I've been anything *but* okay

408

lately. I think she needed me to tell her that to alleviate some of the guilt she's carried all these years. But that's not why I said yes, the real reason was because I didn't want to tell her the truth. I didn't want to tell her about our miscarriages and how I've come close to losing the plot this year.' Josie swallowed to try and shift the emotion that was clogging her throat. 'It would be like telling a stranger.'

'Oh, Jose.' Nik held her tighter. 'That's okay. You don't have to tell her anything.'

'I know,' she whispered. 'And although she says she won't pressure me into getting to know each other better, I think deep down that's what she wants, but I'm not sure I can give it to her. I know I could have looked for her myself, but she was the adult, she was the parent, and she didn't come looking for me. At least Robbie wanted to.'

'So you're not going to see her again?'

'I'll have to, I'm going to be Paige's chief bridesmaid remember? And that's fine. It's not like I hate her or anything.' Even if she did, Josie would be civil for Paige's sake. 'Who knows, maybe in time, I'll get to know her better, but right now, there's other things I want to focus on.'

'Like finding Robbie?'

'Yes, that,' she said, then pulled back a little so she could look at him properly. 'But also you and me and our family.'

His eyes widened in question.

'If this whole thing has taught me anything, it's that family is not about DNA—like you said—it's about what's in here.' She grabbed his hand and pressed it against her heart. 'I don't feel any connection to my biological mother, but I'm glad I've found her, because maybe I didn't think I needed to know about my beginnings, but maybe I actually did. For closure and reinforcement.'

'What do you mean?'

'Whatever happens with Robbie and between me and Rebecca, Mum and Dad will always be my real parents—it's love that matters. They were the ones who gave me that. And you and me? We have a lot of love to give, so I think we should look into adoption after all.'

His mouth fell open. 'What? Rather than IVF or any of the other possibilities?' he asked in a disbelieving tone.

She nodded. 'I know it will be by no means an easy fix either, but I want to give someone love and a place to call home; someone who, without us, might not have the best chance in life. What do you say?'

Nik's look of shock turned into a grin. 'I think you're amazing, Josephine Mitreski. Let's do it.'

*Paige*

'Our parents are going to kill us,' Paige said as she and Sol stood in the entrance hall of a chapel waiting their turn to go inside. She was wearing her mother's dress and Solomon looked sexy as all hell in a dashing charcoal suit, which they'd hired earlier that day. Vegas wasn't called The Wedding Capital of the World for nothing. Not only had they been able to get their wedding licence from the Clark County Marriage License Bureau in a matter of minutes at eight o'clock the day they arrived but they'd easily hired a suit and had fallen in love with this cute little chapel a few hours later. Luckily, they'd had a vacancy that very afternoon.

'They'll get over it eventually.' Sol didn't sound the least bit remorseful as he grinned down at her and the truth was, neither was she. The last forty-eight hours since they'd decided to do this had been the most exciting of her life.

She'd gone home Thursday night, told Sol that he was right—she had overreacted, it wasn't her place to make decisions regarding his kidney—and begged his forgiveness.

He'd pulled her into his arms, kissed her senseless, told her that the twenty-four hours in which she hadn't been talking to him was the worst day of his life. It had given him time to think and he'd come to two conclusions.

One, he couldn't live without her and two, if his mum had sprung something like this on him he'd probably have been furious as well. It was easy to be pious when you weren't actually the one in a situation and he'd apologised for not being as supportive as he should have been. He'd agreed that he didn't want any secrets between himself and Paige and they'd had the best make-up sex in the history of make-up sex.

But afterwards when she'd told him that she'd asked Josie to be her chief bridesmaid, Sol had hit her with a curly question. 'I thought you'd already asked Karis? How's she going to feel about being demoted?'

And before Paige could consider this question, he'd thrown her with another. And another. 'And what about your grandparents? Are they still invited to the wedding? And if they are, how will Josie feel about that? Does she want to meet them? Is your dad okay with Josie being in the wedding party? Is Rebecca? She and Josie haven't even met properly yet, have they?'

'Stop!' She'd held up a hand and placed the other against her forehead to try and dull the roar his questions ignited. Why hadn't she thought any of this through? Even without the kind of revelations that had occurred in her family the last couple of days, weddings were fraught with drama and there was nothing Paige hated more than drama. Right now the thought of her grandparents, her mum, her dad and Josie in the same room ... *Way* too much drama.

'Sorry,' Sol had said sheepishly.

'What do you think I should do then? I can't un-ask Josie but I don't want to hurt Karis either. And I know Jeanie and Grandad did a terrible thing but they've always been so supportive to me. It'll break their hearts if we don't invite them to the wedding.'

She could tell from the expression on his face that he thought that's exactly what they deserved, but it didn't feel that straightforward.

'Do you think we should postpone the wedding until after all this has blown over?'

'No way. Absolutely not.' He'd paused a moment as if deep in thought, then, 'I think we should elope!'

'What?'

He'd grinned that beautiful smile that turned her knees weak and her head to mush every single time. 'The actual wedding was never what mattered to me—it was marrying you and I don't want all this Josie-stuff to overshadow that but I still want to marry you. Let's go to Vegas.'

'What? When?' She'd laughed, unsure if he was joking but the idea was growing on her by the second.

'Tomorrow,' he said. 'If we can get plane tickets and time off work at such short notice.'

'Are you serious?'

He'd nodded. 'I've never been more serious in my life. What do you say, Paige MacRitchie, will you come to Vegas with me and get hitched?'

Thank goodness for the head on Sol's shoulders—at that question Paige had been ready to grab their passports and jump on the next plane, but he did a little online research while she packed their bags. By the time their plane was taxi-ing out of Sydney airport the next morning, he'd booked a hotel, found out where to go to get their marriage licence, what documentation they required to do so and provided her with a shortlist of possible wedding venues. All she'd had to do was sneak into her parents' house and steal the wedding dress. Thankfully her mother had gone to bed early and her father was so happy that she was going back to Sol that he hadn't noticed her leaving with extra baggage.

The plan was to be Mr and Mrs before anyone in Australia even noticed they were missing.

So far, everything was going according to plan.

A round of applause sounded from inside the actual chapel. Moments later the doors flew open and another bride and groom emerged, their faces jubilant.

'Congratulations,' Paige and Sol said in unison as the bride flashed her ring at them and the groom held up their wedding certificate proudly.

'Best thing I've done in my life,' he said, before pulling his new wife into a kiss.

Paige and Solomon stepped aside to let the newlyweds and their entourage exit the chapel. When the small crowd had spilled out onto the streets, an employee held up his hand to them. 'Five minutes and we'll be ready for you guys.'

'Okay, thanks,' Sol said, before turning back to Paige. 'Last chance to back out. Are you sure you want to do this?'

'What kind of stupid question is that? I love you and I've never wanted anything more in my life.'

He grinned proudly. 'That goes without saying. But what I meant was, are you sure you want to go ahead doing this here without our family and friends to celebrate?'

'Yes. A hundred and ten per cent. I didn't drag this big stupid meringue dress halfway across the world and pay for all that excess baggage for the hell of it.'

He laughed, then leant forward, captured her face between his lovely, big hands and kissed her hard.

'I think you're supposed to wait for after the ceremony to do that,' she said, a little breathless, when they finally broke apart.

'Sorry. Just practising,' Sol said playfully. 'And I thought you were crazy wanting to bring that dress with us, but I have to admit, now you're standing in front of me wearing it, looking like the prettiest bride that ever there was, I'm quite glad you did.'

'Me too,' Paige said with a grin she wasn't sure would ever be wiped away. After all the trouble she'd gone to finding this particular gown, it would have seemed wrong not to get married wearing it.

And, this way, at least she would have a piece of her parents and her newly found sister with her when she said 'I do'.

*Josie*

'Oh my God,' Josie shrieked, almost dropping her phone as she stared at the screen.

'What is it?' Nik asked from beside her in the driver's seat—they were on their way to Brenda's house to film the missing persons segment with *This Is Sydney* and she'd been a basketful of nerves all morning. Suddenly that was forgotten.

'Paige and Solomon got married!'

'What?' He sounded just as startled as she'd been. 'Where? When?'

She laughed and, as he slowed the car in front of a red light, angled her screen towards him. His eyes grew wide as he looked down at the photo of a bride and groom in front of the iconic 'Welcome to Las Vegas' sign and he started laughing too. 'They eloped?'

'Looks like. Oh my.' Josie sighed at the sight of Paige in The Dress and her throat grew a little scratchy. 'Doesn't she look stunning?'

The light changed to green and Nik turned his attention back to the road. 'She looks good, but not as gorgeous as you did. What are her parents going to say?'

'I don't know.' Josie wondered if Rebecca had seen Paige and Sol's announcement on Facebook yet. Posted less than twenty minutes ago, it already had over a hundred likes and comments, but she knew Paige's mother was only a recent-comer to social media. 'Not much anyone can say now. Good on them.'

'Let's hope she brings the dress back in one piece,' he said with a chuckle.

But Josie found she no longer cared as much as she once did. In fact, she wasn't sure how she felt about the dress anymore or if she even wanted it back. She posted a quick congratulations on the photo and then popped her phone in her handbag as Nik parked on the street in front of Brenda's house. Clara's car was already there—she'd agreed to come along for moral support—and a silver car Josie guessed belonged to the TV crew had just pulled up behind her.

'They're early,' she said as she hurried out of the car to greet them.

'Morning, are you Josie?' asked the tall and skinny but big-breasted woman who climbed out of the driver's side. With a very dark fake tan and long jet-black hair, she looked like the Barbie's best friend doll Josie had when she was little.

'Yes.' She nodded. 'You guys are from *This Is Sydney*?'

'That's right.' Barbie's best friend held out her hand and introduced herself as Haylee. 'And this is Gayle, my brilliant cameraman.'

Gayle too offered her hand and although her shake was strong and she had a much more casual look than Haylee, she was clearly not a man. It was probably a good thing the station hadn't sent Paige's dad.

'And this is Hunter,' Gayle gestured to the third person beside them. 'He's on sound.'

'Hi, nice to meet you all,' Josie said. 'Thank you so much for agreeing to do this interview. This is my husband, Nik.'

'Need any help carrying anything?' he asked.

'No, these guys have done this a million times. Shall we go inside? Is the missing man's mother ready?' Haylee waved her hand as if she wanted to get this show on the road as Gayle and Hunter retrieved their equipment.

They were greeted by Brenda *and* Clara at the front door. Brenda had on a full face of make-up and what was clearly her best pink dress, but looked even more nervous than Josie felt. More introductions were made and then discussions were had about the best spot to film for both lighting and aesthetics.

In the end, it was decided that Josie and Brenda would sit next to each other on the couch, Haylee would sit on a dining chair angled slightly next to them and Gayle would film from the corner. The trio seemed to know what they were doing and Josie just wanted to get this done—the sooner it was recorded and on air, the sooner someone would hopefully come forward with information.

While Gayle and Hunter set up, testing angles, lighting and acoustics, Nik watched on in fascination, Clara made tea for anyone who wanted it and Haylee got a little bit more background from Brenda and Josie, ready for the actual interview. Her legs crossed, she asked questions and took a few notes on an iPad with a stylus. Josie made the mistake of mentioning how the wedding dress had linked them and Haylee seemed more interested in this than Robbie missing.

'That would make a really good story in itself,' she said, chomping down on the end of her stylus.

Thankfully Gayle chose that moment to interrupt. 'Didn't you say there was a collection of LPs you wanted to feature in the shots?'

The question was directed at Haylee but Josie nodded. 'Yes, I talked about that on the phone, your producer liked that idea.'

'Yes,' Haylee confirmed. 'The personal angle is always best so as well as showing the relationship grandmother and granddaughter have formed, it'd be good for you to tell us a little bit about your passion for music. We definitely want to mention how you were a fan of your father's band—what was it called again? One Road?— long before you knew your connection.'

'One Track Mind,' Josie corrected, anticipation pumping through her veins as she got up to retrieve one box of Robbie's collection. 'Where do you want to put them?'

While Gayle and Haylee argued about positioning and Hunter stood back as if knowing not to get involved, Josie shared a hopeful smile with Brenda. As annoying as Haylee was, she might just be their secret weapon in the hunt to find Robbie. Best case scenario Robbie saw himself on TV, realised how much they cared and came out of hiding, if that's indeed where he was.

'Right, I think I'm all set,' Gayle said.

'Fabulous. Seats please, ladies.' Haylee fluffed her hair a little and reapplied her bright red lipstick as Josie and Brenda took to the couch.

Josie took hold of her grandmother's hand but just as the camera started rolling the doorbell rang.

'Who the hell is that?' Haylee snapped. 'Somebody, get rid of them.'

'I'll go,' Clara volunteered, stepping out of the room into the hallway.

Voices sounded and they waited to start the filming again until Clara had sent whoever it was on their way, but she returned a few moments later with two policemen in tow instead. Josie's scalp prickled at the matching grave expressions on their faces and while she knew instantly what they were here to say, she didn't want to believe it to be true. She tightened her grip on her grandmother's hand and shuffled closer.

'These two policemen need to talk to Brenda,' Clara said, then looked from Gayle to Haylee and Hunter. 'Would you mind waiting in the kitchen?'

As the TV crew left the room, the cops—one male, one female—shut the door and introduced themselves but Josie couldn't have repeated their names to anyone.

'I'm very sorry to have to inform you, Mrs Jones, but a body has been found in an abandoned hut on a property near Armidale. From the information we have we believe it is your son, Robert.'

Josie heard Clara and Brenda both gasp but she was frozen.

'I can't believe it,' she heard Brenda say. 'I guess I knew it was a possibility, but when Josie turned up ... well, I felt sure my Robbie was going to get a happy ending after all.'

'How long has he been ...' Clara couldn't finish her sentence and Josie looked up to see her lips pursed tightly as if she was struggling not to cry. Although she and Robbie had been divorced for over two years, they'd been married a long time and Josie could only imagine how Clara must be feeling right now.

Beside her, Brenda had started sobbing.

But Josie still felt numb. This was not how this was supposed to end.

'We can't be a hundred per cent certain until the coroner has completed the autopsy,' said the man, 'but earlier indicators point to him being gone at least a month, maybe a little longer.'

Clara gasped again and her hands rushed to cover her mouth as if she might be sick.

Nik stepped forward and grabbed a box of tissues from the coffee table, he offered it to Clara, she took one, then he gave the box to

Brenda before squeezing in next to Josie and putting his arm around her shoulder.

She found her voice. 'Have you any idea how he died?' Although part of her didn't want to hear gruesome details, she needed to know. 'Was it natural causes or an … accident?'

'We will be doing a full investigation,' said the female officer, 'but we don't believe it was either of those things.'

'He was murdered?' Brenda asked, her tone incredulous.

'No, we don't think so. There was no evidence of anyone else involved.'

Silence hung in the air as they all digested what this information meant.

Josie's heart cracked at the thought of Robbie all alone at the end, feeling such despair that he didn't feel as if he had any other option but to take his own life. Every few months there was something in the news about the rising instances of middle-aged male suicide, but she'd never been close to anything like this before. She hadn't even wanted to know her biological parents and now she felt ripped apart at the thought her father had died alone and she'd never get the chance to meet him properly.

If only Rebecca hadn't got sick and decided to open this can of worms to give herself peace of mind, Josie wouldn't now have to mourn a man she hadn't even known. She might have still met Brenda and would have supported her through the news about her son, but she wouldn't be feeling so damn confused herself.

After what seemed like forever, Nik spoke. 'Shall I tell Haylee and the others they can go now?'

When neither Clara nor Brenda seemed to hear his question, Josie said, 'Yes, good idea.' The last thing they needed was the media hanging around like vultures to try and get a different, juicier, kind of story.

With a quick squeeze of her hand, Nik stood, slipped out of the room and shut the door behind him again.

'Do you need someone to identify the body?' Clara asked.

Brenda let out a sound like a kitten being kicked and Josie looked to see her grandmother had gone paler than she'd thought possible for a live person. Josie was about to offer to do this, when she realised that even if she wanted to take the burden off Clara and Brenda, she probably wasn't a reliable option considering she'd only met Robbie once.

The cops exchanged a look before the female officer spoke. 'No, that won't be necessary; due to the time since death, in this instance we will use dental records and DNA to confirm identification. However the driver's licence and other cards found with the deceased matched those of the man you reported missing.'

'Ah, of course.' Clara shook her head slightly. 'I'm not thinking straight.'

At Clara's words, Josie suddenly realised that although they hadn't been told how Robbie had ended his life (and she didn't want to ask in front of Brenda), whichever way he'd done so, a body that was a month or so old wasn't going to be pretty. She felt ill at the thought and wondered who the poor person had been who'd discovered him.

'So what happens next then?' Clara asked, as Nik let himself back into the room.

The policeman took a pamphlet out of the file he carried and placed it down on the coffee table. Josie saw the words 'When A Person Dies Suddenly' in bold print on the front. 'This brochure contains information about dealing with the coroner's court. Once you've had time to digest the news, your first step should be appointing a funeral director and they'll liaise with the coroner to arrange a funeral date.'

They all nodded and then Brenda said, 'Are you going to tell us how he actually died?'

'The coroner's report will give you the results of the post-mortem examination, which will likely state cause of death as either fractured cervical vertebrae or asphyxia.' The female officer paused a moment, then, 'But I'm sorry to say your son hung himself.'

'Thank you,' Brenda whispered with an ever so slight nod. It sounded like a weird thing to say but Josie understood—it was better to know these things however appalling and horrific they were.

'Do you have any further questions?' asked the policeman.

'Did he leave any letters to anyone?' Clara asked.

He shook his head. 'I'm sorry, but there was nothing like that found on his person.'

When none of them could think of anything else to ask, the cops made their excuses to leave. The female officer left a card with her contact details and told them to call her if any more questions arose. Nik showed them to the door, then came back and immediately pulled Josie into a hug. Thank God it was his day off and he'd decided to come to the filming with her. She just felt better with him there.

Silence hung in the room for a few long minutes as if all of them were still digesting the news, then Brenda finally broke it. 'Well, today didn't quite go according to plan, did it?'

Josie attempted to swallow the lump in her throat and shook her head. 'Can I get you a cup of tea?' She felt a strong urge to do something.

'I can make them,' Nik volunteered.

Brenda gave them a small smile. 'No thank you. There's not much a cup of tea can't fix, but I think this might be one of those things. I don't think I can stomach anything right now, but you three have one if you want.'

'Do you want me to make you one?' Nik asked Clara.

She shook her head. 'No. I don't think I do.' Then she looked to her mother-in-law. 'Would you like me to call a funeral director, Brenda?'

The older woman sighed. 'You've already been such a help, I don't like to burden you with this.'

'He was my husband,' Clara said. 'It's not a burden.'

It was the first time Josie had heard Clara call Robbie anything other than her 'ex-husband'. She didn't think there was any rush to call anyone but perhaps, like her, Clara felt as if she needed to do something.

'Okay. Thank you,' Brenda conceded and then laid her head back against the sofa as if suddenly exhausted.

Clara slipped into the kitchen—Josie guessed to start making phone calls.

'Is there anything I can get or do for you?' Josie asked Brenda.

'Will you just sit with me a while?'

'Of course.' Josie wasn't planning on going anywhere. They might have only just discovered each other, but she was the only family the older woman had left and she was going to take that role very seriously. She just wished there was something she could do to help in the now.

Once again, she claimed Brenda's hand and Nik, looking unsure what to do with himself, perched on the edge of the recliner. The three of them sat there in not uncomfortable silence as Josie went over and over again in her head what the cops had told them. Just over a month since Robbie had ended it all. Why after all these years had he suddenly decided he'd had enough? If only he'd held on just a few more weeks.

It seemed so unfair.

Josie didn't realise she was crying until Brenda patted her hand. 'Do you need one of these, dear?' she asked, offering her the tissues.

'Thank you,' she whispered as she took one, unsure whether she was sad for herself, for Robbie, for Brenda or just at the whole awful situation.

After a little while longer, Brenda said, 'You're a sweet girl. The saddest part in all of this is that Robbie never got to know you, but I'm so glad I've got the chance.'

'Me too.'

Her grandmother gestured to the box of LPs beside them. 'Robbie would want you to have them. I know you'll look after and love them the way he did.'

'Oh. Thank you.' Overcome with emotion, Josie took a moment before she said, 'Do you think we could put on Robbie's record now or would you rather not?'

'I think that's a lovely idea,' Brenda said and Nik leapt to his feet. 'I'll do it.' He was obviously grateful to have *something* to do.

They were listening to One Track Mind's one hit song when Clara returned to the room.

'That song was about you,' she said simply, looking at Josie as she flopped down into the recliner. 'Everyone thought it was about a woman who'd broken Robert's heart, but he told me not long after we met that it was a love letter to his son.'

'I always suspected as much,' Brenda whispered and Josie's tears that had almost subsided multiplied. It was the saddest yet most wonderful thing she'd ever heard.

The song ended and Brenda looked to Clara. 'How'd you go?'

Clara nodded. 'We've got an appointment to see a funeral director tomorrow afternoon. If you're up for it.'

'I will be.'

Nik cleared his throat. 'I was thinking. Should someone tell Rebecca? You know … before she finds out … some other way?'

They all looked at him as if he'd asked if someone should tell the pope. Yet he was right. It would be terrible if she were to hear the news on the actual news, but even so, the last thing Josie felt like doing right now was going to see her biological mother, which would also mean leaving Brenda. If Paige were in the country she could perhaps give her the message to tell her mother, but Paige was on her honeymoon and this probably wasn't a thing that should be delivered via telephone.

She sighed and was just about to say she'd go, when Clara got in first.

'I'll go tell her. You're right, Nik. She deserves to know.'

'Are you sure?' Josie asked.

'Yes. Unless you want to?'

Josie shook her head. 'Not really. I'd rather stay here.'

'And here's where you should be.'

As Clara stood, Josie did too. She crossed over and gave the other woman a wordless hug; their arms said everything they needed to.

'Do you want me to come with you?' Nik asked, as the women pulled back from their embrace.

'No, I'll be fine. But thank you.' Clara scooped her handbag off the floor. 'I'll be back as soon as I can.'

Josie looked again to her grandmother as Clara left, wondering what she should do next. She tried to remember what had helped after she'd found out that her mother had died, but came up blank. There was nothing that made any kind of death any better. But at least when her mother died, she and her father were swamped with other people who cared about her mother and wanted to offer practical support. They'd been given so many casseroles they'd had to buy another freezer and her dad had still been eating lasagne months later.

But that did make her think of something. 'Is there anyone else we need to inform about Robbie's death?' she asked.

'I don't think so,' Brenda answered immediately. 'I don't have any family left and I don't think Robbie was close to anyone either. Although Clara might have a better idea.'

'Never mind, we'll worry about that later,' Josie said, immediately regretting the question. It was awful to think that someone could die and there were less than a handful of people that gave a damn. She guessed it would be a very small funeral.

Brenda nodded. 'Do you mind if I have a little lie down?'

'No, of course not.' Josie rushed forward to help her grandmother to her feet and down the hallway to her bedroom. 'Nik and I will be right out here,' she said. 'Please call out if you need *anything*.'

'I will. Thank you, dear.' And with a soft smile, Brenda shuffled into her room and closed the door.

Josie let out a long deep sigh and felt Nik's arms close around her.

'He ended his life because of me,' she sobbed, thinking of that guy who'd listened at The Inferno. *She* was the reason for his despair!

Nik pulled back and turned her to look at him. 'What?'

'Robbie was the way he was—and he couldn't handle it anymore—because he never got over giving me away. If I wasn't born or if I—'

'Don't be ridiculous.' Nik gripped her shoulders more tightly than he ever had before. 'I know you're in shock. But this is not your fault. Robert was obviously deeply depressed and could no longer bear the pain. But if you need someone to blame, blame Rebecca's parents. They are the only ones that have anything to answer for.'

*Rebecca*

Rebecca was glad she was sitting down when she opened Facebook Monday morning.

She'd been checking the 'Find Robbie Jones' page obsessively since Paige told her about it and her check-ins had become even more regular since her catch-up with Josie on the weekend. It wasn't that the meeting was a disaster. In theory she'd got what she went for—the reassurance that Josie didn't suffer in her childhood because of her adoption and had had a good life—but it hadn't been like the reunions you see on TV or like the one Rebecca had secretly imagined. She and Josie hadn't thrown their arms around each other, cried tears of joy that they'd finally found the other after all this time and then clicked as if they'd known each other forever.

The conversation hadn't been stilted exactly but it was definitely not comfortable either. It was as if Josie had a list of questions she wanted to get through and once she was done, she hadn't been able to get out of there fast enough. Rebecca had hoped Josie would open up about her miscarriages so that she could offer some kind of motherly support, but Josie had steered clear of anything too personal, except where Robbie was concerned. Despite her standoffish behaviour with Rebecca, Josie didn't appear to have any hard feelings towards her biological father. She knew this was due to the fact Robbie had been vocal about always wanting to find her and although she couldn't blame Josie, it still hurt.

Somehow Rebecca believed that if they did find Robbie, Josie would be more open to getting to know her a little better—especially if she herself somehow helped find him. As promised she'd spoken to her dad on Saturday afternoon and eventually he'd agreed to call someone he used to know who still worked in missing persons. No matter what she said, no matter how angry she got, he was a stubborn man—he refused to acknowledge that he and her mother were ever in the wrong and he refused to call his contact on a weekend. She'd decided to give him till noon today and then call him to see if he'd managed to make contact. This time she didn't plan on letting them push her around and she wouldn't stop pestering until he got her some answers.

She'd also researched private investigators and had a shortlist ready to call once she had the information from the police. Hugh likely wouldn't be keen on spending their money on the search for her ex, but Rebecca contributed to the household income with her piano lessons and this was important.

So caught up in these thoughts as she scrolled through her timeline, she almost went right past a photo of Paige and Solomon standing in front of the 'Welcome To Las Vegas' sign wearing a wedding dress and dark-grey suit.

*Oh my God!* Her fingers froze on the mouse as her heart froze in her chest.

Blinking, she leaned so close to the screen she'd be in danger of giving herself eyestrain in an effort to check she wasn't seeing things.

She wasn't. Paige looked stunning in Rebecca's own dress and the words attached to the post declared that she and Sol had tied the knot that afternoon (it was still Sunday in America). Her first thought was that if she hadn't joined Facebook, she'd never have seen this post. Was this why Paige had suddenly accepted her friend request on Friday afternoon? Rebecca thought it had been a step towards reconciliation but maybe she did so simply so she could rub this in her face.

Tears plopped onto the keyboard as Rebecca realised she'd missed this monumental moment in her daughter's life. How could she and Sol ever have thought this was a good idea? But even as she thought this, she knew the answer. Both her daughters were causing her pain right now and she had no one to blame but herself. Instinctively her hand reached for her mobile phone and before she knew it she was calling Hugh, praying he'd not be in the middle of a shoot and unable to talk.

Thank God he answered after only a couple of rings. 'I was just about to call you.'

'So you've seen Facebook?' She could barely talk past the tears.

'Yes.' His one word oozed disbelief.

'How could she do this to us?'

'Now calm down Rebecca. I know this is a shock and you're obviously upset—'

'Aren't you?' she accused. 'How could they do this? And worse, how could they let us find out about it on social media?'

He took a moment to reply and she realised he was far more likely to be angry at her than Paige over this.

'Obviously I would have preferred to have been there to witness Paige's and Sol's big day, but this is about them, not you, not me, not us! The important thing is they've sorted their differences. And hey, this way, maybe we can spend all the money we would have spent on the wedding on an overseas holiday for us instead.'

Rebecca should have been overjoyed by this suggestion—she'd been wanting to go to Europe for years and more importantly, if Hugh wanted to go with her, it must mean he wanted to fix their problems—but it would probably take her a few days, maybe even weeks, to get over this disappointment.

'Look,' he said, 'I'm really sorry, but I'm going to have to go. We're about to start shooting something with the new environment minister and don't you have to get to a dialysis appointment?' It was a rhetorical question and he continued, 'Try to look at the positives here and I'll be home as early as possible, we can commiserate together then.'

'Okay,' she managed.

'I love you, Rebecca,' he said and then disconnected.

Her heart and head were a whirlpool of emotions—he hadn't said the L-word in days, but oh my, *Paige*! She was telling herself what was done was done (even if she didn't like it), when the doorbell rang.

*What now?* She dumped her phone on the table and headed for the front door. Whoever it was she'd get rid of them quick smart because Hugh was right, she had to be at the hospital soon.

'Clara?' she said when she saw Robbie's ex-wife standing on the doorstep—she was possibly the last person she'd expected to see.

'Hello, Rebecca.'

Thoughts of Paige's elopement were almost forgotten as Rebecca registered the dejected expression on the other woman's face. 'Oh my God,' she blurted, 'has something happened to Josie?'

But even before Clara replied, Rebecca understood that this wasn't a visit regarding her daughter. 'Robbie?' she whispered, sudden terror filling her heart.

Clara nodded solemnly. 'I'm sorry to be the bearer of bad news but we've just been informed by the police that Robert—or at least they're pretty certain it's him—has been found dead on a farm up north.'

Only part of this sentence registered for Rebecca. 'What do you mean they're pretty certain it's him? Is there a possibility it's not? Has someone identified the body?' Weren't there hundreds of middle-aged missing men? It could be any one of them.

'He hung himself, Rebecca.'

Clara's words were like a punch in the gut—Rebecca reached out to steady herself on the door.

'At least a month ago now. The body will already be decomposing, so they're going to use other methods to identify him, but his licence was with him, his bank cards, his description matched those on his missing persons profile.'

'No,' Rebecca whispered, unable to bear the image that had just formed in her head. Would she ever be rid of it?

'I'm afraid so.'

Clara looked as if she were fighting tears but Rebecca couldn't hold hers back—it was like losing Robbie all over again, only this time she knew the heart-shattering truth. He'd taken his own life and she'd played a role in that decision.

There were supposed to be seven stages of grief or something, but she felt all of them all at once. Along with the guilt came shock, disbelief and denial. How could this happen now when he'd been so close to getting what he wanted? Surely fate wasn't that cruel. There was still a remote possibility the police had the wrong guy. The rage she felt for her parents intensified—Robbie may have only ended it a month ago, but they were the ones who started it over thirty-five years ago. She wondered if she would ever be able to speak to them again. And then there was a sadness so intense that she felt the pain of it all over her body. Her grip tightened on the door as she struggled to stay afoot.

'Do you think you should sit down?' Clara asked, both irritation and concern on her face.

'Yes, good idea.' Although, whether Rebecca could make it to the nearest chair she wasn't sure. 'Would you like to come in?'

'No thanks,' Clara said curtly, 'but I suggest you have a strong sweet cup of tea to help the shock. I've got to go.'

As Clara turned to do exactly this, Rebecca asked, 'Does Josie know?'

Clara turned back slowly. 'Yes, we were at Brenda's place about to film a segment on missing persons when the police turned up.'

'Oh God.' The thought of Josie being told there was no hope of ever finding her biological father intensified Rebecca's own agony. There was probably no hope of salvaging any kind of relationship with her daughter now either—Josie would never forgive Rebecca for turning Robbie away all those years ago. And Rebecca couldn't blame her; she would never forgive herself.

'How's she doing?' she found herself asking even though she knew it was a stupid question.

'She's understandably upset, but trying to be strong for Brenda.' Again Clara tried to leave, but this time, not only did Rebecca call out, she also reached out.

'I'm so sorry,' she said, sobbing as she grabbed hold of Clara's arm and then pulled the other woman into a hug.

She hadn't been able to help herself and fully expected Clara to shake her off, but instead Rebecca felt arms close around her, a head sink onto her shoulder and the two of them stood there holding each other for quite some time.

'You were as much a victim as he was,' Clara acknowledged as they eventually broke apart.

'Thank you,' Rebecca whispered, her eyes still an ocean, as Robbie's ex-wife finally made her getaway. She doubted they'd ever be friends, but they were weirdly bonded through their shared love and grief for the same man and the fact neither of their lives had turned out exactly as they'd hoped.

As Rebecca went back into the house, she wondered what to do about Josie. Her instinct was to rush to her and take care of her as she would if Paige had suffered such a heart-blow, but she was under no illusions that Josie wanted that kind of relationship with her and she didn't want to make things worse. She could send her a message, but sending such words of sympathy felt so cold, so impersonal.

Still, she couldn't just say or do nothing. It felt as if she were damned if she did and damned if she didn't.

And what about Paige? Should she and Sol be told about this? Perhaps Josie would message her or would she assume Rebecca would do the honours? As annoyed as she was about Paige and Sol getting married without her, they'd literally only tied the knot a few short hours ago—it didn't seem right to interrupt their honeymoon with such news. She decided to ask Hugh about it when he got home and then her thoughts returned to Josie.

Rebecca desperately wanted her to know she was thinking of her, but what could she do without making everything even worse?

Finally, after a few long moments of contemplation, she had the answer.

She could make a few meals for Josie, Clara and Brenda. Probably the last thing any of them felt like doing was cooking. Decision made, she opened the fridge to check she had all the ingredients necessary for casseroles.

When Hugh returned to the house a few hours later, he found her dishing the last of them into throwaway foil containers. He frowned as he hung his keys on their special hook. 'Shouldn't you still be at dialysis?'

'Oh shit!' *That* had totally slipped her mind.

'Did you skip your session because of Sol and Paige?' He sounded annoyed. 'I came home early to make dinner so you could put your feet up afterwards but,' he nodded towards the rows of containers, 'it looks like you've made enough for an army. I know you're upset but you can't just not go to the hospital.'

He thought she was cooking to distract herself?

'Oh, Hugh.' She let the serving spoon fall into the casserole dish. 'Robbie's dead.'

He stared at her a few moments—his expression dazed. Then he blinked. 'What? Josie's *father*, Robbie?'

'Yes,' she confirmed and then told him everything.

'Fuck.' Hugh rarely swore, saving his curse words for when they really mattered. She appreciated that now.

'Yes. It's all such a horrible mess.'

'So, the cooking? Is that for …'

'Josie and Brenda,' she confirmed. 'But I don't know why I bothered to make it all; after Saturday and then today's news, I'm the last person Josie probably wants to see right now.'

She'd thought her tears had dried up but her eyes prickled again and she swayed a little, both dizzy and tired.

'You don't look so good,' Hugh said, his brow furrowing in concern. 'You should go lie down.'

She *wasn't* feeling so good. 'But what about all this food? All this mess?'

'I'll deal with it,' he said as he put his hands on her and guided her out of the kitchen. She didn't know what he meant by that but was helpless except to lean against him as he ushered her down the hallway and up the stairs to their bedroom. He let go of her only long enough to pull back their doona and then he encouraged her into bed and covered her up like she were a sick child.

'Get some rest.' He leant forward and kissed her on the forehead.

Mentally and physically exhausted, Rebecca was asleep before he'd even shut the door. When she woke hours later, Hugh was sitting in bed beside her, reading his book by lamplight.

'What time is it?' she asked.

He put his book down and glanced at his watch. 'Almost nine o'clock.'

'At night?' She felt so groggy she wondered if she'd slept until the morning.

'Yes. How are you feeling?'

And suddenly all the events of the day came back to her. Robbie. Paige and Sol. *Josie.*

As if reading her mind, Hugh said, 'I cleaned up the kitchen and took all the casseroles round to Josie's place.'

'You saw Josie?' Her heart leapt into her throat. 'How did you know where she lived?'

'I called Paige and asked her for Josie's address.'

'Did you tell her?'

'About Robbie?' He nodded. 'And I didn't see Josie—she was staying the night with Robbie's mother—but I met Nik, her husband, and he said to say thank you for all the food. I told him to give Josie our love and that either of them could call us any time if they needed anything.'

*Oh my goodness.* Her heart brimmed with love for this man.

He spoke again before she could say anything. 'You must be hungry. I know it's late, but can I cook you something or would you just prefer some toast and a cuppa?'

Right now she didn't need anything but him.

'Hugh,' she said, taking his hand as she looked right into his eyes. 'I know Robbie's dead, but even if he wasn't, you would never have to compete with him. I was only fifteen when we were together and yes, things were intense between us. I loved him in the way a teenage girl loves her high school sweetheart, but to be honest, that's not very different from how they crush on celebrities. It was an innocent love, but now I know I didn't even know what love was then.'

436

Rebecca swallowed; she owed Hugh the absolute truth if they were going to recover from this.

'When we met I was still aching from losing my baby and also Robbie. My life felt hopeless. I was broken. And then we got chatting and we became such good friends. I didn't recognise that I was in love with you because my feelings for you went so much deeper than the all-consuming childish passion I had for Robbie. I'll admit I didn't think I was *in* love with you when we got married but I did love you. And over the last thirty years together I've fallen head over heels. You've taught me what real love is. My relationship with Robbie would probably have fizzled out as we grew up, but I know my love for you will never do any such thing.'

A lump had formed in her throat but somehow she managed to say one more thing. 'I do love you, Hugh, more than I've ever loved anyone. I'd be lost without you.'

From now on her mission in life would be to prove this fact.

'Oh, Rebecca.' Hugh pulled her into his arms. 'I love you, too.'

*Clara*

'To what do I owe this unexpected visit?' Siobhan exclaimed with her usual warm smile when she opened the door to Clara not long after she left Rebecca's.

Until that moment Clara had held it together—she hadn't cried when the policeman had delivered the news, she hadn't cried while speaking to the funeral director, she hadn't even cried when she'd shared that weird moment with Rebecca—but she took one look at her little sister and burst into tears.

Siobhan looked momentarily flummoxed—she wasn't used to her stoic sister falling apart—and then she yanked Clara into her arms and held her close. 'Oh darling,' she whispered. 'There, there, it'll be alright, whatever's happened, I'm here.'

'What's wrong with Aunty Clara?' came a voice from down near their hips and Clara drew back to see Zoey and Blake looking up at her with wide eyes.

'I'm fine.' Clara quickly wiped her eyes and tried to smile, feeling embarrassed about being caught in such a mess by her great-niece

438

and great-nephew. She looked back to Siobhan. 'Sorry, I didn't know you were babysitting, I'll leave.'

Siobhan grabbed onto her arm. 'Oh, no you don't. I'll give these two their iPads and they'll be occupied for hours. Just give me one sec.'

'But Mummy said we can't have screen time until after afternoon tea,' Zoey said, her tone disapproving.

Siobhan clapped her hands together. 'Guess it's time for afternoon tea, then.'

'But we just had lunch.' Zoey pouted.

Blake elbowed her in the side. 'Can I have a chocolate brownie?'

'You can have whatever you want, darling,' Siobhan said, ushering them back down the hallway. 'Come on.'

This last order was directed at Clara, so she followed her sister and the kids and tried to compose herself while Siobhan set them up with brownies, poppers and iPads in the theatre room.

'Now, can I get you a cup of tea?' Siobhan asked on her return.

Clara thought of what Brenda had said about the tea. 'Do you have anything stronger?'

'Come into the lounge room and let's see what we can find,' Siobhan said, taking her hand and leading her there.

As Clara all but collapsed onto the sofa, Siobhan went straight for the liquor cabinet—they weren't drunks but she and Neil did have an impressive collection of alcoholic drinks. Thirty seconds later when Siobhan put a glass tumbler of whiskey into her hand, Clara was very grateful of this fact.

She took a sip, screwed up her nose as the liquid burned her throat and then took another. It was *exactly* what she needed. She wouldn't drink too much because she'd have to drive back to Brenda's place soon, but a few more sips wouldn't hurt.

'Have you and Gregg had a fight?' Siobhan asked as she lowered herself onto the sofa beside Clara.

She realised she hadn't yet told her sisters about her split from Gregg—she'd been busy helping Josie and Brenda with the find Rob campaign but also hadn't wanted the lecture she knew they'd give her for the decision she'd made. They wouldn't understand.

'We kind of broke up,' she said slowly, cradling the glass between her hands. 'But that's not what this is about,' she rushed to add before Siobhan could say anything. 'Rob's body has been found.'

It should have been getting easier to deliver this news. But it wasn't. She felt a fresh wave of guilt and sorrow wash over her.

Siobhan gripped Clara's arm. 'Oh my God. When?'

'We're not sure exactly.' But she told her sister as much as they knew.

A tear snuck down Siobhan's cheek. 'Robert might not have been my favourite person in recent years, but …'

'I know,' Clara whispered, not needing her sister to finish her sentence. She felt exactly the same. She might have thought she wished him dead but the reality was something else entirely. She'd never wanted Rob to become just another devastating suicide statistic. Yet—

'So you were with Josie and Brenda when this happened?' Siobhan asked, interrupting this thought.

Clara nodded.

'Will Brenda have to identify the body?' was Siobhan's next question.

Clara shook her head. 'No, and this is going to sound awful— he'll be well and truly on the way to being decomposed, the stench will be terrible—but even knowing how gruesome it would be, I would have offered to do it for her. I kind of want to see for myself that he is well and truly dead.'

This was something she could never admit to anyone else.

'It doesn't sound awful, it sounds understandable,' Siobhan said. 'After all he's put you through while you were married, not to mention the last couple of years, you wouldn't be human if you didn't at least feel some relief that you finally have closure.'

'Yes, I guess, but this wasn't the kind of closure I wanted,' Clara confessed and she wasn't sure relief was exactly what she felt. Whatever it was, it was wrapped up together in a conflicting package with guilt and sadness. 'I know he made my life a living hell much of the time and for the last couple of years all I wanted was for him to leave me the hell alone, but now that he has, all I feel is empty and sad and I hate myself. I hate myself for wanting him gone and for failing him. Not just when we were married and I didn't insist he get proper help but—'

'That's ridiculous,' Siobhan interrupted, 'you tried numerous ways and times. I know you're in shock but I can't let you blame yourself for this.'

'I should have done more to help him try and find his child. And recently, when he got so upset after seeing me with Gregg, I should have gone after him, but all I cared about was my own happiness. He's been dead about a month! Seeing me with Gregg triggered his suicide.'

'You don't know that for sure.'

'Yes I do.' Nothing her sister could say would convince her otherwise. It was the final straw. She might as well have bought him the rope. 'And how can I look at Brenda and Josie knowing this? I couldn't bear being in the same room any longer. It was too horribly sad seeing Josie with Brenda and knowing that had she turned up just a couple of months earlier, there might have been a different ending to this story. When they didn't need someone to identify the body, I offered to go tell Rebecca. I had to get out of there.'

It was also part of the reason she'd taken charge of calling the funeral director, but that break hadn't been long enough.

'Rebecca is Josie's biological mother?' Clara confirmed.

441

'Yes.'

'Wow.' Siobhan let out a long slow breath. 'And how'd she take it?'

'She was a mess. More so even than Josie or Brenda but everyone reacts differently. They're probably still in shock and I think Rebecca's harbouring a lot of guilt. It was weird, actually. Until now, I've hated her almost as much as I hated Rob for ruining my life, but she hugged me and I let her. Suddenly I couldn't help feeling devastated for her as well. I can't imagine how I'd feel if I found out our parents had done something to me like hers did to her and Rob. I don't condone or agree with how she handled the secret, but I can finally see she's not a bad person.'

'That's because you, my dear, are a very good person.'

Clara shrugged; she wasn't sure about that at all right now. No matter she didn't hate Rebecca, she still found herself coveting her daughter. She couldn't help feeling good that Josie had connected with her more than she had her biological mother. What kind of person did *that* make her?

A squeal sounded from the direction of the theatre room. Siobhan let out an exasperated sigh and stood. 'I'll be right back,' she said and rushed from the room.

'Sorry about that,' she said when she returned a few moments later. 'Disaster struck. The wi-fi died for a moment but it's all fixed again now.'

'That's okay.' Clara put her glass down on the coffee table—no longer in such dire need of alcohol. 'I should probably be getting back to Josie and Brenda anyway.'

'Oh.' Siobhan blinked. 'I know this is very uncaring of me when you're so upset about Robert, but you're not going to leave me hanging about you and Gregg, are you? I thought he was perfect for you.'

Clara couldn't help the laugh that burst from her mouth. God, she loved her sister. The Gregg break-up now felt like only a tiny bump in the road, but telling Siobhan would give her a few minutes reprieve from her other emotions—maybe that was her sister's cunning plan—and it would also delay her return to Josie and Brenda just a little longer. She leaned back into the couch and began with the cruise ship fiasco.

'The poor man!' Siobhan exclaimed when Clara told her how she'd ended up missing his comic debut because she was chasing a Rob look-alike.

She agreed, that *was* a terribly unfortunate situation, but it was his ultimatum that had truly ended it all. There'd been a lot of drama over the past week, so perhaps she simply hadn't had time to miss him but the sad truth was she missed Shadow more than she did Gregg. They had jumped into a full-on relationship pretty fast and Clara now had to wonder if the biggest appeal about Gregg was that because he was so different to Rob he came across as better for her than he actually was.

Siobhan shook her head. 'An ultimatum never ends well, and however much I might agree with Gregg that you need to put yourself first, an ultimatum is never fair either. And a man that gives you one isn't right for you. I think you made the right decision. There'll be other blokes.'

'Maybe.' But right now her love-life was the last thing on her mind.

'So what happens now?'

'What do you mean?'

'Well, a lot of things have changed in your life lately—the house is sold, Rob is gone, you've stopped volunteering, things may not have worked out between you and Gregg but you've made a lot of progress in reclaiming your life. So what's the next step?'

'I'm not sure. I might need to sleep on your couch for a few weeks while I work that out.'

Siobhan smiled. 'Don't be silly. You can have the guest room for as long as you need.'

'Thanks. And after that, maybe I'll go overseas after all. Or maybe I'll buy a caravan and travel around Australia. Or maybe I'll just buy a cat and a smaller place to live and take each day one step at a time. Right now, the most important thing is helping Brenda organise Robert's funeral and supporting her and Josie through this nightmare.'

Siobhan rolled her eyes. 'You can't help yourself, can you?'

Clara shook her head. 'No, but whatever Rob was, he was also my husband and Brenda was my mother-in-law. I couldn't save him, but I can sure as hell make sure I don't abandon his mother and daughter in their hour of need.'

*Paige*

When her dad phoned to tell her about the discovery of Robbie's body, Paige's first instinct had been to board the first flight back to Australia, but Solomon had convinced her to at least enjoy a few days of their honeymoon first. After a phone call with Josie who'd assured her there was nothing she could do anyway, the few days extended to almost two weeks. Due to the nature of Robbie's death, the coroner had held onto the body for ten days and Paige and Sol landed back in Sydney the day before the funeral.

They got a taxi straight from the airport to Josie's house.

'She might not be there,' Sol said with a yawn. 'She might be at her grandmother's place sorting any last-minute details for the funeral.'

'Then I'll call her,' Paige said, 'but it's on our way home anyway.'

Sol raised an eyebrow—Josie and Nik's place wasn't exactly on their way—but it was worth the detour as they found Josie at home.

Nik answered their call through the intercom. 'It's the newlyweds,' he called as the door clicked open. He met them in the communal entrance seconds later and gave them both massive hugs. 'Congratulations, you sly dogs, you.'

'Oh my God,' Josie squealed as she pushed past her husband to get to them. 'What are you guys doing here?'

The smile on her face relaxed Paige's heart—she didn't look too bad for someone who had just lost their father.

'Well,' Paige said, 'quite aside from the fact we've gambled away our meagre life savings and spent the rest on flights, food and accommodation, I wanted to be here for you, for tomorrow.'

'Thank you.' Josie pulled her into a tight hug.

'You look like you need a coffee,' Nik said, and Paige knew that comment was directed at Sol.

'Yes, come in, come in,' Josie agreed, 'you can tell us all about your nuptials.'

'So you're not angry we got married without you?' Paige asked.

Josie shook her head. 'I've got too much else in my head to be angry, besides, as I've always said, your wedding should be about the two of you, so it's your prerogative to get married however the hell you want.'

'Let's hope our parents see it your way.'

Nik and Josie laughed. 'You haven't seen them yet?' he asked.

'You're first on our agenda,' Sol said, stifling another yawn and gesturing to their three suitcases—one of which carried the dress—behind them on the floor.

Nik helped Sol drag them into the apartment while Paige and Josie went through to the kitchen.

'How are you?' Paige asked as she sat herself down at the breakfast counter. 'I was so sorry to hear about Robbie. You must be devastated.'

Josie grabbed a handful of coffee pods from a little basket on her bench. 'Thanks,' she said as she started making the drinks. 'I'm doing okay. It was a shock—I so hoped we'd find him—but it's also really weird, being so involved in something so big yet also feeling on the outer. I went with Clara and Brenda to talk to the funeral director but it all feels a bit surreal.'

'I can imagine.'

'Like, I'm sad, really sad—for Brenda, for Clara and also for Robbie himself. I'm heartbroken he wanted to meet me and that never happened, but I'm more upset by the whole situation than I am bereaved. I feel more than I would have had I just heard someone I know talking about someone they know, yet that's really all this is. It's hard to mourn someone you never really knew.' Josie shook her head. 'I'm probably not making much sense.'

'No, you are. Perfect sense.'

'Keeping busy helps. Looking after Brenda and getting to know her, helping her and Clara organise the funeral, it all helps, but seeing you is such a wonderful reprieve from all of it. Thank you so much for coming back.'

Paige beamed at Josie's words as Sol and Nik came into the kitchen.

'Here you are.' Josie handed him the first cup.

'Thanks.' He took a long sip as if it were the elixir of life.

When Josie finished the other coffees, Nik and Sol took theirs into the lounge room. Paige and Josie meant to do the same but they got talking again before they made it out of the kitchen.

'Tell me about the wedding,' Josie said, leaning back against the bench and then taking a sip of her drink. 'How'd you manage to organise flights and everything so quickly?'

'Solomon did pretty much everything. He's amazing.'

Josie grinned. 'Well, you've certainly got that post-honeymoon glow. And I see you did end up wearing the dress. Don't tell me you got married by an Elvis Impersonator?'

'No.' Paige laughed. 'We contemplated that for all of five seconds and then decided it was too tacky. We ended up choosing a really cute little chapel and a gay guy that I kid you not looked like Franck from *Father of the Bride* did the deed.'

'Oh my God, I loved him. And that's one of my favourite movies.'

'Are any movies not your favourite movies?'

'Well, I didn't love the sequel. In fact, I'm sure you'll agree, most sequels are crap.'

Paige nodded. 'Speaking of the dress, I'll get it dry-cleaned and then give it back to you. I promise I took good care of it and there's not a stain or anything on it, but it has been stuffed in a suitcase twice for almost twenty-four hours, so—'

'About the dress,' Josie interrupted. 'How would you feel if I donated it to a charity?'

The question took Paige by surprise—Josie had been so adamant about keeping it. 'What charity?'

'Clara told me about a charity that takes old wedding dresses and makes them into beautiful gowns for stillborn babies. Nothing can bring such a baby back, but having lost three children in gestation myself, I know that grief, I know that heartache, and I like the idea that maybe instead of sitting in a cupboard for moths to feed on, our dress could honour the lives of a few little ones that were taken far too soon.'

'It's your dress,' Paige said, struggling to speak past the tears that had come at Josie's words. 'But I think that's a wonderful idea.'

When the coffee cups were drained, Paige glanced at the time on her phone. 'I suppose I better get Sol home to bed, but is there anything I can do to help for tomorrow? Do you need me to bake something for the wake?'

'Thanks, but I think we're covered. Clara's sisters have taken it upon themselves to do the catering and I reckon there'll be more food than people.'

At this sad admission, Paige took her sister's hand and gave it a little squeeze.

'Thanks,' Josie whispered with a soulful smile. 'How's your mum doing?'

Paige was about to say 'our mother' but she knew Josie didn't yet see her that way and she didn't want to upset her or push the friendship.

'I'm going to see her now,' she said instead.

Josie nodded and then she scooped up both their empty cups and took them to the sink. They found Sol asleep on the sofa in the lounge room.

Nik looked up when they entered and chuckled. 'You must have really worn him out on that honeymoon.'

Paige poked out her tongue at him. She realised as Josie was her sister that made Nik her brother-in-law and she loved the idea that one day her kids would have him as a fun uncle. He'd probably give them bowling balls for their first birthdays.

'Do you mind if I leave him here for a couple of hours while I go visit my folks?'

'Of course not,' Josie said.

'I'd suggest moving him to the spare room, but even if I could carry him, Jose's dad is arriving in a few hours, so he'll need it.'

For a second Paige was confused and then realised Nik was referring to Josie's adoptive father. He must have decided to come all this way for the funeral. 'Thanks.' She hitched her bag to her shoulder. 'I'll just call an Uber.'

'Don't be silly, take my car,' Josie said. 'I'll grab my keys.'

'You okay to drive?' Nik asked when she returned. 'I could drive you if not?'

'Nah, I'm fine. But thanks.' She took the keys and smiled at the two of them. 'I'll try not to be long and I can't wait to meet your dad.'

Sol didn't even stir as the three of them spoke beside him and as Paige drove to her parents' place, she started to feel weary as well. But this conversation was too important to put off. Also, it needed to be had before the funeral—she didn't want the first time she saw her parents after her wedding to be the day they were burying Robbie.

She parked her car outside and for the first time in her life felt jittery as she approached the front door. Should she just go in? Or should she knock? Although she'd spoken to her dad on the phone, their brief conversations had been about Josie and Robbie and about whether she should come home; apart from a quick congratulations, he'd barely acknowledged the wedding. And this was about more than her eloping.

With a deep breath, she visualised putting on her big girl undies, dug her key out of her bag and then let herself into the house.

'Mum? Dad?' Her voice echoed in the almost eerie silence. Had her parents gone out for dinner? She hadn't told them she and Sol would be coming back for the funeral—as far as her dad knew they were still in America.

Within seconds, Molly's head—followed rapidly by her body—appeared from the lounge room and Paige was accosted by excited paws. 'Geez, Mol,' she said, as she gave her cuddles and tried to avoid a slobbery kiss, 'you need a new brand of toothpaste.'

Of course the dog didn't reply, but Paige looked up as a shadow fell over her to see her mother coming the same way Molly had.

'Sweetheart!'

'Hi, Mum.' Paige tried to hide her shock at how harrowed her mother looked. Not just tired but seriously ill—her eyes were so bloodshot it looked like she was wearing fancy dress Halloween contact lenses and she was thinner than she had been in a long while. The knowledge she was responsible for at least some of her mother's anguish made her want to burst into tears. 'Where's Dad?'

'He's gone to get takeaway for dinner. Neither of us were in the mood for cooking. Congratulations to you and Sol,' her mum said, nodding towards Paige's left hand. 'Can I see your ring?'

The question was asked tentatively as if she fully expected Paige to refuse, which wasn't surprising considering the childish and slightly crazed way she'd reacted over this whole adoption surprise. Shame and self-loathing washed over her.

'Yes. Of course.' Paige straightened and, ignoring Molly's whiny protests that she'd stopped stroking her, held out her hand to her mother.

'It's beautiful.' She sounded all choked up. 'And you made such a lovely bride.'

'I'm so sorry, Mum.' Suddenly Paige couldn't believe she'd gone through the most important day of her life without the most important woman in her life beside her. 'I just ...'

But, she shook her head as tears threatened.

There was no acceptable explanation. She'd let her raging fury guide her, she'd let her anger take precedence over everything else that mattered. One thing like this—even though it was a big one—should not wipe out all the years and wonderful ways her mother had supported her. When many parents would have been telling her she was insane for wanting to pursue a career as an artist and steering her towards a degree in law or medicine or something, her mum was buying her paints and easels and taking her to art galleries. She'd always been there for Paige—at one stage she'd even coached Paige's netball team and everyone knew she hated any form of team sport. She'd been a crap coach, but in lieu of anyone else, she'd tried.

Only months ago, Paige had been devastated by her mum's kidney failure diagnosis. The thought of losing her had been both terrifying and impossible to comprehend, yet she'd let something cause a rift between them by choice. Sol had been right—she'd made it all about her.

How could she have been so stupid? And how could she ever make it up?

As tears flowed down her cheeks, her mother closed the gap between them and drew Paige into her arms. 'It's alright, sweetheart. I understand. The important thing is that you and Solomon are together.'

Her gentle reassurance only made Paige wail harder.

Rebecca held her, making soothing noises and stroking her hair as she'd done when she was little, until her sobs finally subsided. Then, 'Let's go have a cup of tea,' she suggested. 'Dad will be home soon and I'm sure he'll have brought enough for an army. Would you like to stay for dinner? Where's Sol?'

Rebecca was acting like everything was normal but Paige couldn't let her go on without addressing their fallout. 'Will you ever forgive me for getting married without you?'

Her mum cocked her head to one side and hit her with a question of her own. 'Will you ever forgive me for keeping Josie a secret all these years?'

'I already have,' she said, and realised it was true. 'I overreacted and I'm sorry.'

'I don't think you overreacted at all. You were hurt, shocked, I get that. I would have been fuming if your father had kept such a secret from me and I wish more than anything now that I'd played my cards differently. I'm glad you and Josie are getting to know each other and, I hope in time, maybe I will too.'

Paige gave her mum another hug. She'd love the three of them to be able to hang out, go to the movies, shop or chat over coffee like normal mothers and daughters do, but she had a feeling it might be a long while—if ever—before that happened. 'I hope so too,' she said and then changed the subject. 'How are you and Dad, now?'

The thought of them splitting up was unbearable, but she was a realist. Her father probably had much more right to be angry and feel betrayed than she did.

'We're good.' Rebecca smiled. 'If anything I think this will make us stronger. Once I'm well again, we're going to use the money we would have spent on your wedding for a big overseas holiday. We might even go to Vegas and renew our vows.'

Paige laughed as relief and happiness filled her heart. 'I think that's a wonderful idea. There's only a few months now until you'll be able to have the transplant. I'm so sorry about saying Sol wouldn't do it—I didn't mean it, of course he will. He'd do it even if we broke up and even if I didn't want him to.'

A serious look crossed Rebecca's face. 'That's sweet of you both, but I've decided I'm going to wait it out on the list for a deceased donor.'

'What? No! Why would you do that?'

'I just don't feel right about doing it any other way,' she said and then held up her hand. 'And you can forget about trying to convince me otherwise, so don't waste your breath. Dialysis isn't as bad as I thought it would be. It gives me a few hours a few times a week to sit back and read or do whatever I feel like doing completely guilt-free. And, I've made some good friends there.'

'Really?'

'Yes.'

Paige couldn't help raising her eyebrows as her mother told her about some of her unlikely comrades. 'A priest?'

'He's the least priest-like priest you'll ever meet. You'd love him.'

Before Paige could respond to that, the door opened behind them and her dad came in to find them still standing in the hallway.

'Paige!' He almost dropped the bag of takeaway food in his hand, but despite her mother's less-than-fabulous health, she reached out and rescued it.

'Daddy.' Paige threw herself into her father's arms. 'I missed you.'

'I missed you too, sweetheart.' He pulled back a little and looked to her mum. 'We both did.'

'I know,' she said, taking his hand. 'And Mum and I have just had a good chat. I'm sorry I didn't let you be there for my big day, but with everything else going on, it just seemed right for it just to be the two of us. In hindsight, I'm a bit sad. It was a beautiful day, but it would have been even more meaningful if the two of you were there.'

'Aw, darling. We'd have loved that too, but plenty of people have an intimate wedding overseas and then follow it back home with a celebration. Why don't we do that?' He chuckled. 'It would give Lisette the chance to show off her backyard makeover after all.'

She'd never known her father knew so much about weddings, but it was a fabulous suggestion. Her wedding to Sol had been the best day of her life and this would give her the chance to relive it all over again. Not to mention use some of Josie's fabulous ideas for a reception. 'Dad, you are a genius.'

'Ah, I don't know about that,' he said, but his smile gave away his pride.

Paige smiled back, but her excitement by the prospect of all that laid ahead dimmed a little when she remembered the reason she'd returned home today specifically. It felt wrong to be feeling so happy and relieved when her sister was about to face one of the saddest days of her life.

*Josie*

Josie had never experienced non-drinking related travel sickness in her life, but as Nik drove to Waverley Cemetery and she listened to her dad and Brenda chatter in the back seat, she felt each and every turn and tiny bump in the road. The moment he stopped, she leapt from the car.

'Can you guys take care of Brenda?' she managed to ask as her dad climbed out from behind her. 'I think I'm going to be sick.'

And then she sprinted into the cemetery and followed the signs to the public conveniences near the entrance. She'd barely even eaten anything for breakfast but as she dry-retched into the toilet bowl, she regretted that decision. You always felt better after a good vomit; then again, maybe even that wouldn't be able to make her feel better today.

'Are you okay?' came a voice from just outside the door.

'Clara?'

'Yes, I noticed you dash in here.'

She almost cried at the sound of the other woman's voice. 'Stomach upset,' she explained and then flushed the toilet.

When she emerged, Clara told her to splash her face with water, then gave her a tissue and a hug.

'Lucky I chose waterproof mascara today,' Josie tried to joke, but she couldn't bring herself to laugh.

'Come on.' Clara took her hand. 'Let's go out and face the music. I want to introduce you to my sisters and I can't wait to meet your father.'

'Thank you,' Josie whispered, and then let the older woman lead her out.

A small crowd had gathered around Brenda, Nik and her dad and it was plain as day that the middle-aged women were Clara's sisters. They were all of similar height, build and colouring. She wondered if people would ever look at her and Paige and see the similarity, although Paige had paler skin and lighter-coloured hair.

The nausea lingered, but she tried to ignore it as introductions and small talk were made. She wished they could get the show on the road and get it over and done with, but Waverley was a busy place and they had to wait their turn. Next in line was a massive funeral if the crowd gathering behind a hearse and two big black cars was anything to go by. At the noise and sheer mass of people, she guessed the deceased was Italian.

She glanced around at the tiny-in-comparison crowd that had formed for Robbie. If it weren't for Clara's sisters, their husbands and children, the attendees could be counted on one hand. And they were more here to support Clara than they were for Robbie; just like Nik and her dad were here for her. Once again Josie fought tears at the hopeless loneliness of her biological father's life and death.

A tap on her back jolted her from her thoughts and she turned to see Paige, Sol, Rebecca and a man she guessed to be Paige's dad standing behind them. She was happy to see Paige and Solomon but didn't know how she felt about the other two.

'Hi,' was all Paige said before giving her a hug. 'How you doing?'

'Pretty crap,' she admitted. 'Thanks for coming.'

'Of course,' Paige said as Sol came in for a hug.

'Hello,' Rebecca said. They also hugged but Josie had felt less awkward hugging Clara's sisters and brothers-in-law and she'd only just met them that day. 'I wasn't sure if I should come but—'

'It's fine.' Josie cut her off and withdrew from the embrace. She didn't want to get into any kind of conversation with her biological mother right now. This day was about Robbie, not Rebecca.

Paige introduced Josie to her dad and they exchanged a polite handshake, before Rebecca retreated to talk to Brenda. Josie thought she had some nerve showing up, never mind actually talking to Rob's mother, but she wasn't about to make a scene and Clara and her dad were looking after her anyway.

As the other funeral party began to slowly walk behind the black cars, Nik exclaimed, 'Holy smokes. Is that Stevie Galloway?'

Clara gasped as Josie, along with everyone else in Rob's funeral party, turned to see a tall man in dark sunglasses swaggering towards them with two other blokes she didn't recognise on either side of him.

The trio singled Clara out and pulled her into their arms. 'Long time, no see,' said the man pushing his sunglasses up onto his head.

Josie was too stunned to be impressed by the fact Nik had recognised the once lead guitarist for One Track Mind, who had gone on to start another band, which had done quite well, and was now a well-respected judge on *The Voice*. She took a closer look at the other two and decided they must be Brad, who used to play drums, and Jonno, the keyboard. If she remembered correctly, Brad was an accountant or something now and Jonno was a piano tuner—either way, Stevie was the only member of the band still in the public spotlight.

If the arrival of Rob's band-mates wasn't overwhelming enough, a number of other well-known Aussie musicians began to appear. By the time the funeral directors announced it was time to start walking, Robbie had quite a respectable crowd and Josie wasn't simply nauseous but shaking at the thought of talking to these people after the service.

Still, trying to put her nerves aside, she stood on one side of Brenda with Clara on the other, everyone else following behind as they walked a short distance to the graveside where the service would take place. Robbie's hearse came to a stop and Nik, along with Clara's brothers-in-law and oldest nephew, carried the coffin to its resting place.

Josie hadn't thought there'd be many people at the service, but there wasn't a small number of mourners gathered on the grass between the graves overlooking the water. Her heart swelled with pride that all these people had come out of the crevices to pay respect to her biological father. If only he'd known how much he was loved and respected after all. If only he'd held on a little longer.

Once the coffin was lowered, the pallbearers stepped back, stooped their heads in respect and retreated. As the celebrant from the funeral home welcomed everyone, Nik came to stand next to Josie and took her hand. Her other one was clutched tightly around Brenda's. The celebrant said a few short words, thanking everyone for coming and then Clara stepped forward to deliver the eulogy. She spoke clearly and with poise but didn't gloss over the ugly parts of Rob's life.

'Robert Jones was born in the rural town of Cobar to doting parents, Malcolm and Brenda Jones. Sadly when he was only two years old, Rob's father died in a tragic mining accident and

Brenda became a single mother. Rob attended Cobar Public School and from an early age showed a gift for music. Although music lessons were expensive and Brenda was struggling to make ends meet during much of Rob's childhood, she sacrificed many other things so he could learn the piano, the guitar and later the saxophone.

'He was good at any instrument he picked up, but his true passion lay in singing and songwriting. Rob had an amazing voice—at his insistence teachers at Cobar High School started a choir and in his second last year at school Rob formed his first band. It was in this group that he met his first love, she was their female vocalist and the two of them hit it off almost instantly. According to his mother, they were inseparable. Both had their sights set on a music career and were undoubtedly far more talented than the others in their high school band.

'What most of you probably do not know is that she and Rob had a child. Although legally forced adoption was a thing of the past, that's in essence what happened with their baby. His girlfriend was sent away to have their little girl and she was adopted into a loving family in Western Australia, but the guilt of his involvement in this and the grief over losing his child was something Rob never recovered from. At first he channelled all this emotion into his music. He moved to Sydney and formed a new band with like-minded individuals—some of whom are here today.'

Here Clara paused and sought out Stevie, Brad and Jonno in the crowd. She spoke about their successes playing in pubs and clubs, and shared a few anecdotes of how the group were like brothers to each other. 'It was Rob's song, "Lost Without You, Baby", that got One Track Mind a record deal. Although he never let on publicly, that song was about the loss of his baby and was written from somewhere deep in his soul.

'I met Rob just as the band's success was kicking off. He had appendicitis and I was one of his nurses.' Clara spoke wistfully about their first few blissful years together. 'Rob was a complex and very driven man, however not long after we were married, I fell pregnant. Sadly we suffered a number of miscarriages and had a daughter who wasn't born breathing. These losses reignited the battle with depression Rob had been suffering since the adoption of his first child. He turned to alcohol to try and deal with this guilt and grief but this only made the black dog worse and he had to keep drinking more and more to numb the pain.

'His band-mates, his friends, his mother and myself all did our best over the years to help Rob conquer his demons, but sadly there was nothing any of us could do and Rob lost this battle two weeks ago. The one thing Rob always wanted was to find that baby he lost to adoption and what makes his passing ever more wretched is that, unbeknownst to him, he did meet the child he'd never been able to forget.

'Rob and his daughter Josephine met outside a pub in Coogee and although they had no clue what they were to each other, they talked and connected on some level. Josie opened her heart to Rob and he suggested she get some counselling, which led her to me. A few weeks after this poignant meeting, Josie came to me and it was only a matter of a few more weeks before we discovered our connection, but tragically by this time, Rob was already missing.'

At this point Clara sniffed—it was the first sign of emotion she'd shown since she'd started to speak. 'Rob and his daughter not only bear a physical resemblance but Josie shares his love of music. Through her Rob's passion will live on and I know he would have been super proud of the wonderful woman she is.'

With one final nod at the coffin, Clara took her position beside Josie and Brenda again. They hugged briefly but tightly as the celebrant took over once again, asking if anyone wanted to say a few words. Josie didn't know what she would say, but felt she should say something and also she wanted to.

With shaking legs, she took a few steps forward and then turned to face the crowd.

'I never knew my biological father personally—or at least I didn't realise until it was too late that I did—but I've known him from a distance for a long time. Those who know me know I sometimes joke about being born a decade or two late because, while I don't mind modern music, my favourite bands and singers are all from the eighties. I found One Track Mind's first LP in an op shop when I was a teenager and I fell in love with their sound. Now that I know "Lost Without You, Baby" was about me, I ...'

But Josie couldn't go on. Tears she so far hadn't shed suddenly burst from her eyeballs and she found her throat so swamped with emotion she couldn't speak. Finally, she too turned to the coffin, silently told Rob she'd never forget him and then retreated.

Nik pulled her close to his side and she stayed there, her head resting against his chest, as others came forward to say their bit. Rob's band-mates made everyone laugh as they shared anecdotes from their times on the road and finished with an apology that they too had never managed to help him.

'We'll always wonder if there was something else we could have done,' finished Stevie Galloway.

At the end of the service the celebrant thanked everyone for coming and invited them all to a celebration of Rob's life at Clara's house. Then, as the coffin was lowered further into the ground, Stevie Galloway started to sing 'Lost Without You, Baby' and slowly the rest of the attendees joined him.

Josie had never heard of anything like this ever happening at a funeral but it felt strangely right. It was the perfect send-off for her father and she hoped somehow he could hear them from the afterlife.

Afterwards while she stood with Brenda and Clara as everyone offered their condolences, she found she was no longer flummoxed about being in the presence of some of her music idols. They were just normal people and told her it was their honour to be there. Stevie Galloway even said she should get in contact with him if she ever wanted to pursue a music career of her own. At thirty-five Josie felt like it was a little late to be starting down such a path and, while she'd loved her time working in musicals and singing in the eighties cover band, since leaving London she'd been happy to keep her singing and acting as a hobby. Besides, she liked her current job, felt she made a difference to the kids, and wanted to focus on her and Nik's family now.

Lost in these thoughts, she was actually surprised when Rebecca appeared before her. Josie hadn't noticed her during the service and had almost forgotten she was there at all. She waited for her anger towards this woman to flare but suddenly all she felt was pity. As she took in her biological mother's bloodshot eyes, she thought about how weird and hard this must be for her as well. And for the first time she noticed a resemblance between the two of them.

They were both ugly criers.

'It was a beautiful service,' Rebecca said, her voice not much more than a whisper. 'I'm so sorry.'

And Josie knew this wasn't the same sorry for her loss that the other attendees had uttered, but an apology that went back years and much deeper.

'Thank you.' She nodded but Rebecca didn't make a move to go.

Instead, she dug into her handbag and pulled out a package wrapped in brown paper. She pressed this parcel into Josie's hands and her voice shook as she said, 'They're mix-tapes that Robbie gave me when we were together and some letters he wrote to me. I'm not sure if you'll be able to find anything to play the tapes on, but the songs are listed on the side and the letters might give you some insight into who he was, our feelings for each other and how much we would have loved you. They're yours. If you want them.'

A lump grew in Josie's throat. She held the precious parcel close and then said, 'Are you not coming to the wake?'

Rebecca bit her lip, then, 'I wasn't sure I'd be welcome.'

'Come,' Clara, who was standing beside Josie, said. 'We should all be together this afternoon.'

And Josie agreed.

Hours later, Josie sat in Clara's lounge room with her grandmother drinking tea. The last of the guests were gone. Clara's sisters and Rebecca had made sure the kitchen was spotless and all signs of the eating that had gone on vanished before they'd left, Stevie Galloway had been collected by his driver a couple of hours ago and Nik had just taken her dad back to their place.

'Well, that wasn't bad as far as wakes go,' Brenda announced as she lifted her china teacup to her mouth. 'It was lovely to see some of Rob's old friends.'

Josie wondered if Brenda was thinking of her son's music mates or Rebecca or both, but all she said was, 'Yes. I'm glad I got to meet everyone and learn more about Rob.'

Clara smiled and took a sip of her tea. Silence fell between them. After making conversation all afternoon, they were content just to sit with each other as they quietly reflected. The day had been better than Josie had imagined it would be and also a much livelier affair. She'd been dreading heading back to Clara's after the funeral, anticipating a very sombre afternoon, but Rob's band-mates' arrival had made the wake anything but.

While the Brennan sisters had done the rounds with food, Stevie, Brad and Jonno had provided plenty of entertainment. In addition to more tales of their time in the band, they'd sung an impromptu concert. They weren't bad, but it was clear that Rob had been the singer in the mix. She couldn't remember who, but someone had mentioned that Rebecca was the singer in Rob's very first band and, after protesting a fair bit, she finally agreed to sing with them.

Josie hadn't been sure how to feel about this and she'd looked to Clara, feeling anxious that this might make her friend uncomfortable, but Clara appeared to be enjoying the music as much as everyone else. Not wanting to be a party pooper, Josie had tried to push aside her irritation and pretty soon she found herself swept away by the music.

Rebecca was really good. Josie had tears in her eyes listening to her biological mother's beautiful voice singing all the words of Robbie's songs, even the lesser-known ones, which only die-hard fans would know. If anybody cottoned onto this they didn't say and neither did Josie, not wanting to upset Paige's dad. He seemed a wonderful man and she could only imagine how difficult this whole situation must be for him.

'Now we know where your angel voice came from.' Another man's voice had jolted her thoughts and she'd turned to see the man who'd raised her as his own standing beside her.

She smiled at her dad as he drew her into his side and kissed the side of her head.

'Thank you for being here today. It means the world.'

As they'd hugged and continued to enjoy the music, Josie realised that just because she'd found out about Robbie, it didn't mean she felt any differently about her dad. Their relationship was as strong as ever. Turned out she had plenty of room in her heart for both her fathers.

And, if that were the case, didn't it also correlate that making room in her life for Rebecca wouldn't take anything away from the precious relationship she'd had with her other mother?

She'd always regret not finding Robbie earlier, always mourn the loss of what could have been, but it didn't have to be that way with Rebecca. When she'd found out about Robbie's death, she'd wanted someone to blame but she understood now Rebecca wasn't that person. Perhaps no one was. This was just a horrible tragic thing.

Josie glanced across to see her grandmother had fallen asleep— her teacup balanced precariously on her stomach—and decided to take the chance to ask Clara something that had been weighing on her mind all afternoon.

'Can I ask you something?'

Clara blinked as if snapping out of a trance. 'Of course. Anything. Anytime.'

'This Paired Kidney Exchange Program that Solomon has volunteered to go on … is it just as good as Rebecca having a direct matching donor? I mean, how does it work? How long does it take to find another matching pair?'

'I don't know a great deal about the program,' Clara began slowly, putting down her teacup on the coffee table, 'but I think the waiting times are fairly good. Definitely better than waiting on the deceased donor list. And recovery rates and longevity of the kidney are far greater than having a deceased donor also.'

But Josie wasn't really interested in those details.

As if Clara could read her frustration, she added, 'If the program works the way it's intended, then the outcome for the recipient would be the same as if they had a matched donor from the start, however, there can be more false starts due simply to the number of people and kidneys involved. I couldn't guess how long it will take for Solomon and Rebecca to find a paired match, but I'd be happy to talk to one of the doctors at work and get some more specific information about the process if you'd like?'

She shook her head. 'Thank you, but I think you've pretty much given me my answer. I don't suppose you happen to know what blood type Rebecca is?'

'I'm sorry. I can't remember, but does this mean you're thinking ...'

'Yes.' Josie swallowed. 'But I don't want to get Paige or Rebecca's hopes up if I'm not a match. Do you think it would somehow be possible for me to get tested as a donor without them knowing?'

'That's a very generous thing for you to consider, but you wouldn't be able to get pregnant until it was over. There'd be a few months recovery after the operation and there's a very small risk to fertility associated with being a donor. The doctors generally don't recommend a woman of childbearing age donate unless all other options have been exhausted.'

Josie knew Clara only wanted the best for her but her mind was made up.

'That may be, but I still want to find out if I'm a match.' Her grip tightened around her own teacup as she added, 'I wasn't able to save Rob, but maybe I *can* save Rebecca.'

'His death was not your fault,' Clara said forcefully. 'You don't need to do this as some kind of penance.'

'I know that! It wasn't yours either.' Josie knew that in their own way each of the women in Rob's life had owned some kind of blame.

'It wasn't anybody's fault.'

They both startled at Brenda's voice. They'd thought her dead to the world.

'We've all suffered some devastating losses in our lives, but some of us can carry on through these things better than others. It's not that Rob was weak or we are stronger, it's just he had a little faulty wiring. We all did what we could to try and help him—maybe it's time to stop beating ourselves up over something we had little control over and seek comfort in the wonderful friendships and relationships we have left.'

Her smile was watery as she looked between them. 'Now, which one of you two are going to help this old girl up so she can go to bed?'

# Epilogue

# February

Coffee- and food-deprived since ten o'clock last night, Rebecca was feeling hangry (a term Josie had recently taught her) as she lay flat on her back on a hospital gurney wearing an unflattering pale blue gown. The small room they were waiting in felt cramped with Hugh, Paige and Solomon in attendance and if any of them asked how she was feeling one more time she was liable to spring off the bed and throttle them. She wasn't sure if the jitters were down to the withholding of her morning caffeine or her nerves over her imminent operation, but either way, the sooner it was over the better.

If they kept her waiting any longer she might chicken out!

'How long till I go in?' she asked no one in particular.

'Mum. You only asked two minutes ago.'

Hugh chuckled. 'She's getting you back for all those long trips we took when you were a kid and you were like a broken record with your 'how long till we get there's.'

'About five minutes if there aren't any hold-ups.'

'Thank you, Solomon.' Rebecca managed an appreciative smile for her wonderful son-in-law and let out a slow breath.

She couldn't believe this was actually happening. In some ways it felt like only five minutes since she'd first been given her kidney failure diagnosis and in other ways it seemed like years. So much had happened since. Back then it had felt like such a big blow, but, as bizarre as she knew it sounded, she was actually now a little grateful for the medical diagnosis that had turned her world upside down. Without it, Paige might never have gone looking for the wedding dress, she herself might not have found the guts to send off for the adoption information and who knows if they would ever have found Josie.

Rebecca's only regret was that the diagnosis hadn't come earlier. If it had they might have been able to save Robbie's life as well as hers.

She thought of Clara and Josie who she'd seen briefly on arrival that morning before they'd been whisked off to another room somewhere down the corridor and sent a silent prayer upwards that the removal of her new kidney went smoothly. She knew she was one of the lucky ones—she thought of Old Biker Dude, Pollyanna and the others who were still enduring thrice-weekly dialysis sessions—but eternal dialysis would be better than the guilt she'd have to endure if anything went wrong. This was a miraculous and selfless act of kindness and she still couldn't believe that someone who was a stranger mere months ago was now giving her the gift of life.

'Shall I put the TV on?' Sol pointed to the monitor hanging on the wall.

'Yes, good idea,' Rebecca nodded, desperate for any distraction.

Two breakfast show hosts were arguing loudly about whether people should be allowed time off work to grieve their pets properly when a nurse with a smile far too chirpy for this early in the morning—she'd obviously had *her* coffee—entered the room with a man Rebecca guessed to be an orderly.

'We're ready for you,' sang the nurse and then looked to Hugh, Paige and Solomon. 'Last kisses for the patient.'

Obediently Paige stepped forward and hugged her. 'Good luck, Mum. We'll see you on the other side.'

Solomon offered her another one of his easy smiles and squeezed her hand. 'Just think of the coffee you can have later.'

Then Hugh leaned over her bed, stroked her hair and kissed her on the forehead. 'I love you, Rebecca, and I think pale blue is very fetching on you.'

'Haha. Thanks.' She tried to smile at him and ignore the butterflies flapping wildly in her stomach. If she was being summoned to the operating theatre, then her donor kidney was likely being whipped out that very minute.

It was too late to back out now.

Hugh, Paige and Solomon watched as Rebecca disappeared down a long corridor and then went into the family waiting area where Nik and Josie were already sitting on uncomfortable plastic chairs, tapping their toes.

'She's in?' Josie asked.

Paige nodded and went over to sit beside her. They clutched each other's hands. 'I hope everything goes okay.'

'It will,' Sol and Nik said at the same time.

'It better.' Hugh added as he began pacing the waiting room.

'Sol.' Paige nodded towards her father. 'Do you want to take Dad to get a coffee?'

'Good idea. Anyone else want anything?'

'I'd love a hot chocolate,' Josie said. 'And a muffin or something. Maybe a sandwich as well, although nothing with salad or cold meat in it. Hmm ... maybe you'd better make it a toasted sandwich or maybe even a sausage roll. Actually, get one of each and a—'

Nik pushed to a stand. 'I think I'd better go with you guys. Paige, shall we get you a coffee as well?'

'Yes please.' As the men started off towards the café, she turned to her sister. 'Got a bit of an appetite there?'

Josie laughed. 'I'd say it's nervous energy but starvation is pretty much a permanent state for me these days.'

Paige smiled, then placed her hand on Josie's stomach. 'How's my future niece or nephew going today?'

Josie glanced lovingly down at the basketball-sized bump in her normally flat stomach. 'Good. Really good.'

She wouldn't be a hundred per cent relaxed until she held her little one in her arms, but she was in her second trimester and her last scan had shown a thriving, healthy baby and she'd finally began to enjoy her pregnancy, which had been an even bigger shock than the first time she'd accidentally fallen. It happened that Josie did share Rebecca's blood type and was also a perfect tissue match, thus making her a perfect candidate for kidney donor. There was just one problem. The results of her blood tests had revealed something else as well.

She was pregnant!

Only this time, she'd been so consumed with the news about her adoption, about Robbie and Rebecca, that she'd overlooked her skipped period and all the other blatantly obvious signs. It seemed stupid in hindsight but she'd put her sheer exhaustion and nausea down to stress and grief.

While on the one hand this had been a joyous surprise, she'd also been terrified that it all might go wrong again and disappointed that she could no longer provide a kidney for her mother in the immediate future. Clara's announcement that she was going to volunteer to be Rebecca's donor instead had been almost as surprising as the pregnancy.

But what she didn't know was that Clara had already decided the night Josie asked her for information that, if at all possible, she wouldn't let Josie do this. At thirty-five Josie might have been nearing the end of her fertility window, but she still had hope, whereas for Clara that boat had sailed. The closest she was ever going to get to a daughter was Josie and, like a mother, she wanted to do whatever she could to protect her.

So, while Josie had been getting tested for donor suitability, Clara had secretly done the same. And, in a strange twist of fate, she had the same blood type as Rebecca. Further testing confirmed she was also a perfect tissue match.

Although Rebecca couldn't understand why Rob's ex-wife would even contemplate sacrificing an organ for her, Clara had proved very convincing. She, Josie, Paige, Hugh and even Solomon had argued that Rebecca would be selfish not to accept this generous offer. Rebecca knew better than anyone how many people were waiting on the deceased donor list and also that a kidney from a deceased person wasn't quite as good a bet as one from a living donor.

It was a wonderful gift Clara was offering, although Rebecca's eventual acceptance wasn't for herself but rather for her family, especially her future grandson or granddaughter.

While she and Josie would perhaps never have the relationship that Josie had shared with her adoptive mother or Rebecca shared with Paige, they were enjoying spending time together and getting to know each other better. When Josie and Nik's baby arrived, Rebecca wanted to be available and as involved as her daughter would allow. She hoped that because the trauma of giving up her first child was now out in the open, she'd be able to enjoy Josie's baby in a way she'd never been completely able to do with Paige. Thrice-weekly dialysis sessions simply didn't fit in with this plan.

Rebecca would miss the camaraderie she'd developed with her dialysis friends, but she'd keep in touch with at least a couple of them and she'd made other unexpected friends during these last few tumultuous months as well. Possibly the most surprising of them all was Clara. They'd liked each other when she'd been in hospital, then the shock of their connection had caused a rift, but they'd bonded again over their grief and guilt about Robbie and their excitement about Josie and Nik's baby.

This little one felt not only like a miracle but also the light at the end of what had been a very dark time for all of them. Rebecca knew that Clara would be as much a grandmother to the baby as she would be and that felt right.

'Here you are, sweet cakes,' Nik said as he, Sol and Hugh returned to the waiting area with their hands full of food and drinks.

Hugh looked much better now he had a soothing coffee in his hands and the men took seats as Josie began to devour her snacks. The five helped each other through the next couple of anxious hours—talking and taking turns to fetch more food for Josie—but when Dr Chopra walked into the room they all leapt to their feet.

A smile split the normally serious doctor's face. 'I'm pleased to say the transplant operation has gone smoothly and both Rebecca and Clara are now in recovery. A nurse will let you know when they're ready to see you.'

'Thank you,' Josie, Paige, Hugh, Sol and Nik said in unison, before they turned to each other and enjoyed a celebratory group hug.

# Author Note

This book began with one simple idea – a travelling wedding dress – and morphed into what it is today, a book that explores a number of serious issues faced in our contemporary world. Although the organisations between the pages are fictional, they are partly based on some wonderful charities and initiatives that we are lucky enough to have in existence in Australia:

**SANDS** Miscarriage, stillbirth and neonatal death support *sands.org.au*

**Beyond Blue** Support for depression and anxiety *beyondblue.org.au*

**Lifeline** If you are having suicidal thoughts, please call 13 11 14 *lifeline.org.au*

**Adoption Jigsaw** Information, counselling, searching services helping people separated from family *jigsaw.org.au*

RACHAEL JOHNS

**Angel Gowns Australia** An organisation making gowns out of donated wedding dresses for angel babies *angelgownsaustralia.org.au*
**Donate Life** Register to become an organ donor *register.donatelife.gov.au*

# Acknowledgements

It's always impossible to know who to thank first when it comes to acknowledgements – and also nerve-racking that I'll miss someone super important (like my mum, or Diet Coke).

I'm so blessed to be able to write 'author' in that space that asks for occupation on the census and I would not be able to do that without all my wonderful readers. Thank you for not only reading but for all your emails, messages, reviews and #shelfies. It's impossible for me to get to every shop in the country to visit my books but thanks to you guys I get to see them on shelves all over the country. I can't wait to hear what you all think of *Lost Without You* and keep those #shelfies coming!

A special shout out to the readers who are part of my online book club – it's been so much fun chatting books with you on a regular basis. If you're not a member and would like to be, simply search 'Rachael Johns' Online Book Club' on Facebook. The more the merrier.

Next I must thank the amazing team at Harlequin and HarperCollins Australia, especially James Kellow, and my wonderfully supportive publisher Sue Brockhoff and her hardworking and enthusiastic team, including Annabel Blay, Adam Van Rooijen, Natika Palka, Johanna Baker, Rob Magrath and many, many more.

Thanks also to my editor for this book, Alex Craig – an absolute genius when it comes to cutting waffle. If it weren't for Alex, this book might just be 1000 pages long.

Big gratitude to my agent Helen Breitwieser for loving and championing this book – I'm sorry about Robbie!

So many thank-yous to the artistic genius Alice Lindstrom, who came up with the beautiful cover for *Lost Without You*. I'm in awe of your amazing talent.

Thank you to the unsung heroes who are bookshop folks and librarians, for all you do to get my books in front of readers. I'm forever grateful.

As always, massive thanks to my writing friends, who are not only happy to brainstorm characters and plot but also put up with my whining when the words aren't coming exactly how I want them to. Especially to Beck Nicholas, Emily Madden, Lisa Ireland, Amanda Knight, Sally Hepworth, Cathryn Hein, Scarlet Wilson, Fiona Palmer, Kelly Golland, Leah Ashton, Tess Woods, Anthea Hodgson, Fiona Lowe, Brooke Testa and Alissa Callen.

Thanks to Dr S who answered my million questions about kidney disease and how finding a donor and having a transplant works in Australia. As usual, any mistakes are my own. And also to my reader Jo McAulay who generously shared with me her feelings surrounding the adoption of her son and my lovely friend Lesley West who spoke openly to me about her grief and her role as a support person for others suffering loss.

The very first seed of this book came when I was listening to a Mamamia Out Loud podcast and Monique Bowley (no longer on the show) spoke about how she'd sold her wedding dress to a listener of the podcast. I think someone mentioned how it could be a travelling wedding dress – a bit like the trousers in *The Sisterhood of the Travelling Pants* – and immediately my writer's brain began buzzing. I started to think about a story that revolved around a group of women who had all worn the same wedding dress. The book you have read is quite different from this original idea, but thanks anyway to Monique for starting it all.

And last but never least, my at-home cheer squad – thanks always to Mum, Craig and my beautiful boys for your practical and emotional support. You are my world and I couldn't do this without your support. xo

# BOOK CLUB QUESTIONS

1. Do you have a favourite character? If so, why?

2. It's said you never get over your first love – do you believe this to be true? Who was your first love?

3. Would you give your kidney to a friend, family member or stranger? Do you think Sol's offer of his kidney to Rebecca is believable?

4. One of the themes of *Lost Without You* is friendship – especially those that come unexpectedly, such as friendships between different ages. Do you have any surprising friendships?

5. Music, and in particular songs, can evoke memories and nostalgia. Can you think of any songs that take you back to a specific time and make you laugh or cry?

6. There are many books written about adoption and how it affects birth mothers and children, but *Lost Without You* also looks at the long-lasting effects of adoption on a father. Do you think this portrayal was realistic?

7. Do you believe Hugh and Paige's anger at Rebecca is warranted? Would you ever keep such a big secret from your family?

8. Was Gregg fair with Clara in his ultimatum?

9. One of the lighter parts of this book is the hunt for Rebecca's wedding dress. Would you keep yours? How far would you go to recover a lost dress?

10. *Lost Without You* deals with some challenging themes and life events, including adoption, suicide, depression, missing persons, infertility and grief. Which of these affected you the most and why?

*Other books by*

# Rachael Johns

*Just One Wish*

*The Patterson Girls*

*The Art of Keeping Secrets*

*The Greatest Gift*

'Full of heartache and joy with a twist that keeps the pages turning...*The Greatest Gift* will appeal to fans of Jojo Moyes and Monica McInerney.'
**AUSTRALIAN BOOKS + PUBLISHING**

'There'll be something you'll identify with in each sister and you'll be questioning your own family dynamics. A story of love and redemption that will surprise you.'
**THE SYDNEY MORNING HERALD** on *The Patterson Girls*

'*The Art of Keeping Secrets* is a compelling and poignant story of dark secrets and turbulent relationships that tackles a range of intriguing real-life issues with careful insight and sensitivity. I fell completely in love with the well-drawn characters of Flick, Emma and Neve. They were funny and flawed and filled with the kind of raw vulnerability that makes your heart ache for them.'
**NICOLA MORIARTY**, bestselling author of *The Fifth Letter*

'A fascinating and deeply moving tale of friendship, family and of course – secrets. These characters will latch onto your heart and refuse to let it go.'
**USA TODAY** bestselling author **KELLY RIMMER** on *The Art of Keeping Secrets*

# Just One Wish

## Rachael Johns

*Three women, three secrets, one life-changing journey.*

Alice has always been a trailblazer as a scientist, activist, and mother. She knew her choices would involve sacrifices, but now, on the eve of her eightieth birthday, she's beginning to wonder if she's sacrificed too much.

Alice's daughter Sappho rebelled against her unconventional upbringing, choosing to marry young and embrace life as a homemaker, but her status as a domestic goddess has recently taken a surprising turn.

Ged, has always been the peacemaker between her grandmother and mother. A tenacious journalist she knows what she wants in life and love, yet when everything in her world starts falling apart, she begins to question whether she really knows anyone at all.

At a crossroads in each of their lives, Alice, Sappho and Ged embark on a celebratory trip together, but instead of bringing them closer, the holiday sparks life-changing consequences and lifts the lid on a fifty-year secret.

Can Ged rescue her family if their story is built on a betrayal?

From bestselling, ABIA award-winning author Rachael Johns comes an engrossing and wise novel about ambition, choices and what it means to be a woman.

**Available November 2019**

# LET'S TALK ABOUT BOOKS!

## JOIN THE CONVERSATION

HARLEQUIN        @HARLEQUINAUS        @HARLEQUINAUS
AUSTRALIA

HQSTORIES        @HQSTORIES